THE WOMAN IN THE PICTURE

JAMES WILSON

The Woman in the Picture

A Novel

faber and faber

First published in 2006
by Faber and Faber Limited
3 Queen Square London WC1N 3AU

Typeset by Faber and Faber Limited
Printed in England by Mackays of Chatham, plc

A CIP record for this book
is available from the British Library

ISBN 978-0-571-22473-9
ISBN 0-571-22473-3

2 4 6 8 10 9 7 5 3 1

For PJW
and for ANRW, TOCW and KW
with love as always

I

Klosterfeld – December 1927

This is it. Too late to change my mind. The engine's flexing its muscles, giving a horsy snort. Even if I ran, I couldn't make it back now.

A hiss. The driving-rods clunk, the coupling chatters and groans. A puffball of dirty smoke breaks around me, tarring my tongue and throwing a shower of ash and grit against my face. My cheeks are too numb from the drizzle to tell the difference between hot and cold.

Eyes stinging, I glance down at the third carriage as it picks up speed. The buttery light and soft shadows give me a pang of loss and panic. There's already someone in the seat I've just got out of: a young man, my age-ish, a student maybe. He's saying something to the old woman with the round glasses opposite. She laughs. He laughs back.

I torture myself by watching until the moving window's foreshortened them into nothing: *That could've been me. But I've banished myself. Banished myself from the land of the living.*

Ridiculous, of course. I haven't banished myself from anything yet, except a few hours' warmth and comfort. And there's no reason why I should, if I don't want to. I can spend the night here, have a meal in a restaurant, see a church in the morning, get a train back to Hanover, be home again in seventy-two hours. *How was Germany, darling? Lovely, thanks.*

There's a small hotel opposite the station: the Stephanie. The green door's lost its gloss, and the tail of the 'p' is missing from the name-board. Must be cheap enough. And staying there wouldn't commit me to anything. It isn't really part of the town at all: just a staging-post on the railway.

The hall has the smell of continental holidays: starch, and coffee, and cigarette smoke. Seems odd to encounter it here, in this context. A handsome, heavily built woman in her thirties looks up from the desk. In my fumbling German I ask if she's got a room for the night.

She nods. 'A single?'

'Yes, please.'

She looks in her book, then gets up and frowns at the rack on the wall. She's wearing widow's black, but it's so close-fitting you can see the plump contours of her body. I find myself wondering if she's Stephanie. By the time she's found the key she's looking for, I've spun a whole story for her: the May wedding in 1914; the husband joyfully naming the hotel after his young bride; the bubble of plans – *We'll work together, fill the place with children, move somewhere grander*; then the Marne, or the Somme, or Passchendaele.

'Room eight,' she says.

'How much is that?'

She says something I don't understand. I nod anyway. She slips me a form, and a stubby black fountain pen.

When I've finished she says: 'Passport?'

If she's as curious about me as I am about her she doesn't show it. She opens it, perfunctorily checks my face against the photograph, then unsmiling scribbles down the number and slides it back again, together with the brass-weighted key. Without another word or look in my direction she calls out: 'Anton!'

An old man in a collarless shirt appears through the door behind her. He has Franz-Josef mutton-chops and moustache, and flint-chip eyes softened by a gluey skim of mucus. I can't catch what she says to him, but it must be something about my nationality, because instead of asking my room number he takes my hand and turns it so that he can see the tag. Then he grunts – seizes my bags – and limps ahead of me up to the second floor. At the door, I give him what I imagine to be a generous tip. He doesn't even look at it, but only grunts again and rams it into his waistcoat pocket with a giant thumb as he hobbles way.

The room's dank, and stinks of mildew: it obviously hasn't been occupied for weeks. The floral wallpaper's scuffed and scabby, and there's a coffee-coloured damp stain on the ceiling from a leak in the roof. I can't help thinking: *Even the Stephanie must have something better than this. And it doesn't seem very full. Perhaps they put me here as a punishment?* It wouldn't be surprising, I suppose, if they were less than friendly towards me. It must be obvious that I'm too young to have fought in the war, but even so . . .

Then another thought strikes me: *What if they decide to make trouble? Telephone the police, and say they have a strange English guest who's behaving suspiciously?* How could I explain what I was doing here? I could lie, of course – *Just stopped off to see the sights* – but it would be hard to sound convincing: my guide-book doesn't mention any sights, and the only address I've got is for a private house. And if they decided to search my luggage, and found the field-glasses . . .

I know I'm being fanciful. But I also know that, having once elbowed its way into my mind, the idea isn't going to be shamed into leaving. If I lie down as I'd intended, I won't be able to rest, or even think. Better to slip out now, without letting them know where I'm going, and get it over with.

I take the field-glasses from my bag, unclip the case, shake out the photograph and slip it into my wallet. I try not to see what's on the back, but can't flick my eyes away in time to avoid it: *Ich liebe Dich*. Then I wonder if I should remove the letter as well. That would help me to cover my tracks if I was stopped, but it might also seem like a kind of violation. In the end I leave it where it is – snap the case shut again – and drop it into the inside pocket of my overcoat.

Outside it's almost dark – the day reduced to a turquoise ribbon on the horizon. To the north is a jumble of black hills, dominated by a lop-sided tower that might be the remains of a castle. A patch of light above the rooftops, diffused into a ghostly fuzz by the thin rain, tells me where the town centre is.

I start towards it, and after a couple of minutes find myself in a wide street lined with shops. Most of the windows are still lit, but the pavements are almost deserted. Between them stretches a sea of wet cobbles, cicatriced by tramlines. The hard still air smells of garlic and fresh bread and cabbages and paraffin lamps – a strange mix of desolation and comfort. A legless man sits on a mat of newspaper in front of a tobacconist's. He's wearing some kind of uniform that bags around his emaciated body in heavy grey folds. He watches me with hyena eyes as I approach, and mumbles something as I pass. I give him two marks.

'Thank you, thank you.' His fingers feel mummified with cold.

I could ask him the way, but I don't want him to know I'm not German, so I hurry on without saying anything. Behind me I hear him calling: 'God bless you!'

There's a cross-roads at the end, after which the main street splits into the two branches of a 'Y' and passes either side of an old square. I'm almost there, and wondering where I should go next, when a girl dashes out of a baker's in front of me, and I have to stop abruptly to avoid knocking into her. She looks up at me, startled, and clutches the loaf she's carrying to her stomach, as if she's frightened I might try to steal it.

'Oh, excuse me!'

'It's nothing.' She can't be more than ten or eleven – too young to know what an English accent sounds like, or perhaps even what being English means. So I pluck up my courage, and ask: 'Can you tell me where Hermann Strasse is, please?'

She frowns and stares – but with puzzlement rather than hostility. Then – slowly so I'll understand – she says: 'I'll show you. Come with me.'

'Thank you.'

A whining tram lurches past. She glances at the bright misted-up interior and shivers.

Suddenly I notice her thin cotton dress and disintegrating cardigan, and realize she must be hugging the bread to soak up the last eddies of warmth from the crust.

She turns, trots ahead of me to the corner, glances back to make sure I'm still following, and scuttles down the road to the right. The sign says: 'Bad Strasse'. It's narrower and gloomier than the street we've just left: the gas lamps are burning, but their anaemic glow scarcely reaches the low barrack-like buildings running along either side. After a couple of hundred yards she stops and points to a road on the left. I can just make out the name fixed to the wall of the first house: 'Hermann Str'.

'Thank you,' I say again. I fumble in my pocket for a coin, but by the time I've found it she's half-way back to the cross-roads.

My throat's dry, and my heart's making an elastic-band pinging in my ears. I tell myself I'm still a free agent: there's nothing to stop me just taking a surreptitious peek and then retracing my steps to the hotel, if I want to, without anyone knowing I've been here at all. But I don't really believe it any more. I've seen where she lived; the corner she must have passed a hundred times on his arm; the Gothic-lettered street sign on its pattern of chipped bricks that must have signified home to her. I can feel them twining themselves into my unconscious and becoming part of that dream landscape that's half a place and half a sensation: Victoria Station; Badger's Wood; the school dining-hall; Hermann Strasse, Klosterfeld. If I back out now, I know I'll suffer for it. I take a deep breath, and start along the road.

The houses here are bigger: square detached villas protected by wrought-iron palings and dripping evergreens. Their air of burgher-ish complacency seems almost obscene – until you look more closely, and see how far it's already been eroded by blotched stucco and overgrown bushes and paths half-eaten by weeds. But number twelve is less run-down than the others: the gate is barnacled with rust, but there's a lamp burning above the door and the plaster's freshly painted. I start to breathe more easily, and feel the knot in my solar plexus loosen. For a moment I can't imagine why, and then suddenly I realize: it makes her seem less vulnerable, and me (in consequence) less guilty. If she's still living here, she's at least got the cocoon of relative prosperity to protect her.

No point debating any longer. I unlatch the gate, and – abandoning any attempt at discretion – scrunch noisily to the door.

It opens almost as soon as I pull on the bell. A slight, dark-haired girl in a maid's uniform cranes her head out, nervously holding on to the handle with both hands.

'Good evening, sir.' She's frowning, and her voice has a surprised lilt that turns the last three syllables into a question. She obviously wasn't expecting anyone to call so late.

'Good evening. I'm looking for Fräulein Brücke.'

'Fräulein Brücke?'

'Yes.'

She seems uncertain what to do. Her lips move and her eyelids flutter, as if she's trying to blink me away. Then she says: 'Wait a moment, please,' and disappears into a room at the back of the house. After a few seconds another woman appears – tall and square-shouldered, wearing an old-fashioned plum-coloured silk dress and a string of heavy wooden beads. I try to project the face in the photograph on to hers, but can't: the cheeks are too high; the nose is too short; and as she strides towards me I see that the coiled snake of her hair is silver rather than gold. She must be at least fifty, and Fräulein Brücke (if that's still her name) can't be more than thirty-five. She stops three feet short of the entrance and squints curiously at me.

'Good evening.' She barely moves her lips.

'I'm sorry to disturb you, but . . .'

She shakes her head, as if disturbing her is the least of my offences. 'My maid said you were looking for Fräulein Brücke?'

'Yes.'

'She doesn't live here any more.' She starts to shut the door.

'Have you got her new address?'

'No.'

'Does she still live in Klosterfeld?'

She shrugs. 'I think so.'

'Do you know where I could find out –' But before I can say any more she's slammed the door.

I retreat to the street, but get no further than the next house. Something's made me light-headed. Shock or relief? I can't tell. Perhaps it's the reaction of a soldier wounded in the trenches: he knows he may always walk with a limp; he can't help a nauseous tremor of guilt at leaving his friends – and yet he's got his passport out of the nightmare tunnels, and back into the sunlit world of Blighty. I've done what I could. I can't reproach myself with having funked it. Next time I wake sweating from the dream I'll be able to say: *Well, at least you tried.*

You don't notice discomfort when you've a reason for putting up with it, but now I suddenly realize I'm shivering. The mist's thickened into a wet fog, prickling the inside of my nose and roughening my throat. My overcoat's sodden with drizzle. When I touch the sleeves they have the clammy stiffness of dead flesh. I'll freeze to death myself inside it, if I can't get warmth. I imagine schnapps, a

Wiener schnitzel, the cheap sense of human contact that comes from hearing other people's laughter.

As I traipse back the way I came, something begins to nag me: why had the woman at number twelve come to the door herself, rather than just telling the maid to say that Fräulein Brücke didn't live there any more? Maybe the girl had mentioned that I was English, and she'd wanted me to feel the depth of her racial anger in person. But her manner hadn't just been hostile: it had been nosy, too – as if there was something shameful in my enquiry, and she was curious to see the man barefaced enough to make it. Perhaps it wasn't who I was she disapproved of, but who I was asking for.

What might Fräulein Brücke have done to earn her enmity? I start to speculate: cheated her over the sale of the house? Or else run off with her husband? Yes – that wouldn't be too surprising, would it, in a country where women outnumbered men by more than two million? And I know Fräulein Brücke lost her own fiancé: I've got his field-glasses in my pocket. Somebody might remember her, and tell me where she lives now. I could try tomorrow at the police station . . .

No: tomorrow I shall be on the train again. The case is closed. Fate has decided it for me. No more flirting with the dead: I'm restored to the world of the living. If I stray from it again, I may never be able to get back in.

And all at once, as if to confirm my citizenship, I hear the world of the living calling me: a heroic little spurt of jazz erupting into the darkness about a quarter of a mile ahead. As I approach it, I discover it's being carried up on a wave of warm smoky air from a basement half-hidden beneath a small block of flats. Above the entrance is an electric sign with three or four broken bulbs: 'Bar Alfred'. I go down the steps, and pull aside the leather curtain at the door.

I'd expected provincial dinginess, but someone's obviously made an attempt at sophistication. The bar runs along the back, next to an iron stove in the corner. To the left is a brilliantly lit little dance-floor, where three couples are Charlestoning with as much verve as if it were still the latest thing. The pianist is on a raised platform behind them. He's pretty good, playing with loose-shouldered con-

7

fidence, and looking up to give me a leisurely smile without losing his way on the keys. The rest of the place is dimmer, the light muted and coloured by thick red lampshades and cigarette haze, but you can still make out the chequered oil-cloth on the floor and the posters of New York and Montmartre and Berlin on the walls.

Two men are sitting at the bar, but my craving for company doesn't extend to joining them, so I find myself an empty table. It isn't difficult: only one is already taken, by a little party of well-dressed women – office-workers having a birthday drink, perhaps. There's a sudden hiccough in their conversation as I sit down, and I can feel their gaze tugging at me. But I resist the pressure to return it, and after a few seconds they relax back into a huddle and begin talking and giggling again.

The waiter maintains the metropolitan illusion by wearing a white monkey-jacket and black tie. He's a dark man with close-cropped black hair that looks as if it would spring into curls if he let it grow.

He swipes a scurf of grey ash from the table with his towel: 'Yes?'
'A Dunkles, please.'
He twitches with surprise as he catches my accent. 'English?'
I nod. He grins, and holds out his hand. I take it.
In broken English he says: 'English, German, American, all friends. Generals, politicians, fabricators' – he rotates a finger against his temple and makes a moronic, rubber-lipped grimace – 'all, how you say? – crazy?'
'Mad,' I say. 'Crazy if you're American.'
'Mad, yes.' He laughs. 'So. A Dunkles. Wait, please.'

When he's gone I fumble for my cigarettes. Most of them are buckled with damp, but I manage to find a dryish one. As I struggle to light it, I'm conscious that one of the women is looking at me again. I lean my elbows on the table and, screened by my own smoke, glance across at her.

She's young, about my age, with a wide mouth and thick tangly hair – attractive in a soft, wholesome, big-cheeked way. When she catches my eye she doesn't turn away, but smiles. There's a movement in my loins – a surly, ill-tempered assertion of autonomy – and a rash of heat spreads up my throat. Her smile widens. I can see the wet pink fold of her lower lip and the gleam of her teeth. No English girl has ever looked at me like that, but the meaning's pretty clear: *I know what you're thinking. And it's all right. I don't mind.*

I try to swallow. My mouth's dry. You can't accuse Fate of being oversubtle: it's making its point with a sledgehammer. Not content with denying me a ghost, it presents me with a warm, live woman instead. My *first* woman, maybe, if I play my cards right. But how *do* I play my cards right? A man of the world would frankly acknowledge his own desire by smiling back, and then amble over and ask her to dance. But I'm not a man of the world – that's the point; and I can't acknowledge my own desire without being embarrassed. And how, in any case, would I feel waking up next to her, and remembering where I was? I'm paralysed. I cover my blushes with my fingers, and let my gaze drift nonchalantly towards the woman sitting next to her.

She's older, this one. That's a relief, at least. Slender, wearing a little hat and a fur-collared coat. She knows I'm watching her, but doesn't respond directly. Instead, she leans close to her companion and says something. They both laugh. It's a charade of joky intimacy, put on for my benefit. Only when it's over does her face swivel towards mine.

Christ. Christ oh Christ. It's impossible to be certain in this light, but it *could* be. This woman's hair is shingled, not wound up in a bun; and her face doesn't have the arrogant, untouched plumpness I remember from the photograph – in fact, it's so fine-boned as to make her seem emaciated. But allowing for the eleven-year difference, and what she must have been through in that time . . . There's surely something about the straight line of the nose, and the upward pull in the right corner of the mouth.

I take out my wallet and lay it on the table, just as the waiter returns with my beer. He misinterprets the gesture, and signals 'no' with a quick wave of the hand, and a pout that says: *No, we're friends, aren't we? I know you'll pay later.*

'Thank you.' It doesn't sound like my voice. Already the dream-world is starting to reclaim me.

As soon as he's gone I nudge the wallet into my lap and flip it open. I'm frightened if it is her she'll recognize the picture, so I tweezer it out and hold it under the edge of the table, tilting it to catch the light from the dance-floor. Still hard to be sure. I glance up and down, down and up, trying to impose the photo-features on to the real face. The nose is very similar, the mouth the same width, though set in a different expression. I remember Bolly telling us in Art that the shape of the ears and the distance between the eyes are the most individual attributes of the human physiognomy. I stare at the ears. They're identical. I use my thumb to measure the distance between the picture-eyes, and then hold it in front of her – fussing with the end of my cigarette to provide a pretext for its strange behaviour. Yes, I think so . . .

And then I know. Her lips stretch and pucker into the same smile. It's unmistakable. *Ich liebe Dich*. She colours, shifts in her chair, and gives me a languorous nod.

My God. My God. I drop my eyes, and begin studying my cigarette packet with a romantic intensity I hope will deter anyone from interrupting me. But it's too late. I sense movement, hear footsteps, and only just have time to palm the picture before she arrives at the table.

'*Guten abend.*'

I glance at her hands. No ring, but a circle of soft white skin where you'd expect to find one.

'*Guten abend, Fräulein.*'

'"*Fräulein,*"' she says, mimicking my accent. Then, in English: 'You are English, or American?'

'English.' I start to get up.

She waggles her fingers to stop me: 'Please. English – that is good. I have many English friends.' She pulls out a chair. 'May I?'

I nod.

'Thank you.' She sits down. 'I saw you looking at me. I think perhaps you are a little lonely, no?'

Panic pinches the air from my lungs. I've been very slow, but now I see: she's been reduced to selling herself. That's why the woman at the house was so sniffy: she thought I was looking for a whore. And I've obviously given Fräulein Brücke and her friends the same impression.

I can't say: *If I'm going to sleep with someone, I'd prefer the other girl*. But equally, I can't tell her I've been looking for her, because then she'd want to know why – and if I explained that, without pre-amble, in a place like this, I'd be bound to upset her and squander any hope I might have of winning her confidence. So I just shrug and grin, and hoist my eyebrows. I must look like a gawky sixteen-year-old, but it buys me enough time to think of something to say.

'It's a relief to find someone who speaks English. My German isn't very good, I'm afraid.'

'Whereas my English is best in the world, no?' She laughs, just in case I am dense enough to take her seriously.

'It's excellent.'

She shakes her head, but she's smiling, and her brow tautens with pleasure. 'Not so very. I used to teach a little, after the war, but it was hard. And then you forget. Is nice to have a chance to practise again.'

'Where did you learn?'

'Oh, that is not so interesting, I think.'

'I'm interested.'

She glances at me obliquely, trying to see if I mean it.

'Really,' I say.

'All right. When I was a girl, we had English friends. Their daughter was older than I am. She came three times to visit us, and after the third time it was decided I should go and visit *them* the next year. Only . . .' She gulps and smiles. 'The next year was 1914.'

I nod. 'That's a shame.'

I can't believe I said it. It was an automatic response. A shame is when you lose your hankie, or spill something on the nursery floor.

'A shame, yes,' she says. She smiles. 'Anyway . . .'

'How did you know them?' I say quickly, in hope of redeeming myself.

'Oh, well, my father was a doctor. He and Harry Brimelow stud-ied together, at University College Hospital.'

'And where did they live?'

She frowns with the strain of remembering. 'Leeds?'

'Ah.'

'That is a nice place, no?'

'I don't think particularly. I've never been there. Rather noisy and dirty, I should imagine. The Yorkshire moors are meant to be lovely, though.' I can hear myself prattling – the words just pour out and skitter off the surface.

I take a breath, and try another direction: 'And what about your father?'

'Please?'

'What kind of a doctor was he? – is he?'

'Was. A *Praktischer Arzt*. What is that? A . . .?'

'A general practitioner?'

'Yes. But anyway . . .'

'Here? In Klosterfeld?'

She laughs. 'Yes! Now, that is enough!' She bends forward and play-slaps my hand, just glancing it with her fingertips. 'I want to hear about *you*.'

'I really don't –'

She purrs scoldingly, and waves a nannyish finger to stop me. 'What is your name?'

'Henry Whitaker.'

She cocks her head to the right. 'Is that Mr. Whitaker, or' – suddenly tilting it to the left – 'Henry?'

'Whichever you prefer.'

'I prefer Henry. And I am Irma.'

'Irma . . .?'

'I have thro-o-own away your surname, haven't I?' she says, chasing it into oblivion with a sweep of her arm. 'So you don't need mine.'

'All right. How do you do?'

She's amused at my formality. She stares at my outstretched hand for a moment before taking it.

'How do you do? Now, Henry, are you going to buy me a drink?'

I nod. 'As long as you promise to tell me something more about yourself.'

For the first time, she's genuinely puzzled. She lifts her chin, and squints at me along the ridge of her nose. I can't help thinking of a gunner taking aim.

'Why?'

I feel the weight of the field-glasses against my thigh. Their mute presence rebukes me: *Don't we belong to her more than to you? Go on: she's asked you directly. Tell her.*

But if I tell her now I'll only succeed in hurting her. The shock of it will make her cry, and the friendly waiter will be appalled, and I'll end up being pitched out of the warm, and back into the numbing desert outside. Better, surely, to get the conversation to the point where it's a natural progression, one tiny step – and then: *It's interesting you should mention that, because . . .*

But before I can say anything she's reached out a hand to touch me again. 'I think perhaps I know,' she says, smiling. 'Sometimes boys, is only natural, can be a little bit shy, don't like to speak what they *really* want. So they say: "Can we just talk?" or something like that. But English gentlemen boys are so well-brought-up, they think is more polite to say: "Can *you* just talk" – no? – "and I listen?"'

'I honestly do want to hear.'

'All right, all right, that's fine.' She squeezes my hand, and her smile deepens. 'I talk, and then, when you're ready . . . We can go upstairs and do whatever you like. Whatever it is, I shan't be shocked.' She laughs, very softly. 'I think you know that, don't you? And that's why you choose me, and not the other one? Because I am little bit older. A little bit more . . .' Her voice drops to a whisper. 'You know I take care of you.'

My mouth's so dry I can't speak.

'I don't do this so much, you know. Only with boys I like. Mmm?'

I nod, and try to swallow.

'Now,' she says, 'what about my drink?'

I raise a finger to summon the barman-waiter. She orders a Helles, and sits studying me silently until he's brought it.

Then she asks: 'How old are you, Henry?'

'I'm nearly twenty-one.'

She makes an odd little jerk, as if I've stung her, and looks down at her own fingers, splayed on either side of her beer mug. Then she shakes herself back to life, and says: 'Well, cheers!'

'Cheers.'

We clink glasses and drink.

'So,' I say, 'you're Klosterfeld born and bred?'

'Excuse me?'

'You've always lived here?'

'Yes.'

'Where, exactly?'

'Oh, well, when I was a girl, before the war, in Hermann Strasse.'
My neck prickles.

'So your father's a doctor, you live in Hermann Strasse – which
number?'

'Number twelve.'

As if I hadn't known.

'Brothers? Sisters?'

'Two sisters, yes.'

'A young man? An admirer?' I thought I said it casually enough,
but she's caught some edge in my voice.

'Yes. Why? Does it excite you, to think of me with another man?'

'No, I just . . . it's just . . . I'd like to hear something about him.'

I know it sounds unconvincing. Her gaze makes a tour of my
face, looking for a crevice that may reveal my true motive.

Eventually she shrinks back, defeated, and flutters her fingers
over my cigarettes. 'May I?'

'Yes. Yes. Of course.'

She takes one. It's still slightly damp: it fizzes when I light it for
her.

'His name was Walther. Walther Luger. He was exactly your age
when I met him. A student at the university here. He hoped to
become a . . .' – she rotates one hand rapidly, and makes a monocle
with the thumb and forefinger of the other – 'how do you say?'

I can't suppress a shiver. She doesn't seem to notice. I say: 'A film-
maker?'

'A film-maker. Yes. What more shall I tell you?'

I smile and open my hand towards her: *It's up to you.*

'He had a dog, Werther, a little English terrier – a Staffordshire?
He could not keep him in his rooms, so he must leave him at home,
but he told me stories about him. All kind of stories.' Her eyes drift
past me towards something I can't see, and she smiles. 'Werther was
a marvel dog. He could say "I am Werther, how do you do?" in
three languages. He would dress for dinner: a white collar and a tie.

Once, when I was ill, Walther sat by me, and I asked him to tell me a story, and he told how hero Werther climbed . . . climbed . . .' – raising her hand – 'how do you say?'

'Vertically?'

'Vertically, yes, up a wall, to save a baby boy in a burning house. He took the child in his mouth, like this, and climbed down the wall again, and laid him before his parents, on the lawn, with a little bow . . .' She tries to make a terrier bow, straightening her arms in front of her and dropping her head between them. 'You know?'

I start to laugh. She catches my eye and begins to splutter herself.

'I hope he got a reward,' I say.

'Oh, yes, of course. A medal and a . . . a . . . ?' She flicks a hand across her chest, as though she's striking a match on herself.

'A sash?'

She nods. 'The whole town came to see him receive it. When the mayor put it on, Werther bowed again and said: "I am Werther, how do you do?"'

'In all three languages?'

'No, only German.' She squeals with laughter. 'Oh, I'm sorry.' She covers her mouth with her hand. Tears are starting to breach the rim of shadow around her eyes.

'And what else?'

'Well . . . he was big, Walther. Big shoulders.' She taps her own. 'About as high as you. In fact, you know? – we make your hair more dark, and give you a moustache and a bit more chin, and cut' – making scissors with her fingers and snipping at my nose – 'something off here, and when you look at yourself in the mirror, you see Walther.' She's still laughing – but as soon as she sits back to appraise her imaginary handiwork, her expression changes: something seems to blot the natural colour from her cheeks, leaving nothing but rouge; her smile cools; and she has to blink furiously to stop herself weeping. 'I'm sorry,' she says softly. 'You do remind me. Not that, so much' – making a frame around her own face with a forefinger – 'but something.' She looks down, and sniffs.

'That's all right,' I murmur. 'I know how you feel.'

My God, English: can't you do better than *I know how you feel*? And even that makes me queasy. I can see how inadequate it is; and

15

yet at the same time there's an admission of weakness about it that seems snivellish and unmanly. If the people at school, or in the J.C.R. at college could hear me, they'd be howling with derision. And what would Daddy say . . .?

No: if I start tugging on *that* thread I'll unravel altogether. Concentrate. Concentrate on this.

I take a deep breath, and force myself to touch her hand.

She starts to cry. 'Please . . . Forgive me.'

'No. I shouldn't have asked you.'

She shakes her head. 'You know, I never before told anyone about Werther the dog. Not my daughter, even. Our daughter.'

'Walther's?'

She nods. 'The last time I see him. Christmas 1916. Three months later I hear . . . I hear he is killed. Two weeks after that, the doctor tell me I am pregnant. So . . . that is why I must do this sometimes.'

I squeeze her hand. Better to say nothing, than another polite formula.

'Is like – you live in a little room, like this.' She crooks her fingers and presses them together to form a box. 'All the rest of the house, is shut up. You don't go there, never, because it make you remember. And if you remember, you can't bear the little room any more. You understand?'

I nod.

'Only you, you' – forcing a smile on to her blotched face and lightly tapping my knuckles, in a ghastly parody of gayness – 'are a naughty boy, that *make* me remember.'

'I'm sorry.'

She shakes her head, burrows in her handbag, and pulls out a large leather purse. Inside are a compact, a powder puff, lipstick, eye shadow. She opens the compact, and – guiding herself with the mirror – dabs expertly at her smudged make-up with a handkerchief. For some reason, I find her little squirrelish gestures as she tries to repair the mask more pitiful than the tears that destroyed it.

After a few seconds I can't stand it any more. 'Please,' I say. 'Don't worry. You look fine.'

Why, I can't imagine – but this sets her off crying again, more violently than before. She screws the handkerchief into her eyes and

16

hunches forward, her thin shoulders lifting and juddering with every sob. I'm conscious that the other women and the men at the bar are looking at us. They must think I've hit her, or said something cruel. I slide my chair next to hers, and put an arm round her. She folds against me, as light and skeletal as a kite: one squeeze, and I could reduce her to splinters. Her head flops so loosely against me that for a moment I'm frightened I've broken her neck. I can smell the salt of her tears, and the acid musk of sweat, and the hot-oven scent of powder.

'Please,' she says. 'Please . . .'

'Hm?'

'Let's go.'

'Go where?'

'Upstairs.'

'But we were just going to . . .' I hear the nervy boyishness in my own voice and can't finish. It's as useless as a sticking-plaster on a bullet wound.

She grabs my wrist, and squeezes it as hard as she can; I can see the bulge of her knuckles, though I feel nothing more than a pleasant pressure.

'Please,' she says.

I gently extricate myself – then get up, walk to the bar, and ask for the bill. I stare at the counter while I'm waiting for my change and don't meet the barman's gaze when he gives it to me so have no idea whether he's amused or curious or censorious. I can't afford to find out. As long as I stay in the strange little world Irma Brücke and I have created for ourselves, I can cope; but I know that the moment I let other people in and start having to answer to them for my actions, I'll be lost.

I leave a large tip on the table, and look around for the stairs.

'No,' says Fräulein Brücke, pointing to the leather curtain. 'There.'

She hurries up to the street, without a glance or a word to her friends, and leads me into the hallway of the block of flats. It's chilly and echoey: the floor bare; the drab walls glistening with damp in the stingy white glow of a single gas-lamp. She trots up to the fourth floor, her quick shallow breath leaving wraiths of condensation in the cold air, and unlocks a door at the back.

17

Before opening it, she turns to me, puts a finger to her lips, and whispers: 'My daughter sleep here in the living room, so we must to be quiet, yes?'

I nod. She takes my hand, and guides me through the darkness. I can see nothing but the blizzard in my own brain, but I feel the sharp jag of a table, and the bump of a stool against my leg, and hear the soft regular sea-noise of the girl's breathing. Then the grunt of a hinge, and Irma saying: 'Wait a moment, please.'

The hiss of gas, the scrape of a match, *whoosh!*

We're in a room about ten feet by eight. Most of it's taken up by the bed, a chair with a torn cane seat, and a brass-bound, military-looking chest that I imagine came from the house in Hermann Strasse. On top of the chest is a white cloth, with scent bottles and a pair of silver-backed hairbrushes laid out on it. Lined up behind them are a Bible, and three or four other books. On the wall above hangs a photograph of a young man in dress uniform. He has dark hair parted down the middle; thick, straight eyebrows; a moustache; and a round chin that seems uncomfortably constrained by his high braided collar. His heavy half-smiling lips are hungry.

Irma looks at me, with the nervous watchfulness of someone who's just introduced two friends at a party. I shift awkwardly. The field-glasses slap my thigh. For a moment I think I'm going to faint.

'I'm sorry,' I say, 'could you tell me where the bathroom is?'

She points out the way we came. 'Second door to the right. You perhaps have to wait. Old Mrs. Müller . . .' She smiles suddenly. 'Sometimes we think she live there.'

I go back through the sitting room, teasing out the way with my fingertips. The second door on the landing is locked and my attempt to open it provokes a whine of complaint from inside. I take a few steps back and wait, trying to block out the sounds of a violent fart-storm punctuated by groans and whimpers. Eventually an old woman in a dirty black dress comes out and hobbles off, scowling. I bat the door back and forth to fan the fumes out, then edge inside. No deep breaths here. The floor's wet, and the lavatory's stained with an ulcerous streak of fudge-coloured shit. I piss it away, trying not to retch; then stagger out again, panting.

At the entrance to the flat I hesitate. This really is my last chance.

Perhaps I'm deluding myself, but I feel my whole destiny depends on what I do now. I can go back in and lose what's left of my virginity to the fiancée of the man who . . .

Don't think about it. Whatever you decide, don't think about that now.

Or else I can creep out, write a note of explanation in the morning, leave it for her at the bar with the field-glasses . . .

That'd be better. Cleaner. More honest. And would keep things more or less as they are. I wouldn't wake up tomorrow to find the walls between the different compartments of my life irrevocably ruptured, with God knows what results . . .

I begin to hot-foot it down the stairs, but almost at once I start to slow again. She won't get the note for at least twelve hours; and in the meantime she has to survive the night. I see her waiting – coming to look for me – discovering me gone – throwing herself on the bed. *Why has he done this to me? Am I too old for him? Doesn't he find me attractive?* The image of her lying there, hurt and alone, balloons into a tumour, squashing every other thought out of my head. Before I reach the next landing, it's paralysed me.

I exposed myself to him. I trusted him. Oh, God . . .

All right, all right.

I tiptoe up again, and through the open door. In my eagerness to get back and reassure her, I stumble over the bed. A shuddery wave passes through the girl, carrying her to the edge of waking.

'Mummy?' she murmurs.

'I'm a friend of Mummy's.'

She casts off again with a sigh, and drifts back into sleep.

Irma is standing on the far side of the bed. She's turned out the gas-lamp, and is lighting two candles on the chest, which give it the air of a shrine to St. Walther. Her clothes are piled on the floor. She's barefoot, but wearing a red kimono, with the fur-collared coat draped around it for warmth.

'Hullo,' she whispers, turning towards me. 'You were a long time. Was it Frau Müller?'

I nod.

She giggles. 'I'm sorry.' She's quaking so much the match in her hand blows itself out. 'Brrr. You mind if I get in bed?'

'Of course not.'

She shrugs off the fur-collared coat and scrambles under the blankets, pinching the kimono shut with one hand, then reaches the other towards me, fingers spread wide. When I lean forward to take it, she shivers and smiles: 'Oh, you are so nice and warm!'

I'm near enough now to see that she's removed all her make-up, except for the lipstick. Her face looks more lined, but also more girlish, somehow.

She colours slightly under my gaze, and her mouth flickers anxiously. 'I think is better, no? I don't like I pretend with you.'

'Much better.'

'You don't pretend with me?'

Jesus. That almost stops me. Should I tell her, even now? I want to. I want her to know the truth, to shoulder my burden gladly, to let me shoulder hers. And then, when there's no deceit between us, when we've willingly accepted each other's loss, I'll be relaxed and open enough to do what *she* wants.

'Do you dream about him?' I say.

The little furrows between her eyes deepen. 'Yes, sometimes. But you don't answer my question. I think you pretend. You don't like me like this?'

It's no use. I should have done it before, if I was going to. Now I'd just be inflicting another wound, and disqualifying myself from making it better.

'No,' I say. 'I do. You're beautiful.'

Her eyes flood, and she bites her lip. 'Will you come to bed now?'

'Yes.' The word sticks to my tonsils. I have to cough to free it.

As I start to undress, I think of all those stories I've heard of prostitutes robbing their clients while they're asleep. What if *she* tries, and finds the field-glasses? I carefully fold my overcoat, then hang my sports coat on the back of the chair so that the wallet's clearly showing. If she wants my money, she won't have to look far.

Then I remember: the wallet's where I put the photograph.

I'm down to my pants and socks now. I say: 'Would you mind looking away a minute?'

She giggles. 'Why? – are you shy?'

'A little.'

She fans her fingers over her eyes, a child playing hide-and-seek. I quickly take out the picture and transfer it to another pocket. Then I finish stripping, and pull back the sheet.

She's tinged blue with cold, and so thin that the roundness of her little breasts seems a gesture of defiance. I lie down beside her. She rolls over, nuzzles my neck, and starts to stroke my hip and thigh. I suddenly shiver.

'Sorry. Am I freezing?'

'It's not that.' My throat's so tight I can barely say it. 'It's just . . . I'm afraid I've never done this before.' That, at least, is true.

'I know,' she says, smiling. 'Neither had Walther. Neither had I. That's nice, no?'

I don't want to think of Walther, or my parents, or William, or the skeins that wind our stories together. Some day – tomorrow probably – I'll have to deal with them; but the only responsibility left to me tonight is *kindness*.

I turn, hunch her head on my arm, and kiss her. She tastes of beer and cigarettes and something less personal: a kind of warm composty damp, the tang of the primeval soup. Her tongue darts against my teeth, then swims into my open mouth. I hear myself moan.

She pulls back. 'I hurt you?'

'No.'

She kisses me again. Her hand finds my erection. I grimace, and pull away.

'You are sure?'

'Hmmm.'

She takes my hand, and guides it down over her belly. Her breath starts to come more quickly. She presses my neck and pulls at my waist, urging me on top of her. As I turn, I'm startled by Walther's steady beatific gaze. I lever myself up, and blow out the candles. But he's still there, sod him. A glimmer of moonlight from the window catches his pale cheek.

'*Meine Liebe . . .* ,' she says. '*Meine Liebe.*'

She draws me into her. Her eyes are shut, but leaking tears. She squirms and thrusts against me, crossing her legs over mine, slapping my back, razoring my shoulder with her nails, as if she's trying to snap the bonds that keep us separate and burrow her way into

21

my skin. God knows what she's imagining. If *I* knew, it would kill me, I'm certain of it. I'm surrounded by the dead, and only my ignorance is keeping me from joining them. One moment of empathy, and I'll cross the divide. And perhaps that won't be so bad . . .

'*Oh, meine Liebe . . . Ich liebe Dich.*'

I'm not thinking any more: the sensation's too overwhelming. I lick the lobe of her ear, and whisper: '*Ich liebe Dich.*'

She cries out, then her eyes roll up beneath the lids, and her lips stretch into a rictus. I'm no longer myself: I hear a yelp from my mouth, and feel the banks bursting, and whatever was me flowing into her.

No: death's not so bad.

It's dark when I wake up. For a moment I can't remember where I am; then the unfamiliar warmth at my side reminds me. I'm conscious of having experienced some immense change, but I've no idea what I feel about it. To know that, I need to be on my own somewhere, with time to think.

I get up, and fumble on my clothes. The wallet's where I left it. I'm certain it's not been touched. I need to pay her something. I grope for my matches, edge round the bed, find one of the candles, and light it – standing with my back to her, so she won't be disturbed by the glow. What should I give her? I haven't a clue. I take out a ten-mark note. Seems a bit mean. Twenty . . .?

I hear her stirring behind me. I turn round.

She's propped up on one elbow, blinking sleepily. 'What do you do?' she says – and then, seeing the wallet: 'No!'

'I'm sorry,' I say. 'I don't know how much . . .'

'Nothing.'

'Oh, no, I must –'

'Nothing! You write to me, all right? You promise you write to me?'

'All right, but –'

'No!' She's almost crying.

'All right.'

I feel I ought to kiss her, but she doesn't seem to expect it. When I take a step towards her, her eyes widen into a startled stare. I stop, and say: 'Well, goodbye, then.'

'Goodbye.'

I take the candle to guide me through the other room. As I pass, the child moans and turns in her bed. I glance down at her.

God: Fate knows no shame. It's the girl who showed me the way to Hermann Strasse.

I take the twenty marks, and slip it under her pillow. I hope her mother will understand: not the settlement of a debt, but another act of kindness.

I snuff out the candle and leave it inside the door, then make my way down the piss-smelling staircase to the street. It's still drizzling. The moon's gone. I huddle inside my coat, and start back towards the Hotel Stephanie.

In the morning, I take the ten o'clock train to Hanover. I'm quite calm, but beneath the solid crust that enables me to get my ticket and find my seat and stow my luggage, I know my life's no longer viable. It can't be, in a universe where Irma Brücke slowly freezes to death.

I look at the rain-specked window, and the numb grey winter countryside beyond it. Should I get out at the next stop, and go back, and try to save her? I couldn't: there's no alchemy to turn pity into what she wants. And even if I could, what about the ten and twenty and forty million others?

Tell someone about it, then – at least I can do that. But who? Mother? The language doesn't exist. William? No problem with language there: the more *fucks* and *shits* and *whores* the better. But only because they're words we *can't* use with our parents. The rest would embarrass him as much as *fuck* would embarrass Mother. He'd simply jettison it, and reduce the whole thing to gossip: *Henry Whitaker's a bit of a dark horse, isn't he? Do you know what I heard he did in the Christmas vac . . .?*

Turn it into a story? A book? Try to get it published?

Unimaginable.

I *can* go on writing, of course. I *must*. But only for myself.

A grey-haired pastor in the opposite corner glances companionably at me. He doesn't see me at all. I've walled myself in: no-one knows I'm there, and I can't get out. I'm running out of air already . . .

And then, suddenly, I see a loose brick.

I get up, take my pen and notebook from my bag, and start to draft a letter:

Dear Mr. Maxted,

You won't know me, but I am a great admirer of your work, and have an idea for a film which I think you might find of some interest:

A young man – let's call him Gilbert Smith – is haunted by dreams of his father, who died in the war. Hoping to find the exact circumstances of his father's death, he calls on another officer, Lieutenant Taylor, who was with him at the time. It turns out that Captain Smith was shot at close quarters during an assault on German lines, and that Taylor then shot the German who killed him. He still has the dead Boche's field-glasses case, which he now gives to Gilbert. Inside, Gilbert finds not only a pair of binoculars, but also a letter from the dead German's fiancée, and a photograph of the girl.

Far from laying his father's ghost, this discovery only troubles Gilbert more. He can barely sleep, and when he does he is visited by even worse dreams, involving not only Captain Smith but now also the German and his fiancée, in a triangular relationship that can never quite be resolved. [Imagine a montage sequence, showing the three faces, such as you used in Mr. Murgatroyd; *I think it could be very powerful.] He finally decides to go in search of the German officer's fiancée, in hope of bringing them both some peace of mind, by explaining the tragic connection between them, and returning the field-glasses and the letter to her.*

But when he goes to the address on the letter [a train moving through the darkness; a blur of lighted carriage windows; then the desolate reality of a provincial German town at night; a half-empty hotel; a scowling receptionist] he finds the girl no longer lives there, and the present occupant doesn't know where to find her. Disconsolate, he wanders the streets [plenty of opportunity here for your wonderful night-work: the gloss of rain on the cobbles; gas-lamps burning through swirls of mist] until at length he takes refuge from the weather in a dingy basement bar.

And there, sitting in a corner, he sees a woman . . .

II

35675 Eventide Road, Mason, Oregon 97400
E-mail: miranda@pfizerfamily.com

March 30

Dear Mr. Arkwright,

   Thanks for your letter, which the studio finally passed on to me a
couple of days ago. It's been years since I worked there, so I guess
it probably lay in an office someplace gathering dust, until
somebody recognized the name. At least they didn't just throw it
out, which they could have done. Anyway, that's why you've had to
wait so long for a reply.

   No, I'd no idea there was a "Henry Whitaker Centenary
Committee." It sounds like an interesting project, but I don't think I
could contribute much to it: I've been living in the States for thirty
years (way more than half my life), and am totally out of touch. To
tell the truth, my younger self doesn't feel like me at all now. And
even when I do succeed in half-imagining myself back inside her
head, I can't come up with anything that would interest you much,
I'm afraid. I was only seven when my mother died, and after that I
lived most of the time with my grandmother (when I wasn't at
boarding school) – which means I really don't have too many
memories of my father at all, and most of the ones I *do* have are
quite hazy. I guess the overriding impression, looking back, is that
he was permanently *puzzled* – just couldn't understand why he
was having to scratch around making dull little films about the Coal
Board or free milk in schools, when he thought (or so I assume,
from what happened at the end of his life) that he ought to be in
Hollywood, astonishing the world. He'd had some success as a
documentary-maker in the 1930s, I believe (well, of course he had:
that's why you're commemorating him), so perhaps everything
afterwards felt like a bit of a let-down. But you'll know more about
that than I do: I've never even seen any of his pre-war work.

   So: thanks for the invitation, but I honestly don't think there'd be

25

much point me trying to write a memoir of him, or coming over to address your conference.

On the question of my mother: yes, he did meet her in Germany at the end of the war. He was making a documentary about refugees; she was living in a displaced persons camp – with, from what I was able to gather, several thousand other people from all over Europe. Her maiden name was Stimpel – or, at least, that's what it said on her identity card – but I've no idea where she was originally from. I don't remember them ever talking about it in front of me; and the one time I asked her who her parents were she was so upset that I knew I must never, ever raise the subject again. I was used to storms and appalling moods, of course: she was a desperately unhappy woman – though since I had no-one to compare her with, I didn't fully realize just *how* unhappy until after her suicide. But her reaction on this occasion was particularly frightening. She wasn't angry or reproachful: she just seemed to disintegrate, like a cartoon house collapsing into a straight line. Everything that made her recognizably *her* – the walls and gables and windows, as it were – just disappeared. Nothing left but a featureless sea of misery.

My father did try to trace the rest of her family once, but every scrap of information that might have helped him had disappeared. My mother couldn't even remember what they were called, apparently: she'd say a name (he told me, in a whisper), and then almost immediately start wondering if she'd dreamt it. I can only have been six or so, and it really freaked me that human beings could just completely *vanish* like that. *Death*, even at that age, I could sort of understand – but the idea of being totally erased from other people's memories was something truly, mysteriously awful. Though I have to say my father didn't seem too bothered about it: in fact, I got the impression (though of course it's easy for a six-year-old to be wrong about this kind of thing) that he was actually rather *pleased* to find that my mother didn't have any relatives – as if being anonymous was somehow part of her attraction for him. That's really as much as I know.

As for friends: I don't think my parents really had any – not, at least, in the sense of people they visited together, or who came to see them. I knew who Christopher Morton Hunt *was*, of course, but the only time I saw him was at my mother's funeral – and then he hardly spoke a word to anyone. During the 1930s, my father had obviously been pretty close to Arthur Maxted, and – as you know – they continued to keep in touch until the end of his life. But Max had decamped to Hollywood long before I was born, so for most of the time it was a pretty long-distance relationship: Christmas cards, and the occasional letter. Not what you could really call *friendship*.

The person in the village we were actually closest to, I guess, was Flo Torridge, who used to cook and clean and take care of me. I imagine she must be dead now, but you could try to contact her daughter June, who was about my age and played with me when her mother brought her to our house. I don't know if June married, and if so what her name is now, but it shouldn't be too hard to find out.

Anyway – hope this is some help. Seems to me you have your work cut out: there can't be that many people left who actually knew my father, but tracking them *all* down is still going to be a big job. Good luck with it!

Best,
Miranda Pfizer

III

Milstead – February 1928

''Ere?' says the cabby. 'Or in there?'

'Here's fine,' I say. Stars are driven to the studio. People like me walk.

I get out and pay him. Beyond the fence I see lawns, and a tooth-paste squiggle of drive leading to a long, single-storey, flat-roofed slab of a building punctured with metal-framed windows. Immediately behind that rise the stark red-brick walls of a much larger structure that might be a hangar. The whole place, in fact, has the look of an aerodrome: everything there just to accomplish one outsize purpose. The glamour's in the product, not the production.

There's a painted sign standing at an angle to the entrance: 'Milstead Studios. British Imperial Pictures'. Next to it is a white-washed hut. As I approach, a gate-sergeant pokes his head through the sliding window.

'Morning,' I say.

'Morning, sir.'

'I'm here to see Mr. Maxted.'

'Mr. Maxted . . . Mr. Maxted . . .' He squints at a list pinned to the wall. 'You've got an appointment, have you?'

'Yes. Eleven.'

'What name?'

'Whitaker.'

He picks up his telephone and dials. 'Miss Weedon, please. Miss Weedon? Ronnie at the gate. There's a Mr. Whitaker here, for Mr. Maxted.'

I hear the distant whistle of a female voice. He frowns as he listens to it, pressing his temples as if he's trying to ease a headache. Maybe I've got the wrong day, or the wrong time, or dreamt the whole thing.

'All right,' he says, and clunks down the receiver. 'There, sir. The girl at the desk'll show you the way.' He points towards the one-storey building.

I can't help noticing that half his middle finger's missing, though he disguises it well, by folding the others to the same length. He catches my glance and says: 'Wipers.'

I feel myself stiffen. But that's stupid. Why should I be surprised? Think of the numbers involved.

I say: 'My father was at Ypres.'

'Really, sir?' His stare screws into my face. 'A . . .?'

'Captain Whitaker. Frank. First Sherwood Foresters.'

'I don't think I knew him.'

'No. Well, anyway – thank you.'

The first bend in the drive takes me to the left, showing me an untidy huddle of ancillary buildings exiled from the main block. One has a tall smoking chimney: the powerhouse, presumably. Next to it is what looks like a large barn with double-width, double-height doors. That must be the workshop. As I watch, a boy staggers out of it, dancing clumsily with a fat-arsed, splay-legged Chippendale chair, and almost collides with two men carrying a Tudor fireplace inside. I don't know why, but the sight of them gives me a caffeine jolt of elation.

At the last bend I hear an engine behind me and side-step on to the grass. A little green van grumbles past and stops in front of the entrance. A big, sandy-haired man gets out, clutching a pair of leather gloves. He pulls them on absently, ambles to the back, gingerly lifts the handle, leans inside – and then the doors whip open with a clang and the biggest mastiff I've ever seen springs on to the concrete. I flinch instinctively. It senses the movement, freezes for a second, then lunges towards me. Without thinking, I lift my hands to protect my throat. The dog stops with a gargling choke, its eyes bulging. I look up, and see the man holding the other end of its chain.

'Oops, sorry,' he says. But he's smiling: obviously my reaction amused him.

I smile back, trying to recover my dignity. 'What's its name?'

'Hector.'

'Hullo, Hector.' I hold my fist out. The dog frowns at it.

29

'I wouldn't do that,' says the man. 'He's been baited.'

'All right.' I withdraw my hand as nonchalantly as I can. 'What are they making? *The Hound of the Baskervilles?*'

The man shakes his head. '*Shadow* something.' He flicks a sheet of paper from his pocket and scans it. '*Shadow on the River*'.

'Who's the director?'

'No-o-o idea. Here, boy.'

I push open the glass door. The hall's as functional as the outside, with bare electric bulbs and stark white walls. The only decoration is a few framed film posters. To the left, a receptionist sits behind an open partition.

'I'm here to see Mr. Maxted.'

Her hand moves towards her telephone. 'Is he expecting you?'

'Yes. The chap rang them from the gate.'

The hand stops. 'Down there, turn right, third from the end on the left.'

Down there's a stuffy windowless corridor that runs the whole length of the building. The doors all have name-plates on them. I finally reach one that says 'Mr. A. Maxted', and knock.

A young female voice says: 'Come in!'

The door's so flimsy I feel I'm going to pull it off its hinges. As I open it, a school-staff-room smell of sweat and smoke and paper spills out. The girl's sitting at a table in the window. She's my age, or even younger, with springy gold-flecked brown hair drawn back behind her ears. In front of her is a typewriter, with a sheet in the carriage. A half-open internal door leads to another office, presumably Maxted's. I can see the corner of a bookcase, and a desk with an empty chair tucked under it.

'Hullo,' says the girl, getting up. 'I'm Nicky Weedon. You're Mr. Whitaker, I expect?'

'Yes. How do you do?'

She laughs and tilts her head sideways as we shake hands. She's tall and slender, with a strong nose and a big mouth that bisects her face when she smiles.

'Mr. Maxted's on set, I'm afraid.' There's a slight hesitation before 'on set', as if she's still not used to film jargon. She glances at a clock on the opposite wall and nervously straightens her frock.

30

'Do sit down. I shouldn't think he'll be terribly long.'

I find a chair by the door, and pull it out so I'm facing her. 'What's the film?'

'Something called *Shadow on the River*.'

'Is there a dog in it?'

Her eyes widen. 'Yes. How on earth did you know that?'

'I met it on my way in.'

'Oh, oh, I see. Yes, it's going to attack poor Greta Szagy. She doesn't like dogs at all, but Mr. Maxted insisted.'

'And who's Greta Szagy?'

'Haven't you heard of her?'

'No – I mean, who is she playing?'

'Oh, oh, Betty. The heroine. I did offer them Jojo, but they said he wasn't frightening enough.'

'Is Jojo a mastiff?'

She shakes her head, takes a framed photo from her desk, and hands it to me. It's a portrait of a smiling golden retriever with its tongue hanging out.

'I can see their point,' I say.

She giggles and flushes. A rash of faint freckles dapples her face. 'Anyway,' she says. 'Would you like some coffee or something?'

'Coffee would be lovely.'

'Right.' She smiles. '"O.K."' She seems flustered. She sucks in her lips, stares at the telephone for a second, then suddenly pounces on it. 'Hullo? Operator? This is Miss Weedon. Can you put me through to the – to the – the Coffee Department, please?' She knows it's wrong: her colour deepens, and she avoids my gaze. '*Coffee*,' she says. 'Who do I need to speak to, then? I'm trying to order some coffee for Mr. Maxted's visitor.'

'Please don't worry, if it's a problem,' I say.

She flutters her fingers to shoosh me. 'Oh, oh, all right. Yes, please. Hullo, is that the canteen? Could you send some coffee to Mr. Maxted's office, plea–?' She stops with a despairing *oof*, and starts tugging at a loop of hair. 'Well, what –? Who –?'

'Really, it doesn't matter,' I say.

She clamps a hand over the mouthpiece. 'Are you sure?'

I nod.

31

'Well . . .' She grimaces, then says into the receiver, 'No, don't bother, that's all right,' and drops it so quickly you'd think it was burning her. 'Sorry,' she says. Her face is feverish-red now, and the freckles have darkened into blotches. 'Usually the coffee just appears, so I've never had to do this before. But this morning it must have appeared on the stage.' She laughs. 'Whoops. "Appeared on the stage" – that sounds rather funny, doesn't it?' She crooks one arm against her side to make a cup-handle, and takes a little bow. '"Also starring: a teaspoon".'

I smile.

She takes a deep breath: 'As you'll have gathered, I'm afraid, I'm a bit of a new girl here. My typing and shorthand aren't bad, but everything else . . .' She shakes her head.

'Is this your first job?'

She nods. 'I'm just mad about films. I'd have been perfectly happy being an usherette in a cinema, actually, if my parents had let me.'

'But they don't mind your being a secretary?'

'Not awfully. Well, I think maybe my mother does. My father's a bit, you know, more modern.'

'Well, they must be pleased you landed this. I mean, Arthur Maxted . . .'

'Yes, wasn't I lucky?' Her blush was starting to fade, but now it deepens again. 'The thing is, my brother knows Val Farrar. So when Mr. Maxted started here, and said he wanted' – her voice dropping to an awed half-whisper, as if she's worried the other directors might hear, and start demanding the same treatment – 'his own *secretary*, Val put in a word for me . . .'

I've no idea who Val Farrar is, but I'm not going to admit it. 'Ah,' I say. 'And that helped?'

'I think it must have done, don't you?'

I shrug. 'Only if you were pretty good in the first place.'

She gives an *oh, no, really* grimace, and glances down at her typewriter.

'And are you enjoying it?' I ask.

'Oh, yes, yes, of course. Though it can be a bit daunting sometimes. To go on to the set and suddenly find yourself rubbing shoulders with Betty Balfour or Ivor Novello or Greta Szagy.'

Why am I surprised to hear her use the word *daunting*? I shouldn't be: it's unfair and lazy of me. She wouldn't be here at all if she were stupid.

'But of course,' she says, 'it's frightfully exciting, too. Sometimes I sneak in there for a few minutes and just *stare*. It's like being a child again. Watching the magician at a birthday party.'

I feel myself smiling. 'Yes, I know exactly . . .'

'Do you?' She crouches forward suddenly, her hands on the edge of the desk. 'I say, would you like to go in now?'

'All right – if you're sure he wouldn't mind.'

'Well, don't you think it shows we're keen?'

'I suppose so.'

She gulps – nods conspiratorially – and gets up. I follow her down the corridor, trying to quell the feeling that I've been trapped into joining a raid on the tuck-shop. At the end she turns right. In front of us is a black door with 'Studio A: Stage' painted on it. She turns the handle silently, and edges it open with her elbow.

A narcotic smell of fresh paint, wood resin and hot celluloid hits me. I can sense the cavernous space from the current of warm-cool air that eddies across my face, but all I can see is a square of black, fraying into grey along one edge. A man's voice that seems to be coming from half a mile away says something I can't hear. A moment later there's an echoey clatter that might be the sound of pebbles hitting the bottom of a well.

Nicky Weedon eases the door to, cushioning it with her fingers so as not to make a noise. Around us I can just make out the skeleton of the studio: tiers of steel rods clamped together, and trailing ropes and cables. It's as big as a small cathedral. Pressed against the walls are paint-pots, ladders, buckets, rolls of canvas, chairs, sofas, window-frames, a gramophone, the front of a car. On the floor are piles of tripods and black-shelled lamps. You can imagine the scarab crunch if you stepped on one of them. As I inch along behind Nicky Weedon, I'm careful not to.

The set is at the far end. It's so brilliantly lit I have to half-close my eyes to see what it is: a desolate Thames-side wharf at night. The edge is marked by three squat bollards; the ground is a vipers' nest of chains and hawsers; there's an unlit watchman's hut in one corner. The river scene beyond is painted in Turnerish *chiaroscuro*, with a hazy moon above St. Paul's making a wrinkle of white on the inky water. Along the far bank indistinct little blobs of yellow peep mysteriously out of the mist. They could mean danger or sanctuary – you can't tell. The romance of it makes me shiver with pleasure.

After twenty feet or so Nicky Weedon stops in the lee of a canvas flat leaning against a stack of mattresses. I station myself close behind her and we cautiously peer round the frame. Maxted is perched Buddha-like on a tall chair, stage right. He's heavier and younger than I imagined, with a plump unlined face and small intent eyes. He's bending down, saying something to a boyish, floppy-haired man on a canvas stool beside him. The cameraman stands in front of them, shoulders hunched and neck craned as he peers through the eyepiece. Next to him, holding a slate-board, is a spotty-faced chap who looks about sixteen. Three or four other people are dotted about, though I can't immediately see what they're doing.

Maxted straightens, and shouts: 'Action!' A woman runs on to the set, her hands bobbing in front of her in an operatic gesture of panic. It takes me a moment to recognize Greta Szagy beneath the mask of make-up. She totters to the edge of the wharf, glances down as if she expects to see something in the water, then strains on to tiptoe and stares first up the river, then down it. A sudden noise distracts her. She turns, just in time to see the door of the hut open, and the mastiff leap out at her, tugging so violently at its chain I'm afraid it'll snap one of the links. She backs away, stumbling over a bollard, and stands cringing on the brink, her face pulled into a mimic grimace of horror.

It suddenly strikes me that though the camera's been following her, I can't hear the sound of the mechanism. I lean close to Nicky Weedon, and whisper: 'Is he filming?'

She twitches her head: *No.* It's a tiny movement, but enough to catch the eye of the floppy-haired young man, who glances across at us and smiles. Nicky Weedon acknowledges him with a waggle of her fingers.

'All right!' shouts Maxted. 'Again!'

Greta Szagy glowers at him, then hurries off the set. The dog is dragged back spluttering, and the hut door closed. A wireless-murmur of conversation erupts among the technicians. The words are lost to me, but the tone's impatient, aggrieved even, and there's an undercurrent of subversive laughter.

'Action!'

Greta Szagy reprises the whole routine, tracked by the silent camera. Maxted still isn't satisfied. She does it again, but this time the gestures are less graceful: her fists beat the air, and when she trips against the bollard she's so close to falling that she has to thrust her hands out to save herself. At the end, she frowns anxiously up at Maxted. He shakes his head, and she gives a despairing wail.

'Please!' she says. Her voice has a phlegmy rasp, and her accent's almost impenetrable. 'The dog scare me. We make take now, please.'

'*I'll* decide that,' says Maxted.

She stamps her foot, but is too close to tears to reply. The technicians mutter and shift uneasily. The floppy-haired young man walks over to her, says something in her ear, then touches her elbow and guides her gently off the set.

After a few seconds he reappears alone, and calls up to Maxted: 'A couple of minutes?'

Maxted nods. The young man wheels round, and makes his way towards us.

'Hullo, Val,' says Nicky Weedon.

'Hullo, shrimp.' He turns to me. 'Are you the chap who's here to see Max?'

'Let me introduce you,' says Nicky Weedon. 'This is Mr. Whitaker. Mr. Whitaker: Val Farrar, the first assistant director.'

'How do you do?'

'How do you do?' He holds on to my hand a moment, and looks directly at me, inquisitive but friendly. 'She's still awfully correct, isn't she? We're not that formal here, as a rule. Tend not to *mister* very much.'

'I'm Henry.'

He nods and smiles.

Nicky Weedon blushes painfully, and stumbles: 'He – Mis– Hen– I thought it might be rather fun for him to see how it's done. I hope that's all right?'

Val Farrar pulls a face. 'I expect so,' he says absently, glancing towards the set. 'Max is in a bit of a mood today. As you can probably tell.'

'How?'

'Well, he's not really giving poor Miss Szagy any direction at all, is he? Just letting her stew in her own juice. Obviously got out of bed the wrong side this morning.'

'Perhaps we should go back to the office, and leave him to it,' I say.

'No. He'll have seen you. You'll just have to brazen it out. That's the only way to deal with Max.' He turns towards me again. 'Anyway. What do you make of it all?'

'It's marvellous.'

He nods.

I'm conscious that Nicky Weedon's looking at me, waiting for something more. I hear myself saying: 'It's like being inside a giant head. All this lumber' – sweeping my hand towards the pile of mattresses and a wobbly tower of furniture beyond crowned with a heavy-framed Victorian picture of cattle by a highland stream – 'all this random accretion of odds and ends lurking in the shadows. And the job is to drag bits of it it out into the light, and use them to form a coherent world.'

Neither of them speaks: they're too surprised. I'm pretty surprised myself – that's not the sort of thing you say to strangers, particularly when you want them to give you a job.

I try to redeem myself: 'Anyway, I thought it was fascinating, what we were watching just now. What exactly's the story?'

'Oh,' says Farrar. 'Greta's a publican's daughter. Father's a drunk, mother's a harridan. One day she brings home a handsome young man. But he isn't all he seems.'

'Poor girl. Isn't it a shame?' says Nicky Weedon.

Farrar laughs. 'Turns out he's more interested in the pub than he is in her. The back overlooks a bank, you see . . .'

Out of the corner of my eye I see one of the technicians bustling towards us. An electrician, maybe: he's wearing gloves, and has a pair of pliers stuck in his belt. Farrar hears him coming and spins round.

'Val,' says the man urgently. He stops, and jerks his head towards the set.

'Right,' says Farrar. 'Here I am.' As he hurries off, he calls back over his shoulder: 'But it's all right. She meets a nice policeman. Ask Duplicity for a leaflet about it, if you really want to know.'

My puzzlement must be obvious. Nicky Weedon whispers: 'He means Publicity.' Her voice is apologetic.

I look at her. She's still blushing. Farrar's facetiousness embarrasses her, for some reason.

'Camera!' calls Maxted. The pimply boy holds his slate-board in front of the lens. The motor whirrs. 'Action!' Greta Szagy runs on to the set. The wretched woman is frantic now: she looks as if she's flying for her life, and when the dog appears she trembles and starts to cry. Afterwards she doesn't even look at Maxted, but slumps down on one of the bollards, her head in her hands.

'That'll do!' shouts Maxted. He levers himself out of his chair and drops on to the floor, landing with surprising nimbleness on the balls of his feet.

Farrar says something to him. He looks in our direction, nods and calls: 'All right! Close-up!' Farrar walks over to Greta Szagy and lays a hand on her shoulder. The cameraman and his assistant start moving the camera. Maxted waddles towards us.

'Oh, dear, I hope –' says Nicky Weedon.

Maxted's face is pale but damp, giving it the sickly glint of a trout's belly. His doughy features are completely impassive: the only clue to what's he thinking is in his little eyes, which are bright with anger or satisfaction. He nods at me and says: 'You're Herr Whitaker?'

'Yes. How do you do?'

He takes my hand but doesn't bother to reply. Instead he looks at Nicky Weedon and says: 'What's he doing on the stage?'

'I – I –'

'Sorry,' I say. 'It was my idea. I've never seen a set before, and well, you know . . .'

I expect him to let me off the hook: nod, or shrug, or say *It does-n't matter*. Instead, he just continues to stare. But there's something histrionic about his displeasure – the jutted chin; the little sniff – that makes me think he's acting it. Is it that he simply enjoys dis-comfiting people, or is he testing me in some way? Did he even guess that, if he kept me waiting long enough, Nicky Weedon would bring me here, and give him a chance to gauge my reaction?

Remembering Farrar's advice, I return his gaze and say nothing more.

Finally he looks away and says: 'Well, you're here now. And that silly bitch has wasted us enough time already. I'd have been out half an hour ago if she knew how to act.' He glances at his watch. 'Ten minutes, while they're setting up the next shot.' He starts towards the door, with an irritable little flick of the wrist to make me hurry. 'Miss Weedon, keep the predators at bay. No hawkers. No tele-phone calls. No anything.'

He moves with the lumbering speed of a wounded buffalo. I'm a couple of inches taller and three stone lighter than he is, but I have to break into a trot to keep up with him, and by the time we reach the outer office Nicky Weedon is ten yards behind us. A pile of papers marked 'Mr. Maxted: urgent' has appeared on her table in our absence, but Maxted doesn't even glance at it. Once inside his own room he kicks the door shut, and deflates in the swivel chair behind his desk.

'Sit down,' he huffs.

I don't know what I'd expected – stacks of film cans on the floor, maybe; or smoky production stills lining the walls; or at least a sug-gestive prop or two, like the murderer's razors from *Mr. Murgatroyd* – but certainly not this. The desk's bare, except for a telephone and a cigar-box and an ashtray; there are three filing-cabinets, and a small bookcase, so neat you'd think no-one ever touched anything in it; the only other furniture is my leatherette-covered chair, which looks as if it's been pinched from a dentist's waiting-room. The one hint of individuality is a German railway poster, showing a view of the Alps.

'Cigar?' he says.

'No, thanks.'

38

He takes one himself, pokes in the end with a matchstick, but doesn't light it. 'So? What'd you think?'

'About what?'

'What you saw in there?'

'It was very interesting.'

'How about the girl?'

I shrug. 'She was obviously upset.'

'Well, she would be, wouldn't she, if she'd lost her lover and a mastiff went for her? And an audience who see *that*' – jabbing his cigar towards the stage – 'will *know* she was upset. You think they would have done if I'd just told her that's what she was meant to be feeling, and let her skip around being tragic, like Madame Butterfly?' He says 'areeound'. He sounds like a sweet-shop owner.

'They'd have got the idea.'

His eyes narrow. He's caught the coldness in my voice. 'That's the trouble with a lot of you chaps,' he says. 'You think it's all right to knock a tart about, but not an actress. An actress is a *lady*, if she isn't a chorus girl. Have to handle her with kid gloves.'

He opens a drawer and pulls out a few typewritten pages. I recognize the ziggurat shape of the address at the top: it's my letter. He slaps it on the desk.

'Would you be happy if people just got the *idea* of this?'

I hesitate. 'No.'

'No. You want them to get the feeling.'

'Yes.'

'Well,' – drawing himself up, and pulling a mournful face – 'you got to make the girls cry, then. How would she do for your whore, do you think – Miss Szagy? For Fräulein . . .?' He starts searching through the sheets for the name:

'Mayer,' I say.

'Yes, Mayer. Miss Szagy's under contract to us. Could you see her in the part?'

Does he mean it? Is he actually thinking of *making* the film, after all?

'Well, she's a bit young. Fräulein Mayer has to be at least thirty.'

He shrugs. 'That could be arranged. What about colouring, though? Is she blonde? Dark?'

39

'Mousey. At least, that's how I imagine her.'

'Features?'

I try to conjure up Irma Brücke's face. 'Straight nose. Sad eyes: she's really been through it. A charming smile, though. A bit lop-sided.'

'Tits? Miss Szagy's are rather large, as you'll have noticed.'

'Not ver–' I begin. Then I see the brilliance in his eyes and the tinge of pink on his cheeks, and realize what he's doing. 'Well, any-way, it doesn't matter, I suppose,' I say, trying to sound off-hand. 'She's fictional, so we can make her whatever we like.' But it's too late: his tongue darts out and dabs his lips, and he gives a diabolical little smirk. He knows I'm describing a real person – and what's more, he knows I know he knows.

He watches me for a few seconds, idly rotating the unlit cigar in his mouth, and then says: 'You don't mind, do you?'

'Mind what, sir?'

The 'sir' makes him smile. 'My juices are a bit peculiar,' he says. 'But looking at this,' – chopping my letter with his hand – 'I'd say your juices are a bit peculiar, too. That's why I asked you to come here. I thought we might be two of a kind.'

My mouth's dry. I've no idea what to say.

'It's a good story,' he says. 'You've got an eye. You've got a feel. It'd be a nice queasy little picture. Unfortunately, there's not the faintest chance they'd let me do it.' He removes the cigar and strokes the wet end with one finger: a Brobdignagian baby, play-ing with a giant nipple. 'You heard of the Cinematograph Films Act?'

'No.'

'Passed last year. Meant to protect our film-makers. A proportion of every cinema presentation has to be British. So young directors are given twopence-halfpenny to shoot bland little movies that won't offend anybody. A dollop of suburban English spud to go with the American meat. People like me are luckier. We get a couple of bob to make bland bigger movies. A bit of bully-beef to stick on our own plates. But most of it's the same kind of material. You know: gentleman crooks. Love against the odds. Sinister master-criminals. Rogues nobbling racehorses.'

I grimace. 'It doesn't sound very different from what we were doing before.'

He makes a barking sound. It takes me a second to identify it as a laugh.

'Well, you may be right. But in the old days you could at least sneak in a bit of real murder occasionally.' He slices his hand across his throat. 'Or a madman in a slum. Or even an English boy meeting a German whore, who turns out to be the fiancée of his father's killer.'

'Couldn't we call it a war story?' I say hopefully.

'Too many of them already, old son. It's old hat. People want to forget the war.'

No-one's ever called me old son before. I'm surprised to find I like it.

'We're Jack and Jill, you see. Tumbled all the way down to the bottom of the hill, and have to start climbing again. So this' – returning my letter to the drawer – 'has to go back here, I'm afraid. And maybe in five years, or ten, we can have another look at it.'

'And how do we get to that point?'

'I continue making bland pictures – but try to nudge them, an inch at a time, in the right direction, so that they start to look a bit more like real movies. But to do that, I need allies. People like you.'

'You mentioned the story department . . .?'

'Yes. They're looking for someone. I'm not God – at least not yet; so I can't promise anything. But I could shove your name under their noses.'

'What would I be doing?'

'Finding stories, developing treatments, working with writers. It's an important job. Especially with sound coming. In a couple of years nobody'll be making silent films any more; they'll all be talkies. There'll be a lot of new technical constraints. Pretty much everything'll have to be shot in the studio – so more drawing-rooms, more libraries. And we'll be needing real dialogue. The question is whether it'll be' – breaking into a ladylike falsetto – '*Oh, darling, I'm so unhappy, cook's left us.* Or something a bit more . . . queasy.'

I laugh.

His lips twitch. He says: 'There, you see? The future of the British film industry's in our hands.'

I can't tell whether he's being serious, or joking, or just trying to flatter me. 'Thank you,' I say.

'Is that *Thank you for thinking of me*, or *Thank you, I'm interested*?'

'Thank you, I'm interested.'

He must sense my hesitation. He frowns, and says: 'Nobody starts *out* as a director. Unless he's the Prime Minister's son, of course. You're not the Prime Minister's son, are you?'

'No.'

'Then you're buggered, I'm afraid. But for the rest of us the story department's as good a way in as any. If you stick with it, you could be an A.D. before you're twenty-five. And by then there might be something worth A.D.-ing on. Anyway –'

He suddenly cocks his head towards the outer office. The next instant, I hear the muffled buzz of a man's voice talking to Nicky Weedon. I can't be certain, but I think it's Val Farrar's.

'Got to get back, I'm afraid,' says Maxted, looking at his watch, '– make sure Miss Szagy cries again for the close-up.' He stands up. 'You're a Cambridge boy, aren't you?'

'Yes.'

'Reading – is that the word – English Literature?'

I nod.

'You ever come across a book called *New Year's Eve* by Mabel Penney?'

'No.' I try not to smile, but can't help it.

'What's funny?'

'Oh, nothing. It's just I know her nephew, that's all.'

'Do you, now?'

'And I think he'd be amused to hear her novels described as "literature".'

He stares at me and his mouth opens in a fishy gape. I can't imagine why, but I've obviously just gone up several notches in his estimation. *Thank you, Christopher.*

'Well,' he says finally. 'Why don't you go away, get hold of a copy, and send me a three-page treatment by the end of next week?'

The end of next week! I almost say: *that's impossible*; but then think better of it. 'All right.'

He nods. 'See if you can quease it up a bit. That'll give me something to show them.' He's already moving when he puts his hand out.

I catch it in passing. 'Goodbye.'

He doesn't even reply.

Farrar stands outside the door: a collie waiting for a troublesome sheep. He lets him pass, then pirouettes and follows him into the corridor – keeping so close behind that they'll collide if Maxted stops. Nicky Weedon watches them out of earshot, then turns anxiously towards me.

'I'm awfully sorry. I didn't get you into trouble, did I?'

'No, I don't think so.'

'I should have known. He can be a bit –' Her smile manages to be rueful and conspiratorial at the same time. It clearly says: *Isn't it funny? We're the sort of people we are, and he's an oik, and you have to be careful with oiks – especially brilliant ones, like that . . .*

'Really?' I say. 'A bit what?'

'Oh, you know . . . touchy.'

'What's he touchy about?'

She squirms. 'Oh, oh, you know . . .'

'No, I don't,' I say – but with enough of a smile to prevent it being a reproach.

'Well, it can't have been terribly easy for him, can it? – leaving school when he was fourteen. And with parents like that . . .'

'Why, what did his parents do?'

'Not *did* – do. They're still doing it.'

'What?' I grab the chair opposite her, whirl it round on one leg, then sit astride it with my arms resting on the back. Relaxed. Brotherly. *You can tell me.*

'Well, what Val said' – lowering her voice, and glancing towards the corridor, to make sure we're not overheard – 'is that they keep a lodging-house in Brighton. Called' – whispering now – 'Lovely View, of all things.' She quivers with a noiseless giggle.

'He's done very well, then, hasn't he?'

'Yes, yes, he has.' My failure to laugh has rattled her. She tries a different tack: 'I'm sure you and he would get on. What you said in there, about being inside a giant brain – it's just the kind of clever thing he appreciates.'

'Well . . .' I still don't know why I said it myself. I shrug and get up. 'We'll see.'

'Are you going to apply?' she says. 'He really is a great director. The only one we've got that could compare with an Eisenstein, or a Griffith. People will see that, I know they will, if he ever gets the chance to make the kind of films he should.'

She's surprised me again.

'I think I might,' I say.

IV

35675 Eventide Road, Mason, Oregon 97400
E-mail: miranda@pfizerfamily.com

April 27

Dear Alan Arkwright,

Thank you for the e-mail, and your very kind comments. I don't actually write for a living now; I haven't for years. But it's reassuring to know I can still manage to string a few words together when required.

O.K., let's start with the worst: how can I be so sure my mother's death was suicide, and not an accident? It's true the coroner recorded an open verdict – but then that's what coroners generally *do* do in these sleeping-pill and alcohol tragedies, isn't it, when there's any room for doubt at all, to spare the family? And there *was* just enough doubt in my mother's case, because she didn't leave a note – or if she did, my father quietly destroyed it without telling anyone about it.

Maybe you think I'm being paranoid here; but I know for a fact that he suppressed at least one other vital bit of evidence that would, I'm sure, have tipped the balance if the coroner had known about it. Just a few days before her death, she found out that my father had been seeing another woman. There was an appalling row, which I heard from my bedroom: shouts, and thumps, and one dreadful wail of despair that I'll never forget, because it was so wild – so *shameless* – that it made a little china figure on my dressing-table rattle against the mirror. The next day she was quieter again, and I childishly imagined the storm had passed. But now it seems pretty obvious that she never really recovered from the shock.

I was too little to go to the inquest myself, of course, so it was only years later, not long before he died himself, that I discovered my father hadn't even mentioned any of this – and I have to say it made me pretty mad. (That, if you've done your research, is the

45

background to the interview I did after his funeral, when I said he'd "tortured my mother to death, and then covered it up." I was a lot younger and angrier then, and I wouldn't put it quite like that now – but it's still fairly much what I believe.)

On the big question of why he married her in the first place, I really don't have an answer. But if what you're trying to say – as I guess, reading between the polite academic lines, it is – is that they seem to have been a crazy mis-match, then I wouldn't disagree with you. The younger, angrier me, I suppose, would say it was megalomania – that he was turned on by the idea of taking a shattered personality and rebuilding it in his own image – or at least according to his own specifications. Certainly that might account for why he seemed glad (no, *glad*'s the wrong word: *relieved*?) that he couldn't trace any of her family – which meant that he was free to play Svengali (or Dr. Frankenstein) without any competition from her earlier life. And it might also explain why he seemed obscurely disappointed in her a lot of the time – as if she was failing to live up to some *idea* he had of her, though of course he'd never come right out and say it. Example: she loved all the trashiest bits of 50s English life: *Music While You Work*, and Lyons chocolate Swiss rolls, and electric tea-makers, and ding-dong doorbells, and *Woman's Own* magazine. For her, I think, they represented a refuge from what she'd been through: a kind of bright plasticky stage set, where – whatever was happening in the wings – you knew you'd be safe. But for my father, they were evidence of everything that was horrible about the modern world: proof we were living in a "Sergeants' Britain," as he put it, where the last vestiges of real culture were being swept away by a tidal wave of dross. So it really made him angry when she said she wanted one of those kitsch doll things to stick on top of the biscuit tin, or a flight of plaster ducks like the one in the Torridges' hall – as if she were letting him down, somehow, by having such vulgar tastes. And she could never understand, and always ended up crying, and asking me, *Vhy is it wrong to like beautiful things, Poppet?*

But if I'm honest, I have to admit that wasn't the whole story. There were odd, mysterious moments of intimacy and tenderness,

46

too. Once, for instance, I remember seeing them holding hands at the kitchen table and weeping with laughter together over the photograph of a grim-looking man in a homburg hat in the paper. Another time I couldn't sleep, and came downstairs to find them dancing to the radio in the twenty square feet of available space in the little living-room. I'll never forget my mother's smile as she beamed over his shoulder at me: *Can you believe it, Poppet?* I'm *the cat the sun's decided to shine on.* She looked happier and serener than I'd ever seen her, or saw her again.

Unlikeliest of all (so unlikely I sometimes wonder if I dreamed or imagined it; but it *feels* like a real memory) was her birthday one year, when I was woken by a snipping noise from the garden just after dawn. I glanced out of my window and saw my father in his dressing-gown, gathering a huge armful of honeysuckle. When I went in later with my present, it was strewn all over the bed. Again, it's my mother's face I remember best: she looked stupefied, but delighted, too. Her cheeks were streaked with tears and startling smears of yellow pollen that made me think of an Indian brave in war-paint.

So obviously there was some genuine feeling there – some passion and affection, however odd and twisted – but I really don't know where it came from. Looking back, it seems strange I never thought to ask him about it. But you didn't, when I was growing up. That was the whole problem with 50s England: people wouldn't talk about that stuff at all. So all I can say, really, is that he always seemed to be moving to the rhythm of some orchestra the rest of us couldn't hear. But as to what it was, your guess is good as mine. Better, probably.

Re the other people you mention: William Malpert was pretty much a household name when I was a kid. But I had no idea – until you told me – that my father had ever known him, so I can't tell you anything about him that you couldn't get from half a million other people who listened to the radio in the 50s. And as for the name "Omar" – that means nothing to me at all, I'm afraid.

Anyway, sorry I can't do more – but I hope this is some help. I'm glad, at least, that the lead I gave you last time worked out. How

amazing that Flo Torridge is still alive! Please give her – and June –
my love when you see them.

Good luck with the rest of the search.

Miranda Pfizer

V

The Lantern House – October 1928

'Will she fight, do you think?'

Christopher shrugs. 'I really don't know, I'm afraid. She's just an aunt. And a rather disapproved-of aunt, at that. I've met her perhaps five times in my life.'

'Disapproved-of – what, by the rest of the family, you mean?'

He nods.

'Why?'

His hands tighten on the steering-wheel. He hunches forward to peer at the road straggling up ahead of us. 'I'm not sure, to be honest.'

'Because of what she does?'

'Oh, no – producing pap for the middle classes is quite acceptable. No, there was a scandal of some kind, a year or so before I started at Dulwich. I don't know what, exactly, because no-one ever talked about it. But whatever it was meant she had to leave London in a hurry and go to earth in Kent. Anyway,' – rushing on before I can ask him anything more – 'I don't see why you have to talk to her at all. Surely, if British Imperial have got the rights to the book, they can do whatever they like with it?'

His worldliness startles me. He must have changed more than I thought. I glance across at him. Yes, it isn't just the new glasses and the neater hair: his face seems longer, and more shadowed. The mess of adolescence has finally ebbed away, leaving nothing but one enormous pustule in the corner of his mouth.

'Apparently she's a friend of Lady Hopkirk's,' I say.

'Who's Lady Hopkirk?'

'The new chairman's wife.'

'Ah.'

'She persuaded her husband to buy it – or at least, that's what we all assume. And he gave it to Max. The only problem is: Max hates it.'

49

'Why don't they get someone else to make it, then?'

'No-one else will do. Max is the star director.'

'Yes, well, I suppose that is a bit difficult,' he murmurs – but in a disengaged voice that says: *But it's just cheap trash. Why should either of us be interested in a detective story?*

'When he asked me to do the treatment, I thought it was just an exercise,' I say. 'So I pulled out all the stops. Made it as bilious as I could. Put in things I knew would never be allowed on a screen. And then, to my astonishment, my first day in the job, he told me he'd passed it on to a writer and was waiting for a script. So I suddenly realized: he must have given it to me in the first place in the hope that I'd throw him a lifeline, by turning it into something he liked. Which I now have to try to sell to your aunt.'

'Why can't he sell it himself?'

'He's very busy.'

'Still, if it's that important to him . . .'

'I think he feels it might be easier . . . for someone of our background . . .'

'Ah, dear old England, eh?' He nods agreement with himself, then drifts into some train of thought of his own that makes him frown and press his lips with concentration. I guess it must be something to do with *Hamlet*, and decide to leave him to it.

Then he surprises me again: 'So. What's the plot?'

'What? Of *New Year's Eve*?'

He smiles. 'Yes.'

I understand what he's doing now: trying to get me to condemn myself out of my own mouth. Being forced to describe the story, he thinks, will show me its deficiencies more effectively than any argument he could muster. My spirits flag, but I'm not going to give him the satisfaction of appearing apologetic about it.

'Well,' I say, sounding as jaunty as I can, 'it's actually quite ingenious. An elderly millionaire called Vincent da Silva invites eight people to dinner on New Year's Eve. They're an odd assortment: his own doctor; a Labour M.P.; a barrister; a retired brigadier; an industrialist; a bishop; the Provost of an Oxford college; and a blind novelist. Could be a nice scene, I think: imagine' – making a film-frame with my hands – 'lots of candles, and the walls dappled with sinister shadows from da Silva's collection of oriental art. Anyway, as the evening progresses, it becomes clear why the guests are there: da Silva knows something damaging about all of them, and he's been blackmailing them for years.'

I pause, expecting Christopher to laugh, or to say: *You'd have to be a pretty stupid blackmailer to introduce your victims to each other*. But he remains silent, his ear cocked towards me – as though he's giving the book the benefit of the doubt and waiting for me to tell him why it's worthy of his attention.

It's a bit unnerving, but I answer the question anyway: 'The thing is, he's ill, he knows he hasn't got long to live, and this is his last chance to get revenge. Because for all his money, you see, he's always been made to feel an outsider here. Now he's going to turn the tables and humiliate the country that humiliated *him*. The guests, you'll note, have been carefully selected, so that every pillar of British society is represented.'

Christopher nods. Not even a derisive smile. I wouldn't have though him capable of such restraint.

'Half-way through the meal, da Silva is called away to the telephone. When he hasn't returned after half an hour, the doctor goes in search of him. He comes back a few minutes later to say that da Silva's dead. He found his body in the library. "I can't be sure until there's an autopsy, but I'd say someone poisoned his food. I've 'phoned for the police, and they're on their way."'

'Ah.'

'Shortly afterwards, Inspector Holbrook turns up. He interviews the guests one by one, saying that they are under suspicion of murder and that their only hope is to tell him the truth. Gradually he prises their secrets from them – but they all deny poisoning da Silva. Finally, he tells them they're free to go – all except the doctor, who must accompany him to the station.'

I stop, and look curiously at Christopher. He seems completely impassive. Can he be so cold-blooded that he doesn't want to know the dénouement?

He isn't. After a few seconds he mumbles: 'So – he's the murderer, is he?'

'Wait wait wait. There's a twist, which we only discover thanks to da Silva's young secretary, Charles Wymering. He thinks there's something odd about the inspector – and his suspicions are deepened when, after Holbrook's gone, he finds someone's broken into da Silva's safe. So he rings up the police station – only to be told no such person as Inspector Holbrook exists.'

'But surely – if the doctor had telephoned the police . . .?'

'He hadn't telephoned the police. He'd telephoned Holbrook, who's an actor. They're in cahoots, you see. The doctor knows da Silva has a dicky heart, so he arranges for Holbrook to ring up in the middle of dinner, impersonating a man that da Silva had driven to suicide the year before. They think the shock of believing he's heard a ghost will be enough to kill da Silva, and they're right. Once he's out of the way, they plan to pinch his valuables and then assume control of his blackmail business themselves. They've got all the relevant information, remember, from Holbrook's interviews?'

'Ah. Clever.'

'But Charles's prompt action foils them, and they're picked up at Newhaven, trying to make their escape.'

'Is that it?'

'Pretty much. Apart from some love interest between Wymering and the blind novelist's daughter, Angela.'

'*Pas très cinématique.*'

'No, but it could be worse. They've just given us a new story called *Tiddlywink*. About a boy and his dog. It's completely unfilmable. And worthless, to boot.'

'*Tiddlywink?*'

'I swear.'

'Who on earth would call a dog that?'

'Tiddlywink's the boy.'

'Oh, my God!'

I nod. 'Max says he'll cut his throat if they make him direct it.'

Christopher laughs.

'But he thinks if we can bring off *New Year's Eve*, he'll be spared. And they'll maybe give us a shot at something a bit more ambitious.'

'Such as . . .?'

'I was thinking of suggesting *Markheim*.'

'What's *Markheim*?'

He knows perfectly well, of course. But I'm not going to get defensive.

'A Robert Louis Stevenson story.'

'Ah.' Magnificently chilly: a Victorian dowager determined not to notice the dog-shit on your shoe. He pauses, to let me feel the depth of his contempt, then goes on: 'So. What are you changing? In *New Year's Eve*, I mean?'

I mustn't let him rattle me.

'Well,' I say. 'I've tried to make it a bit more visual. Dramatize the guests' stories, so we can see why they're there. And I've darkened some of their guilty secrets, to make them a bit more credible. The novelist's not a plagiarist, he's a pornographer. The doctor isn't just someone who cheats at cards, he's a drug-addict and an abortionist. And I've managed to hint that he and Holbrook might be more than simply partners in crime.'

'What – lovers, you mean?'

I nod. Christopher splutters. The wheel slips in his hand, and as he grabs it again the car lurches so violently that for a second I think we're going to end up in the ditch. Sweat breaks out on my fore-head. The breeze plasters it against my skin, making me shiver. I have to take a deep breath before I can go on.

'And in my version, they get away with it. At the end you see each of the victims in turn opening a letter from them, demanding money. And then the very last scene is Holbrook and the doctor toasting each other on their balcony on the Riviera.'

Christopher gives an incredulous squeal. Adolescence has rushed back on to his face, turning his cheeks beef-red and reactivating the dead volcanoes of his acne. His shoulders shake. He's a boy in the changing-room again, sniggering at a piece of smut he can scarcely believe he's heard.

My God: if that's *his* reaction, how on earth is his aunt going to respond?

Just after eleven we get to Tenterden. It's a graceful jumble of shops and weather-boarded cottages and fine Georgian houses strung out along either side of a wide High Street – the kind of place Daddy would have loved. Looking at it, I feel his hand on my seven-year-old shoulder, and hear the ghost of his voice: *See that, old man? The cleverest chap in the world couldn't have* planned *anything so lovely. It just grew naturally. That's the real glory of England.*

'I think I need a break,' says Christopher, yawning. He stops the car in front of the church, and stretches his scraggy arms in the air.

'Have we got time?' I'd rather keep going: the motion dulls my anxiety.

He glances at his watch. 'It can't be more than twenty miles. It'll take us an hour, at most.'

We have coffee in a Tudorish tea-room called the Spinning Wheel. It's the soul of cosiness: oak furniture polished to a tawny glow; steamy air scented with the nursery smell of jam and cakes. At the table next to us a couple of women in hats are talking about the harvest festival. One of them, a wispy-haired spinster with wrinkled-peach cheeks and gold-rimmed spectacles, looks frighteningly like my idea of Mabel Penney. I try to ignore her, but my gaze keeps drifting guiltily back to her mild, sweet-natured face.

Afterwards, Christopher prowls up and down the High Street, taking pictures with his folding camera. In one cottage, a red-faced man who might be a retired colonel glares out through a diamond-paned window. Christopher instinctively shrinks back – then pushes himself forward again, blushing, and carefully presses the shutter, before turning and ambling back along the pavement. The man twitches his moustache and wags an angry finger. I smile at him apologetically.

'What the hell are you doing?' I say, catching Christopher up.

'This is Elsinore,' he says. 'And that's Polonius.'

'What, *that* old dug-out?'

He nods. 'I'm going to be doing it in modern dress. Did you notice his suit? Quite extravagantly tweedy. Perfect for the sententious Mr. P.'

'Isn't it a bit English?'

'My Elsinore *is* England.' He pauses in front of a newsagent's, and photographs a notice in the window: 'Missing tabby. Martha. Please get in touch with Mr. and Mrs. Martin at the Forge. Telephone: 239.'

As we go on again, he says: 'What do you think this place would have looked like fifteen years ago?'

'Pretty much the same.'

'Exactly. It's a lie, isn't it?'

I shrug. 'It just didn't get shelled, that's all.'

'That's one bit of luck for the French. At least they can't pretend that nothing happened. But Gertrude and Claudius can pretend. The court's still there. The castle.' He sweeps his hand towards a freshly painted house, its four-hundred-year-old timbers as elegantly bowed as a ship's. 'Everything appears to be the same. But really they've reduced the world to chaos. That's the heart of Hamlet's predicament, isn't it? Their greed and folly have ruptured his relationship with the past, and robbed his life of meaning.'

I feel suddenly sick and giddy, as if I've drunk too much. When we get to the car, I have to lean against it for a few seconds to catch my breath.

'Are you all right?'

I nod, and open the door. My head's stopped whirling, but I still have a strange sense of dislocation. Christopher cranks the engine, then gets in beside me, jabs it into gear, and lets in the clutch with a jolt. As we glide past the White Lion Hotel it seems to buckle, as if it's no more than an image painted on a flat. The original must exist somewhere – but somehow I can't reach it.

'Do you ever feel cheated?' I say. 'As if there's an invisible membrane shutting you out from everything?'

'Of course I do. It's our generation's job to feel that.'

A mile or so after Tenterden we get our first glimpse of the marsh: a grey-green quilt of oddly shaped fields and hillocks, stitched together by dykes and low hedges hunched against the elements. Suddenly I can breathe easily again, as if someone's just opened a window in an overheated room. The desolation makes it real: this isn't cosy England, but an England of smugglers and convicts and Napoleonic prisoners of war. As we descend through Appledore, I finally catch an exotic whiff of sea and sheep and salty wind-dried grass. For the first time in hours, I feel a spasm of hope. If she chooses to live in a place like this, we may get on after all.

The Lantern House is at the end of a tussocky track running alongside a canal. It's a lonely spot: the only other buildings you can see are a couple of wonky tar-painted huts toppling into a muddy creek about a mile away, and beyond them a small church standing all alone on a little rise. The house itself is square and heavy and coarsely classical, its red-brick walls weather-beaten and seamed with lichen. At one end is a squat glass-topped tower, rather like a stunted lighthouse, which must have given the place its name. I'm still peering up at it, trying to work out what it is, when Christopher suddenly yells 'Jesus Christ!' and stamps on the brake. I'm thrown violently forward, and have to fling out a hand to stop myself going through the windcreen.

There's a soft feathery thud, then an enormous Rhode Island Red shoots out from under the bumper, squawking with outrage. I can see sweat on Christopher's forehead, but he tries to appear nonchalant.

'That is the biggest bloody chicken I've ever seen in my life,' he says. 'I don't know how I managed to avoid it. Wouldn't have been a good start, would it, to go in with blood on our wheels?'

We leave the car where it is and scrunch up the short drive. Just as we reach the front door it opens suddenly and a pair of clumber spaniels bound out to greet us. Behind them is a wiry woman with cropped grey hair, wearing a Tyrolean felt waistcoat and a purple skirt that hangs awkwardly off her hips. She glances tentatively from me to Christopher. It must be so long since they last met that she doesn't know what he looks like now.

'Hullo, Aunt Mabel,' he says.

'Christopher!' She takes his hand in both of hers and gazes into his eyes, but isn't sure what to say next. He's clearly uneasy, too.

He flexes his angular shoulders and hurriedly directs her towards me: 'This is Henry Whitaker.'

'How do you do, Mr. Whitaker?' Her manner with me is noticeably different: brisk and formal. I barely feel the pressure of her bony fingers. 'Did you have a good journey?'

'Yes, thanks.'

She nods, and turns back to Christopher. 'Well, I expect you're ready for a drink, aren't you?'

She leads us through a tile-flagged hall, and into a chilly sitting-room with a couple of logs hissing in the heavy iron grate. Another woman stands by the fireplace. She's bigger and taller than Mabel Penney, with the swelling belly of a rugger player gone to fat. She's wearing a green Viyella dress, but obviously isn't used to it: it's much too tight, and smells of mothballs. Her silver hair is curled above her ears, giving it the appearance of an eighteenth-century man's wig. The overall impression, in fact, is of a Hogarthian squire inexplicably dressed in modern women's clothes.

'Hilary,' says Mabel, 'I'd like you to meet my nephew, Christopher. Christopher, this is my companion, Miss Boucher.'

'How do you do?'

'How do you do?'

'And his friend, Mr. Whitaker.'

We shake hands. I feel I'm being gripped by a pair of blacksmith's tongs.

'Sherry?' says Miss Penney.

'Or would you like some of my parsnip?' says Miss Boucher.

They start moving simultaneously towards the drinks table. The sherry's in a decanter. The parsnip's in a scuffed old port bottle with a hand-written label stuck on it.

'Sherry would be lovely,' says Christopher.

'Are you sure?' says Miss Boucher. 'Parsnip's jolly warming on a day like this.'

He freezes.

I go to his rescue: 'I'd love to try some, if I may.'

'Of course you may.' Her craggy face flushes pink and breaks into a crooked smile. Half her teeth, I see, are missing, and the rest stained brown with rot or nicotine. 'Your friend's a plucky fellow, Christopher,' she says, uncorking the bottle and pouring out a glass of hazy amber liquid. 'The kind of man who made this country what it is.' She starts to shake with laughter. No sound comes out except a faint whistle, with a phlegmy wheeze at the end. 'Here we are,' she says.

She watches to see my reaction. It looks like a urine sample. Smells like one, too. But mercifully she's right: the *taste* is rather comforting.

'It's delicious,' I say.

'Capital.' Is she being ironic, or does she naturally say *capital*? 'We'll join you, won't we, chaps?' She pours half a tumbler for herself, then holds it out and tilts it towards the two spaniels. I assume this is some kind of strange joke, but to my astonishment they both trot forward eagerly and lick the rim, quivering.

'That's enough!' she says, pushing them away again. 'A bit tiddly's all right, but you can't have your dogs falling over.'

I'm conscious of Miss Penney at my elbow. She's struggling to get by with two glasses of sherry and looking nervously at Christopher to try to gauge his reaction to Miss Boucher and the spaniels. She won't be reassured by what she sees: he's leaning against the back of a chair, watching their antics with incredulous disdain. She clears her throat and makes a humming noise that must mean *Excuse me*.

As I step back to let her past, an eddy of smoke suddenly billows from the fireplace and swirls around her ankles. She coughs and says: 'Oh dear, I'm afraid the weather's going to be nasty.'

We all look out of the window. A tumult of charcoal-edged clouds, slashed here and there with paper-cuts of silvery light, is rushing towards us from the horizon.

'Are you going back tonight, or will you be staying somewhere?' she asks, handing Christopher his drink.

'Going back. Thanks.'

'Well, if it gets too exciting, we can always find you a couple of beds here.'

'That's very kind, but –'

'Not kind. Just practical,' mutters Miss Boucher. 'Storms here can be awful. You wouldn't send the Kaiser out in one, unless you're a black-hearted devil.'

'Yes, well, anyway,' says Miss Penney quickly. 'Good health, everybody!'

We all raise our glasses. I edge towards Miss Penney, hoping to ask when we can discuss the book, but before I can say anything she's turned her back on me and is facing Christopher again.

'So,' I hear her say, 'how are your parents, and Judy? You must give me all the news.'

My skin prickles, but I tell myself it's all right: she's no reason to feel offended by me – or at least, not yet. It's natural she should be glad of the chance to talk to her nephew after so long. Perhaps she's hoping it will lead to a rapprochement with the rest of the family. That would account for her embarrassment at Miss Boucher's eccentricity – if you're trying to prove your respectability, you want to appear as *un*eccentric as possible. From her point of view, in fact, *I* may be the 'B' movie, and Christopher the first feature, rather than the other way round – which should, perversely, make my job easier, because it would suggest she doesn't actually care terribly about *New Year's Eve*, and so won't put up much resistance to my ideas for it.

'I hope you're going to flabbergast me,' says Miss Boucher suddenly in my ear.

I smile. 'How?'

'With filth about the film world. You hear such tantalizing things, don't you? – but our lily-livered press leaves pretty well everything to the imagination.' She takes a mother-of-pearl cigarette box from the mantelpiece and opens it. 'Gasper?'

'No, thanks.'

She scrabbles one out for herself. I light it for her. She inhales deeply, half-closing her eyes with pleasure, and says: 'Sometimes, when I can shake off Mabel for the afternoon, I sneak into Mr. Petty's in Rye and exchange a grubby halfpenny for the *Daily Mail*. But even that titillates more than it gratifies, doesn't it?'

'I just know a lot of hacks, I'm afraid.'

'No, no.' She wags a thick finger reeking of tobacco, then lays it on my lapel. 'You can't fob me off with that. Even hacks must gossip. More than the rest of us, probably. That pert young woman Greta Szagy's one of yours, isn't she? I can't believe there aren't a few stories about her.'

'Well, I do know, from personal experience, that she doesn't speak very good English. And tends to cry a lot.'

'Really?'

I describe the scene I saw being shot from *Shadow on the River*. She's as engrossed as if I were telling her I'd found Greta *in flagrante* with Ivor Novello.

When I've finished, she gives a squawk of delighted outrage: 'My

God, I'd no idea! Your Mr. Maxted must be a monster. If he'll do that in public, what does he get up to when he's alone?'

'Not a great deal, I suspect.'

'Oh, come now.'

'No, really. I'm sure he leads a blameless domestic life. He keeps all the unsavouriness for his films.'

'You should see yourself, Mr. Whitaker. You can't even look me straight in the eye. You're just being a good chap, aren't you, and protecting him?' She leans towards me and half-whispers: 'It'll be perfectly safe with me, I promise. I won't let on to a soul. Except maybe a few sheep, if I really can't contain myself.'

I'm saved by the sound of the gong in the hall.

'Ah, shall we go through?' says Miss Penney. She takes Christopher's arm and starts towards the door.

'Don't think you can escape that easily,' says Miss Boucher, laughing and waggling her glass. 'We'll see if a bit more booze can't loosen your tongue.' She breaks the end off her half-smoked cigarette and leaves the rest in the ashtray, presumably to finish later. Then she taps my elbow, to urge me after the others.

The dining-room's even colder than the sitting-room, and smells slightly of mildew. In the middle is a mahogany table laid with heavy Victorian silver and battered mats showing hunting scenes from Jorrocks. We're waited on by a red-faced girl in glasses.

'This is Alice,' says Miss Penney, sitting down, as if it were quite normal to introduce servants to guests. 'Her mother cooks for us. We're very lucky to have them both looking after us.'

Alice blushes, and half-curtseys. 'I'm ever so pleased –' she begins, then stops as she sees Miss Penney's smile, and giggles: 'Is that wrong?'

'No. It's very nice. Thank you.'

I sit opposite Christopher. Behind him there's a grandfather clock with a funereal rhythm and huge ornate hands. Every portentous tick reminds me that there isn't very much time: I need to get on to the subject of the book. But it's difficult. Throughout the soup the conversation remains stubbornly superficial. Miss Penney talks about her mother's watercolours, one of which hangs above the fireplace. Miss Boucher explains how she breeds her giant Rhode

Island Reds: 'It's perfectly simple. They call it eugenics now, but it's straighforward common sense: you just get your biggest cock and let it loose on your biggest hen.' Christopher smirks behind his napkin, but she doesn't seem to notice. The odd thought strikes me that, for all her roguishness, she may not actually know that 'cock' has another meaning.

The next moment Alice appears with a vast roast chicken. 'Here we are,' says Miss Boucher. 'The proof of the pudding, etcetera.'

There's a brief lull as she starts to carve. I feel Max's breath on my neck, hear his voice in my head: *Come on, old son, get a bloody move on. That's the trouble with you people. Don't know how to cut to the action. That's why you can't make films.*

'I hope none of us gets called to the 'phone,' I say. 'That would be rather sinister, wouldn't it?'

Miss Boucher laughs.

Miss Penney looks genuinely puzzled: 'Mm?'

'Like Mr. da Silva.'

'Oh, yes, yes. Poor Mr. da Silva.' She blushes slightly, then turns to her left. 'So tell me, Christopher, are you still directing plays?' There's a tiny pause before the 'directing', as if it's a dangerous activity: *Are you still racing Bentleys, and running guns?* 'I seem to remember that was your passion, wasn't it?'

'One of them. Yes, I'm going to be doing *Hamlet*, next term.'

'What, at Cambridge?'

'Yes. The Festival Theatre.'

'So you're staying on, are you?'

'For the time being.' He nods towards me, with a rancid smile. 'I know Henry couldn't wait to get out, but I actually quite like the place.'

'And who's going to be playing the Prince?'

'A fellow called William Malpert. I'm setting it in the present.' He quickly outlines his ideas for the production, enjoying playing the *enfant terrible*. Miss Penney seems gratifyingly perplexed.

When he's finished, she says: 'Well, it does sound very . . . very interesting. Most unusual.'

'But you won't get the girls to come,' says Miss Boucher. 'They like seeing chaps in knickerbockers and hose.'

A gust of wind rattles the window and spatters it with raindrops. Miss Penney turns towards it. The sky has darkened to the colour of an old bruise. She clicks her tongue, and says: 'That looks rather ominous, doesn't it?'

'We should hurry up and get out for a walk, before it sets in good and proper,' says Miss Boucher.

I'm desperate now. The whole day seems to be slipping away. I can't think of a more delicate approach, so I burst out: 'What about the book?'

'Mm?' says Miss Penney.

'We will have a chance to talk about it?'

'Well, I don't really think there's an awful lot to say . . .'

'But you don't know yet what I'm going to suggest.'

She swallows and glances shamefacedly at Miss Boucher. Even before she speaks, I know what's coming:

'I was rather uneasy when I got your letter, Mr. Whitaker. I couldn't quite imagine what you had in mind. So I spoke to Lucy Hopkirk, and she arranged for a copy of the er . . . of the *treatment* . . . to be sent to me.'

I take a deep breath. 'And what did you think?'

'I thought . . . Well, to be frank, I couldn't see why everything had to be so sordid.'

'Sordid.' I let the breath out again. 'Well, yes . . . But then, *killing* people's a bit sordid, isn't it?'

Miss Boucher cackles.

'My readers expect murder,' says Miss Penney. 'They don't expect . . . all those other things.'

'Has anybody filmed one of your stories before?' I'm being disingenuous: I've done my research, and know the answer already.

'No.'

'It's a very different medium.' I turn so I can't see Christopher at all. I daren't risk catching his eye. 'You can be subtle in a book – suggest all kinds of nuances with a word or a phrase. In a film, you can't. Everything is literally in black-and-white. The characters' motives have got to be strong and clear. You've no opportunity to explain niceties.'

'But such *awful* motives. I mean – Dr. Dickinson. He's the sort of man you might meet at a dinner party. Well, of course, that's where you do meet him, isn't it? I just can't believe he'd do anything so *horrible* as – as the things you have him doing.'

'He does deliberately frighten an old man to death.'

'Yes, but – Oh, dear –' She sniffs. Her eyes are suddenly bright with tears. Her lip's trembling. She looks down and thrums her fingers on the table to steady herself.

'Why don't you ring the bell for our pud?' says Miss Boucher.

Afterwards Miss Boucher finds a couple of old coats for Christopher and me and whistles up the dogs. When she opens the door the wind knocks the handle out of her hand and pushes her back into the hall.

'Aagh!' she says, staggering forward again. 'I'm afraid that settles it. You'll have to stay. Can't motor back to town in this.'

We troop outside and start along the canal towards the little church, screwing up our faces against the rain. It's hard to see and almost impossible to talk: the words are just whipped away from you, so you can't even hear them yourself. Miss Penney, in any case, makes it quite clear she doesn't *want* to talk to me: she strides purposefully ahead with Christopher, and then – when I catch them up – drops back to join Miss Boucher. By the time we turn for home again I've more or less abandoned all hope of being able to discuss *New Year's Eve* at all.

But then, just as we reach the drive, Miss Boucher suddenly stops and says: 'Right – I'll ask Alice to get us some tea. And then Christopher and I will make a census of the beds and decide who's going to go where.'

'And perhaps you, Mr. Whitaker,' says Miss Penney, 'would like to come with me?'

It's so neatly done that it must have been pre-arranged – though when I can't imagine, because they barely seem to have spoken to each other. I follow Miss Penney past the front of the house. She unlatches the door of the tower, gropes for an electric torch hanging just inside, then switches it on to guide us up the twisting staircase. The room at the top is obviously her study. It's octagonal, with bookcases and cabinets on four sides. The others are entirely taken up with big windows that shiver in the wind and fill the place – even in this weather – with soothing pearly light. In the middle is a little iron stove on claw feet. It's still quite warm: she must have been working here this morning, before we came. In front of it are a pair of tattered armchairs.

'Do sit down,' she says.

'Thank you.'

She settles herself opposite me and I brace myself for a dressing-down. So it's a surprise when she smiles appeasingly and says: 'I hate weepy women,' she says. 'I'm sure you do, too. You must think me very feeble, after my performance at lunch.'

'No, not at all. It's quite understandable that you should feel strongly about the characters you've created.'

She purses her lips and murmurs: 'Hm.' It's half a laugh, as if the idea has never occurred to her before and she finds it amusing.

'I'm just sorry you saw the treatment before I had a chance to explain what I was trying to do.'

She shakes her head. 'I'm a complete novice when it comes to film, Mr. Whitaker. For all I know, you may be absolutely right about it. And I wouldn't want you to imagine I was so self-deluded as to suppose that Dr. Dickinson and the rest are more than mari-onettes. I really don't care very much *what* happens to them. It's just . . . I would much rather you left them as they are.'

She looks away from me quickly and busies herself feeding the stove from a pock-marked copper scuttle.

'I'm sorry,' I say. 'I don't quite understand –'

'No, I know it must sound contradictory.' She clears her throat, noisily riddles the coals with the poker, then sits up again and scru-tinizes my face to see if she's said enough to satisfy me. And immediately realizes she hasn't.

'Oh dear, oh dear,' she says. 'This is exceedingly difficult.'

I should, of course, go to her aid: *That's all right – you needn't say any more – naturally, we'll respect your wishes.* But that would be to throw away my last frail chance of persuading her and returning to the studio in triumph. So I keep quiet, and watch her struggling with herself.

Eventually she says: 'We've been here nearly ten years, Mr.

Whitaker. We lead a very quiet – well, you can see the kind of life we lead. It might look rather isolated, but we've managed to put down a few roots. I do the flowers sometimes, in the church in the village. Hilary generally has a stall at the vicarage fête. There are two or three houses where we're invited to tennis parties in the summer and drinks at Christmas. It's not what I'd have imagined for myself when I was younger, but you adapt, don't you? *Ivy's got to go where the wall takes it*, as my nurse used to say.'

'It sounds a rather ideal existence, for a writer.'

'Yes, it is. We're left pretty much to our own devices. Nobody pries, or makes a fuss. And I don't think anyone will, as long as I keep on turning out detective stories, and don't upset the apple-cart. But this film you want to make most definitely would upset the apple-cart, I'm afraid.'

'Oh, surely people are a bit more tolerant than that, aren't they?'

She shakes her head. 'We'd have to move again.'

'I find it very hard to believe . . . I mean, you could tell them, couldn't you, that it wasn't your fault? – that we'd taken awful liberties with the book?'

She doesn't reply at once, but looks sadly at the fire. Then she turns abruptly back to me and says: 'Do you chaps still talk about honour? Honour bright, word of honour – that sort of thing? Men did, all the time, when I was a girl. But perhaps everything's changed.'

I've no idea why she's asked me, or how I'm meant to respond. I almost say: *I suspect those kinds of ideas have been rather devalued by the war*; then I think better of it, and decide simply to throw a question back at her instead.

'Why?'

She sighs. 'You put me in a very awkward spot, Mr. Whitaker.'

'I'm sorry –'

'No, I'm not blaming you.' Her hands are clenched together, and she nibbles at her lip before going on: 'Christopher hasn't said anything to you, has he?'

'He did mention a scandal, some years ago.'

'But not . . . what it was?'

'No. His parents never told him.'

'No, I can't imagine they would. So you see . . .'

'Miss Penney,' I say, 'you really don't have to justify yourself. I'll just go back and say you don't like my ideas.'

She looks at me uncertainly: a child suddenly told she doesn't have to take her cod-liver oil after all.

Then she sighs and says: 'Well . . . Yes . . . Thank you. If you're sure that's all right.'

'Of course.' *Damn*. Max is tut-tutting in my head, but what else could I have done?

'I'm sorry I dragged you all the way up here for nothing. And that I wasn't more helpful.'

'It doesn't matter,' I say, getting up. I can hear the irritation in my own voice: it sounds staticky and brittle.

She hears it too: 'Does this mean the film won't be made, do you imagine?'

'I don't know. That's not my decision.'

She stands up herself and hovers by her chair, smiling tentatively. 'What if it were your decision?'

I shrug.

As I start towards the door she says: 'It's a bit daunting, you know.'

There's a plaintiveness in her tone that makes me stop and turn. She's standing in front of her chair, kneading her hands. 'Having you and Christopher here,' she says. 'I mean . . . I know what you were taught to think at Cambridge. About the kind of books I write. Christopher told me.'

'They didn't teach us anything about them.'

'No. That's the point, isn't it?' She knows it sounds snappish, and sugar-coats it with a grin. 'I suppose it's just pride, really, but I'd hate you to leave with the impression that I don't *know* how limited they are. Or that *New Year's Eve* is the – the' – laughing – 'the pinnacle of my literary ambition. Look.' She opens a cabinet next to the desk. It's divided into four compartments, each of them half-filled with stacks of paper. 'These are my more serious efforts.' She lifts one of the piles out, grunting with exertion. 'They won't see the light of day till after I'm gone, but then, I hope – Well, maybe you'll be surprised.'

I start towards her to take a closer look. Immediately she turns away and begins to slide it back again. But her hands are shaking,

66

and the top few sheets graze the shelf above and start to slide off. I lunge forward to save them. As I do so, I catch sight of the title page: *The Black Moon*, by Sylvia Plumtree.

'There you are,' I say.

But she's frozen: her hands clamped on the mansucript, her eyes shut.

After a few seconds she mutters, through gritted teeth: 'Did you see?'

'What?'

'The name.'

'Sylvia Plumtree?'

She nods.

'Shouldn't I have done?'

'Did you recognize it?'

'No.'

She unfreezes enough to finish putting the papers away and close the cabinet. But she's still very tense: the tendons in her neck are bulging.

'Please,' she says. 'Sit down again.'

I return to my chair. She perches opposite me, then closes her eyes again and lifts her face towards the ceiling, as if she's appealing for divine guidance.

Finally she looks at me again and says: 'Well, I have to tell you now, don't I? You'll only find out some other way, if I don't. That would be even worse.'

Dusk is beginning to fall. There's an oil-lamp on the desk and another hanging from the ceiling, but she doesn't light either of them.

'How well do you remember the war?' she says.

'I was eleven when it finished.'

She nods. 'You'll know everything got terribly jostled, then. I'd been living with my mother in Blackheath, then suddenly I found myself as a rather elderly land-girl on a little farm in Bedfordshire. The whole place stank of cabbages. After a few weeks I put my back out and was ordered to bed. I was very bored. And a bit lonely, I expect, too. I occupied myself scribbling a novel. About . . . about . . . Well, perhaps you can guess . . .'

I take a huge chance: 'The . . . The love between two women?'

She doesn't say I'm right, but I can tell I am.

She swallows, then goes on in little more than a whisper: 'It came out in 1918, three months before the armistice. At least I had the gumption to use a *nom de plume*. I took it from the plum tree I could see from my window. But otherwise . . .' She shakes her head. 'I was a complete idiot. I'd no idea the stir it would cause. *I hesitate to suggest that Miss Plumtree is in the pay of the Hun. But why else would she mock the gallantry of our fighting men and the quiet strength of their wives and mothers by showing us such a warped and unnatural example of womanhood?*'

'Who said that?'

'Lady Grylls, in *The Record*. I can still remember it, word for word.'

I grimace.

'Two or three other journalists took up the refrain. One of them went to the trouble of uncovering my real identity. It can't have been terribly difficult for him. Then he wrote to me, saying he would blazon it across every paper in the country if I ever . . . if I ever . . . *exposed the sewer of my filthy imagination again.*'

What can I say? *Oh, dear* or *How awful* or *Poor you*? As useless as *That's a shame* to Irma Brücke. I lean forward and look directly at her, hoping my eyes will express what I can't find the words for.

'He's now an editor, I believe,' she says. 'So you see why . . . I mean, the film . . . It isn't hard to guess what he'd make of abortionists and drug-addicts and pornographers. Not to mention the other thing you hint at.'

'Yes.'

'It was a dreadful misjudgement on my part, I'm afraid. I should have known better, but there you are. You make a mistake, and you're lumbered with the consequences for life, aren't you? – like those poor girls who have babies.' She hesitates a moment. 'You're not shocked?'

'No.'

She nods. I wonder if I should elaborate? Confide in her? I start to formulate an explanation in my head: *Actually, I admire your*

courage. I write myself, after a fashion. But I'd never take the risk of
showing anyone . . .

But before I can say anything, she goes on: 'Have you thought of
going into the church? You'd make a good confessor. I've never told
our vicar what I've just told you. I've never told anybody.' She sighs
and stares at her feet. Then she slants her watch towards the last
patch of daylight and jumps up. 'Oh, my word!' she says. 'Come
on. Tea, tea, tea.'

I expect Christopher to interrogate me the next morning, but he
barely speaks at all until we're in Tenterden again. Then he says: 'I
really liked the look of that sponge cake,' and parks jerkily in front
of the Spinning Wheel.

The same women in hats are sitting in the window. They glance
oddly at us as we come in. I wonder whether it's just because we
were there yesterday, or whether perhaps they suspect we're lovers.
Then I wonder if *they're* lovers. Miss Penney and Miss Boucher
probably don't look very different when they go out.

Christopher's silent until the coffee arrives. As he absently plops
the sugar into his cup he says: 'So – the question is – visible, or not?'

'What?'

'The ghost. Hamlet's father.'

'Oh. Well. That depends on what you think it is.'

'What do *you* think?'

'I think . . .' I try to remember my essay on it. 'I think you can't
simply dismiss it as an illusion.'

'So it's really there?'

'Well . . .' The words start to form themselves into an argument.
I feel its undertow pulling me in. 'We mustn't be anachronistic.
Shakespeare wasn't a product of the Enlightenment. Whatever he
believed himself, for the bulk of his contemporaries the supernatu-
ral was real. They'd have looked at the ghost and thought: *Ah, a
ghost.*'

'Ye-es.' His left hand's still stirring, as if he's forgotten to tell it to
stop.

'But I *do* think we can perhaps see the first hints of modernity in
the way he handles it. You compare it with a medieval mystery play,

say. *There* you know exactly where the devils and angels come from, and they're just as real as the human characters. Not so Hamlet's dad. *He* seems only half-present, doesn't he? And his provenance is left maddeningly uncertain.'

He nods, but he's frowning.

'No?'

'Maybe.' His arm twitches. He wants to make a *go on* gesture, but suddenly realizes he's still holding a teaspoon, and has to drop it with a clatter.

'Hence all those critical debates about whether he's a Catholic or a Protestant ghost, from purgatory or from hell. I think we've got to assume that if he'd considered the point important, Shakespeare wouldn't have been that vague about it. Which means that it's not the theological aspect that interests him, but the *psychological*.'

His face relaxes. 'Yes. I see.'

'So you've got one foot in the world of Dr. Dee, and the other in the world of Dr. Freud.'

'Mm, that's very good.' He stares at me for a moment, then laughs and says: 'Will you tell me something?'

'What?'

'What someone with *your* mind is doing in the world of Mabel Penney?'

'Give me five years,' I say. 'If I haven't saved British cinema by then, I promise I'll give it up.'

'All right.' He stares for a moment at the silky surface of his coffee, then looks up and says: 'By the way, what was that note she handed you just as we were leaving?'

I press my fingers against my inside pocket. I can't help smiling.

'Nothing,' I say.

VI

35675 Eventide Road, Mason, Oregon 97400
E-mail: miranda@pfizerfamily.com

May 25

Dear Alan Arkwright,

Thanks for the message: glad my letter was some help. I'm sorry, though, that it left you feeling "slightly confused." So I'll try, just this one more time, to elucidate. But I'm afraid that really will have to be it.

You want to know what evidence I have for saying that my father was having a relationship with another woman. That's simple: I saw them together, less than a week before my mother died. *She*'d gone to London that morning (after days of gentle coaxing by my father; I remember noticing how unusually nice he was being to her) on a rare shopping expedition by herself. *I*'d been sent to play with June Torridge for the afternoon – but June and I had had a bust-up about one of her dolls, and I'd rushed home in tears. As I passed the sitting-room window, I saw my father sitting on the sofa, talking to a strange woman.

They weren't doing anything particularly compromising. But I sensed at once, somehow, that I was looking at something I shouldn't have been. She was leaning towards him, her feet neatly folded under her, one arm draped along the back, so that her fingers touched his shoulder; he was slumped in the other corner, legs crossed, his hands folded over one knee. The thing that really struck me – though I probably wouldn't have known the right word for it then – was how *familiar* they seemed. To my seven-year-old mind, a man should only look like that with his wife. And this wasn't his wife.

I began to back away; but the woman must have noticed the movement, because she glanced up suddenly. Her expression – it still comes back to me, almost intact, if I shut my eyes – was real horror-movie stuff: she gasped; her eyes boggled; her outstretched hand whiplashed back to cover her mouth. For a second I couldn't look away. When I did, my father was on his feet, gawping at me and supporting himself on the arm of the sofa like an old man. I was shocked to see that he had been crying.

I ran inside, hoping to get upstairs to my room before they could catch me, but they were already waiting for me in the hall, like the bride and groom at a wedding reception. My father hovered in the doorway, pale and fidgety. I think he was still too shaken to think of anything to say. The woman was doing slightly better: she even managed to smile, though it looked like a big effort. She held out her hand and said: "Hullo. You must be Miranda."

I felt, somehow, that it'd be betraying my mother to say anything, so I just stared at her. She was about my father's age (early forties?), well dressed in a tweed-skirt-and-labradors kind of way, and with a discreet whiff of new leather about her – it made a big impression on me, this – that reminded me of a shoe-shop. She waited for me to reply – and, when she realized I wasn't going to, smiled again and said: "I've got a little girl, too. Called something-or-other" – I think it was Susie. "I'm sure you'd be friends, if you knew each other."

There were tears in her eyes. I thought she was going to start crying, like my father. I pushed past her and raced up to my room. They didn't try to stop me.

I never saw her again or found out who she was. But, in case you think I just childishly misinterpreted some perfectly innocent meeting (with somebody from a film company, say), you could tell from my father's behavior that *he* didn't see it that way at all. He told me two or three times that what had happened was a secret between him and me; the woman, he said, was an old friend who'd been upset about something and it would only make *Mummy* very unhappy if she found out about it, so I must promise not to mention to her what I'd seen. After my mother's death, he couldn't bring himself to talk about it at all. The one time I tried to raise it with him, years later, he just got up and hurried out of the room, without saying anything. A guy, it was pretty obvious, with something on his conscience.

Which takes us on to your second point: what, exactly, do I mean by saying that my father "always seemed to be moving to the rhythm of some orchestra the rest of us couldn't hear"?

Let me give you an example: the last time I ever saw him.

It was the summer of 1970. He was in Hollywood, working on that last big crazy project of his – the "tribute" to my mother that never came to anything. I'd finished my "A" Levels, but was still at school. On July 3 the headmistress came to find me, just before supper. She had bad news: Dinah Maxted had called from Hollywood to say that my father had suffered a mild heart attack. He was back at work, but in view of all the complications the doctors figured he might have another one at any moment, so I should get there as soon as I could. Dinah's dad would pay for the ticket.

I went the next day. It was a twelve-hour flight to L.A. Dinah met me, and drove me to the studio. A bunch of people were leaving the cutting-room just as we arrived. Inside, we found my father in a wheelchair, looking at some rushes with the editor. I hardly recognized him: the cancer had eaten another ten pounds in the three months since he'd left, and when he turned towards me I saw the lipless, big-eyed face of a concentration-camp victim. Ironic, really, I suppose, when you think of the film he was trying to make.

He nodded and sort-of-smiled, but his attention was on the screen. I looked to see what he was watching. There was a white flash of clapper-board, then a shot of a crowd of people in 30s clothes gathered in front of a railroad station. One figure stood out: a young fair-haired woman in a fur-collared coat, who seemed suspended in the middle of the chaos, like the calm heart of a tornado. As I watched, she suddenly looked in our direction and smiled. My father wheezed something that I couldn't make out. I assumed he was angry, because she'd broken the first rule of film-acting: never show you're aware of the camera. But he must have asked to see it again, because the editor ran the film back, and showed us the same episode a second time. And then a third. At the fourth, my father made a choking noise, and I noticed he was crying – huge tears squeezing themselves out over the papery skin under his eyes. I asked if he was O.K. After a few seconds he managed to mutter: *It's all right.*

73

"*What*'s all right?" I said. "You mean *you* are?"

He shook his head, and stretched his hand towards me. I reached out, but he withdrew it again. It took me a moment to realize he didn't want me to *hold* it but to *look* at it. He made sure I was watching, then made a shaky thumbs-up sign. After a couple of seconds he couldn't keep it up any longer and dropped it in his lap. Then, all at once, his eyelids flickered, and his head sagged.

I thought he was dying. I yelled at the editor that we should get help. The guy was very calm about it – *It's OK, he's just worked up* – but called the nurse anyway. While we were waiting for her, I asked why my father had been so crazy about that shot. The editor didn't know; he just said that when my father had first seen it, he'd called the rest of the crew in and asked if they remembered noticing the woman while they were filming. When they all said they didn't, he'd got very excited, and wanted the guy to run it again. And then I'd arrived. "And you're his daughter, right?" he said.

"Yes."

"Well, the only thing I was thinking was, maybe that lady reminded him of your mom? When she was young?"

I told him she looked nothing like her: my mother was dark, like me. "And, anyway," I said, mimicking my father's thumbs-up, "what was this for?"

The guy just smiled and shrugged. "Sorry."

The nurse arrived and wheeled my father away. I don't know if he ever spoke again, or even recovered consciousness. He died just before two the next morning.

People were very kind to me afterwards – especially the editor. I asked him if I could look at the rest of the movie, so as to try and figure out where the shot of the smiling woman would have fitted in, and what it could have meant to my father. The guy gave up a whole day to showing them to me. I guess maybe he liked having a young English girl around the place – though I have to say he never tried to make a move on me.

Naturally, I was in a bit of a daze – trying to deal with my feelings about my father, and my excitement about America (it was absolutely love at first sight: I already knew, even then, that I never wanted to go back to England), and – inevitably – a huge dose of guilt that these totally contradictory emotions were torrenting through me at the same time. And, of course, when he died, my father hadn't even finished shooting, let alone editing, so all I got to see was a lot of undigested raw material, in no particular order – and, as I know from my own time working in television, even the greatest movie in the world's going to look a bit of an ugly duckling at that stage.

But, even allowing for all that, I can confidently say that it was the worst dog's breakfast I have ever sat through in my life. All I can remember of it now is a jumble of weird, disconnected images (a cloud of moths appearing from nowhere; strange figures in uniform popping up and vanishing again; a close-up of a mouth with wobbly false teeth). There was no evidence of a story. And, even if there had been, the continuity was so crazy that it would have been unfollowable. In one scene, you saw the heroine (if that's what she was meant to be – it was impossible to tell) getting into a car; in the next, she was getting out again – but her clothes and even her hair had changed, so she was barely recognizable as the same person.

I just sat there shaking my head.

The editor said: "And you know what it was going to be called?"

"No."

He grinned. "*Ordinary.*"

I tried not to laugh, but I couldn't help it.

I remember feeling confused afterwards, and depressed, and astonished that a man like Arthur Maxted should have used his influence, and even gone so far as to put up some of his own money, to help my father make such a pile of incomprehensible junk. But (and this is the significant point) the fact that I found it incomprehensible junk didn't surprise me at all. In fact, I'd have been amazed if I hadn't. Because nothing Henry Whitaker did ever made sense to me. I just never had a clue what was going on in his head.

Hope that's a bit clearer.

All best,

Miranda

Sorry, I forgot: "Omar." I can only repeat what I told you before, I'm afraid: the name means nothing to me. I have absolutely no idea who he is/was; or why William Malpert should have imagined he knew "the true story" of my parents' marriage; or what that story is. If you ever find out, please let me know.

VII

London – May 1929

'Morning, Ronnie.'

'Morning, Mr. Whitaker.' He touches his cap, then drops his hand to cover his mouth. But the missing half-finger leaves an arrow-slit, through which I can see the twitch of a smile.

I know it's stupid to say anything, but my skin feels grated raw. Tiredness, I suppose. And nerves.

'Yes, I know I'm late. I didn't leave last night till after midnight.'

'Oh, really, sir?' But his eyes say: *Well, you should manage your time better, shouldn't you? You don't know what it's like to have a real job.*

No, of course not. I only know what it's like working twelve hours a day, struggling to turn a dreadful script into a merely bad one. But you can't out-suffer a gate-sergeant, can you? I simply nod and walk on, biting my lip.

It's not even eleven o'clock yet, but already the heat is thudding off the whitewashed walls. Inside, the atmosphere is thick and woolly with yesterday's cigarette smoke. Nicky's left her door half-open, presumably to create a draught. I stick my head in. She's gazing wistfully at something in her lap, just below the edge of her desk.

'Hullo.'

'Oh, oh!' Her fingers flutter to her throat. The other hand flips over what she was looking at, then picks it up and shuffles it into a pile of papers. But I can see what it is: the picture of her dog. 'You made me jump!'

'Sorry. Is he here?'

'No. Well, he's *here*' – drawing a loop in the air, to lasso the whole studio – 'but not *here*, if you see what I mean.'

'They're not shooting today, are they?'

She shakes her head. 'He's gone to see Sir Basil.'

'What – about the script?'

77

She nods.

'I thought he wanted to discuss it with me first?'

'Yes, well, he was in a bit of a hurry, I think. You know they're going on location tomorrow, for *Second Helpings*?'

I nod back.

'So that's why, I suppose.'

So: he must either hate it or love it. But wouldn't he have told me, if he'd hated it? Given me another chance?

Not necessarily. I can visualize him now, his pendulous belly grazing the edge of Sir Basil's desk; hear the rhythm of his voice as he splutters: *Look at this. We've been struggling with it for months, and it's still rubbish. Simply isn't going to work.*

'Did he say anything about it?' Yes, yes, stupid again: I shouldn't reveal my insecurities. But I'm suddenly light-headed and short of breath. I feel I'll faint if I don't know.

'No, just that I was to ask if you'd mind waiting.' She glances up at the clock. Her face, I notice, is pearled with sweat, but she isn't flushed; in fact, she seems paler than usual, and there are purplish crescents under her eyes. 'He won't be terribly long, I expect.' She suddenly catches my expression: 'What?'

'Are you feeling all right?'

'Yes. Why?'

I dab my cheek.

Frowning, she mirrors me. 'Oh, oh, that,' she says, relaxing again. She splays her hand and examines the glistening fingertips. 'That's just the weather, I'm afraid. It gets like an oven in here.'

'You've got the look of a girl who hasn't been sleeping very well.' *Or one that's been crying her eyes out*, I almost add. But that would be to breach the thin line between friendly concern and intrusiveness.

A faint wash of colour spreads from her jaw to her ear-lobes. 'Have I?'

'A bit.'

She takes a stab at a smile. 'Oh, dear, I'll have to start wearing make-up.'

I straddle the visitor's chair and rocking-horse it across the floor till I'm directly opposite her.

'What is it? Aren't you happy in the new flat?'

'Well . . . No, it's fine, really, I expect.'

'No, it isn't.'

She gives a startled, rabbit-in-the-headlights smile, as if she can't imagine how I knew that. Must be easy being a mind-reader. 'The thing is . . .' she says, 'I'm just not sure . . . I mean, do you *know* Clapham?'

I shake my head. Then I remember William. 'But a friend of mine from Cambridge has just moved there, and he's got pretty rarefied tastes. It must be a decent enough place, if he's prepared to grace it with his presence.'

Her face glows with relief. 'What's his address?'

'Oh, I haven't got it with me, I'm afraid.' *Or anywhere else, for that matter.* But if I tell her that I'll have to explain why, and risk rubbing the lustre off William's endorsement. So I just say: 'What about the girl you're sharing with – sorry, I forget her name?'

'Pippa.'

'Does she like it?'

She shrugs. 'Yes, I think so.'

'Well, what does she say?'

'She doesn't say anything very much. She works in town, you know, and so she's really got her own life, and . . .' Her voice wavers suddenly. She takes a gulp of air to steady it, and hurries on: 'The other evening I was there all by myself, and the people upstairs were playing their gramophone far too loud and thumping about the place, as they always do, and I was staring out of the window and wondering if I could escape on to the common, it looked so peaceful and nice. I was just about to get my coat on when seven or eight boys – young men, I don't know what you'd call them – suddenly sort of exploded out of the bushes. Two of them were fighting, the rest were all just standing around jostling each other and jeering. And then one of the fighting ones got knocked down, and the others started kicking him. It was awful; I didn't know what to do. I was going to 'phone for the police, but then thankfully a bobby turned up, and they all ran off.'

'What, even the one on the ground?'

She nods.

'Well, he can't have been very badly hurt, then, can he?'

'He looked badly hurt. There was blood all over him.'

'Probably just a drunken brawl. You see quite a lot of that sort of thing even in Cambridge. Town picking on Gown outside a pub, or vice-versa. Rugger players and college eights on the rampage. Happens all the time.'

She shrugs again. 'Still. It doesn't make me feel very comfortable.'

'No, of course it doesn't.'

Her gaze has sagged towards the floor. I stare at her intently, trying to prise it up again. After a few seconds she responds – catches my eye – blushes – and glances hastily towards the window.

'You making love to my secretary?'

We both shoot round: neither of us heard him coming. He's looming in the doorway, seams bulging. He looks bigger than ever – but lighter too, somehow, as if someone's filled him with helium.

'I want a word with you,' he says, glancing towards his office, and shovelling the air with his pudgy hand.

I follow him in, then linger by the door to shut it.

'Leave it,' he says. 'Don't want to suffocate.'

He takes off his coat and hangs it over the back of his chair. His shirt is blotched with sweat. His tie straggles listlessly and ends in a scrumpled heap on the ledge of his stomach, as if it's lost the will to go on.

He glares at me. 'You know what I've a mind to do?'

Six months ago I'd have been scared. Now I'm just impatient. 'No.'

'I've a mind to go to the Ritz bar, order a magnum of champagne, and toast myself for having had the mother wit to make them give you a job here.'

My palms prickle. I can hear my heart thudding in my ears. 'So he liked it, did he?'

'I'd have one glass,' he says. 'Then' – his gaze side-stepping mine and settling on the Alpine scene behind me – 'I'd get up and leave. And tell them to pour the rest of it down the plughole.'

He wants me to say: *Why wouldn't you bring it back for me? Or invite me in the first place?* But that'd only give him another current of air to ride, and carry him further into the stratosphere.

After a few seconds he says: 'Yes, he liked it. He just couldn't imagine how you got Mabel Penney to agree to it. So I enlightened him.'

'What!' I know as soon as I've said it that it's a mistake. I've never told him about my conversation with Mabel Penney. I've never told anybody.

'Yes. I said: "It was feeling his cock inside her that did it, Sir Basil. He'll do anything for British Imperial, that boy."' He leers, turning his baby lower lip inside out. '"You should bear it in mind," I said, "next time you want something out of your missus. Invite him over to Hopkirk Hall, and get him to give her a good rogering."'

I press my mouth shut and bite my tongue. There's a sudden rattle of typewriter keys from the next room. Out of the corner of my eye I can see a thick bramble of hair and half Nicky's face. It's still pale, but there's a vivid pink welt above the cheekbone.

Max gives a tiny smirk. 'And he's agreed we can shoot it in Germany,' he says.

'Really?'

He nods. '*You don't need to convince me. I'm sure you're right. Germany's the place for it. All those clever technical chaps.*' He doesn't even try to catch Sir Basil's accent, but somehow he's got his manner exactly. '*Because, you know, Max, Art's the thing with this picture. Art's the thing –*'

'*Art?*'

He nods. '*And we're going to show those foreign chaps we know how to do it.*'

I can hear Christopher's derision in my ear: the whistle of indrawn air through his nose; the click of his tongue. What can I say? Of *course* it's ludicrous. I try to keep a straight face, but an odd spluttering sound forces its way between my teeth.

'Don't snigger, old son. The marriage has been announced between Sir Basil Hopkirk and Art. And you're the best man.'

I've been fighting laughter for so long that I can't hold it back any more. I gulp and wheeze in the struggle to fill my lungs; my shoulders ache; Max shimmers out of focus, till I'm glimpsing him through the surface of a pool.

'Yes, yes,' he grumbles. 'All right . . .'

81

I'm blurrily aware that he's looking at me, one eyebrow raised, trying not to laugh himself. But I can't stop.

Suddenly he glances up and says: 'Ah, Sir Basil –'

That stops me. I turn towards the doorway. It's empty.

'Sorry,' he says. 'Easier than slapping your face, or sending Miss Weedon out for a bucket of water.' He clicks open the cigar box and tilts it towards me.

'Thanks.'

He fumbles two out, snips off the ends with his cutter, then hands one to me and lights them both. There's no noise, suddenly, except the click and grind of the lighter, and the drone of a bee outside the window. Nicky must have heard my hilarity and stopped typing again, in hope of discovering the cause.

'It may not be a love match,' says Max finally. 'But it's still bloody useful for us. For a start, *artists* don't have to make sentimental pictures about plucky animals. Which means we're relieved of *Tiddlywink* duty.'

'That's good to hear.'

'It is indeed, old son, it is indeed. So I won't be casting a collie. And you won't be stuck in your cupboard all summer, writing lines for a ten-year-old brat. And what's more –' He sucks in a mouthful of smoke, then slowly releases it. 'What's more is, he's agreed I can take you with me.'

'What – to Germany, you mean?'

He nods. 'As an A.D.'

Silence. He blinks at me through the haze: a fat cat full of salmon.

I can't think what to say. And then I hear myself saying something anyway: 'Well, that's really first-rate.'

First-rate? What's *first-rate* got to do with the twinge in my solar plexus and the moth-blizzard of images in my head – Irma Brücke; the cathedralish gloom of the Babelsberg studios; a German technician (white coat, glasses, crinkly hair – I could draw him), smiling at my ignorance; the flicker of 'Second Assistant Director: Henry Whitaker' on a screen; Irma Brücke, Irma Brücke . . .?

But then that's the point, isn't it? Pictures are stronger than words. They're *truer*. That's why I'm here.

Sorry, Christopher.

'What about the censors?' I say.

'Sir Basil's taking the script himself. This afternoon.'

'Is that a good idea?'

'He knows O'Connor personally. And I'll be going with him, in case they've any' – another smirk – 'technical questions.'

'Wouldn't it be better to wait?' It sounds childish, I know. I *feel* childish: something I've been saving up for for months is in my hands, and I'm suddenly terrified it'll be snatched away again at the last moment. 'I'd have thought they'd be more likely to be convinced if you showed them what you and the German wizards could do with it?'

Max shrugs. 'We're already costing him three thousand more than he bargained for. He doesn't want to go to the expense of shooting sequences that have to be cut out later.'

'No, I can see that, but surely – with a *fait accompli* –'

He stares at me, absently tapping the end of his cigar against his teeth, as if he can't decide whether to believe the desperation in my voice. Then he nods abruptly, snatches up a pen, scribbles something on a piece of paper, and slides it across to me.

'That's my number at home. Give me a ring tonight. I'll let you know how it went.'

'What time?'

'Oh, I don't know. Seven? Eight?' He pushes back his chair and floats to his feet. 'And take the rest of the day off. You're all wrought up, old son.'

'Thank you.'

He's already in Nicky's office. I drift out in his wake. As he disappears into the corridor, Nicky looks up at me. Her eyes are misty with admiration.

'Well,' she says. 'Congratulations.'

She's giving me her biggest smile, but there's a kind of wistfulness about it that tightens my throat. Yet another case in point: trust what you see, not what you hear. And what I see is: *I wish I had wonderful news, too. But I suppose I'm not clever enough.* 'You're going to be too grand to talk to me soon,' she says. 'I feel I ought to curtsey.'

She starts to get up, but her skirt catches the wobbly tower of papers next to the typewriter and decapitates it. The top half slithers towards the floor. She tries to grab it, but too late: there's a thud, and a brittle snap.

'Oh, oh!' She bends down and retrieves the photograph of her dog. I'd forgotten it was there. She must have, too.

'Is it broken?'

'Yes. Oh, poor Jojo!'

'Let me look.'

She hands it to me. The picture's undamaged, but a long meandering crack bisects the glass from the top right-hand corner to the bottom left.

'Oh, damn and blast!' she mutters. It's the closest I've ever heard her come to swearing. Her eyes are pricked with tears. She tries to smile again, but her lip's quivering too much, and springs out of shape.

'I'll go and find Stuart,' I say. 'See if he can help.'

'Oh, really, it doesn't matter. It isn't anything –'

'Yes, it is.'

The stage is unusually dark and cool: no arcs, I suppose. As I step into the familiar void – breathing the smell of pine and paint and scorched dust that would tell me where I was even if I were blindfolded; glimpsing the snake-pits of cables and the shadowy mountains of props around me – I'm conscious that my feelings about it have changed. Before, I was a visitor from some remote corner of the Empire, allowed to approach the metropolis on sufferance only; now, I shall be a citizen (however lowly) of the metropolis itself. An A.D. *belongs* here. It's his world; he commands its resources; one day, if he's lucky, he'll be elevated to the purple himself, and allowed to use them to make his own film.

Half the *Second Helpings* drawing-room has gone. It looks as if a shell has hit it. Three or four carpenters are demolishing the rest. One of them catches my eye and grimaces as he wrenches at a nail with the claw of his hammer. I know him by sight, but not his name. Must start making the effort: I'll be giving him orders soon.

'That being difficult?' I say.

'It's a bugger. They could put a gun on it, and launch it. Save building another ship.'

84

'What about disarmament?'

He laughs. 'I forgot about that.' And then, as the nail finally comes free: 'Huh, there, you fucker!'

Stuart's in the store-room, scanning the shelves. He looks towards me, then quickly back again.

'Well, hullo, there,' he says. As usual he gets round the problem of what to call me by calling me nothing. 'You wouldna happen to have seen a teapot, would you?'

'No, I'm afraid not.'

'It should be here. They had it last week.' He takes a pencil from behind his ear and strokes his fine coppery moustache with it. 'Um. Um. What would anyone do with a teapot?'

'Break it?'

'Aye, maybe you're right.' He stands back and cranes his neck to look at the top shelf, then suddenly loses interest and turns away. 'Oh, well. What have you got there?'

'It's a picture.'

'Nice dog.'

'It's Miss Weedon's. It fell on the floor, and she's rather upset about it.'

'That's a shame.' I can't tell if he's being sarcastic or not. He slips a fingernail into the fracture, gingerly prises up one edge of the broken glass and squints at it. 'Aye, I think we've got something that might do.' He glances at his watch. 'All right. Tell you what, er, er . . .'

'Henry.'

'Aye, Henry. You wait here a minute, and I'll see what I can find.'

'You sure?'

He nods.

'Thanks very much.'

Wait here. So he still doesn't want me violating the sanctity of the workshops. But at least he's started to call me Henry. That's progress.

Only after he's gone does it hit me: I'm so tired I can barely stand up any more. It isn't surprising, if you think about it: I've had three hours' sleep, and nothing to eat since tea-time yesterday. Nervous excitement kept the strings artificially taut until I'd had my interview with Max, but now they've suddenly gone slack, and I'm buckling at every hinge. The heat is pressing on my shoulders. If I don't sit down I shall faint.

There's no chair, but the library steps are wide enough to perch on. I know I mustn't give in to sleep, but I can't keep my eyes open. Pictures start to form in the darkness behind them: Irma Brücke's flat; the photograph of Walther; Nicky Weedon lying on the bed beneath it . . .

Stay awake.

'You're in luck,' says Stuart.

I open my eyes and stumble to my feet. I've no idea how long he's been there, but if he'd noticed that I was asleep he gives no sign of it.

'Ozzie's making a French window,' he says, holding the picture towards me. 'There was a broken pane, so he didn't even have to nick the glass.'

'Oh, that's splendid.' It takes me a moment to visualize Ozzie: the little fellow with the swimming eyes and the strawberry nose. 'Yes – he's done a very nice job. Miss Weedon will be pleased.' I slip my hand into my pocket. I hate this part of it. 'Do you think he'd . . .? I mean, I'd like to buy him a drink.'

He shakes his head, and gives a man-of-the-world smile. 'Och, that's the last thing Ozzie needs.'

'Really?'

'Aye, don't fash yourself; it's all part of the service.'

I gulp. 'And what about you? Can I . . .?'

He's still smiling, but his Horlicks-coloured face turns cowrie-pink. 'The next time we're in the pub together, all right?'

'All right. Thanks very much.' I must remember to find out which pub he goes to, and make sure we coincide there.

Nicky's watching for me, head tilted to see into the corridor. 'Oh, oh,' she says, as I hand the photo back to her. 'You really didn't have to!'

'Honestly, it's nothing.'

She blushes. 'You've got much more important things to do than –' But she can't finish. Something closes off her voice, and her eyes flood. She must be in a bad way to be so affected by a small kindness.

86

I need a bath – a meal – bed. But I won't sleep if I just abandon her like this. Or rather I'll sleep for an hour – and then wake up and find I can't get off again. I imagine myself lying there in the late-afternoon light: my conversation with Max seeping back into my consciousness, giving my spirits a champagne-lift; then suddenly the memory of her saying *You're going to be too grand to talk to me, soon*, and the champagne turning flat.

So it's selfishness, really: knowing her misery will blight my happiness, if I don't do anything about it.

I hesitate for no more than two seconds. 'Nonsense. You heard Max. I'm actually a gentleman of leisure all of a sudden. So why don't you let me take you out for a drink in Clapham this evening?'

'What!?'

'And you can show me the sights.'

'Really? Do you mean it?'

'Of course. Let's meet at Clapham Junction. Say six?'

'I'd love to!'

I can smell the bitter edge of my own sweat, and the fusty sweetness of my socks. But I know I won't even get as far as the station if I don't have something to eat first, so I slink into the canteen and edge my way to a table by the open window, keeping my head down to avoid meeting anyone's eye. Then I light a cigarette, and look about discreetly. I get a few nods, but not from people who might want to join me, or invite me to join them. The only real danger comes from Val Farrar, who's a few tables away on the same side of the room. But he's busy comforting an obviously distraught Greta Szagy, nodding encouragingly and reaching out every few seconds to pat her hand, and his attention can't escape the gravitational pull of her face.

'Hello, sir,' says the waitress.

I wave my cigarette to fumigate the air around me. 'Sorry. I was up all night.'

She smiles. She's used to it. 'What would you like today?'

I order the steak-and-kidney pie. As she weaves back towards the kitchen Val turns to intercept her, and – as luck would have it – spots me. When she's gone he nods at me and beckons.

I get up, but stop a couple of yards short of their table: 'This probably isn't a good idea. I'm afraid I'm not fit for human company.'

'Really? Why ever not?'

I pinch my rumpled shirt.

'Oh, don't worry about that. We don't mind a bit of a pong, do we?'

Greta's hunched forward, staring at a mound of uneaten mashed potato on her plate. She shakes her head.

'I gather congratulations are in order?' says Val. He half-gets up, holding out his hand. I take it and sit down, angling my chair as far from Greta as I can.

'Thanks. Who told you?'

'The great man himself.'

'Ah.'

'He seemed pretty cheery about it all, I must say.'

'Yes, well, it'll be nice – all of us going to Germany together.'

'Not all of us,' he says softly.

'What?'

He shakes his head slightly, telling me to keep my voice down.

'But surely –' I mouth.

'You and Greta and Max. But not me. That' – darting his eyes towards Greta and scarcely moving his lips – 'is what *this* is about.'

'Why not?'

He shrugs. 'He doesn't feel he needs both of us, I suppose.'

'Oh, God, I'm sorry. It never even occurred to me. I just thought there'd be two A.D.s instead of one.'

'Well, that's decent of you, old man. But I'm sure he made the right choice. You do know Mr. da Silva *et al.* far better than I do. And I'll be all right. I'm being given my own film.'

'Oh, that's tremendous, Val! What is it?'

His glum expression gives me the answer before he says it: '*Tiddlywink*.'

'Ah.' What can I say? *Tiddlywink* has become a studio joke. Example: *What would Sir Basil do if he caught you in bed with his wife? Fire you. What would he do if he caught you in bed with his secretary? Give you* Tiddlywink *to direct.* Or the one I told Val last week, apropos of German reparations: *If they really want the Germans to suffer they'll let them keep their money and tell them to make* Tiddlywink *instead.* Val haw-hawed, and bought me a drink on the strength of it. It's hard to retreat from a judgement like that.

He understands my predicament, and is nice enough to get me out of it. 'I know,' he says, with a rubbery-lipped grimace. 'I must have done something awful in a previous existence. It was this or coming back as a dung-beetle.'

I laugh.

He shakes his head. 'Anyway, I'll just have to make the best of it, won't I? But poor old Greta's taking it a bit hard. Aren't you, m'dear?'

'*Greta?*'

He nods, and lays a hand lightly on her shoulder. She angrily twitches it off. Why should *she* be upset? She's too young to play Tiddlywink's mother, and the only other female character is a shop-girl, who appears in just one scene. I can imagine Max being cruel enough to suggest her for the rôle: the prospect of condemning her to working with a dog for three months would be irresistible. But surely Sir Basil would never agree to squander our female star on such a tiny part? And who would play Angela in *New Year's Eve* . . .?

Val sees my perplexity. 'No, no, no,' he says, smiling, 'it isn't that. *Her* grouse is that she's being dragged off to Germany, and has to leave her lovely Mayfair flat – which is perfectly understandable, of course –'

'No, not just this, stupid!' says Greta, looking up suddenly. I'd have expected tears and blotches, but her eye-shadow's unsmudged and her complexion plaster-smooth. Only the flecks of spittle when she speaks show how angry she is.

'Well, no,' murmurs Val. 'There's also the question of Charlie. Her new um . . . who unfortunately can't go with her . . .'

'And what about you, you silly . . . oh-oh, I don't know what you are! You don't go with me neither, do you? So I have no-one who will keep that pig from me.'

'Well, you'll have Henry here. That's why I asked him to come over: so that you could have a bit of a chat. Max takes much more notice of him than he does of me –'

'Oh!' She gets up, pushing back her chair so violently that it topples on to the floor. As she starts towards the door she almost collides with the waitress – who manages, just in time, to swoop her tray out of the way and gracefully land it on our table. There are two cups of coffee on it, quaking in their saucers.

'Sorry,' says Val, taking one. 'There's been a bit of a change of plan. We won't be needing that now. And bring Mr. Whitaker's lunch here when it's ready.' He watches her out of earshot, then rolls his eyes and mutters: 'Oh, Lord!'

'Here,' I say, offering him a cigarette.

'Thanks.'

I light it for him. He stares at the table-cloth, scratching the side of his mouth with his little finger.

'A damn nuisance,' I say. 'The whole mess. Is there anything I can do?'

'Don't think so, old man. These things are sent to try us, as my nurse used to say.'

Should I offer to have a word with Max? Or would that only rub his nose in it more?

Before I can decide he goes on: 'There are times when I think I'd just like to go off and run a pub. Some pretty place in the country somewhere. Marry a nice girl. Couple of kids. Log fires in the winter. Garden in the summer. Roses. Stocks. Tobacco plants. You know: all those lovely smelly things.'

I nod. I can't tell if he's being half-serious, or merely showing his *sang-froid* by making a joke of what's happened.

'It'd be doing pretty much the same thing really, wouldn't it? Giving ordinary people a bit of pleasure. A bit of entertainment. Only this time you'd be doing it directly. Not through all this.' He waves his hand above his head, trailing a pennon of smoke. 'Sets and cameras and lights and laboratories and what-not.'

I can't tell him that's exactly what I like about it. So I murmur: 'Yes, I know what you mean.'

'And gossip and back-stabbing and who's sleeping with whom and bloody temperamental actresses.' He catches my smile, and starts to laugh. 'God, you think of all the chaps out there who'd give their eye-teeth to be in my position. Having lunch with Greta

90

Szagy. Listening to all her little secrets. Giving her a shoulder to cry on. Tell them you'd rather be chewing a sandwich and talking about dogs with Nicky Weedon and they'd say you were ripe for the loony-bin. But that's the honest truth. You know where you are with a girl like Nicky. You don't have to worry whether the next thing you say is going to touch a raw nerve and cause a scene.'

'No, but even she can get blue sometimes –'

'Ah, the counsel for the defence! *My client may be difficult – but then what woman isn't, your honour?*' He jerks back, as if I've slapped him. He's blushing, and has the martyred grin of a cornered schoolboy persecuted by bullies. 'I can see you and Greta are going to get on marvellously.'

It's the first hint of resentment he's given me. I can feel an answering prickle of heat in my own face. I want to yell: *Don't blame me – it's not my fault if I'm better at this than you are.* Then my internal monitor intervenes.

I close my fingers, and dig the nails into my palms. 'All I mean is', I say, astonished at how calm my voice sounds, 'that I saw Nicky this morning, and she was pretty miserable. Almost in tears.'

The change in him is just as abrupt. He leans towards me, eyes wide with concern. 'Oh, really? Poor kid. Why? I hope some bastard isn't breaking her heart?'

'I don't think it's that. I think she's just a bit lonely in her new flat.'

'Well, it goes to show, I suppose, doesn't it? Life's simply not fair. Even the nice ones get it in the neck.'

'Especially the nice ones.'

He looks at me oddly for a second. Then the beam of his gaze is broken by the arrival of the waitress with my steak-and-kidney pie.

When she's gone again he stubs out his cigarette and lumbers to his feet. 'Well, I think I'll be popping along,' he says. 'See you later.'

''Bye, Val. *Bon courage.*'

He nods. ''Bye.'

As he saunters towards the door, I drive my fork into a hard carapace of pastry, splitting it in two and spraying the tablecloth with gravy.

*

91

She's already at the station when I arrive, standing in a little back-water next to the entrance, where the wall protects her from the mill-race of people spilling into the street. She blinks when she sees me, as if she can't quite believe I'm there – can't quite believe she has the power to draw someone half-way across London for no other reason than to be with *her*.

'Hullo.'

'Hullo.'

'I haven't kept you waiting, have I?'

'No.' She's blushing, and she knows it, and it makes her grin with embarrassment. 'This is awfully nice of you.'

'No, it'll be fun. About time I got to know Clapham, anyway. It's the topic of the moment at all the best parties. I shan't be able to hold my head up unless I can discuss its finer points.'

She giggles.

'Where do you want to go?'

'Well, it all depends –' She looks round for inspiration, but can't find any in the clutter of sooty, heavy-featured Victorian shops and banks and gin-palace pubs stretching in both directions. 'Actually,' she says sheepishly, 'I don't really know anywhere, I'm afraid.'

'The only place *I* know is the station buffet. So unless you want a cup of milky tea and a biscuit . . .'

She laughs. 'The common's nice.'

'Let's go to the common, then.'

We let the stream of returning office workers carry us east, past a billowy department store with a cupola that would look more at home in Knightsbridge; and then – a couple of hundred yards fur-ther on – turn down a street of shabby, buttoned-up houses set back behind tiny front gardens. There are lace curtains in most of the windows. Two or three of them twitch as we pass, and behind one I glimpse a bony-nosed old woman scowling out at us. You can't miss her disapproval, though it's hard to know of what – the fact that we so obviously don't live there? The possibility that we might be in love, and sleeping together?

'Do they always do that?' I ask.

She knows exactly what I'm talking about. 'Yes. I just try to ignore it.'

Poor Nicky. No wonder she feels uncomfortable here. But then I think: *What if the old woman's a widow?* She lost her sons in the war, and every young person she sees affronts her by reminding her of them – by saying, in effect, I'm here, and they're not. For a second, a tide seems to tug at my ankles, drawing me to her door . . .

No: that's absurd. What you have to do is take those experiences, and turn them into art. How would you manage it, in a film? First you'd establish your sympathy with the young couple – see them laughing and talking together, feel the drop in temperature as the old woman's face appears at the window; then you'd move the camera inside her house – show the young people from her point of view, before gradually pulling it back until you see the photograph of two boys on the piano . . .

Then I remember my conversation with Max this morning, and my neck and shoulders tighten with excitement: soon I might actually have the power to do it.

'I always feel I'm out of the woods at this point,' says Nicky. 'No more bears lurking behind trees.'

We've emerged, suddenly, on to a wide busy road, with a huge stretch of green beyond. It's laid out with the apparent artlessness of an eighteenth-century park: an asymmetrical network of paths entices you in to a nymphs-and-swains landscape of lawns and little copses. The illusion's only marred by the centrepiece: instead of a half-glimpsed temple to Pan there's an all-too-visible iron bandstand, where a band of red-coated soldiers are thumping out jingoistic marches.

'There you are,' she says – with the wistful pride of a homesick schoolboy showing Mummy and Daddy his dormitory: 'the common!'

'You're right. It's lovely.'

The air is thick and dusty, and smells of grass and sap and engine fumes. There's something indolent about it, as if it can't be bothered to move and doesn't see why anything else should, either. Fighting lethargy, we amble across the road, and start towards a cluster of buildings in the distance.

'I hope that's a pub,' I say.

'Yes. The Windmill. And there's a garden there, so you can sit outside.'

'That sounds nice.'

'It is. Rex took me there once. My brother.'

'Your brother?'

She nods.

'I didn't know you had one. You've never talked about him before. Mother, yes. Father, yes. Dog, several times. But not brother.'

'That's not quite true. I did mention him, when you came for your interview. But –'

'Oh, yes, of course you did! I'm sorry.'

She shakes her head. Not reproachful, but resigned, as if it's in the natural order of things that she should remember our first conversation and I should forget it.

'He's a friend of Val's,' I say, trying to redeem myself.

'Yes, that's right.'

'You thought he might have had something to do with your getting the job?'

She nods, and colours. But not with pleasure: she isn't smiling. Perhaps the idea of it still bothers her.

'Well, you can put that out of your mind, at least. Max says you're the best secretary in the place.' Not strictly true: he says she's the *tastiest* secretary in the place. But near enough. '*The day Sir Basil snaffles Miss Weedon for himself is the day I resign, Henry.*'

I've guessed wrong. My Max-imitation's a cheap trick, but it's normally guaranteed to make her laugh. Not today: she seems not even to have noticed.

'Well,' she mutters, 'that's awfully nice. Thank you.' But it's half-hearted: a well-brought-up girl going through the motions.

I can't think what to say next. And neither can she, apparently. But somehow it doesn't matter: the warmth of the evening and the sound of the band seem to excuse us from talking.

Even though the fields beyond are carpeted with houses now, the Windmill still has the air of a large, unpretentious farm-house. The open front door hints at polished flags and joints of beef and jugs of cream, and ducks from a nearby pond lollop through the garden,

94

foraging for crumbs and bits of dropped sandwich. The place is already thronged with people, and I look round nervously, wondering if William is among them and what I should say if he is: *Hullo, William, this is a colleague of mine . . . Hullo, William, have you forgiven me yet?* But mercifully there's no sign of him – or of anyone I know.

Most of the outside tables have gone, but we manage to find one in a cool shady corner everyone else has overlooked.

'What would you like?'

'Oh, oh, a half of bitter, please.' Not what I expected. And it obviously shows, because she smiles and goes on: 'I know: everyone thinks I must like shandy. But I was brought up on beer. Daddy says it's our national drink, and everybody used to have it, even women and children, and it never did them any harm; it made us the hardiest people in the world. In the old days it was actually women who brewed the stuff – did you know that? They were called brewsters.'

I nod. I *must* remember: she's not as simple as she seems. I claim my chair by draping my coat over the back, and go to get the drinks.

'Well,' I say, raising my glass.

'Here's to *New Year's Eve*,' she says. 'And – and – you. The new A.D.'

'Thanks. And to you, Nicky. And the flat. And Clapham.'

'Thank you.'

'And while we're at it, we shouldn't forget Val, and – and *his* new project.'

'Yes,' she says. But her voice is flat, and she doesn't catch my eye. So: it's the thought of *Val* that makes her glum.

'Why do you look as if you've suddenly got a toothache?' I ask.

'Do I? Oh, sorry.' She gives a quick appeasing smile, as if I've surprised her pilfering paperclips. She hesitates for a second, then decides there's no point in further concealment: 'Did you – did you tell him I was down in the dumps?'

'I may have mentioned it. Why – shouldn't I have done?'

'It's just that I think, you know, being Rex's friend, he feels sort of responsible for me. It's awfully sweet of him, of course, but it can be a bit . . . I mean, this afternoon he popped in, pretending to be looking for Max, when he knew perfectly well he wasn't going to be

95

there. Then he said, *How are things going?* You know, trying to be casual about it. And when I said *fine*, he said that's not what he'd heard, and would I care for a spot of dinner tonight, to cheer me up? So I had to explain . . .'

'Oh, you should have said! I'd have perfectly understood!' But then I realize: that sounds as if I'd have been quite happy to forego her company if someone else had stepped into the breach. Which is true, of course, but horribly rude. So I try to joke my way out of it: 'You've got to take the best offer you get, Nicky. And dinner beats a drink any day.'

She shakes her head and takes a gulp of beer. Her glass, I notice, is half-empty already. The muscles in her face are tense, giving it the flat planes of a cubist painting. She wants to say: *I'd rather be with you.* But she can't: that would be fast, and risk putting us both in an awkward position.

The beer's starting to work in my head. I must must must be careful.

'The thing is,' she says, 'I'm afraid everyone must think I'm making a mountain out of a molehill. Clapham isn't so awful, really –'

'Well, *this* certainly isn't.'

'Not when you're *with* someone, no. But the problem is I'm usually not. Pippa's only here two or three nights a week. And I never know which nights. And when she does deign to turn up she makes it perfectly clear she'd rather be somewhere else.'

'Where?' I say.

'With her – with – Oh, it's a long story.'

'Tell me.'

'She met a man – at work. From everything she's said about him I think he seems completely unsuitable, but within a week she'd got the most terrific crush on him. It was just, you know,' – holding up her hand, and miming a domino being knocked over – 'like that. And I think – well, I *know* – she – she stays at his flat. In Earl's Court.'

She's blushing, and her voice has dropped almost to a whisper, but there's a flash of what-the-hell recklessness in her eyes. It's obviously a relief for her to get it off her chest. And to be talking about something other than Val.

'And do you know what's so silly?' she says. 'She was Mummy's idea. *Pippa's such a nice sensible girl. I'd feel much happier if you were sharing with her.*'

'Oh, I see. She's an old friend?'

'We were at school together. She was Head Girl. *You'll be company for each other. And just in case anything does, you know – well, she'll be there to stop you going off the rails, won't she?*' She drains her glass with an impulsive flick of the wrist. '*Her* stop *me* going off the rails!'

I laugh.

'The whole thing's just so – so cheap and sordid. Honestly. His name's Dennis. He's twelve years older than she is, and he's got a wife already, only they're separated, and he's letting her divorce him. And then he's going to marry Pippa. Or so he says.'

'Do her family know?'

'Oh, goodness, no! There'd be hell to pay. When her mother rings up I have to say "I'm afraid she's not back yet." And then I have to 'phone *his* place, and Pippa rings her from there, pretending she's at our flat and has just got in. I'm sure the poor woman's starting to suspect something. One of these days she'll ask me about it outright, I know she will, and I really don't know what I'm going to say then. I'd make a rotten actress, I'm afraid. That's why I have to do this' – waggling her fingers over an imaginary typewriter – 'rather than this' – smiling and fluttering her eyelids at an invisible camera.

I smile, and reach out my hand. 'Would you like another –?'

'Yes, please,' she says promptly.

I get two halves, and give one to her.

'Thank you,' she says. 'I'm sorry, I'm not being an awful bore, am I?'

I empty the other half into my pint glass. 'No, of course not.'

'The trouble is, you're too kind. You just let me rattle on. My silly little problems must seem dreadfully trivial to you, when your head's full of scripts and budgets and actors. And actresses.'

'Not a bit. I'd far rather make *Pippa and Dennis* than *New Year's Eve*. It's a much better story.'

She grins. Her eyes are moist: some protective film has suddenly melted. 'She's very pretty, isn't she?'

'Who?'

'Greta Szagy.'

'Greta? Yes, well –' Should I tell her what Val said at lunch today? No: that would be unfair to both of them. 'I suppose so,' I say at last. 'But she's not really my type.'

She forces herself to hold my gaze. Her mouth quivers uncertainly: she can't judge the right degree of smile. 'What is your type?'

'Oh, I don't know.' *German whores.* But even that's not right. *One* German whore. And I wouldn't want to be *married* to her, in any case. 'I'm not sure I believe in types, really. I mean, would you say Dennis was Pippa's type?'

She laughs. 'You see? You're changing the subject again. I tell you all about me, and you won't tell me anything about you.'

There's a snap of anger in my head: why should she imagine I'd unburden myself to a secretary? Then I catch her eye, and wilt with shame. I expected gauche coquettishness; instead, I see such intelligence and warmth and frankness that for a second I think: *Perhaps I could actually tell her. Perhaps she's one person who wouldn't judge me, or think I was mad.*

But no: remember Jojo. And Mummy and Daddy and Rex and Pippa and the school where she was Head Girl. Remember Germany's coming up . . .

'My life is in my art,' I purr, in a Russianish voice.

Her face seems to collapse slightly: I'm reminded of a deflating air bed. But she's too well bred not to play the game, so she smiles and says: 'Oh, I hope not. That would make you, let's see' – ticking off the cast of *New Year's Eve* with her fingers – 'a drug addict – a blackmailer – a cheat – a – a –' She can't quite bring herself to say *pornographer* or *abortionist*.

'Which reminds me,' I say, laughing, and glancing at my watch. 'I'm meant to be phoning Max tonight to find out how it went.'

'What went?'

'The visit to the censors.'

'Oh, oh, yes, I'd forgotten about that.' She looks uncomfortably at her glass. 'I'm sorry, am I holding you up, then?'

'No, of course not. But it does mean I should probably be pushing back not too late. So I'm afraid I won't be able to match Val's invitation.'

'Oh, no, I wasn't expecting you to! I shall be fine!' There's a forlorn brightness in her expression that almost makes me relent. But having found a way out, it'd be madness for me to go back in again.

'You generally fend for yourself, do you? In the evening, I mean?'

'Oh, yes! I'm only a humble working girl, remember. The idea was that Pippa and I would take it in turns. Her strong point's pastry; mine's eggs. So I've eaten an awful lot of eggs recently.'

'But not much pastry.'

She shakes her head. 'No. Thanks to Dennis.'

'But I'm sure they're the best eggs in London.'

She blushes. 'I'm not bad, actually, though I says it myself as shouldn't.' She pauses a second, scanning my face, and for a moment we're caught in a hall of mirrors: I know what she's thinking, and she knows I know. The beer has made her almost bold enough to say it: *Why don't you come to dinner with me some time, and I'll show you?* But then she decides it'd be too forward, and looks away. 'Daddy says my omelette's better than one he had once at the Colombe d'Or in St. Paul,' she says. 'I really don't mind cooking at all, in fact – it can be quite relaxing, when you've spent the day getting hot and bothered at the office. The problem's having to sit down and eat it all by yourself, when there's all that racket coming from upstairs.'

'What – it feels as if there's a party going on, that you haven't been invited to?'

'Yes.' She hesitates – gulps awkwardly – stares boggle-eyed at her glass – and mutters something I can't make out above the hive-buzz of our fellow-drinkers.

'What?'

'Not just a party. They make the most extraordinary noises.' She tries to laugh, but can't look at me. 'Sometimes I think there must be some huge animal up there, with all the squeals and groans I hear.'

Poor kid. Can she have pitched up living underneath a bordello? Or is it just some hearty young couple who don't mind the world knowing about their lack of inhibitions? I say: 'Would you like me

99

to have a word with them? It might come a bit more easily from me.'

'What? Oh, no, you really don't have to do that!'

'I'd be happy to.'

'Well –'

'Come on. No time like the present.'

'But have you got time?'

'Yes, if we go now.'

'All right.' She giggles: a schoolgirl challenged to a dare. 'Thank you.'

We drink up and leave.

The sun's lower now, giving the grass a scorched yellow tinge and slanting into our eyes as we start back westwards across the common. But there's no chill yet: the air's still a dense fug, and the beer seems to have hollowed out my thighs, making it an effort just to walk. And it must have had the same effect on her, because we both settle into silence again, without any awkward little spurts of conversation.

But there is a difference this time: I'm suddenly intensely aware of her as a physical presence – as if, having made my decision, I can't help wondering what's behind the closed door of romantic entanglement. I can feel the warmth of her body radiating through its thin insulation of cotton; see the neat little escutcheons of sweat under her arms; smell the oil of her hair, spiked with a kind of curranty sharpness. At one point she brushes against me, and the skin of my bare arm is so oversensitive that I make an involuntary gasp. I'm conscious of an abrupt movement of her head at the edge of my vision, but I don't want to make matters worse, so I resist turning to see her reaction.

I must do this quickly, and make my escape.

'See?' she says. 'You can hear it from here.'

She points ahead to an ugly red-faced mansion block cluttered with gables and pinnacles. It's in a group of equally stand-offish buildings on the far side of the road bordering the common, where they're safely protected from *hoi polloi*. From an open window on the second floor there's a frenetic shriek of dance music, shrilly defying the ponderous beat from the bandstand far behind us. A dim figure inside the room is moving in time to it, though I can't see whether it's male or female, or whether or not it has a partner.

'Yes,' I say. 'I take your point. Let me see what I can do.'

We cross the road. A thin drive running behind the narrow strip of garden takes us to a bad-tempered black front door that wheedles complainingly as we open it. The entrance hall is cool and dim and has the institutional smell of floor-polish and long-since-eaten fish. As we climb the stairs, the memory of Irma Brücke's apartment building suddenly superimposes itself on my senses, and I have to blink it away.

'You wait here,' I say, when we get to her floor. 'Better if I do it on my own.'

I go up the next flight – brace myself – knock – and wait. Ten seconds – twenty – thirty: nothing. He or she or they can't have heard.

I knock again, more loudly this time, and bellow 'Hullo! Hullo!' at the keyhole. A moment later the music stops. There's the soft click of a switch, and then the quick irritable *slap-slap* of slippered footsteps.

'Yes?' says a young man, yanking open the door. I can't see him clearly: he's turned on the hall light, so that he's half in silhouette. But he sounds angry.

'Hullo,' I begin. 'I'm a friend of –'

He suddenly interrupts me:

'Good God! What are you doing here? Have you come to apologize?'

I'm so startled it takes me a second to realize it's William.

VIII

Mason, Oregon
June 1

It's 3 a.m. Hode's asleep. I could wake him. But for some reason I'd rather tell my computer about it instead.

Not a bad dream. A bad *memory*.

How old am I? I'm seven. We're in the – What's it called? Not the living-room. The sitting-room. Twelve feet by twelve, smelling of damp and coal-smoke. In the middle, so big it squashes everything else against the walls, is the sofa. Mummy's stretched out on it, her head propped on one of the arms. I lie facing her, warming my feet between her legs, my calves scratched by leaking horse-hair. Despite the fire, it's cold. A draught from the window nudges past the curtains and fingers my neck. The only light comes from the lamp with the scorched shade, and from the glow of the radio dial. (Radio? Or wire-less? I'm not sure. And what was that stuff it was made of? Something that made me think of crusts whenever I touched the smooth ridged surface. That's it: Bakelite.)

We're listening to *Niddle at Nine*. Mummy strains to understand the jokes, her eyes unfocused, her dark eyebrows pressed together with concentration. But as soon as she hears laughter she relaxes and joins in. The first few isolated chortles make her grimace and purse her lips; as they gradually fuse into a chorus she begins to shake and giggle. Tonight there's a soloist: a braying man whose delighted shrieks have the rest of the audience howling and fighting for breath. Mummy matches them, squeal for squeal: her mouth lolls open; she's weeping, and shaking, and clutching her hair with both hands. I'm a little bit frightened, but also pleased, because it means she's happy. And soon I'm squealing myself, without knowing why.

All at once I feel another draught. Daddy's come in. He walks to the fireplace, and stands there scowling. Mummy watches – taking her cue from him, now, rather than from the audience. In a few seconds, the hilarity has congealed. I taste it on my lips, like cold porridge.

The room is silent, except for the click of the coals and the whisper of the curtains and the chatter of *Niddle at Nine*.

And then, suddenly, there's a new voice on the radio. A woman. Saying something that makes me stiffen: *Bot vee hartly know each odder.*

It's the first time I've ever heard anyone else who talked like that. A huge shadowy animal starts to stir in my tummy. I clench my fists and stare at my own feet. I want to throw myself forward and hug Mummy, but I know it won't be enough. I'm too small to protect her. Mummy will shake, and moan: *Vhy are dey laughing at me?* and I won't be able to stop it.

I force myself to look up. To my astonishment, Mummy doesn't seem to have noticed anything.

But Daddy has. He lunges towards the radio – but not quickly enough to stop us hearing a man's voice replying: *I know you are the one.*

Daddy switches it off, then has to steady himself on the mantel-piece, breathing deeply, his head drooped towards the fire – as if (it suddenly strikes me now) he's afraid he's going to faint.

Finally he says: "You really shouldn't let her listen to rubbish like that."

I've never seen him so angry before. He's trembling. Color pumps into his cheeks, then ebbs away again, leaving blotchy islands of pink. There are bubbles in the corner of his mouth. As he stalks out of the room I hear him muttering something under his breath.

Fucking Omar. I'll kill him.

It's the only time I ever hear him use that word.

The laughter's gone: Mummy's crying now. The sight of her seems to break some sea-defense in me, and a tide of feeling rushes in, tug-ging at my guts.

"Mummy," I say.

She looks at me blankly. A silver thread of snot dangles from her nose.

I somersault towards her and cling to her neck. "Mummy –"

"Vhat is it?"

"The other day – when you went to London – and I was playing with June –"

I feel her stiffen. This must be something really big. Perhaps I shouldn't say, after all.

"Tell me. Tell me, Poppet."

I try to think of something harmless to tell her instead, but I can't.

"Vhat?" I can hear the dryness in her throat. "Vhat happened?"

"I came home early. And saw Daddy with a –"

That's why I told Arkwright the name "Omar" meant nothing to me.

IX

Berlin – September 1929

'This is a joke?'

'No. Well, yes, actually, I suppose you could say it is, in a way. The joke's the English censors.'

'*Senses?*'

'Cens*ors.*'

'Oh, oh.' But he's more puzzled than ever: the white icing of make-up folds into a frown. 'They let me say *I murder babies with a spoon?*'

'No, they wouldn't let you say that. That's the whole point. *Max* wants you to say that. What the audience will see on the *title* is: *It's not my fault if I'm lucky sometimes.*'

He stares at me, then slowly shakes his head. He's a good actor: even his head-shaking's expressive. It says: *Either I'm stupid, or you're mad.*

One day I'm going to machine-gun the entire British Board of Film Censors.

'Listen,' I say. 'Gerhart. You know a book called *Alice in Wonderland?*'

'Yes, yes. Of course.'

'Well, this is a bit like that. I wrote a script, hinting that Dr. Dickinson is an abortionist. Abortionist?'

He nods.

'So in this scene I had da Silva saying: "Strange that a young lady apparently in the very pink of health should have been obliged to enter a nursing-home. *Your* nursing-home, doctor." And then *you* saying: "I don't know what you're talking about."'

'Ah.'

'But the censors insisted I should change it – turn him back into a card-cheat, as he was in the book. So da Silva has to say: "Strange that young Lord Garraby should be so unfortunate as to lose a

thousand pounds in one evening. Almost all of it to *you*, Doctor."
And you reply –'

'"It's not my fault if I'm lucky sometimes."'

'Exactly. All very Queen of Hearts.'

He smiles, and shakes his head again. A spike of dark hair breaks
free and flops on to his forehead. Immediately, the performer's
instinct takes over: he catches it on his finger and – glancing into the
mirror – carefully smoothes it back, pouting with concentration,
impervious to me or scripts or the capriciousness of officialdom
until it's in exactly the right place.

'Anyway,' I say, when I've got his attention again, 'Max's idea is
to use *their* titles, but suggest what *we* want visually. We'll shoot
your lips in close-up, and the quicker members of the audience will
realize that you're *not* saying: *It's not my fault if I'm lucky sometimes.* Then we'll hint at what you *are* saying with all sorts of
subliminal images. That's why –'

'Subli–?'

'Subliminal. You know.' I flicker my fingers at the very edge of his
vision. 'Like something you see out of the corner of your eye. You
know it's there, but you're only half-conscious of it.'

He nods.

'So that's why Greta gasps, and drops her spoon. And then you
bend down and pick it up for her. We'll have another close-up there,
just to stress the point. And –'

He raises a hand to stop me. 'All right. I understand now. And I
try to do how you say.' He levers himself up with an eloquent sigh:
a sadder but a wiser man. 'But my goodness, you are right, old
chap. I feel quite like Alice.'

I follow him back out of the dressing-room. My muscles have the
loose trembly feeling you get when a door you've been pushing at
unexpectedly springs open. But then I glimpse the clock in the corridor and my solar plexus tightens again. I've been focusing all my
attention on Gerhart. Now he's dealt with, there's nothing to insulate me from the bigger problem that I've been wrestling with for a
fortnight, and is now suddenly urgent: what am I going to do about
tomorrow? In twenty hours, I shall either be on a train, or I'll have
missed the opportunity.

Time to decide, Henry.

All right, all right. We've got to get on . . .

I hurry Gerhart on to the stage. I expect to find Max with his back to us, sulkily finishing the close-up of Greta, but he isn't there at all. Jimmy and Colin are perched on the edge of the camera trolley, playing cards, and the German crew-members are huddled in the corner, drinking coffee – all except Rainer the Wizard, and the Greek-god-looking young camera assistant whose name I can never remember, who are up on one of the lighting rostra, arguing about the exact angle of an arc.

I'd much rather leave them to it, but I know if there's a hitch I've got to get it sorted out before Max comes back, so I force myself to go over to them and call up: 'Problems?'

Rainer shakes his head – but only after a split-second's delay that suggests he isn't sure.

'Do you want me to ask Jimmy to come and have a look?'

I can just imagine Jimmy's sighs and grumbles if I did, so it's a relief when the camera assistant says: 'No. Please. Let me show you.' He checks the tilt of the lamp again, switches it on, then climbs down – giving me a disarming smile, as he reaches the ground, that somehow implies we're in this together: two ambitious young professionals who know perfectly well what they're doing, but are forced to indulge their stick-in-the-mud elders. Rainer the Wizard follows slowly, muttering under his breath. The camera assistant glances back at him, then smiles at me again.

'Now,' he says. 'If you'd care to look through the camera, I think you'll see what I mean.' His English is even better than Rainer's: almost accentless, and with perfect intonation. Maybe he guesses what I'm thinking, because – as if to prove the point – he gives a knowing twitch to his eyebrow and adds: 'There won't be a *shadow of a doubt* about it, you know?'

It's impressive enough that he even knows the phrase: to be able to make a double meaning out of it is remarkable. I find myself laughing – not at the humour, but at the virtuosity of it. He flushes with pleasure, and starts towards the set.

'Sorry,' I murmur, as Rainer and I stroll over to the camera, 'but I *keep* forgetting that chap's name.'

'Karl-Maria Glocke.'

'Karl-Maria. Karl-Maria. That must be why I find it so confusing. Sounds half-man, half-girl to me.'

Rainer sniffs. The meaning's unmistakable: half-man, half-girl's not too far from the truth. But then he softens the effect by saying: 'But I think he is very, how do you say – *talented*?'

I station myself next to the camera, while Rainer squints through the viewfinder. Karl-Maria checks we're ready, then picks up a spoon and holds it a foot or so from the edge of the set, creating a huge shadow on the wall behind him. Even with the naked eye I can see that it's extraordinarily black and sharp, as if someone's scorched the image into the white paint.

'*Ja*,' mutters Rainer grudgingly, straightening up. 'Very good. Much more good than your Chimmy, I have to say.' He shouts something in German to the young man, who smiles and nods, then puts the spoon down again and makes his way back to us.

'That looked excellent, Karl – Kar–' I say.

'Why don't you just call him K.-M.?' says Rainer, laughing.

'Would that be all right? I would find it easier.'

'Of course,' says the young man.

'Anyway. Very good work. Well done.'

'Thank you.' He says it pleasantly enough – but with a kind of briskness that suggests he doesn't need my congratulations: he *knew* it was excellent already. Too off-hand. Too cocky. I decide to reassert directorial authority.

'But now you'd better go and kill that arc,' I say. 'We don't want Max finding the place ablaze when he comes back.'

Don't watch to see how they take it: just assume they'll do what you say. I turn, and walk towards the set. By the time I get there, the light's gone.

Most of the cast are still in their places at the table, impervious to what's been going on around them: they're slumped back in their seats, laughing and shaking their heads at something Fritz Frankel is saying. Only Hugh O'Donnell has decamped altogether, to one of the director's chairs, where he sits with an open notebook in his lap and a pencil in his hand, watching the rest of them with an air of patrician amusement.

He looks up as I pass him and says: 'Ah, Henry.' And then, checking that Gerhart's back in his place and out of earshot: 'All better now?'

'I hope so.'

'Thank you, Nanny. Ugh' – running a pudgy finger along the tight rim of his dog-collar – 'these things are quite *punitive*. I suppose that's why they wear them. Far worse than a hair shirt. Anyway, I can see I'm going to have to develop a *temperament*.'

'I beg your pardon?'

'Well, it seems the only way to get a moment of your time. No-one ever pays any attention to an old war-horse like me who just does what he's told, do they?'

His mouth's smiling, but not his eyes: they're big and wet, and full of some hunger I can't quite identify, and don't want to. So I grin quickly, and shrug, and say: 'Where's Max?'

'Oh, he was *taken short*, as he was pleased to put it. Though not *so* short that he didn't have time to name last night's sausages as the guilty party and describe in gruesome detail the effect they'd had on his insides. It was rather like one of those operas where the hero stabs himself, and then spends five minutes singing: "I die!" We were treated to a whole *aria* of *gurgling* and *burning*.'

I laugh. 'Yes, I can imagine.'

'I now have a considerably more intimate acquaintance with his internal workings than I should have sought. Or, to judge by their glazed expressions,'– nodding towards the table – 'they would have sought, either. Though most of them, of course, were protected from the full import by their unfamiliarity with the word *squits*.'

I laugh again, and start to pull away.

'No, no, don't go,' he says, reaching out and patting the arm of the chair next to him. 'I want to know what you think of my idea.'

I can't immediately come up with an excuse that won't offend him. It's pretty obvious, after all, that we're all in the same boat: unable to get on with anything very much till Max is back.

'What idea?' I say, sitting down.

He taps his knee with his notebook. 'Well, I don't know why, but watching Max's disquisition on his guts seemed to rouse my slumbering muse, and a rather lovely thought slipped into my head.

Almost fully formed.'

Oh, God, I'm not immune, even here. I know the next line already: *I was wondering if you'd mind just casting an eye . . .?*

Before he has time to say it, I rattle out the stock answer: 'It's a very tricky business, Hugh. And I haven't got much influence, I'm afraid.'

'Yes, yes, yes,' he says, mock-slapping my hand. 'Don't worry: I'm not one of those dewy-eyed *ingenus* I'm sure you meet all the time at parties, who think you can get them into pictures. It's nothing to do with films at all. I merely want to canvas your literary opinion.'

'Oh, I see; you're planning to write a book –?'

He shakes his head. Dropping his voice to a stage-whisper, he says: '*Une pièce de théâtre.*'

'A *play?*'

He nods, and cocks an eyebrow towards his fellow-actors. 'Listen.'

I listen.

Fritz is in full flood: 'So she go upstairs. And I go after, saying, you know, *Please, please, don't bodder, I'm sure you very beautiful young woman.* "No, she say"' – slipping into a wavery falsetto and sucking his lips to make the cratered face of an old crone – '"I show you. I want you to *see.*"'

'I predict *moths*,' murmurs Hugh.

'*What?*'

'Moths,' he mouths, then twitches his head to divert my attention back to the story.

Fritz is saying: 'She go to a big trunk by the window. She stand there, and she say: "My veddink dress, Herr Frankel. Is in this box fifty year now. I never take it out. I never show nobody. But I show *you.*" And she bend down, and she lift up the lid, like this. And you know what?'

'Moth, moth, *moth*,' breathes Hugh in my ear, pitching the third 'moth' an octave higher to turn it into a little song.

'Out come a great cloud, like this,' says Fritz, making a graceful arc with his long-fingered hands, 'of *motts.*'

'What did I tell you?'

'You've heard it before.'

He smiles, and nods at Boris Zinik, who's frowning, and looking to Greta for guidance. Greta pouts and shrugs. Fritz notices their perplexity.

'Motts,' he repeats. '*Motte. Papillons de nuit.*'

Boris still doesn't understand. He shakes his head.

'There, you see?' says Hugh. 'Quite sublime. All these fellows dressed up as stuffy English club-men, and half of them can't speak English properly. Some of them can't speak English at all. And there isn't even a *lingua franca* for them to fall back on.'

As if to illustrate the point, Fritz resorts to sign language – cupping his hands into a pair of wings and fluttering them. Boris gazes at him in astonishment.

'They are very little. They eat clott,' says Fritz. 'And this is what happen here. They have eat the dress. Nothing left but one tiny piece of silk thread.' He measures the tininess between thumb and index finger.

It's this detail, for some reason, that finally seems to enlighten Boris. He nods energetically, and mutters something I can't hear.

'The possibilities for misunderstanding are *endless*,' says Hugh. 'It'd be *perfect farce*.'

He's right, of course. What English audience could resist the humour of a spluttering Russian dressed up as a brigadier in the Indian army?

'And, what – it'd be set in a studio, would it?'

'A studio remarkably – nay,' – leaning confidingly towards me – '*eerily* – like this one.'

'You could call it the *Tower of Babelsberg*.'

He's mystified for a second, then jabs the air with his pencil and says: 'Ah, yes, very good! It seems so dazzlingly obvious, though, doesn't it? Such an absolute gift. You imagine every playwright in the country must have had the same idea, and is even now toiling away at it in his garret, wrapped in newspaper against the cold. But I don't think anyone else has actually *done* it yet, have they?'

There's a chorus of shuffling and chair-scraping at the table, but Fritz fails to take the hint. 'And another remarkable thing . . .' he begins. I watch the others subside hopelessly in their seats. My neck tenses with embarrassment. But it's not my job to prevent one of the actors boring the rest, so I force myself back to Hugh.

'I don't *know* anyone who's done it . . .'

'I shall start scribbling this very evening, in my hotel room.'

'But –'

'No *buts*, dear boy. Nothing ventured, nothing gained. And it'll distract me from distressing thoughts of all you young things going out and *wallowing* in the fleshpots.'

'God, if only you knew!'

He laughs, making the ridge of fat round his collar tremble.

'It's just I think the danger is that by the time you'd finished it and got it on, it'd be rather *passé*.'

He's genuinely puzzled. He half-expects another joke. The corners of his mouth pucker in readiness.

'No-one'll be making films like this in a couple of years.'

'Why? Because of the er – *speakies*?'

I nod.

'But I have it on the very best authority that *they're* just a passing *craze*. They won't last more than –'

'What authority?'

He doesn't like being challenged. He blinks at me, and ruffles his shoulders.

'I mean, I know some people think that,' I say, trying to sound less combative.

'Well, it was your chairman, as it happens.'

'Sir Basil?'

He nods. 'At our *envoi*. He was telling me about the technical limitations. To do *this*, for instance,' – waving towards the set – 'you'd have to dangle one microphone over the middle of the table. And everyone would have to stay put, as I understand it – at least while they were talking – because if they got up and moved about you wouldn't be able to hear them.'

'Here, you'd just have to dangle it over Fritz, and everyone else could do what they liked,' I say.

But Hugh is not to be disarmed. He pays me off with the most perfunctory smile, and goes on: 'Then you'd have to have four cameras at different angles, sealed off in little boxes to prevent the microphone picking up the sound of their motors – which I think you'd have to admit, might rather spoil the illusion. You couldn't vary the speed of the film, apparently. You couldn't do long shots – or not with dialogue, anyway. You couldn't do any of the things, in fact, that make the cinema an *art*.'

'And Sir Basil believes Art will prevail, does he?'

'Hm?' He catches my tone, but it baffles him: unlike Max, he doesn't see anything intrinsically ludicrous about bracketing the name 'Sir Basil Hopkirk' with the word 'art'. 'Yes, I think he does. He says as soon as the novelty's worn off, people will realize that watching a speakie is like being trapped in a particularly dull theatre. And then they'll start clamouring for the real thing again.'

'Well, I have to say, I'm not happy about it myself, Hugh. The thing I've always *loved* about film is its freedom from the constraints of language. Its capacity for the grand emotional gesture. Its *operaticness*.'

His mouth twitches. You can't say 'operaticness'. I almost snap: *My point entirely*. But it might sound rude – and he probably wouldn't get the irony of it, anyway. So instead I say: 'But we're just going to have to try to preserve that as best we can under the new regime. Better techniques will be developed. People like Max will find a way.'

I regret it even before I've finished saying it. Hugh stiffens: a dog that's suddenly sniffed a bone under the rug.

'*Max*?' he says. '*He*'s not proposing to turn Judas, is he?'

I'm cornered. If I tell him Max's plan now, it'll be common knowledge before the end of the day – and might well leak back to Milstead, so scuppering the whole project; if I don't, he'll realize within a week that I've lied to him – which could end up being just as disastrous, if (as he probably will) he complains about it to Sir Basil after we get home, because it suggests we know we're doing something we shouldn't.

'Well –' I begin.

And then Hugh looks past me and says: 'Ah, I can ask the man himself.'

I swivel, and see Max bobbing towards us. My back turns cold and a gobbet of sweat starts to dribble down my spine.

'I do hope he's washed his hands thoroughly, don't you?' murmurs Hugh.

It's the sight of his collusive little smirk as he says it, and the way he squirms in his chair, that suddenly decides me. A sickly wave spreads through me, as if someone's bandaged me too tightly and I can't breathe properly. Englishness is claiming me for its own. If I don't assert myself against it, I'm lost.

So that's it: I'm going tomorrow.

Summer is shrinking. At 6.30 a.m. an autumnal mist hides the *chiaroscuro* of sun and shadow, and the air's so sharp your face feels it's getting a second shave. The trams have already started, but the few delivery-boys and street-cleaners I pass still have the furtive *camaraderie* of people who work while the rest of the world's asleep. And I must exude the same twilight air, because as I turn towards the station, a smartly coiffed woman in a fur-collared coat emerges abruptly from an apartment building and glowers at me – as if she's the harbinger of the new morning, and I've no business lingering after she's appeared. Sensing her hostility, her little dog rushes at me, winding its scarlet leash around my leg. As she disentangles us, muttering curses under her breath, I catch a whiff of sandalwood soap from her freshly bathed skin.

In the main street, the breeze feels fresher and you can hear the distant *zizz* of a big city waking up. After three weeks of seeing nothing beyond the studio and the hotel and the short journey between them, I'd almost forgotten I was *in* a big city. The sulphurous air is tinged with the smell of roasting coffee and hot bread and sweet pastry. It makes my mouth weep with hunger – not only for food and warmth, but for the promise of the day ahead. No script; no schedule; no sulky Max; no actors' temperaments; no having to goad them back to work after lunch with their bellies full of suet and cabbage: just, for once, an unfilled page, waiting to be drawn on.

The mist is starting to thin. Through it you can see newspaper-sellers and street traders setting up their stands, and glimpse the shadowy contents of shop windows. They look more prosperous than I remember them from two years ago: pyramids of hats, and serpentine displays of tinned foods garlanded with tinsel, and groups of elegantly dressed mannequins turned to stone at some fashionable party. There's more live flesh in evidence, too. As I arrive at the station a large black car glides up to the entrance, and a grey-uniformed chauffeur gets out and opens the back door. After half a minute a round head appears, covered in sparse, sleeked-back black hair; then a body so bulky that it has to come at the gap sideways – giving the odd impression that you're witnessing the birth of a giant baby. He's followed by a valet, who helps him into his overcoat and stands patiently holding his hat while the man-baby fusses with his cuffs and strokes the crumples from his trousers. Then they both set off briskly towards the platforms, through a crowd of gaunt men in oil-smeared overalls, who turn to watch them pass with unsmiling, stony-eyed faces. That's something else I don't remember from last time: obvious class-hostility. Maybe I simply didn't see it. But there *is* a kind of edginess in the atmosphere that seems new: the sense of yeast starting to work below a calm surface. Perhaps it's just that when people are less depressed, they're less resigned, too. But I still feel my neck prickling when I have to run the gauntlet myself, and can't help glancing back to see if I've been subjected to the same treatment. I haven't: the only person looking at me is a short man in a tweed suit a few paces behind me – and he meekly lowers his head the instant I catch his eye.

I get my ticket, then walk along the platform until I spot an empty window seat in a quarter-full carriage. Before sitting down I drop my bag in the place opposite. Trying to keep the overheated machinery of cast and crew and director oiled and functioning for the last month has exhausted my stock of emotional energy, and I've only got three hours to replenish it – which means avoiding casual conversation at all costs.

I close my eyes and pretend to sleep. Nobody's going to wake someone and ask him to move his luggage unless it's occupying the last seat. Around me I hear the shuffle of feet – the squeak and thump of suitcases – the growing murmur of voices. But the ploy seems to work: no-one disturbs me. When the whistle finally goes and the train stutters into motion, I leave it a couple of minutes just to make sure, and open my eyes again.

An old woman in round glasses is staring at me. 'Is this seat free?' she says.

'Yes, of course.' I scrabble the bag up and put it in the rack.

'Thank you.'

She sits down with a grateful sigh, muttering something about her feet. She's just like the woman who sat opposite me last time. She might, in fact, *be* the woman who sat opposite me last time.

Everything happens twice, Christopher told me, just after we'd first met. He was quoting somebody – I can't remember who. *The first time as tragedy, the second as farce.*

The woman cranes her neck and peers up at the sky. 'It's going to be another lovely day,' she says in schoolmistressy German.

'Yes.' My only hope, I realize, is to hide behind the book Christopher sent me. I get up again. I've just opened the bag when the train lurches over a point, and the contents spew out. I manage to grab *Pudovkin on Film Technique*, but my sweater drapes itself over the woman's knees, and the field-glasses graze her ankle as they clatter to the floor.

'Oh! I'm so sorry!' I'm conscious of four or five faces turning to see what the commotion is.

The old woman smiles and shakes her head. 'It doesn't matter.' She hands me the sweater, then bends down and picks up the binoculars case. 'I just hope they aren't broken.' She slips her thumb under the clasp, as if to look inside.

I snatch the case from her. 'Thank you, I'm sure they're fine.'

'Oh!' She's startled by my abruptness, but poised enough to turn it into a joke. 'What have you got in there? Not a gun, I hope? You're not a Communist, are you, going to murder us in our beds?'

The elderly couple next to me and the mother and daughter opposite them nod and chuckle.

Yes: this is going to be farce.

I wrap the glasses in the sweater – stuff them back into the bag – then sit down again and open Pudovkin. On the title page Christopher has scribbled: 'To Henry Whitaker: A useful guide, I hope, through your chosen jungle. Christopher Morton Hunt, September 1929'. It seems curiously formal, as if he wrote it to be read by posterity. Only the phrase *your chosen jungle* hints at the derisive tone of his accompanying letter.

I riffle through the book, and select a passage at random:

Kuleshov maintained that the material in film-work consists of pieces of film, and that the composition method is their joining together in a particular, creatively discovered order. He maintained that film-art does not begin when the artists act and the various scenes are shot – this is only the preparation of the material. Film-art begins from the moment when the director begins to combine and join together the various pieces of film. By joining them in various combinations, in different orders, he obtains differing results.

He's right: I know he's right. But I'm so distracted I can only half-assimilate what he's saying. I start again, looking for key words: *artists act . . . scenes are shot . . . only the preparation of the material . . .*

'Your friends have been busy, look!' says the old woman loudly. There's a chorus of knowing laughter from the other passengers. I glance up. She's pointing out of the window at a dingy block of flats. The cement skin's badly cracked, and in some places has crumbled away altogether, leaving ulcerous blotches of pink brick. On one of them someone has daubed a huge white hammer-and-sickle.

Of course – *that's* where the tragedy-and-farce quote came from: Marx.

I try to think of a light response. It's impossible: in my present state I probably couldn't do it in English, and in German it's completely beyond me. But then the conversational baton seems to pass to the elderly couple: the wife clicks her tongue and mutters something about riots and strong leaders; her husband says something I can't understand; and in thirty seconds I've been completely forgotten.

I return to the book: 'To be able to find the requisite order of shots or pieces, and the rhythms necessary for their combination – that is the chief task of the director's art.'

Indisputable. Brilliant. But it's no good: I just can't take it in properly.

I close my eyes again.

Immediately I see Irma Brücke. What am I going to say to her? *I wanted to know how you were, of course. But I also wanted to tell you something: why I was looking for you before. It bothers me that I never explained. It makes me feel fraudulent – as a man, as a . . .*

What if she laughs at me? Or has simply forgotten all about me? Or else cries, and says: *But I thought you really liked me?*

That's all right. I'll know how to react when it happens. I'm older now . . .

And then I do sleep.

If I have any dreams, I don't remember them.

Klosterfeld is wavery in the heat. Someone's carefully painted in the amputated tail of the 'p' on the front of the Hotel Stephanie, but in the merciless light you can clearly see it's an artificial limb: the colours don't quite match and there's a drippy line along the join. The hills to the north seem almost welcoming, their two-dimensional blackness softened to a glossy magpie-feather green. The wonky tower on top doesn't seem sinister any more, just pitifully old and tumble-down.

The first time as dream, the second as waking.

The main street is crowded with mothers and children and young couples and old men wearing collarless shirts and baggy jackets. I weave between them, keeping a look-out for Irma Brücke and her daughter, but see no familiar faces at all. In the square at the end, forty or fifty people are gathered round a platform draped with N.S.D.A.P. crosses. All I clearly make out of the speaker is his high forehead and the glint of his gold-rimmed spectacles, but I can hear the waspish little surges in his voice as he tries to goad his audience into anger. He's not having much luck: they're attentive but sober, shifting and twitching in the sun, responding with no more than an occasional bovine low of agreement.

I turn off into Bad Strasse. The bar's still there, though there's no sound coming from it. The door to the block of flats stands open, presumably to cool the stairwell. I hesitate a second, then force myself inside. It was indecisiveness that did for me before: I'm not going to make the same mistake again.

It's even dingier than I remember. There's the same old smell of piss and mildew and burnt cooking-fat, despite the ventilation. The mould on the walls has dried to a black scum, but the first damp days of autumn will bring it back to life again. I have to breathe through my mouth to keep myself from retching.

Keep going. Keep going.

I climb to the fourth floor, knock on her door and wait. No answer: no footsteps. I knock again, then press my face against the thin panel. Nothing but the same murmur of traffic I can hear more loudly with my other ear. She must have left the window open – which means she can't have gone away. I consider leaving a note, but what would I say? *Please stay in, and I'll come back?* That'd only work if I was sure she'd want to see me – and I'm not.

I trudge downstairs, and out into the street again. Two years ago I'd have told myself I'd done what I could, and given up at this point. Not today. She must be here somewhere, and I'm going to find her. I rehearse a few German phrases in my head, then descend to the bar. My eyes can't immediately adjust to the gloom after the brilliance outside, and for a moment I'm reduced to blindness. But I sense emptiness: the air has a sour day-after-the-party staleness, and I can only hear two or three muted voices, which break off abruptly as the leather door flops shut behind me. I hover inside the entrance for a few seconds, until the black shapes of furniture start to differentiate themselves from the surrounding grey.

'Good morning.'

I can't see who said it, but it must be addressed to me. The tone's cautious, and slightly puzzled, as if they're not used to strangers here.

'Good morning.'

I start towards the bar. Behind it, the pale blob of a face suddenly flowers in the darkness. I blink, and recognize the barman. He clearly doesn't recognize me. He watches quizzically as I approach, then slaps his hands on the counter and says: 'Yes?'

'I'm trying to find someone called Irma Brücke. Have you any idea where she might be?'

I try to sound off-hand – a long-lost cousin, or a lawyer come to tell her about a legacy. But I'm no Gerhart. He stares at me so intently that I feel myself starting to blush, and have to struggle to hold his gaze. He thinks I'm looking for a whore. Which of course I am, in a way.

'I understand she lives there,' I say, pointing towards the flats. 'But there was no reply when I knocked.'

He stares at me a moment more, then flips a rag from the pocket of his apron and starts to wipe the counter.

'You don't know her?'

He says nothing, but begins rubbing furiously at a particularly stubborn ring. From the corner of the room I hear the clink of a glass. I turn, and see a couple of middle-aged men sitting at a table. One of them's looking at me, but abruptly jerks his head to avoid meeting my eye. He drains his glass – clears his throat – then gets up and walks heavily towards the lavatory next to the empty dance-floor. I wonder if he's a plain-clothes policeman, and the barman's frightened of admitting that prostitutes ply their trade here.

I lean forward, and whisper: 'But I met her here. Less than two years ago. She was over there, with some friends.'

He shrugs. 'I'm sorry. I can't help you.'

I wait for him to say why not, but he ignores me. After a few seconds he treats me to a little dumbshow by spitting on his cloth and then returning to the stain with renewed ferocity. You could film it, and people would know exactly what it meant: *I'm in my own world, and you don't exist for me any more.*

I preserve what dignity I can by waiting a few seconds longer, and then retreat to the door, giddy with an odd feeling of looking-glass *déjà vu*. I seem to be making the same journey as last time, but in reverse order: *then*, it was the woman at the house who was offended by my enquiries about Irma Brücke, and the bar that delivered her to me . . . By that logic, if I go to Hermann Strasse, I ought to find her there.

The first time clockwise, the second anti-clockwise.

I'm still standing outside, smiling at this idea and trying to come up with a more rational one, when a voice behind me says: 'What do you want with Irma Brücke?'

I spin round. It's the fellow who was looking at me in the bar. He's half-way up the steps, shading his eyes with his hand as he squints into my face.

All at once, a new thought strikes me: perhaps he's her fancy man, and the barman thought there'd be trouble if he heard me asking for her.

'I'm a friend of hers,' I say carefully.

'A friend?'

I nod. 'And I've got something that belongs to her, and want to return it to her.'

He lumbers slowly up the last few stairs, watching me the whole time. 'You're not from round here?'

I shake my head.

'England?'

'Yes. I happened to be working in Berlin, and –'

He draws his thumb quickly across his wet lower lip, then jerks it over his shoulder.

'Down there,' he says. 'This side of the road. I can't remember the number, but you'll see the plate by the door. Dr. Becker.'

'Why? Does she work –?'

But he's already walking hurriedly towards the town centre.

'Thank you!' I call after him, but he just hunches his shoulders and breaks into a little trot.

I hoist my bag and set off in the other direction. From somewhere behind me a roar of applause suddenly erupts, then fractures and subsides into the murmur of a dispersing crowd. The N.S.D.A.P. meeting must be over.

It doesn't take me long to find the house: it's just past the entrance to Hermann Strasse. It's tall and grey, with big square windows staring out between slatted shutters, and a cheese-wedge roof. On one side it's connected to its neighbour, but on the other there's an archway with a wrought-iron gate leading to a courtyard and a garden beyond. This, presumably, is the tradesman's entrance. Should I try that, or the front door? It all depends, of course, on what she does here: I can imagine her equally easily as a doctor's receptionist, or as a housekeeper. But to ask for a housekeeper at the front door would be a bigger *faux pas* than looking for a receptionist at the back, so I lift the latch of the gate and walk in.

The yard's cobbled, with a small coach-house and stable bracketing one corner. The stable door's open, and in front of it stands a boxy black car. The stones around it are dark and shiny and flecked with soap bubbles, as if somebody's just washed it, but there's no-one to be seen. Gusts of steam are coming from the kitchen window, laced with the hot tang of boiling bacon. From inside I can hear the metallic *clack* of saucepans. There's someone *there*, obviously. Perhaps I'll find it's her: red-faced, her hands swollen to dumplings, her beefy bare arms sprinkled with flour . . .

As I cross towards the back door, I catch sight of something white moving in the garden. I stop and look: it's a hat. The woman who's wearing it is sitting beneath a big lime tree. I can only see her shaded face and the back of her deck-chair, but from the angle of her neck I can tell she's looking at me, too. My footsteps must have alerted her.

I'd better explain myself.

I switch direction, taking off my hat as I go. She starts to get up to meet me – sinks back – tries again, and this time just manages it. I can see why it's a struggle for her: she's enormously pregnant. Even the front of her loose cotton smock is stretched taut by the bulk of her belly. As she starts towards me her bare legs look too spindly to bear the weight.

There's a little ornamental gate between the courtyard and the garden. She stops a few feet short of it and lifts her head to see me better. Sunlight floods under the brim of her hat.

I stop too. 'Irma?'

'Oh, my God!' she says, and covers her mouth with her hand. She gawps at me for a second, then starts to sway from side to side. I move forward to help her, but before I can get there she's steadied herself by catching hold of the gatepost. A needle of light jabs my eye. I glance down. There's a thin gold wedding ring on her finger.

'What do you do here?'

'I came to see you.'

'Oh!' She's almost hyperventilating. She tightens her grip on the wood. Finally she blurts: 'How . . . how do you find me?'

'I asked at the bar.'

'Bar Alfred?'

I nod.

She rolls her eyes. 'I am surprised. They do not like me there. They are all Communist.'

'It wasn't the barman who told me.' I start to describe the man who followed me.

Before I've finished, she nods and says: 'Ah, yes, now I understand. That is Mr. Rudiger. He is Communist, too. But he think my husband is a good doctor, because he save his child.'

'You're married to Dr. Becker?'

'Yes,' she says quietly. The tension in her face suddenly eases. She looks healthier than I could have imagined: her cheeks have filled out since I last saw her, and pregnancy has flushed them with colour. But the mark of what she went through before is still there, in the deep furrows creasing her forehead and the mesh of fine lines round her eyes.

'You are surprised, I think?' she says, smiling.

'No, no.' I am, of course. Astonished.

'He is a good man.'

'I'm sure. I'm glad.'

'Thank you.' She glances past me. 'But he will come back here. Very soon now. So –'

'Ah, I see.' I'd visualized her outraged, grateful, bemused, startled. The one possibility that had never occurred to me was that she might feel compromised. 'I'd better be going, then.'

'I think so, yes. I'm sorry.'

'But before I do – there's something – Can I just say . . .?'

'Quick, please.'

'When I was here the last time . . .'

'Oh, that is nothing. Nothing now. So: you don't worry any more, all right?'

'All right. But there's something I should have explained –'

'No, no, no. You don't have to explain nothing. I know you are a nice boy. You didn't do nothing wrong.' She squeezes through the gate, lays her fingertips on my arm, and pushes me gently back into the courtyard. 'Now,' – nodding towards the archway – 'you go that way. My husband probably come through –'

She stops abruptly, and cocks her head. For a second, I can't hear anything. Then a man's voice calls out: 'My darling?'

Irma steps away from me, softly clicking her tongue. I turn to face the house. There's an open French window next to the back door. A man stands in it, looking out at us. He's about forty, slightly built and not very tall, wearing an elegant linen suit and gold-rimmed spectacles, and crumpling a large soft hat in his hand. As Irma meets his gaze he throws up his arm in greeting. She raises her own in reply.

'Come and meet our visitor,' she calls, in English.

'With pleasure,' he replies.

What on earth is she going to say about me? He doesn't look an easy man to deceive: his mouth is wide and sardonic, and his wispy ginger hair is swept severely back from his forehead, as if he's determined to impress even the most unobservant with his intellectuality. There's something unnerving about the way he moves, too – rising up on the ball of the foot with every step, in a kind of dressage display of fastidiousness. But as he approaches he smiles at me pleasantly enough, before turning to Irma for an explanation.

'You remember,' she says, 'that I mentioned my father studied in England with a Dr. Brimelow?'

'Oh, yes, of course. But surely' – studying me with eyes the colour of Glacier Mints – 'unless he has discovered the elixir of eternal life . . .?'

'This is his nephew. Mr . . .' She laughs. 'I'm sorry, you must tell again. I am not so good with names. All I think about' – patting her belly – 'is this little one.'

Has she genuinely forgotten, or is she just pretending? Even in this extremity, the answer seems crucially important to me. If our encounter was really that insignificant to her, then I've fatally misjudged some fundamental part of my life. It's a struggle not to glance at her, but I daren't take the chance.

'Whitaker,' I say. 'Henry Whitaker.'

'Yes, of course, Mr. Whitaker. My husband, Dr. Becker.'

He dips his head, then holds out his hand. 'How do you do?'

'How do you do?'

We stand looking at each other. I try to guess the questions that must be going through his head, and which one he's going to fling at me. The knack of successful deceit, I know, is to keep it to a minimum. Telling the truth whenever you can not only reduces the chance you'll contradict yourself, it also gives an air of credibility-by-association to your lies.

'Your uncle is well, I hope?' he says at last.

'Yes, thank you.' I do a quick calculation: if Brimelow's the same age as her father, and she's thirty-two or three, he's likely to be sixty-five or so. 'Quite fit. But looking forward to retirement.'

He smiles. I'm terrified he'll ask me something else about the Brimelows: all I can remember is that they lived in Leeds, and it's almost certain that he knows a name or a date or an anecdote that will catch me out. So before he can speak again I say: 'Anyway. I mustn't intrude on you any longer.'

I start to edge round him, but he immediately puts out a hand to stop me. 'Oh, you're not intruding, Mr. Whitaker, not at all. This is a great honour.' He speaks almost without accent. 'Please. We are about to have lunch. We'd be delighted if you would stay and eat something with us. Wouldn't we, my dear?'

'Yes, of course.' I avoid looking at her, but I can hear the strain in her voice.

'That's very kind,' I say. 'But I really ought to be pushing along.'

He pinches my sleeve to detain me, then pulls a watch on a gold chain from his top pocket.

'Where are you – *pushing along* – to?'

'Berlin.'

'And you came from Berlin this morning?'

'Yes.'

'Just to see my wife?'

'Well, I . . .'

He studies the watch. 'I left the house two hours ago. You were not here then. Less than two hours is not so long for a social visit. Particularly after such a journey.'

'I know. But it was this or nothing, I'm afraid. I'm working on a film, you see . . .'

'But you are not working today?'

'No, but . . .'

'And there is a train to Berlin this afternoon. So. You will take a glass of beer, at least, before you go?'

I hesitate. I could simply bolt, of course; but that would be bound to make him suspicious, if he isn't already; and the last thing I want to do is to leave poor Irma in the lurch and spend the rest of my life

125

wondering if I'm responsible for unravelling her marriage. But if I stay, on the other hand, and he finds me out . . .

'Ah, I see you are weakening,' says Becker. 'It is this' – pointing up at the sun – 'and the word *beer*. Together they are irresistible. You take our guest into the garden, my darling. And I will go and ask Else.'

I lift a finger to signal *wait*, but he's already about-faced, and is walking away from us.

'I'm sorry,' I say.

She sighs and shakes her head.

'I wouldn't have come, of course, if I'd realized. It's just it never occurred to me . . . you know . . . that you might . . .'

'No, it never occur to anyone. Except Willi. Anyway, we better . . .'

She turns, and leads me through the little gate. Three curly-armed cane chairs are arranged around a table under the tree. On one of them a cat lies dozing, its gold-tinged fur dappled by light from a hole in the canopy of leaves.

'How did you come –?' I say, as we sit down. 'I mean, have you and he known each other for a long time?'

'No. Well, in a way, you could say so, I suppose. He was a friend of my fiancé.'

'Walther?'

She nods and blushes. Because she's pleased I remember, or uncomfortable that she gave away so much about herself the last time I was here? I can't tell.

'They were in France together,' she says. 'Willi was a doctor, you know? In the army. Walther did not speak much about me, I think – but once he showed Willi a picture I sent him, and said: "That is the girl I will marry." Then when Walther was killed, he try to find the picture, or some letter or something, so he can write to me. But there is nothing. He think perhaps is in his – how do you call it?' She flexes her thumb and forefingers into a pair of 'O's, and holds them in front of her eyes.

'Field-glasses?'

'Yes. Field-glasses case. But that is missing, you know? Stealed, I think' – she makes an odd gargling sound that it takes me a second to identify as an aborted giggle – 'by the English.'

God, I should have remembered: Fate's always a flashy showman when you come to Klosterfeld. What do I do now? Own up, and give her the binoculars? That might provoke a fit of hysterics – maybe even send her prematurely into labour. But if I *don't*, I'll never get another opportunity. I'll be denying her the truth and the chance of accommodating her life to it. And the consciousness of my own failure will corrode me.

I reach into my bag.

'Perhaps he find me anyway,' she says. 'But after he come back to Germany he is very busy. He work with the poor people in Berlin. And he has his own wife, and she is not so well. In the head, you know? She has to go to' – drilling her finger into her temple – 'the – how do you say? *Psychiater?*'

I grip the binoculars case. 'Psychiatrist.'

'Psychiatrist, yes. Then she die. To the funeral come a . . . a colleague, another doctor. Willi does not know him so well, but when they talk after he tell Willi that before the war he was at the university here in Klosterfeld, and he was a friend of Walther Luger. And all the other students were jealous because Walther was engaged to a beautiful girl' – she smiles, and waves the compliment away with her hand – 'or, you know, some nonsense like this.'

'That's understandable,' I say. 'List–'

'Anyway,' she goes on. 'He come here. Nearly two years ago. He tell me about Walther. About how he . . . how he died. Walther was a real German hero. He and his men, they were . . . *in der Minderheit sein?*'

'Outnumbered?'

She nods. 'But Walther doesn't run away. He stand still. And he succeed to kill three of them.' She shows me the number with her fingers, in case I missed the scale of his achievement. 'Including the English officer. Before he is shot himself – in the back.'

The case is slithery with my sweat. 'It was a tragedy for all of us,' I say, easing it up.

'Yes,' she says. 'But not the same. *You* did not lose so many. *You* were not betrayed. *You* were not forced to pay.'

It's the first time I've known her angry. Seeing it provokes an answering surge of rage in me. 'My father –' I begin.

'He is killed also? I am sorry. But still, it is not the same.'

'It's just the same,' I say. 'Look.'

I take the case out and put it on the table.

But the change in my voice has alerted her. She turns abruptly away, blinkering her right eye with her hand. 'Please,' she says. 'I don't want to look at nothing.'

'Irma . . .'

She bats the air to shut me up. 'A pregnant woman, she must be careful,' she says. She's breathing rapidly again, making the words choppy. '*Blutdruck*, you know? What is that?'

'Blood pressure?'

She nods. 'So. We talk about something else, please. We talk about – Oh! Here come Willi.'

I glance into the courtyard. Becker is walking gingerly towards us, clutching a tray to his belly to keep its cargo of bottles and glasses from wobbling off.

'Now,' she mutters. 'You drink your beer, all right? Quick. And then you go.'

I shiver. I can feel the sun on my skin, but it doesn't warm me. Perhaps I should get up and go *now* – without a word, leaving the field-glasses on the table. It's unbearable to think she sees me just as a tiresome dreg of her former life that has to be sluiced out and then forgotten. If she won't allow me to explain the real connection between us, then let her work it out for herself.

I've got about five seconds before Becker's near enough to see the case and recognize it for what it is. Once that happens, of course, there's no way out: whether I stay or go, he'll know he's been lied to and guess the reason. But what if he does? It's not my responsibility to protect them. If anything, in fact, I should be doing the opposite. These people are my enemies. They venerate the man who killed my father. And they dismiss *my* loss as less than *theirs*.

So bugger them. Let them suffer.

'Here we are!' calls Becker, as he nudges the gate wide. 'Relief is at hand!'

He says it in English, but looking at Irma, with an uxorious smile.

She makes a noise that's half-sigh and half-moan. I glance across at her. She's staring at him, her mouth open, her eyes big and swimmy. Her cheek and jaw are blotched with patches of white.

As casually as I can, I reach out my hand for the binoculars, and drop them back in the bag.

Becker edges between us, puts the tray down and unloads a flagon of lemonade and two bottles of beer. He gives us a glass each, and takes one for himself. There's another one left on the tray. Irma frowns at it.

'Effi,' says Becker. 'She'll be joining us in a minute.'

She replies in German: something to do with having got too much sun already.

'She'll be all right,' says Becker, in English. 'She was in the shade for most of the meeting. And out here she'll be as cool as a cucumber, won't she?'

I can't help laughing. 'Did you use to live in England?' I say. 'You speak just like a native. Better than most natives, actually.'

'You're very kind.' He gently picks up the cat. It's so relaxed it just dangles from his hands as he sets it down. 'I did, as it happens,' he says, taking its place. 'Though not entirely by choice. I was a – a guest of your government for two years.'

He must mean a prisoner of war. I feel myself blushing. But Irma spares me having to respond by suddenly pushing herself to her feet, then leaning heavily on the table, as if she's frightened of passing out. Becker and I get up, too, but she nods us back again.

'No, you stay, please,' she says. 'I will be back in a moment.'

'Shall I come with you?' asks Becker, but she shakes her head. He watches her start slowly towards the house, then turns to me and says mildly: 'She was very fond of your uncle, Mr. Whitaker. And of your . . . your cousins. But they are – how shall I say? They are part of something that no longer exists. So you are' – groping for the right expression, then softening its effect with a smile – 'a kind of ghost, I suppose. And of course this weather doesn't help. Or her . . . condition.'

This is torture. 'I'm sorry,' I say. 'I should have thought.'

He shakes his head. 'Oh, no, please. You couldn't have known. I'm glad you came. And I'm sure she is, too. She is a strong woman, Irma. Only sometimes you forget you are strong, when always you are told you are weak.' He starts pouring the beer, his face blank with concentration. 'I am curious, though,' he murmurs, 'how you happened to find us?'

It's too off-hand. My neck prickles. What do I tell him? If I mention Bar Alfred, he'll immediately guess I've been here before, because no stranger would think of wandering in there to ask directions. And if he knows anything about Irma's past (and it's hard to see how he couldn't), he's bound to realize *why* I went there, and put two and two together . . .

'My wife did not, I think, write to Dr. Brimelow,' he goes on, before I can come up with an edited version, 'to *say* she was getting married? They have not communicated since before the war, I believe?'

'No,' I say, trying to sound as casual about it as he does. 'But when my uncle knew I was coming to Germany, he suggested I should look her up. Well, look the *family* up.'

He watches the foam rise above the rim of my glass, then stop just before it spills.

'But you did not have the address?' he says.

My saliva's thick and gluey. 'I was lucky. I saw someone coming out of a bar, and asked him. And it turned out he's a patient of yours.'

He frowns. 'Really?'

'A Mr . . . Rudiger, I think his name is.'

His face suddenly relaxes. He even smiles. I wonder if I've misjudged him: perhaps he was just being polite, and a guilty conscience made me see it as something more sinister.

'Ah, yes,' he says. 'Rudiger.' He pauses for a moment, then looks curiously at me. 'Did he say anything about me?'

'Only where you live.'

He nods. 'That is good. I have hopes of Rudiger. He is like a dog. But a good dog. A brave dog. He needs a new master, that is all.' He lapses for a moment into some thought of his own, then shakes himself out of it. 'Anyway. That is why she seems a little shocked, I think.' He slides my glass towards me, then raises his own. 'Your very good health.'

'And yours.'

He takes a sip, licks the froth from his upper lip – then freezes, the tip of his tongue still showing.

130

After a moment he nods, and says: 'Let me show you something.'
He reaches inside his coat for his wallet. One of the compartments
is fat with small photographs. He riffles through them, then slips
one out on to the table.

'Here,' he says, skewering it round so that I can see it. 'This is
how she was when I first met her.'

It's the photo *I'd* have got, if I'd thought to take one last time.
She's in front of the block of flats, huddled into her fur-collared
coat: her face pale, except for the sooty shadows under her eyes; her
head tilted to one side, parodying coquettishness; her mouth just a
diagram of a smile. Next to her stands her daughter, arms crossed,
frowning into the lens with an expression that says: *You can make
my mother perform for you, but you won't make me.*

'When was this taken?' I say.

'Christmas twenty-seven.'

Christmas twenty-seven. Jesus: not long after we'd slept together.
Not much of a testimony to the effect I had on her.

'There, you see. That is what you look like when you are beaten
into believing the lies about you. *You are weak. You are worthless.
You should be ashamed of your country. You should be ashamed of
yourself.*' He starts suddenly, and glances down: the cat has jumped
into his lap. He begins to stroke it absently. 'Why' – lowering his
voice – 'should a German woman be ashamed of having the child of
a German hero? Why should a German man be ashamed of making
her his wife, and bringing the girl up as his own?'

It suddenly strikes me just how much courage it must have taken
for him to do what he's done: marry Irma, and then – instead of
hurrying her away to somewhere where no-one knows her – brav-
ing a barrage of gossip and tongue-clicking and back-biting to
brazen it out with her in her home town.

'You cannot wipe this out,' he says, craning forward to see the
picture himself, and spreading his fingers above it. 'But you can do
something. You can love. You can give back a little pride. A little
self-respect. And then, you see –' He gestures towards the house.

'Yes,' I say. 'An astonishing transformation.'

'Thank you. It is hard sometimes. But I am very –' His voice is suddenly constricted. He clears his throat to free it. 'I have failed before,

you see. With my first wife. She was unhappy, and I . . . I surrendered my responsibility for her to an alienist. Dr. *Rosen*.' He watches me closely, to see if I've caught the significance of the name. His eyes are rimmed with tears. 'That was a mistake. He only made her feel *more* ashamed. More powerless. More contemptible. There is no nobility in human life. No greatness. The only reality is the sewer. Everything else is illusion.' He pauses and nods, acknowledging the inevitable. 'In the end she . . . she put her head in the oven . . .'

'I'm sorry.' *Sorry?* It's nothing: a stone dropped into a well. I can hear the emptiness echoing around it.

His grimace turns into a watery smile. 'No, *I* am sorry,' he says. 'It is not very English, is it, to talk about these things? I am embarrassing you.'

'No, of course not.' But my cheeks tell him the truth.

'One day,' he says, 'they will try to take your empire away from you. The Bolsheviks, or the Americans. And you'll be too polite to say anything. And then *phht!* – nothing left except strawberries and cream.'

'I'm sure we'll find a way of losing the Empire anyhow, without any help,' I say.

He manages a little laugh. 'Did I understand you to say you are working on a film?'

I laugh back. 'You don't *have* to change the subject –'

He holds up his hand. 'No, no, I should like to hear about it. Film is a great interest of mine.'

'It probably isn't what you mean by film at all. Just a silly little mystery, really. We're doing our best with it, but it'll only confirm all your worst suspicions of English culture, I'm afraid – if *culture*'s the word.'

He says nothing, but smiles, and waits patiently for me to go on. There's obviously no escape, so I outline the story of *New Year's Eve* as quickly as I can, watching him all the time for the first sign of amusement or contempt. But he listens respectfully enough, and when I get to the point when 'Inspector Holbrook' is exposed as one of the criminals, he nods and says: 'Ah, very clever.'

'Clever, maybe. But not exactly *Nosferatu*, or *The Cabinet of Dr. Caligari*.'

His nose puckers, as if I've pushed a dog-turd under it.

I say: 'Well, *I* should love to make something that effective.'

'They are effective, yes. But not in the right way. They tell us we are in the grip of our own dreams. Our own madness. And that is dangerous, I think.' He leans forward abruptly, squashing the cat so hard against the table that it yelps and hurls itself into the void again. 'It is my belief', he says, 'that the cinema has the potential to be the most powerful cultural force in human history.'

'Well, I absolutely agree with you there. Though most of my friends wouldn't –'

He dismisses my friends with a shake of the head. 'But no-one has begun to *harness* that potential. Except perhaps the . . . the Americans. Just a little.'

'What about the Russians? Eisenstein? Pudovkin? Do you know' – suddenly remembering Christopher's book, and reaching into my bag for it – '*Pudovkin on Film Technique?*'

He takes it and flicks through the pages, but I can tell from his eyes that he's not assimilating anything. After a few seconds he hands it back, murmuring: 'Yes, perhaps you are right. The Bolsheviks begin to understand it, too. They see' – waggling a finger at his glasses – 'the same thing: that in the coming struggle, the victor will be the nation that most efficiently puts the full might of the cinema at the service of the cause.'

'You think there's going to be another war?'

He smiles. 'Of course. Why should we imagine we are at the end of history?'

I can't think of a reply that wouldn't sound ludicrously inadequate.

'So that is why,' he goes on, 'we need a different kind of German cinema, before it is too late – a cinema that helps us rediscover our racial pride and our common purpose.'

Why have I been so slow? My own anxieties must have blinded me. It's only the oratorical ring of *racial pride* and *common purpose* that finally makes me put two and two together.

'Were you addressing a meeting in the square this morning?'

'Yes, that's right.' He's not remotely shamefaced, just surprised. 'But I don't remember seeing *you* there?'

'I just saw the glint of your spectacles.'

He laughs, and leans forward to refill our glasses – so giving me time, mercifully, to find a way of nudging the conversation in another direction.

'I think German cinema has every reason to be proud already,' I say. 'Technically, it's streets ahead of anything we can do. That's why we're here, of course.'

He says nothing: he's too busy preening himself, carefully wiping his wet fingertips on his handkerchief.

'I mean, look at sound,' I say. 'Who invented the Tri-Ergon process?'

'We did,' he says, looking up. 'And what did we do with it? We sold it to Mr. Fox. An *American Jew.*'

Oh, God. 'Well, yes. But still –' Still what? My stock of anodyne phrases is empty.

'But still, yes.' His gaze drifts past me. There's a calm vacancy in his eyes, giving the impression that he's disconnected them from the external world and is looking at something inside his head.

A woman's voice calls from the house, getting suddenly louder for a second as the back door opens, but he doesn't seem to hear it.

'But I think it will *rebound*,' he says finally. 'Is *rebound* the word? Mr. Fox hopes to become very rich, selling us our own invention. And he will. But he and his friends underestimate the power of *hearing*. The cinema will no longer be dumb. The audience will no longer be deaf. They won't be satisfied any more by decadent cosmopolitan films that are the same everywhere – except for the language in which the titles are written. They will demand to hear the authentic voice, the true spirit of their own nation. And that is our oppor–'

'Herr Doktor!'

We both turn. A stout white-haired woman in an apron is hurrying towards us. There's something alarming in the way she moves: rocking from side to side with every step, hands flapping, as if all her available energy's going into moving her legs and there's none left over to control her other muscles.

Becker jumps up, calling out in German: 'What is it?'

I can't catch any of the reply: she's too out of breath, and speaks with a strong local accent.

'Mr. Whitaker, my wife has pains, I'm sorry, I must go,' says Becker. He doesn't look at me: he's already running towards the house. Only when he's half-way across the courtyard does he glance over his shoulder and call: 'Goodbye!'

I watch them through the back door, then gather up my bag and slowly follow them. The beer's made me heavy, and anaesthetized my emotions. I don't feel anything very much, except a sluggish curiosity: is Irma really going into labour? Or is she merely faking it, in order to get me off the premises before I betray myself, or her daughter appears and recognizes me?

If that's what she's hoping, she's too late. As I walk past the end of the house and into the street, I catch sight of the girl herself, watching me from an upstairs window. I nod and smile at her, but she just goes on staring, as glum and suspicious as she was in the photograph. *You can change my mother's life, but you can't change mine . . .*

I buy a ham sandwich and another beer at a bar in the square, then make my way to the station. In the bustle on the platform is a little man in a tweed suit who looks familiar, though I can't place him. But there's an electric sharpness to the sensation he triggers in my head that tells me my acquaintance with him is recent and trivial rather than old and profound. Was he one of the drinkers in Bar Alfred, perhaps? No, too well dressed . . .

And then I get it: the man following me into the station in Berlin this morning, who averted his gaze when I looked back at him. He must have been making exactly the same journey as I was today. I wonder what his was for – a family visit? a wedding? (his leather bag might be a camera case); a business appointment? – and whether it was more successful than mine.

I dare myself to go and ask him. To my astonishment, I find I'm starting to edge in his direction.

And then the train comes, and I sink into my seat, and before we're even moving again I'm asleep.

It's only the next morning that what's happened really hits me. I'm quite calm about it. All I feel is that wintry sense you get when you finally pack your model trains away in the attic: a mix of shame and puzzlement that the enchantment lasted so long, and a faint tingle of sadness that it's over. The one thing I must do now is make sure no-one finds the field-glasses by accident. I consider several hiding-places, but am haunted by the fear that if the chambermaid *did* find them she'd assume they must be stolen. In the end I simply wrap them in a dirty shirt and stuff them into a corner of my suitcase. Goodbye Irma Brücke.

It's three minutes past nine when I get to the projection-room. Max scowls at his watch but says nothing. Next to him sits Jimmy, arms folded, smiling sourly at my discomfiture, and then the young camera assistant, K.-M. – who must be there at Max's insistence because of the work he did with the lighting. It's no wonder, then, that Jimmy's in a bad mood. Beyond them is Rainer the Wizard, who doesn't look at me at all, but perches bolt upright on the edge of his seat, craning his neck to see the blank screen.

Max paddles his hand impatiently to hurry me into my chair, then glances back at the projectionist and nods. The machine clacks, and the screen fills with a dazzling pattern of light and dark. The light is the bare wall. The dark is split into two: Greta's shadow, and Gerhart's next to her. As the shadow-Greta starts lifting a spoon to her mouth, the shadow-Gerhart turns to talk to her. We see the motion of his lips. We see Greta flinch – freeze – and drop the spoon. And then the shadow-Gerhart bend down to pick it up.

Theoretically, the next shot is impossible: it shows something no-one could actually see, because the table would be in the way. But it doesn't matter. Nobody will be thinking about that.

The shadow-Gerhart retrieves the spoon from the floor, and lifts it up till it's exactly parallel with the shadow-Greta's waist. He weighs it in his hand for a second – then jabs it suddenly towards her, with a curving motion that makes it clear he's aiming for her groin. You don't actually see it reach its target, because its small shadow dissolves in the larger darkness of her body. But you *do* see her hand shoot up, the fingers fluttering in an unmistakable gesture of pain.

'Then the close-up,' says Max, as the tail of the film flap-flaps on its spool. 'Anyone who can lip-read'll realize what he's saying.' He chuckles. 'Then they'll see the title, and they'll think, *Hold on a*

136

minute – that wasn't: "It's not my fault if I'm lucky sometimes." It was "I murder babies with a spoon.""

And he's right: it's so crisply lit and perfectly shot that the *meaning* will seep into their consciousness, even if the words contradict it. In fact, the contradiction may actually add to the effect: when a title doesn't say what you expect, you automatically think back to what came before it, looking for an explanation.

'Well done, Jimmy. Well done, K.-M. Well done, Rainer,' I say. 'And well done, Max. It's brilliant. But do you think the censors will allow it?'

Max shrugs. 'What can they do? If they say anything, I'll just tell 'em they've got dirty minds.'

We have a few more minutes of assorted lips and eyes and hands, then the long sequence when da Silva is called away to the telephone. Max watches stonily, occasionally scribbling something on his pad or grumbling under his breath or making a faint train-whistling sound through his nose.

When it's over he slaps the notebook shut and turns to Rainer and Jimmy. 'Right,' he says. 'We'll be with you on set in five minutes. For the big moment. All right?'

They get up, nodding and smiling, and shuffle past us to the door. Max waits, drumming his fingers on his knee, till their footsteps have faded to a whisper. Then he turns to me and says: 'I'd like you to do it.'

'What?'

'It.' Nodding towards the stage. 'This. Now.'

'What – direct it, you mean?'

'No. Say it.'

I'm at a loss. He's always spared me his practical jokes up till now, but perhaps he's decided to punish me for being late. But when I meet his gaze his eyes don't flinch and his mouth doesn't twitch.

Finally I say: 'I thought you were going to ask Hugh?'

'I'm asking you instead.'

'But I'm not an actor.'

'That's the point. *An ac-tor speaks like this.* I don't want the audience to feel they're in a theatre. I want them to feel the real world has suddenly sliced in' – violently slashing the air in front of me with his hand, so that I jump involuntarily – 'like a knife.'

'Why don't you do it?'

'Voice like a drain, old son. They'll think I'm a plumbing prob-lem.' He gets up, and taps my arm. 'Come on. Your chance of a place in history.'

I'm still not certain he's serious as he leads me into the corridor. I half-expect to be greeted by spluttering laughter when we walk on to the stage. But the atmosphere's quiet and tense: everybody watching us, their faces clamped into grins of contained excitement.

They've built a set for the library in one corner. There's a desk with a bookcase behind it and just enough floor for da Silva to col-lapse on. Above the desk dangles a microphone. Fritz is already in his chair, waiting patiently with one hand on the telephone receiver while Rainer the Wizard fusses with the light on his face. Max sits me down opposite him. From his soundproof booth, Jimmy checks that I'm not compromising the shot.

'Here,' says Max, handing me a script.

'I know what it says.'

'So you do.' He retreats to the edge of the booth and pulls on a pair of headphones. 'Say something to me, darling.'

'Hullo hullo hullo.'

He winces. 'Nearer.'

'Hullo hullo hullo.'

'Mmm . . . Better. Again.'

'Hullo hullo hullo.'

'All right. Lights. Action.'

The arc floods the side of Fritz's face, throwing a jagged triangu-lar shadow on to the bookcase. He picks up the telephone and holds the receiver to his ear.

Max looks at me and nods.

'Mr. da Silva,' I say, 'I am the ghost of the past.'

X

35675 Eventide Road, Mason, Oregon 97400
E-mail: miranda@pfizerfamily.com

June 30

Dear Alan Arkwright,

I don't quite know how to write this.

Strange rumors have been reaching me. A couple of weeks ago, while he was listening to the BBC on the internet, my son Michael caught part of an interview with you about my father. Needless to say, he couldn't remember it word for word – but he was pretty sure he heard you claim to have discovered new evidence proving that my mother's death was an accident rather than suicide. He also said (though he was less sure about this bit) that you seemed to be suggesting that the suicide story had been deliberately put about by Henry Whitaker's daughter (i.e. me), in an attempt to discredit him.

Is this true? And if so, why didn't you tell me, before announcing it to the world? I would have thought, frankly, that's the least you owed me.

I realize, of course (and he realizes it, too), that Michael may simply have got the wrong end of the stick. But I have to say I'm really quite upset about the whole thing, and would appreciate a response. Since you haven't replied to my e-mails or phone messages about it, I'm guessing maybe you've been away. I hope that's the explanation, anyway. Which is why I'm sending this registered, to make sure you actually get it.

Best,
Miranda

139

XI

London – April 1930

'I've no idea *where* he is,' I say. 'Let's just start rehearsing it, and hope he turns up before we're ready to shoot.'

The make-up girl helps Hugh on with his mask, then smooths his wig back over the seam. I position him and Graham in the window.

'Lights, please!'

The arcs come on. Rainer really *is* a wizard: the figures are so sharply defined they look as if they've been cut out of black paper.

'Now,' I say.

Graham and Hugh turn. It's nothing: just two very similar men – twins, perhaps? – looking at each other.

'More slowly,' I say. 'I'll count *one-two-three*. At *three* you should be in full profile. You've got to get there at exactly the same moment. Ready?'

They do it again. It's better, but I still doubt whether it'll give the audience that immediate thump-in-the-solar-plexus we're after. I put a hand on K.-M.'s shoulder.

'May I take a squint through here?'

'Of course.'

If anything, it looks even feebler through the camera. 'What do you think?' I say, straightening up.

He shrugs: *See, I've learned to know my place now.*

'Oh, come on,' I say.

'I'm not the director.'

'But if you were?'

He shrugs again. I hear the door opening behind us and feel the weight start to lift from my shoulders. But when I turn, I see it isn't Max, but Nicky, carrying her notebook and her copy of the scenario. She smiles brightly when she catches my eye, but her forehead's runkled with worry.

'What is it?' I say, as soon as she's in hailing distance.

'Max's wife's just 'phoned. He won't be coming in, I'm afraid.'

'Why not?'

'Well, I didn't talk to her,' she says – just crisply enough to remind me that she's a continuity girl now, not a secretary. 'But I gather it's something personal. Anyway. We can't afford to lose a day, so he says you'll have to go on and finish without him.'

My stomach suddenly feels as if it's about to take off into the ether. 'God, it *would* have to be today, wouldn't it? First Jimmy, and now Max.'

She grimaces ruefully. 'I know. It really is the most awful luck.'

'And I'm not even sure about this shot.'

'Oh, dear.' She purses her lips, and shifts her weight from one foot to the other, uncertain whether to stay, or go to her table.

'Here,' I say. 'Come and take a quick dekko at it, will you?'

She puts down her papers. I manoeuvre her behind the camera. 'Can you see?'

'Yes.'

'Right – Hugh – Graham – ready, please. One-two-three.'

They go through it again.

'Now,' I say. 'What was happening there?'

'I don't know. I'd say it was someone looking at himself in the mirror, only it was the wrong angle. What it reminded me of was one of those optical-illusion things where you're either seeing a white vase or two silhouettes facing each other, and your brain can't decide which it is, and keeps switching between them.'

'It's meant to be the big moment – when Markheim suddenly realizes that the stranger he's been talking to all this time is really himself.'

'Oh, oh, gosh. Well, I must say, I didn't get that. Perhaps I'm just being very slow.'

'No, you're not. And anyway, you can be certain that ninety-nine per cent of the audience will be a good deal slower. So how else could we do it?'

She blushes and laughs. 'Oh dear, I don't really think I'm the right person to ask.'

'Actually, you've given me an idea.' And she has: the mirror. There was one hanging amongst the junk in the shop. And it's still there, because the set's been left standing for the final scene.

I shut my eyes, try to visualize how you'd do it, then cup my hands and call: 'All right, everybody: no Max today, I'm afraid. So you're going to have to do this not only with the assistant cameraman, but with the assistant director, too.' I almost add *so please bear with us*, but then I remember that if you don't want to be bullied, you shouldn't show weakness. Instead I say as breezily as possible: 'We'll shoot this now, and then I want to squeeze in another couple of shots which aren't on the list.'

I'm braced for a challenge – or at least a chorus of groans. But everyone just nods, and begins setting up. Perhaps I'm starting to grow into the job.

We do three takes. The third one's flawless: perfectly synchronized, and beautiful, in a balletic way. But – to my eye, at least – it still doesn't do what it's meant to.

I call K.-M. and Rainer over to me, then tell the others to take a break.

'It's nothing to do with you two, or the actors,' I say, 'but I don't feel that's quite right. I want to give Max an alternative. What I'm thinking is: we have the stranger silhouetted in the window, as before. But Markheim's not standing next to him; he's still in the back of the shop, at the bottom of the stairs. Then as the stranger turns, Markheim catches a glimpse of his face in the mirror and realizes it's himself.'

They both look puzzled. Is it a language problem, or do they think what I'm asking for is technically impossible? I beckon Nicky over from the continuity table, and try the idea out on her. She colours with pleasure at being consulted.

When I've finished, she says: 'But won't it just look as if Markheim's seeing his own reflection?'

K.-M. nods. My confidence starts to seep away.

I clench my thigh-muscles, trying to hold on to it. 'Well,' I say, 'I think there *is* a way of doing it that'll avoid any confusion: by establishing Markheim's point of view so far away from the mirror that he could *only* see the stranger in it.'

K.-M. looks from left to right, taking in possible camera positions, then shakes his head. 'Very difficult.'

'But possible, I think. We're doing, what?' I count the M.L.S. in the scenario. 'One, two, three, four, five medium long shots of Markheim at the bottom of the stairs? That'll really hammer home the fact that he stays there the whole time the stranger's talking to him. Then we'll just add one more, showing his reaction when he sees the face in the mirror. If he's still in the same position, it'll never occur to the audience that he might have moved in the meantime.'

'No, perhaps not,' says K.-M. 'But the problem will be the other way.' He walks over to the staircase, and puts his foot on the first step. 'If we shoot from *here*, you won't see anything in the mirror – or at any rate, not clearly enough to know what it is. And if we get closer, it won't look, you know, as if we're seeing through his eyes any more.'

'I think there's a way to do it with an M.L.S., if Rainer can light it,' I say. 'Anyway, let's get the bottom-of-the-stairs shots out of the way, and then see. If it doesn't work, we've only wasted the reaction shot.'

'All right.' I expect it to be followed by a 'but', but instead he startles me by murmuring: 'Nothing ventured, nothing gained.' It's something he must have picked up from Hugh, I suppose.

I explain what I want to Graham. He grasps it immediately: we barely have to rehearse. But still everything seems to take five or six minutes longer than I think it will. By the time we've finished, we're running three-quarters of an hour late. When I ask K.-M. to move the camera I can sense the edginess of the assistants.

'We'll give it till one, O.K.?' I say. 'If we haven't cracked it by then, we'll abandon it.'

My heart thuds in my throat. If I mess this up, I'll have lost the respect of the crew, and Max will be furious with me. But I know I'm right – and if I can carry it off, I'm pretty certain he'll agree with me, though he may not admit it.

Rainer, at least, is indefatigably eager. He puts a couple of arcs just outside the set, then angles the light in through the window so that it will leave Hugh in silhouette but catch the surface of the looking-glass. We rehearse the move a few times, shifting Hugh's position until it gives exactly the effect I want: of something dark and mysterious that can't quite be grasped in the mundane world but suddenly becomes clear and three-dimensional when it's glimpsed in the mirror, as if behind the glass there's another reality altogether. Seeing it gives me a tremor in the gut.

But K.-M. isn't satisfied. He peers through the camera, then shakes his head.

'There's too much light from the glass. It'll burn everything else out.'

'Why don't you use a nigger?' I ask.

He frowns at the mirror. 'I don't think that will help. Look.' He gestures me behind the camera, then holds his hand out next to the lens, making an impromptu screen. 'See? If you cut the light, you cut the image, too.'

He's right. But I'm not going to surrender my darling without a struggle. 'Couldn't we put something on the glass to mute it?' I say. 'Grease, or something?'

'I think then you have a problem with continuity.'

'Oh, come on – the last time the audience saw it was when Markheim first came into the shop. They'll never remember what it looked like.'

He's not listening: he's thinking. After a moment he nods to himself, then says something to Rainer in German. Rainer nods too, and they walk quickly over to the mirror together. Rainer squints through the window at the light, before turning and measuring the angle of the reflected beam, using his fingers as a protractor.

He ponders for a few seconds, then calls to me: 'Yes, I think he is right. I can do something for you, I am pretty sure.'

'Abracadabra,' whispers the second Camera Assistant, and the clapper boy gives a stifled guffaw. But Rainer doesn't seem to hear them.

I don't want to intrude by going too close, so I stay on the set, trying to guess what he's doing from the sounds I can hear: the squeal of tape; the snap of scissors, the soft flop of card hitting the floor. After half a minute or so the quality of the light striking the mirror starts to change, though so imperceptibly that it's hard to decide how, exactly. The closest I can come to it is to say that it appears to be more intense, as if it's being wound in on itself.

'There,' he says, walking back on to the set. 'Try that.'

144

We try it. The first time, Hugh's in the wrong place, and all we get is the top of his head. But when we do it again, his head's perfectly framed in the glass.

'Shall we go for a take?' asks K.-M.

'Ye-es.' But something's still bothering me, something I hadn't noticed before. Try as I may, though, I can't quite identify it.

'O.K.,' I say. I can hear the reluctance in my own voice, but no-one else seems to catch it. 'Ready, Hugh?'

'I shall be ready for lunch, soon,' murmurs Hugh. 'Assuming I am permitted to remove this.' He taps the mask. 'Otherwise I'll be obliged to suck my steak-and-kidney pud through a straw.'

Damn. Damn. That's it: now I can see the mask clearly, I realize that viewed full-front it doesn't look *quite* enough like Markheim's face.

For a moment, I'm paralysed. Then I brace my shoulders and say: 'Look, I'm sorry, I don't think this'll really do. The audience are going to have less than a second. If they just glimpse a facsimile in the mirror, rather than Markheim himself, a lot of them won't know what it is. And even the ones that do won't get the full impact of it. They'll have to ask themselves: *What was that?* Then they'll think: *Ah, yes, Markheim.* What they *need* to do is feel it *here*.' I tense my stomach, then hit it with my clenched fist. The thump's loud enough to make two or three of the crew jump. 'You know? Without thinking about it at all. So – I'm afraid we're going to have to dress Graham up as the stranger, and shoot him.'

There's a murmur from the technicians. The second camera assistant shakes his head. 'Oh, come on,' he mutters, not quite able to look me in the eye. 'Chances are Max won't even use it.'

It's a direct challenge to my authority. Even the clapper-boy looks startled at his tone. Do I remind him curtly who's in charge? Or would that be over-defensive, and weaken my position further?

Before I can decide, K.-M. comes to my aid. 'But still,' he drawls, 'we must do our best, mustn't we? Even if it finishes on the cutting-room floor, we don't want someone to find it and say: *Ha! That was all they could do*.' And he steps decisively back from the camera, daring the A.C. to protest again.

The make-up girl says she'll need ten minutes. I remove myself to the continuity table. I'm not going to argue with a camera assistant; I'm not going to try to ingratiate myself with him. A bit of distance is what's required.

Nicky smiles. 'I do think you're doing well, Henry.'

I shrug.

'No, honestly.' She hesitates. Her throat tightens. 'I'm really proud of you.'

'Well, thanks ever so,' I say, in a shop-girl voice. She laughs. *Phew*: I've deflected her. Why does it make me so uneasy when she says those things? I tell myself it's because they're worthless praise: the only real test of how I'm doing is whether or not the shot works.

'I think I'll just pop out for a spot of air,' I say.

'Mm. That sounds nice.'

'Why don't you join me, then?' I'd rather be on my own, but what else can I do?

We leave through the outside door. The early-morning haze has thickened into a stippled layer of cloud, rubbing out the black shadows and making the grounds look remote and dream-like after the *chiaroscuro* world of the stage. I offer Nicky a cigarette. She says *No, thanks*. I take one myself, and light it. She grows wavery and indistinct behind a curtain of smoke. I know she's watching me, but I can't think of anything to say. I feel as if I'm vanishing inside my own skull.

'You look like Hamlet,' she says finally. 'Just after he's seen his father's ghost.'

'Do I? Oh, God, I'm sorry. I'm just a bit preoccupied, I suppose, with what's going on in there. If this doesn't come off . . .'

She smiles, and shakes her head. 'It won't be the end of the world. You need a break, that's all. You've been overdoing things. Just think: you've only got to get through this afternoon. And then tomorrow . . .'

'What's tomorrow? Oh, oh, yes, I know –'

'Aren't you looking forward to it?'

'Hmph . . .'

'Oh, come on! It'll be fun, won't it?'

'Well, it'll be *something*. I'm not sure *fun*'s the word, from what I've heard about the play.'

146

She could say: *He's your friend,* but she doesn't. She just smiles, and raises her shoulders, and opens her hands in a *please don't spoil it* gesture.

The A.C. appears to summon me back to the stage. K.-M. must have sent him: the poor chap's wriggling with embarrassment and still can't bring himself to look at me.

Graham's already in position, practising the move. We only have to go through it twice before he's ready. I watch carefully during the first take, and know at once from the spiders-crawling-on-my-skin sensation it gives me that we've got it. No-one seeing it could fail to realize they're looking at Markheim's own face. The effect will be as shocking as my voice on *New Year's Eve.*

K.-M. knows it too. He nods at me, bright-eyed. 'There, see? You did it.'

'We *all* did it.' I cup my hands and call: 'Thank you, Graham. Thank you, Hugh. Thank you, Rainer. Thank you, everyone. All right. Lunch.' And then, turning back to K.-M., I say: 'And thank *you*, especially.' I hope he understands why I've singled him out: not just for his photography, but for his support, too.

'It was a pleasure,' he murmurs. 'Señor Buñuel and Señor Dali would be proud of you.'

I feel myself blushing. I'm pleased, of course – but more than that, I'm surprised: an English cameraman, I'm certain, wouldn't even know who Buñuel and Dali were.

As we start together towards the canteen, a thought suddenly strikes me: 'I say, K.-M., tomorrow night Nicky and I are going to be going to see a chap we know in a new play. Would you like to come along?'

It seems to throw him, for some reason: perhaps, after all, he's not so self-assured as he appears. 'Oh, I am – I am so sorry,' he stutters, a flush of red spreading up from his throat to his face. 'But I am doing something else. Another occasion, perhaps?'

'Yes, yes, of course.'

Nicky runs to catch up with us, and slips a hand through my arm. 'Happy now?'

I nod.

She gives me a quick squeeze. 'Good.'

And I am. I can't say I don't care what happens to my shot – of course I do. But even if they throw it away – even if they fire me for insubordination – I'll go to my grave knowing I've created at least one moment of art.

The theatre's stifling, the seats cramped and punitively bony. The play – I mustn't be uncharitable about it; it's well enough crafted, I suppose. But the words are butterfly-light tokens, so removed from the emotions they're meant to represent that they don't even stir the hairs on your skin as they pass – don't stir the hairs on *my* skin, anyway. But then I'd have been very surprised if they had. This is England, after all.

The one thing that sustains me is the secret knowledge of my *Markheim* shot. I keep seeing it again, sensing its impact in my belly. But even so, fifty minutes into the second act I'm starting to wilt. When William ambles on with a wheelbarrow, I want to scream: *Hurry up, for Christ's sake!*

'I'm going to build a bonfire, Mummy,' he says, with a bitter-sweet smile. We're so close I can see the snakes of sweat eating his make-up, and the blotches of paint on the heap of paper leaves in the barrow.

'Why, darling?'

'Because, Mummy, they're dead.'

He turns, slowly takes up the barrow, and wheels it off at a funereal pace – his stage-mother staring after him, holding a handkerchief to her open mouth.

It's a moment or two before the audience are certain it's over. Then they give a collective gasp, and erupt into applause. I hear Nicky sniffing, and look towards her. Her cheek's spangled with tears. She senses my glance and tries to smile at me, but can't control her mouth properly and gives me a gummy leer instead.

'Sorry,' she whispers.

'Why? That's what it's for.'

But my own eyes are obstinately dry. Thank God.

'Oh,' she says. 'That was – Oh! Here they come!'

She cranes her neck to see over the man in front of her, clapping furiously. She's still clapping when the house lights come up. I slip my hand under her elbow. She twitches as if I'd given her an electric shock.

'Let's go,' I say. 'Or we'll never get a drink.'

The bar's already packed when we get there. I install Nicky at the last free table, and join the crush at the counter. The barman's a big, wheezy fellow who does everything infuriatingly slowly, scanning the shelf for glasses as if he's no idea where he put them, and painstakingly retrieving every bottle cap after he's levered it off and clattering it into a box. It takes me five minutes to jostle my way to the front and buy three pale ales. I arrive back at the table with them just as William appears in the doorway. I barely recognize him: instead of the ballet boy outfit I was expecting, he's wearing an open-necked white shirt and an unactorish grey sports-coat. He catches my eye, waves a couple of fingers at me, and starts edging in our direction.

'You dying of thirst?' I say, handing Nicky her beer.

She laughs. 'No, I'm fine. Thank you. Gosh, I feel frightfully honoured, don't you?'

'Why?'

'Well, because, you know, we know *him*. The star.' She nods at William.

If he thought he could avoid being recognized, he was wrong: two middle-aged women, their faces pink with adulation, have intercepted him, and he's acknowledging their compliments with modest little bobs of the head.

'I think *star*'s overstating it a bit – for the juvenile lead in a new play at a theatre club.'

'No, it isn't. Everyone'll be looking at us and saying: *Who* are *those people?*'

'I hate to shatter your youthful illusions, but I think it's extremely improbable that anyone will be the slightest bit interested.' I take the edge off it with a smile, but it still sounds harsh.

What made me put her in her place like that?

She flushes, then smiles herself as William detaches himself from his admirers and saunters towards us.

'Hullo, Henry. Hullo –' He's still debating between *Nicky* and *Miss Weedon*.

149

'Hullo.'

He turns to me. 'No Christopher?'

'Haven't seen him.'

'Hm. I did write to him – telling him about it.' He gives an odd little shiver, and stares at the table for a moment. Then he shakes himself, and looks sweetly at Nicky. 'Well, anyway.'

'That was marvellous,' she says.

'Did you enjoy it?'

'Oh, I can't tell you how much.'

'I'm so pleased.' He pulls out a chair and sits down. 'One never knows, you know. Sometimes you'll say something you think's killingly funny, and you won't get so much as a titter. Other times you'll deliver a line so dull you can barely remember it – you know, *Pass the mustard, Mildred*; or *Goodness, it's starting to rain* – and find the whole place suddenly heaving with helpless merriment.'

Nicky laughs. 'We didn't make too many howlers tonight, did we?'

'No, no: you were the perfect audience.'

'Well, it isn't very difficult, is it? With a play like this? I mean, it works like a piece of music. The allegro. Then the slow movement. It made me think of Chekhov.'

'Yes,' I hear myself drawling. 'It's painfully obvious that's exactly what it was meant to do.'

There: I've done it again. Why, when she's absolutely right? Am I just annoyed that she keeps confounding my expectations of her? Surely I'm not such a bastard as that?

She seems not to have noticed, but William has: he tilts his head forward, gives me a curious oblique glance that could prise the back off a watch, then wags his finger at Nicky and says: 'Careful, or you'll end up in the book.'

'Book?' She looks from him to me and back again, trying to gauge if he's being serious. 'What book?'

'He keeps a book – didn't you know that? Writes down all the absurd things we lesser mortals say and do. I caught him writing about *me* once – though needless to say, he wouldn't let me see what he'd put.'

Blood floods my neck and throat. I brace my arms and pinch the edge of the table. I'm going to fling it over – walk out – never speak to him again.

'But *I* don't think what you said was absurd at all,' he says, smiling at Nicky. 'In fact, I thought it was the most perceptive thing about *Leaves* I've heard. *Much* more perceptive than the blasted critics. You wouldn't like to come *every* night, would you?'

She laughs again. My rage evaporates – leaving me cold suddenly, despite the heat. He was right: I deserved a slap in the face.

'Here,' I say, sliding his drink towards him. 'Something to wet your whistle.' It sounds awful: grudging and brittle. I force myself to add: 'And seldom has a whistle warranted wetting more.'

'Thanks.' But he doesn't meet my eye. If I'm not going to offer my opinion, he's too proud to solicit it.

'You were very good,' I say. 'Very restrained.'

'Ah, restrained,' he murmurs. You can barely hear it, but the venom in his voice is unmistakable: perhaps my criticism of his Hamlet still rankles.

He says to Nicky: 'If Henry had his way, you could get a knighthood for restraint.'

She turns to look at me. Her face is hot with excitement and drink. There's a directness in her gaze I haven't seen before – flirtatious and mocking at the same time.

'Yes,' she says. 'I can believe that.'

The skin between my shoulder-blades prickles. I say: 'Only in the acting. I think we could do with a good deal less of it in the words. If the mixture were a bit thicker, the poor old actors wouldn't have to work so bloody hard to squeeze every last drop out of it.'

'Ah,' says William. 'Hear the clatter? That's the toy-cupboard door. Here comes Henry's hobby-horse: *the paucity of modern English.*'

His voice is too quiet: he's really wounded. I've underestimated his commitment to this play.

'It's no-one's fault,' I say. 'Barrett Trayne's just a product of his time, like all of us.'

'Well, *there*'s a profound observation,' says William. 'I wish I had a bit of paper so I could write it down. *Products of our time.*'

'Here,' says Nicky, opening her bag. Then she catches William's expression, and stops.

I manage a smile. 'And it's a time that regards language as a way of hiding what you feel, rather than expressing it.'

'Well, personally,' says William, 'I've no desire to be acquainted with other people's feelings. Or to acquaint them with mine. I can't imagine anything drearier than meeting a perfect stranger and having to listen to him maunder on about his soul. I think it's rather amusing to live in a world where nobody means what they say. The real art is to do it better than everyone else.' He smiles at Nicky. 'Isn't it, Miss W.?'

'Um.' I can hear the slither of her bag as she nudges it back under the table. She's staring at him with that trapped-rabbit gaze. She can't tell if he's really asking her opinion, or simply making fun of her.

He isn't doing either, of course; he's signalling a truce. For a moment, it incenses me: you can't just unilaterally decide to get out of the ring and start talking to the referee. Then I remember the *Markheim* shot again. I fold my arms, hugging it to me. Arguing's pointless: wait till they see *this* . . .

'Well,' I say, accepting terms. 'We're not going to resolve the issue tonight.'

William smiles. 'No.' He gropes in his pocket, pulls out a silver cigarette case I've never seen before and offers it to Nicky. She studies the elegant line of Sullivan Powells as if she's not quite sure what they are, then decisively reaches out and grabs one.

'Thank you.'

'Henry?'

'Thanks.'

He takes one himself, and snaps the case shut. I just have time to glimpse the inscription on the front – *To W. from B.* – before he's magicked it away again.

'Here,' I say, holding a match for Nicky. She almost blows it out – then gets the idea that she has to suck, and flinches as the smoke makes her eyes smart. When I turn to William, I find he's looking anxiously towards the door.

'William?'

He jerks back: a naughty boy surprised playing with himself. 'Oh, right, thank you.'

We stare at each other through the haze, listening to Nicky's strangled coughs and gurgles as she wrestles with what must be her first cigarette. It isn't that we haven't got anything to say, just that neither of us seems able to say it. I want to mend fences by praising tonight's performance, but I can't think of a way of to do it without seeming – implicitly at least – to damn *Hamlet* yet again, and so opening old wounds; *he* sits stiff-shouldered at the table, looking awkwardly behind him, then glancing curiously into my face, as if he's challenging to me call his bluff and try to find out what's really going on in his head.

'It's awfully stuffy in here, isn't it?' says Nicky suddenly. She's pink with the effort of trying to get her breath, and is holding her cigarette at arm's length, letting the smoke coil placidly up to the ceiling. 'Could we – I mean, why don't we think about moving on?'

William grimaces. His eyes widen with panic and for a second I catch a glimpse of what's behind them: not *amour propre* about his acting, but some sea-sick anxiety about his private life – and how much he can say about it in front of Nicky. Then an invisible hand brushes the frown from his forehead and his mouth curves back into a matinée-idol smile.

'Move on where?' he says.

'Oh, I don't know – a pub, or somewhere. Or' – darting a quick look at me, that seems to prick my cheek – 'we could all go back to my flat, if – if – you know . . . I've got some beer. And I did get a bottle of malmsey, just in case.'

Malmsey? Oh, God: that's my fault – I remember telling her once that he liked it. He probably hasn't touched the stuff since he hung up his green velvet cloak and broad-brimmed hat at the end of our second year, and embraced Communism.

'That's terribly sweet of you,' he says. 'The thing is, though, I promised the others I'd go and have dinner with them a bit later on. And you – well, you two have already eaten, I take it?'

He knows damn well we have: I asked his advice about restaurants.

'Oh, dear, that's a shame,' says Nicky, crestfallen. Then she brightens suddenly. 'I know: maybe we could just have a pudding or coffee or something with you, and then go back to Clapham together? I mean, it would be sense for us to share a cab, wouldn't it?'

'Yes, perfect sense,' he says. 'The only thing is, Barrett was hoping to do a bit of work on the script afterwards, and I offered to help him . . .'

He tries to look off-hand, but he can't keep a pink tinge from his ears and throat. Of course: the *B* on the cigarette case. Barrett Trayne must be his lover. *That*'s why he was so defensive about the play.

'Well, we could wait a bit, couldn't we?'

'Yes, but – honestly, Nicky, I've no idea how long it'll take. I may even end up sleeping on his sofa. He'll probably be giving us notes in the morning, and it'd be a bit silly for me to trek all the way home and then all the way back into town again, wouldn't it?'

'All right. Well . . .' She gulps and nods, blinking her smoke-reddened eyes. Greta Szagy could never convey disappointment so directly. I tell myself it's nothing: she'll have forgotten about it in half an hour. But it doesn't feel like nothing: it feels as if she's drowning in misery.

'Could we make it another time?' murmurs William. He leans towards her, props his chin on his palm, gazes directly into her face with that cat-like stare that says: *You are the most fascinating person in the world.* 'Maybe when the run has settled down a bit? I'd love to come and drink malmsey with you *then*, I really would.'

Yes: the malmsey. That's the detail that particularly haunts me, for some reason.

'Of course,' sniffs Nicky. 'That would be lovely.'

'Good.' He reaches out and quickly touches her hand. He can be so oleaginous sometimes you'd think someone had squeezed him from a tube. 'I'll look forward to it. You'd better be ready for me, though. I shall tap on your door when you're least expecting –'

A sudden drop in the level of noise behind him makes him stop and turn. The rest of the cast has arrived, led by a sun-tanned young man in an open-necked shirt who stands inside the doorway, scanning the room.

William gets up and waves at him. 'Barrett!'

154

The young man smiles and comes towards us.

As he approaches, William says: 'Barrett, I'd like you to meet Nicky Weedon. My poor long-suffering neighbour.'

'How do you do, Miss Weedon?'

'How do you do?'

'And this is Henry Whitaker. An old –'

'Oh, yes, I know about Henry Whitaker,' says Trayne, taking my hand. 'The most frightening man in England.'

'Really? What's William been telling you about me?' I say, laughing.

'Well, you were the voice on the telephone, weren't you? In *New Year's Eve*? *Mr. Da Silva, I am the ghost of the past –*'

'Ah, that, yes.'

'I thought it was an absolute coup. Suddenly to have someone *speaking* in a film. And saying *that.* I almost jumped out of my seat and ran gibbering from the theatre.'

I'm smiling with relief, but still have that odd feeling of let-down you get when you're expecting another step on the stairs and it isn't there.

'Well, ten words is a rather slight claim to fame, but *faute de mieux*, I suppose.'

'Oh, I don't know. *I'll* never inspire a moment of terror like that, if I'm writing plays till I'm eighty. Anyway, I don't want to seem dreadfully anti-social, but' – turning to William – 'did you explain?'

He nods. Trayne smiles at Nicky. 'It's just there's a table booked, and then we've got an awful lot to get –'

'Yes,' she says. 'I know.' She tries to smile back, but her face won't co-operate: the muscles have seized up, as if she's being turned to stone.

I reach out and touch her arm. 'Come on,' I say. 'Let's go. I'd love a sip of malmsey, if I'm invited.'

We barely have to wait for a taxi. The driver's a blue-jowled man in his forties who exudes disapproval – though why I can't imagine, since half his fares at this time of night must be young couples. When I say: 'Clapham Common, please,' he nods and clicks his tongue, as though it's an address in Gomorrah, and exactly what he would have expected.

'Well,' I say, as we settle into our seats. 'I'm glad you enjoyed it, anyway.'

'I did. Very much. Thank you.' Her voice is thin and constrained.

'Not at all. It was a pleasure.'

'Was it?' She smiles and tries to look at me – but as soon as her gaze meets mine, it bounces away again.

'Well, *pleasure* might be overstating it a bit. But *interesting*.'

She doesn't respond – just stares out of the window. I almost add: *Barrett Trayne ought to be executed for crimes against literature* – but then I realize that if she was going to laugh she'd have done it already. I'm sick of being facetious, anyway: it makes me hate myself. So I'm happy just to sit back and watch the Morse code of street lamps and headlights flash up on her face: *dash dash dot; dot dot dash dash*. There must be a message in it, if I could only read the letters.

Several times I hear her drawing in her breath as if she's about to say something, but – after a tantalizing pause – it always comes out as a ragged sigh instead. I tell myself to leave her alone: she'll speak when she's ready. But when we reach the West End, the gulf between the glittery bustle around us and the dark silence of the cab quickly becomes unbearable, and I suddenly hear myself saying: 'I know it'd have been nice if William could have come with us. I'm sure he'd have preferred it, too, if he hadn't had to work.'

She shrugs.

'No, I mean it. Theatre's like that, I'm afraid. A hard mistress.'

'Mm.'

'You obviously don't believe me.'

She turns sharply, forcing herself to look at me. 'It just made me think of Pippa, that's all. That's exactly the kind of thing *she*'d say. *It'll be easier for work in the morning. I'll sleep on the sofa* – when it's about a hundred yards closer to work than we are. And she's obviously got no intention of going anywhere near a sofa. Except maybe for a – you know, a gin and tonic or something. And a bit of ca*noo*dling.'

I'm so surprised that I can't help bursting out laughing.

Her face darkens in the half-light. 'Is he a – a –? You know? A –?'

'What? A pansy?'

'Yes. A pansy.' She doesn't flinch as she says it: her tone's curious rather than embarrassed. It occurs to me in the same instant, first, that she's growing up, and second, that whatever's bothering her, it isn't William: she's talking about him too easily, and with too much relish.

'Well?' she says, misunderstanding my silence. 'Is he? I mean, I suppose he must be, only I've never met one before –'

'I expect you have, actually.'

'Well, not one that I've known about. So –'

'You probably just couldn't tell. They wouldn't tend to advertise it, would they?'

'No.' She hesitates, then says very quietly: 'But anyway. You haven't answered my question.'

But the question's changed: I can sense it from her sudden stillness, and the limpet-grip of her eyes on my face. She's not just asking about William, now, but about me, too.

I feel myself on the edge of a precipice. Half of me wants to jump back, screaming: *I'm sorry, but I don't really see that's any of your business*. The other half wants to close my eyes – spread my arms – and topple gently forward. I try to find an answer that'll keep me where I am.

Finally I think I've got it: 'Well, I'm not sure how easy it is to say, really. I mean, quite a lot of chaps go through a queer phase – you know, at school, and so on – and then grow out of it, and are perfectly normal. But William – well, I suspect he won't grow out of it.'

'That's what I thought. Oh –!'

The cab's slowed suddenly to avoid a party of young men and women in evening dress spilling off the pavement in front of a nightclub. Nicky and I are thrown together, thigh against thigh. She gasps, but doesn't move away. My hand brushes hers as I reach for the door to push myself upright again.

'Goodness!' she says. I can feel her breath on my ear, and the tickle of her hair on my neck.

'No harm done.' I lean forward and call to the driver: 'Well saved!'

157

He doesn't reply. He's pale and rigid with fear or anger. Sticking out of his pocket is a half-folded biblical tract. I can just make out the title: 'The Wages of S–' .

'Is it true?' says Nicky, as I settle back in my seat. She's whispering, trying to prolong our enforced intimacy. 'About the book?'

'Mm?'

'You know. The one he was talking about. Where you write everything down?'

'Well' – raising my voice, to dissipate the churchy atmosphere – 'everyone keeps a diary from time to time, don't they? I'm sure *you* must have.'

'But I think – I mean, I got the impression this is something different, isn't it?'

'In degree, perhaps. Not in kind.' I want to add: *He really shouldn't have mentioned it at all.* But that would only heighten the sense of mystery.

She's on the point of saying something more, but changes her mind, and looks out of the window again instead. I'm happy to do the same: I'm still swaying on my cliff-top, and half an inch in any direction now might prove fatal. I shut my eyes to steady myself. Lightning-flash images invade the darkness: the pallor of William's body; the smooth brazil-nut hollow where his buttock joins his thigh, and Barrett Trayne's fingers stroking it; Nicky unbuttoning her dress, and rucking it up around her waist, and lifting it over her head. I don't need to imagine the warmth underneath: I can still feel a tingle where my leg touched hers, as if she had burned off the top layer of skin.

The familiar debate starts clanging in my ears: *Why shouldn't you? Why shouldn't you?*

Same old reason. Because she's a virgin. Because it would mean something to her that it wouldn't to me.

Perhaps it would mean the same thing to you. You're starting to feel jealous about her, aren't you? Wasn't that why you were so horrible to her? You couldn't bear the thought of her being more interested in William than you?

I open my eyes again. We're juddering down half-empty Whitehall. Ahead of us is the Cyclops face of Big Ben.

'Ah,' I say. 'The mother of parliaments.'

She stiffens and glances at me, as if she can't believe my inanity. Then she looks away again, murmuring something I can't hear.

'What?'

She hesitates, then replies in a stage-whisper: 'I said, I wish I knew what you'd written about me. That is, if I'm important enough for you to have written anything.'

'Of course you are.'

I've trapped myself – but what else could I have said? She's quiet as we turn on to Millbank.

Then she goes on: 'The thing is, Henry, I don't know what I am.'

'Well, I do. You're a very nice, very bright girl.'

'No, I don't mean that. I mean – you've been awfully sweet to me: taking me out, and everything. But other people seem to be boyfriends and girlfriends. Or else they're engaged, or what have you. And I don't know what we are.'

I'm shocked. Shocked to hear her saying it. Shocked at myself, for assuming she never would, and not even bothering to think of an answer. Frantically, I try to find one now. *Oh, really? I thought we were human beings.* No: it's too late for jokiness. *Well, I always thought we were just friends.* A slap in the face – and do I really want to close off the possibility of being something more? *I'm queer.* Ditto – and a lie, to boot. *Come here, silly* – and kiss her.

That's what I want to do: my whole body feels shorn and tremulous without the pressure of hers against it. But that would be a lie, too. And one it'd be impossible to retreat from.

Jesus.

I stare out of the window. A knot of workmen stands in front of a coffee stall by the Thames. Beyond it I can see the lights of Vauxhall Bridge and their blurry mirror-image in the water. What do they remind me of? Something marvellous that's also connected with Nicky, so that being with her now feels oddly apposite. It's a second before I get it: the set for *Shadow on the River*, the first time she took me on to the stage at Milstead and I saw the painted flat. There's the same shivery sense of mystery; the same tantalizing promise of another, more intense life, hovering just outside your grasp. Except, of course, that with the flat the promise recedes as you approach it – whereas here, if you got close enough, it would eventually reduce to light-bulbs and cables and the oily skin of the river.

'Sometimes I wonder if you're just being kind, and you don't really like me very much at all,' she says suddenly, as we start to slow for the junction. I can hear the anguish in her voice: she must have been hoping that if she waited long enough I'd get her off the hook by saying something, but I've left her with no alternative but to spell it out.

Guiltily, I rush to reassure her: 'Oh, that's not true at all!'

She shakes her head. 'I just mean in, you know, the way a man likes a girl. And if that's it, you've only got to tell me, and of course I'll understand.'

I start to speak, but she's determined to finish now, and hurries on, staring down at her feet.

'But then other times I think maybe it's something else: that you don't *trust* me.' She reaches out and fumbles for my hand. 'And I . . . I just wanted to say that you can. I don't think there's anything you could tell me that would stop me liking you.'

William. Irma Brücke. The dream.

I say: '*I murder babies with a spoon.*'

She looks up sharply, shaking her head impatiently. 'There, you see? You're not taking me seriously. You think I'm not old enough, or strong enough, to understand.'

We've reached the bridge. Sure enough, I can see the network of wires and bolts and fittings that create the distant illusion of romance. Even now, God help me, I can't escape a tremor of disappointment.

It's not *her* that isn't old enough: it's me.

'I mean, I know something happened in Germany,' she says. 'I don't know what, exactly, but it's pretty obvious you didn't just make it all up.'

'Make what up?'

'Oh, you know – the story you sent in. About the field-glasses, and the poor woman who's had to become a . . . a prostitute. And Max said when you were there last year you sneaked off secretly one weekend, to see someone in a place called Klosterfeld. So putting two and two together . . .'

160

I'm suddenly so cold I start to shiver. 'How the hell did he know that?'

She shrugs, blushing. 'Perhaps he saw your ticket or something. Anyway, all I'm saying is, it doesn't matter. I'm not a school-girl any more.' She takes my hand again, squeezes the wrist, pulls it very gently towards her.

You do realize you'd have to marry her?

Well, would that be such a bad thing? You've got to come home at some point, if you're ever going to grow up.

'I'm not asking for any promises, or anything, Henry. You don't have to protect me.'

I lean across and kiss her.

She starts with surprise, then whimpers and opens her mouth so I can find her tongue. Her fingers press my neck as if she can't quite believe she's finally touching it. And when we stop to get our breath she presses her cheek against mine and murmurs in my ear: 'Oh, thank goodness. Thank goodness, thank goodness, thank goodness.'

We're both shaky when we get out of the cab, *brrr*ing in the sudden cold, then hugging each other again for warmth, laughing at the novelty of it, as the driver sifts a coin at a time through his bag for change. I give him a huge tip, but he doesn't even say thank you. As he drives away, I catch a glimpse of his face in the mirror, glowering back at us.

She holds my hand while she's leading me inside and groping for the key, as if she's frightened that if she lets me go I'll vanish again. I want to tell her it's all right, I won't back out now. But there's no way of saying it that won't sound boorish and graceless.

She's obviously spruced the place up in anticipation of William's visit. The bulbous Victorian sofa's covered by a jazzy pink-and-black bedspread that still has the sweet woolly smell of the shop. There are a couple of modern lamps with opaque glass shades that look as if they were bought at the same time. Lying on the table is a big book about Cézanne.

'Right,' she says. Her own flat seems to puzzle her: she glances around, blinking in the light, as if she's not sure where anything is.

'Malmsey. Malmsey. That's what we need. Ah, yes.' She squats in front of a lacquered *chinoiserie* cabinet, takes out a bottle and puts it on the table. 'Now. Glasses.' She starts towards the door, then stops as she passes me. 'Sit down. Sit down. Please. I'll be back in a sec.'

I've burned my boats: I'm going to stay. If she doesn't want to go to bed with me tonight, I'll sleep on the sofa. And if she does, then . . .

You haven't got a French letter. What if she gets pregnant?

Then I'll have to marry her that much sooner, won't I? It wouldn't be the end of the world.

I can rub toothpaste on my teeth, get a shave on my way to work in the morning. My notes are at home, but I should be able to defend myself. It'd help, though if I could re-read the end of *Markheim*, just to refresh my memory. I start to scan her bookcase. She's got more than I'd have expected: a couple of Mabel Penneys; an Agatha Christie; but also *The Idiot* and *Mansfield Park* and – yes, Chekhov. But no Stevenson that I can see . . .

There's a sudden crash, followed by a despairing 'Dash it!' from Nicky. I rush out into the kitchen. It's cold, and smells of fried food and gas. She's staring at a diadem of broken glass on the floor.

'Oh, hullo,' she says. 'Sorry, you didn't have to – I just –'

'Where's the dustpan and brush?'

She opens a cupboard, and takes them out. While she's sweeping up I stand behind her, my shin pressing her bum. When she stands up again she's shaking so much the glass fragments rattle in the pan. I put my arms round her and pull her to me.

'Are you sure malmsey's really what you want at the moment?'

She pulls away just enough to be able to turn and look at me. There's no bashfulness or coquettishness in her expression – just a kind of frank curiosity. She's very still for a second, then gently rests her forehead on my neck.

I prise the dustpan from her hand, slide it on to the table, then start moving her towards the door in a clumsy two-step.

When we get to the hall, I whisper: 'Which is your room?'

'There.' It sounds sticky. Her mouth must be as dry as mine.

I reach for the handle, and push. The bed's straight ahead. I half-lift her on to it. The pillow has the curranty scent of her hair. In the wedge of light from the hall I can see a moth-eaten teddy-bear poking out from under the sheet, and a picture of Nicky and Jojo on the bedside table.

I kiss her throat, and start unbuttoning her dress. She crosses her hands across her chest, and makes a whining sound that means *no*.

I feel a jolt as if I'd touched an electric fence. 'Sorry,' I say. 'I shouldn't be doing this.'

'No. I want to. It's just the door.'

I get up and close it.

'Is Pippa still likely to be coming in? At this hour?'

She giggles. 'She might.'

I blunder back to her. She's finished unbuttoning the dress herself. I help her to pull it off. As I undress myself, my eyes adjust to the darkness and I see the faint glow-worm phosphorescence of her skin against the brown blanket. She's still wearing her underclothes.

When I lie down next to her she says: 'What do you want me to do?'

'You don't have to do anything.'

'Just tell me. Please.'

I start to fumble with her brassière, but can't unhook it. She slips her hands behind her and does it herself. Then, without prompting, she removes her knickers and discreetly nudges them on to the floor.

'There,' she whispers, turning towards me. 'I'm all yours.'

I start to stroke her. She shivers. I half-pull her off the bed and tug at the bedclothes so we can get underneath them, but they're so firmly fixed it takes me three or four goes to jerk them free. She must still make her bed the way she was taught to at school. I've strayed somehow into a girl's dormitory, and ended up seducing the Head Prefect.

You'd think it'd be off-putting, like the thought of fucking your sister. But it isn't. It's exciting.

You must be a monster.

Only if I let her down. And I'm not going to, am I? I'm going to marry her.

That's what you say.

I am. I am.

163

No way out.

'Henry,' she murmurs, as I worm my way under the sheet. I can feel her straining to see me in the dim light of the street lamps, trying to square the looming bulk in front of her with the details of my face. 'Henry,' she says again, as if to reassure herself that it is really me.

Her breasts are bigger than Irma Brücke's. She gasps when I kiss them – whether with pleasure or ticklishness, I can't tell. I slip my hand between her thighs. She clenches them involuntarily.

'Relax,' I whisper.

'Sorry.'

What did I do with Irma Brücke? Not very much – that's the truth of it: she choreographed everything, drew me into her at the right moment. Nicky won't let me know when she's ready. She probably won't know herself.

I roll on top of her, as gently as I can. She spreads her legs, but I can't get inside her. Her teeth are clenched. Breath hisses between them. It's clearly hurting her. After a few seconds I stop and lever myself off.

'Sorry. This obviously isn't a good idea.'

'No, no, please.' She puts her hands in the small of my back, presses me down again, then lifts herself to kiss me. That movement does it, for some reason. We both of us cry out. The next instant she makes another noise: an unsteady panting moan. It takes me a second to recognize it as laughter.

'Are you all right?'

She nods.

'I'm not hurting you?'

'No,' she says. But immediately bites her lip. She's staring at me, eyes wide, as if she's trying to fathom what I'm feeling, and decipher what she ought to do.

What she ought to do, of course, is tear me, try to eat me. But how could she know that, unless her instincts tell her? Until thirty seconds ago she was a virgin. Did Irma Brücke know it, when she fucked the man who killed my father?

I shut my eyes. I'm in Klosterfeld again. I feel Irma's nails in my back, and her tongue in my mouth, and see the holy image of St. Walther gazing down on us.

164

'Henry,' says Nicky, stroking my face. 'Henry. Henry.'

I open my eyes again. She's crying. I kiss the tears away.

Then all at once it's over.

I subside on top of her, stunned. My own body has ambushed me.

'I'm sorry,' I say. 'That wasn't very satisfactory, was it?'

'It was lovely,' she says.

I roll away, and find myself looking at Jojo.

This is what I'll come home to every day of my life.

I wake suddenly in the middle of the night. I've had the dream again. Nicky stirs next to me, and murmurs something I can't understand. For a long time I can't get back to sleep. I lie there, cold with panic, taking deep breaths to try to calm myself. When I at last drift off again I dream I'm in the lavatory with Nicky. Both of us are naked. We can't get the door to shut properly. After a minute or two Max bursts in. 'Ah, that's what we'll do with Markheim!' he says, smirking: 'Have him fucking in the lav.'

I finally come to at 7.30. Nicky's standing by the bed, holding a tea-tray. She's wearing a grey flannel dressing-gown with frayed lapels. It must be the one she had at school.

'Good morning,' she says. 'How did you sleep?'

'Fine. Fine. How about you?'

She blushes slightly and smiles. As she hands me my cup she says: 'Did you have a bad dream or something?'

'Why?'

'I heard you crying out. You said *Daddy*.'

I take a sip of tea. What shall I say? I've got to tell her something. 'It's just . . . It's just a nightmare I get sometimes.'

'About your father?'

'Yes.'

'What happens in it?'

'Oh, it's . . . You know the sort of thing. You must get them, too.'

She shakes her head.

I smile. 'I won't burden you with mine, then.'

She draws her dressing-gown tighter around her, and sits on the edge of the bed. 'Please.'

'It's nothing. Really.'

She reaches out and takes my hand – not possessively, presuming on our new relationship, but tentatively; just as she did in the taxi. *You can trust me.*

'Well –'

Come on. If you're going to marry her, you can't not.

'Well, it probably doesn't sound anything very much, I expect. I'm in Westminster Abbey. It's dark, but with strange oblique light coming in through the windows. Like the stripes on a mint humbug.'

A chance for her to laugh, if she's embarrassed. But she doesn't. She just nods.

'I'm standing in front of the tomb of the Unknown Warrior. And suddenly the ghost of my father rises up from it, like that, as if the feet are hinged, somehow. I look around at the other visitors, but none of them seems to have noticed. It's just me and him.'

'Oh.' She squeezes my wrist.

'He's staring straight at me. And moving his lips. But the only noise that comes out is a kind of strangled groan. Like this.'

The noise of it shocks me.

She says: 'You think he's trying to tell you something, but you don't know what?'

'Yes.'

'Last night you probably wondered if it was: *What are you doing with that girl?*' She doesn't smile. She's quite serious. I'll never underestimate her again.

'Yes,' I say. 'But I'm sure he'd approve, really.'

'I hope so,' she says. She leans forward and kisses me. Her hair tickles my cheek. 'Thank you for telling me.'

XII

London
July 17

Three a.m. again. But it's not memory that's keeping me awake, this time: it's discombobulation. My biological clock is eight hours adrift, and I haven't caught up with myself yet. The fuggy little room where I'm writing this has that stale-tobacco-half-covered-by-carpet-shampoo stink you get in low-rent motels everywhere, so if I shut my eyes I can still imagine myself just a few hours from home – holed up in some fleabag in Gallup, New Mexico, say, or Boise, Idaho. It's only when I open them again, and see a broom closet with internet facilities and a distant view of Victoria Station, that I start to assimilate where I am.

But even London's not quite what I expected. I knew it must have changed, but I was still half-braced for the tourist posters – smiling bobbies, and red-coated guardsmen, and cheery cockney bus conductors. I hadn't realized just how *multi-ethnic* it's gotten. I was afraid I'd have the old sense of people glancing oddly at me, and thinking to themselves: What's *she* doing here? Surely she doesn't *quite* belong? But anyone from anywhere would look like they belonged here now. It's such a relief to open the door and find yourself in an ocean of turbans and dreadlocks and baseball caps. Your own small peculiarities dissolve away to nothing. You're – blessed state – *invisible*.

Deep England will be different, I know. That's when it'll *really* hit me that I'm 5,000 miles from the nearest person who cares about me.

I tried calling Hode a few minutes ago. He wasn't home. It's so strange: all day, I've been storing up little incidents and observations to tell him, and now I can't.

My plan was to go after Arkwright right away – no calls or e-mails to let him know I was coming or give him time to escape. It was too early to check in, so I left my bags at the hotel reception, took the tube to Paddington Station, and got on the first train to Slough. I'd expected a strange sense of *déjà vu*, but the scene from the window

167

was unrecognizable. It looked like a Disney version of *Bladerunner*: old houses sprayed with graffiti; derelict factory yards strewn with wrecked cars and interspersed with trim parks where little old ladies were walking their dogs; then fields, and even the remains of a farm or two, spliced at the horizon with a different reality, where almost-static 747s were stacked up over Heathrow.

Davey Brooker University, it turns out, isn't really in Slough at all, so all I got to see of the town was a litter of shopping-mall buildings straggling round the edge (almost all of them, shockingly, put up since I was last here), and looking like a Lego model of an American suburb. And it isn't really a university, either – just an overgrown poly-technic. After looking at a map I couldn't understand and asking a couple of students who don't know their way around their own cam-pus, I finally discovered that the Department of Historical Studies was half-way up of one of the towers.

An elevator took me to the fifth floor and set me down in a gray cor-ridor lined with identical doors. The fourth one along was marked: "Dr. A. Arkwright." Above the name-plate was a tired-looking sign-up form for meetings. One of its tape brackets had come unstuck, making it flop at an angle. The final date, I noticed, was last week.

I knocked, but there was no answer. I tried the handle. Locked.

At the end of the corridor I found a half-open door marked "Office." I tapped lightly on the frame, then put my head inside. A girl of nine-teen or twenty was sitting at a desk piled with papers, working at a computer. When I told her I was looking for Alan Arkwright, she stared at me big-eyed, as if I was crazy. He wasn't there, didn't I know – he'd gone away? Away where? Abroad, somewhere, she thought, but she couldn't be sure, because he hadn't told anybody. He wanted complete privacy to finish his book.

She was a nice kid: when she saw my reaction, she said, oh, dear, was I all right, and would I like to sit down for a minute?

So I did, and she went and fetched me a glass of water, and we started talking. She had a sympathetic face, and I guess maybe I felt I didn't have too much to lose now, so I told her more than I probably should have done. When I said I'd come all the way from the States to see him, because I'd heard he'd been saying some pretty horrible things about me and he never answered my calls, she shivered and said that didn't surprise her. I asked her why not. She shrugged: *He's just a bit of a funny bloke, that's all.*

And then she told me all about him. He's only about thirty-five, she said, but he always wears a tie – not just naturally, like you see old men doing sometimes, but more as if he's making a statement: telling everyone else off for *not* wearing one. The other lecturers don't like him at all. Most of the students don't, either. But there's a little gang of four or five of them, mostly third-years, who are always hanging around his office.

What's *that* like? I asked.

She hesitated a second, then took a key from her drawer, and said she'd show me. She led me back down the corridor and unlocked the door. *There*, she said. And started to giggle.

It was pretty strange. The bare bones were standard-issue modern office: metal desk, computer, construction-kit shelves full of creased paperbacks. But all the spaces in between were crammed with images from a different world altogether: black-and-white photographs of men in suits and women in hats, or wearing Ginger Rogers hairdos and brilliant lipsticked smiles. Most of them were mounted in silver or ebony frames, and arranged in devotional little clusters that made me feel like I'd strayed inside a private chapel. Some of the faces I didn't recognize at all: others seemed to lift the edge of faint childhood memories – though whether because I'd seen them before, or just because there was something familiar about the style, I don't know. There were only two that I could put a name to: Trevor Howard in *Brief Encounter*; and (a bit of a jolt when I saw it) Henry Whitaker. Not quite the Henry Whitaker I remember: this was a formal portrait that must have been taken before I was born, at some point in the 1930s, when his skin still had that frightening perfection you lose by the time you're thirty. But there was no mistaking the flop of fair hair, and the beaky nose, and the look-how-detached-I-am smile.

I asked the girl if I could have a quick look round. She hesitated again, then nodded and said yes – as long as it really was quick.

She stood guard in the entrance while I went inside. I don't know what I was hoping to find, exactly: I was just a hunting dog casting about for a trail. Behind the door was a filing-cabinet, with a bottle of dry sherry and four glasses on top of it. The bottom drawer was marked "Whitaker." I longed to open it – but I knew she wouldn't let me, of course, so I moved on to the desk. One end was piled with hefty thesis manuscripts, with another picture of my father leaning against it: just a snapshot, this one, taken at about the same time and showing him with two other young people, a man and a woman, all of them dressed in period costume, as if they were taking part in a play.

At the other end of the desk stood one of those plastic towers that people have now instead of in- and out-trays. I glanced perfunctorily at it, and turned to scan the bookshelves. And only then realized (the way you do when your brain lags behind your eye sometimes) that I'd seen the name Whitaker there, too, in the middle basket.

I turned back again. It was on the dull-looking cover of a journal called *Cultural History Review*. The second item: "Henry Whitaker and the Succubus: the Strange Decline and Fall of a Quiet Genius." By Dr. Alan Arkwright.

I waved it at the girl. Could I borrow it? No: if it got lost, or I sent it back damaged, she could lose her job. Copy it, then? Not without a special card – which was available, unfortunately, only to faculty and students. But she did very nicely say I could look at it in her office, and she'd return it when I'd finished.

So that's what we did.

I skimmed most of it: I just wanted to see, really, what he had to say about my mother and me. It turned out to be pretty much what I expected, only a bit nastier, and hedged about with weaselly protestations about how he knows he's "offending against all the shibboleths of political correctness." Poor Mummy, of course, was the "succubus"– a term he used (he was at pains to point out) "in the medieval sense of a creature that swallows its victim's breath." Her crime, apparently (I was so scandalized by this bit that I copied it down) was to "elbow her way into Whitaker's life at the moment when he was at his most vulnerable, and establish herself as a kind of black hole at the centre of his universe, sucking the almost boundless light of his compassion into her own misery, diverting his vital energies from the humane, understated documentaries that were his *forte* into a monstrously ill-judged memorial to her suffering."

To be fair, he does stop short of out-and-out revisionism: he admits the camps existed, and that – like millions of other people – my mother (whom he unctuously refers to as "Romona") endured "appalling horrors," which were the cause of her "unmanageable neurosis." But there's no such excuse for me, of course: I'm just "an old-fashioned feminist," who deliberately perpetuated the myth of Romona-as-victim by claiming that Whitaker "drove his wife to take her own life." This, he says, reprising what he said in the radio interview, he can now "prove is a lie." Just *how* he can prove it, we won't know until he publishes his book – which he hopes will lead to "a fundamental re-evaluation of Henry Whitaker, and his long-overdue recognition as a master of documentary film, and a key figure of mid-twentieth-century British culture."

But he's given me a clue. The evidence, he says, came from someone who knew the couple well, and who clearly remembers the day my mother died. That someone, by a simple process of elimination, can only be Flo Torridge – whose name, of course, he actually got from *me* in the first place.

The irony of it. The ingratitude of it. Why don't I feel angrier than I do?

Must be the jet-lag. Even my emotions are still somewhere over the Atlantic. It'll probably still be a day or two before they finally get here.

Meantime, I guess, I've no choice but to steel myself to go and look for Flo.

XIII

London – October 1932

Is it the solitude? The break with routine? The time of day? I don't know; but as I clop down the stairs to the platform I suddenly feel nineteen again. Everything – the echo of my own footsteps, the whine of the approaching train, the fusty-wardrobe smell of the hot air it gusts into the station – seems to tingle some nerve I'd forgotten having. The effect's a strange hybrid: half loss, half possibility.

To get to West Ham I have to make three changes. Each one leaves me feeling freer and lighter. By the time I finally emerge I'm almost levitating. Nobody in the thin straggle of people on the pavement knows me. And nobody who knows me has the least idea where I am.

It's still almost dark, but the sky to the east is grazed with streaks of red. I hail a southbound bus and clamber on to the top deck. To begin with, I can see nothing but lights, but within a few minutes the rising sun has begun to give some shape and colour to the world. My first reaction is disappointment: we seem to be passing through a vast desert of dust and rubble where hundreds of houses have been demolished to make way for a new road. It's too open, too anonymous, too undefined, despite the distant ribbon of water hemming it in. For a moment I wonder if I'm too late. Perhaps the landscape I'm looking for has already gone.

Then, suddenly, we're *in* the landscape I'm looking for. To the right, on a loop of the river, are the derricks and chimneys of the East India Dock; to the left is a grid of close-packed little streets – and beyond them, breathtakingly huge, the Brobdignagian expanse of the Royal Docks stretching away into the mist. Imprisonment and escape in a single dramatic image. Exactly what we want.

I get out at North Woolwich Station and walk back the way I've just come. There's a spectacular shot at the end of pretty well every road: a black ziggurat of crates, as alien as a Mayan monument, blocking out the sky; a giant crane sending a faint spider of shadow scuttling over a wall as it turns; most dream-like of all, the middle section of an ocean liner, towering so monstrously over the sooty terraces leading you towards it that it appears to belong to a different order of reality altogether. *God*, I think: *if only K.-M. were still here, and I had him and a crew with me now!* But then it strikes me that even if I did, I wouldn't know what to tell them to do – so I shrug off my frustration, and start scribbling notes and taking snaps with my Kodak.

After forty minutes or so I've covered ten pages and exposed a dozen rolls of film. The hungry cavity behind my eyes feels sated. I've the comfortable sense that I've got six times as much material as I need – which, experience tells me, makes it a reasonable certainty that I've got about enough. Now all I have to do is find the house. That's going to require some care. When we build the interior in the studio, I want every detail to be right.

Where should I start? I stand back, and scan the names of the little roads: Taylor Street; Berwick Street; Thacker Street; Herman Street . . .

Herman Street. Hermann Strasse. The association gives me an odd fluttery thrill. I tease myself: *Go down Herman Street, and who knows where it'll take you? To Irma Brücke again? Or to some other encounter you'll never be able to tell anyone about?*

I go down Herman Street. At the far end looms another part of the gigantic liner, linked to the squalid, everyday, human-scale world only by a spindly gang-plank running from the promenade deck to the quay. The sight of it sends the same adolescent shiver through me that I felt going down into the tube this morning. On my neck, suddenly, I sense the weight of the life I've started to make for myself – a knobbly shell, I visualize it as, or else a dimly lit, over-stuffed room, full of bulbous shapes that have to be negotiated, reducing every movement to no more than a nudge. For a moment, I'm consumed by the fantasy of casting it off – bluffing my way on to the ship – hiding in a steamy corner smelling of oil and sea-water – and eventually starting again in Cairo or Nairobi or Rio de Janeiro. Different name. Different education. Different job. Different morals.

Stop it. You've got stowaways on the brain. Concentrate on what you're doing.

Half-way down the street there's a little alley leading off to the left. Six or seven emaciated children are huddled round the entrance, bony shoulders hunched inside clothes too big for them, the boys' hands in their pockets. When they catch sight of me, they start trickling a soccer ball back and forth, as if to prove that – despite their conspiratorial air – they're only playing. But as I approach them they seem to lose their nerve, and stop again, drawing together in a line and staring at me uncomfortably. After a few seconds a girl of ten or so breaks from the others and takes a few steps towards me. Her pale face is smudged with dirt, and there's a stain that looks like raspberry jam on the front of her dress.

'Are you a reporter?'

'No.' I can't help thinking of Irma Brücke's daughter. 'Why? Is there something I should be reporting?'

She shakes her head. But her eyes betray her, drifting away towards the alley. I turn to see what she's looking at.

It's little more than a courtyard, really: just five houses deep. My first thought is: *This is the perfect place. You could re-create the whole thing on the stage.* Then I notice that the door of the nearest house is open and there's a man standing in front of it. He's maybe fifty, with short grizzled hair, wearing a grubby vest stretched tight by the swell of his belly, and a pair of grey flannels held up by a piece of string. His thick bare arms are ledged with fat. There's a dribble of blood running from the edge of his nose to the corner of his mouth.

His jaw sags when he sees me. Then he just gawps at me, oyster-eyed. It's hard to read his expression, but I don't think it's hostile. More *shocked*.

'Swatting a fly,' he says, finally. 'That's all it was. Swear to God.'

The sound of his own voice seems to rouse him. He hitches his trousers, and splays his feet, ready to defend himself. Between his straddled legs I suddenly notice a pair of women's shoes jutting out over the door-step. They're at an ungainly pigeon-toed angle, as if she's lying twisted on her side.

'I told 'er,' says the man. 'Little Lascar fellow, 'e was. Any father'd 'a' done the same. You'd 'a' done it wiv yours.'

Impossible to tell whether the woman's dead, or only injured. Should I barge my way in and try to find out? The man probably wouldn't let me inside the house. And even if he did, and she was still alive, I wouldn't know what to do to help her.

I turn back to the girl. 'Anyone here with a telephone?'

She shakes her head. I should have guessed.

'Where would I find a policeman?'

She glances at the fat man, then shrugs and says: 'Dunno.'

'All right,' I say quietly, struggling to sound off-hand. I look round and find the street sign: Berry Court. Then I edge my way through the knot of children and continue walking in the direction of the ship. *Don't hurry. Don't look back. Make them think you noticed nothing, and are just getting on with what you came here for.*

It works. No-one follows me. At the bottom of the street, almost at the water's edge, there's a cross-roads. I turn left, and find myself in front of a pub called the Rising Sun. A few doors down, on the other side, is a café, with a little shop next to it. And in front of the shop, talking to a woman in an apron as she cleans a big tin sign for Camp Coffee, is a policeman.

Thank God.

I hurry over to him.

'Excuse me –'

'Yes, sir.'

I briefly tell him what I've seen. My appearance seems to interest him more than my story: while I'm talking, he eyes me up gravely, as if trying to deduce what someone dressed like me could be doing here.

When I've finished he merely nods and says: 'Right, sir. Thank you. I'll see to it.'

He starts towards Herman Street. I follow him for a few paces, then stop when I realize he isn't waiting for me.

'Do you want me to show you the way?'

'That's all right, sir. I know Berry Court. And old Jimmy Duke.'

I'm conscious of people gazing at us from the café.

'But surely – shouldn't I come with you?'

'Better not, sir. This isn't the first time. We're more likely to get somewhere if there isn't too much fuss about it.'

He crosses the road, walking purposefully, but not rushing. I stand and watch as he disappears into Herman Street. What should I do? *This isn't the first time* suggests the woman probably isn't dead, at least – but it also suggests that her father beats her regularly, and that even the local constable tacitly accepts it. If I insist on going along, I'll look like a busybody, and may end up making the man more violent. If I don't, I'll be haunted by the knowledge that I just turned a blind eye to her suffering, like everybody else.

The sensible thing, I decide eventually, is to wait until I get home – then ring up the police station, and explain the situation to the inspector. That would more or less force him to take action, without my being directly involved at all.

I write down *Jim Duke, Berry Court*, and make a note of the time. I've just finished when a movement in the café window distracts me. I turn towards it, and blink.

Most of the glass is opaque with condensation, but someone's wiped a smeary hole in the middle of it. And there, staring out at me, is someone who shouldn't be here.

Christopher Morton Hunt.

He gives me an odd crooked smile and beckons to me. I push open the door and walk inside. For a second I feel so displaced that I have the odd sense of having blundered into the war: there's a ferocious noise of hissing steam and clanging pans, and a thick haze hanging in the air through which I can just make out four or five shadowy figures as hunched and turned-in upon themselves as men sheltering from an attack. Then I catch the whiff of fat and cheap bacon and cigarette smoke, and hear the sound of a child starting to wail somewhere in the back, and I know where I am again.

Christopher's sitting by himself, with a folded newspaper and the remains of breakfast in front of him. His eyes, the line of his nose, the gawky geometry of his face are unmistakable; but everything else is so different I wonder if he's trying to disguise himself. His hair's dull and matted, he hasn't shaved for two or three days, his sports-coat's frayed and crumpled, and the thick fisherman's sweater he's wearing underneath it is nibbled away by holes.

'He– He– Henry,' he says. I haven't heard him stutter since our first year at Cambridge.

'Jesus! What on earth are *you* –?'

He glances round nervously. I take the hint, and shut up. He prods a chair towards me with his foot. I pull it out and sit down, as casually as I can.

'Ha– ha– have you had breakfast?'

'No.'

'Would you like something?'

The smell makes me want to retch. 'Maybe just some tea.'

He nods towards the counter, and calls softly: 'Syl! Wh– when you've got a minute, please.'

'Are you all right?' I say.

'Yes, yes. Why? You mean' – hooking a thumb through the biggest hole in his sweater and yanking it towards me – 'because –?'

I nod. 'Where have you been all this time? Nobody's heard anything from you for . . . for God knows how long.'

'I haven't heard from you.'

'I sent you a wedding invitation.'

'Wedding? You're –?'

'I am.'

'God, I'm sorry.' He thrusts a hand across the table. It's cold and loose-skinned despite the fug. 'Congratulations. It never reached me, I'm afraid. It may not even have reached my parents. They're not at Blackheath any more, and the new people don't seem to be terribly good at forwarding stuff. And I told my mother not to send anything on to me, in any case . . . Is it anyone I know? Your wife, I mean?'

'I don't think so. Her name's Nicky. We met at the studio.'

'Ah, so you're still in films?' It sounds flat, almost bored – as if he hasn't the energy to conceal his disappointment that I haven't moved on to something more worthwhile.

'Yes. Did you happen to see *Markheim*?'

He shakes his head. ''Fraid not.'

'It did pretty well. There's one moment in it I'm particularly proud of. Max was kind enough to say it was the key to the whole thing. It was on the strength of that, actually, I was asked to do *this* picture. It's nothing very grand. Just a miserable little *quota quickie*. But I have at least managed to get a small part for William. And I'm hoping it may lead to something a bit more, you know . . .'

177

'Well done.' As off-hand as if I'd told him I'd won five quid at the races. 'So, what – she's an actress, is she?'

'Who? Oh, no, no, she was Max's secretary. And then a continuity girl –'

'Ah.' He studies me, as if trying to understand why I'd settle for anything so unglamorous. I'm suddenly aware that I don't want to talk about Nicky: she's something small and vulnerable, burrowed inside me, and I doubt my ability to do her justice, or to explain our marriage in anything but vapid clichés that would have him curling his lip. *What a girl! She's an absolute angel, old man . . .*

So before he can ask anything else, I say: '*Why* didn't you want your mother to send things on?'

'Oh, you know' – dropping his voice – 'she'd insist on addressing them to *Christopher Morton Hunt, Esq.*' His eyes suddenly drift past me. 'Ah, Syl.'

I turn. The woman's standing at my side.

'Yes, Chris?' She's small and monkey-featured, with raggedy gingerish hair pinned up under a cap. In one arm she's holding a sniffly eighteen-month-old girl.

'Can we have two more teas, please?'

She nods, then twitches her shoulder in my direction. 'Who's this, then?'

'A friend of mine. Henry Whitaker.'

''Enry Whitaker.' She gives me a shrewd appraising glance, curious but not unfriendly. 'In the same line of business, are you, love?' Then, before either of us has time to say anything, she notices my overcoat. 'No, you're not, are you?' she says. 'Right.'

She leans forward to collect Christopher's plate. As she picks it up, the child suddenly knocks it out of her fingers with a petulant *No!* It clunks back on to the table, sending the knife and fork skittering on to the floor.

The woman clicks her tongue exasperatedly. 'Oh, you little devil!' She raises her hand to smack the girl.

Christopher quickly reaches up and says: 'Why don't you leave her with us, Syl, while you get the tea?'

He must have done this before: she doesn't even hesitate. 'All right, then, Chris. Ta.'

The child pouts and cries as her mother leaves, and lets out a fart I can smell three feet away. I'd always considered Christopher more fastidious than I am, but he seems completely undismayed. He puts her on his knee and bobs her up and down, whispering: *This is the Way the Ladies Ride.* After a few bounces she relaxes and starts to chortle.

'Very good,' I say. 'Where'd you learn to do that?'

He shrugs. 'You soon pick it up. When you're living in the sort of places I've been the last few months.'

'Mm?'

He smiles. 'Oh, you know: lodging-houses; mill-workers' cottages – that kind of thing.' He stops jigging the little girl and lowers his face close to hers. 'It's no good expecting Nurse to do the dirty work there, is it, Cath?'

I'm sure she doesn't understand what he's saying, but the tone's enough to tell her what's required. She solemnly shakes her head.

'All right now?' he says.

She nods, pulls speculatively at his nose, and then, when she finds it won't come off, begins to explore his coat, lifting the lapel and sticking a finger through the button-hole. He watches her for a couple of seconds, then I sense I have his attention again.

'So,' I say. 'What were you doing there? In the mill-workers' cottages, and so on?'

'Oh, well, I er . . . Research, I suppose you'd say, really.'

'For what? *The Duchess of Malfi* in clogs?' I regret it the instant I've said it. It'd seem cheap and sneery anywhere, but here it sounds awful. I look round: nobody else appears to have heard.

Christopher has the grace to laugh. 'I'm not sure, at the moment. I'm just spending a few weeks at a time in different places, talking to people. Taking notes. And photographs. I'll probably try to do a book, eventually. If I can find a publisher.'

'A novel, you mean?'

He shakes his head. 'Novels just slither off the surface, don't they?' He swallows, and blushes. 'Sorry . . . I mean, I know you were thinking of doing something. And I'm sure it would be awfully good. Only –'

'Don't worry. I'm not thinking of it any more.'

He nods, as if he supposes I must independently have come to the same conclusion he has, and for the same reasons. 'I want to do something rooted in fact,' he says. 'So that it can't be ignored. Can't be dismissed as invention. People have to be confronted with the –'

''Ere you are,' says Syl, flittering up with two white mugs of tea. She slides them in front of us, then stands back and taps the side of her nose. 'I know what it is,' she says. 'You're an old college chum.'

'Yes, that's right.'

'You was just passin', and you see 'im 'ere, so you come in.' She squints at my camera and notebook. 'You ain't official, are you? To do with the Board, or the Means Test, or something?'

'No.'

'That's all right, then. Come on, Cath.' She holds her hands out. The little girl shakes her head. She's found a book in Christopher's pocket, and doesn't want to give it up. The woman snatches it from her, slaps it on the table, then gathers the child in her arms. As she carries her off, squirming and shrieking, she calls over her shoulder: 'Give us a shout if you need anything.'

'All right, thanks,' says Christopher. He watches her out of earshot, then turns to me again. Her suspicion's obviously infected him: he's chewing his lip, and his eyes are wide with anxiety. 'Yes,' he murmurs. 'What exactly *are* you doing here?'

'Well – research, really, like you . . .'

He doesn't seem to be listening. He cranes his neck, trying to read what I've written on the notebook.

'I'm looking for locations,' I say. 'Mr. Ribbon, our hero, is a stowaway. You can do the inside of the ship in the studio, but you can't really have it coming into port. So I'm squandering half the budget on a couple of minutes here in the docks . . .'

All at once, before I can stop him, he's reached out and grabbed the notebook. I'm so incensed, I almost snatch it straight back again. But that'd be childish and give the impression I was trying to hide something – so I simply sip my coppery tea and wait for his reaction.

After a few seconds he says: 'How do you know Jimmy Duke?'

'I don't.'

'Then why's his name here?'

I explain. As I'm talking, I can see his face gradually relaxing.

When I've finished, he nods and says: 'That's very gentlemanly of you.' To my surprise, it doesn't sound sarcastic. In fact – it suddenly strikes me – I haven't felt the rasp of his contempt at all. Whatever's happened to him since we last met seems, if nothing else, to have made him a nicer person.

'Not gentlemanly, particularly. Just human.'

He shrugs. 'The trouble is, it's a useless gesture. Worse than useless.'

I can't help bridling. 'I doubt if it'd feel useless to her, if it stopped her getting hurt again.'

He shakes his head. 'All you're doing is shoving sticking-plaster on a lump of gangrene, and thinking you've made it better.' He sees the heat in my face and smiles. 'Sorry. Sorry. It's just when you realize what's going on . . .'

He shakes his head again – at himself rather than me, this time – and starts working some stray grains of sugar on the table into a spiral with his finger. I remember that distracted fiddliness well: he's gathering his thoughts. I prepare myself for a lecture – on the true nature of tragedy, probably, or the irrelevance of my outmoded ethics to the modern world.

But in the end he just looks up and says sadly: 'Look, don't think I'm not sorry for her, too. I am. You couldn't not be. She catches it every time he's been drinking, poor girl – and quite often even when he hasn't been, nowadays. I know: I'm staying just round the corner from them –'

'God!' I burst out, before I can stop myself. 'How do you stand it?'

He shrugs again. 'It not that hard. I'm lucky: at least I've got my own room. And I'll be moving on in a couple of weeks. He *can't* move on: he's trapped here. And if you succeeded in rescuing his daughter, he'd only take it out on somebody else – somebody even weaker and more pitiful than she is. It's elementary psychology. Think of school. Fagging. You systematically humiliate a boy by giving a prefect absolute power over him. And what does he do? He doesn't take a poker to his oppressor, does he? He just grins and bears it, until he's old enough to have a fag of his own – and then systematically humiliates *him* in exactly the same way.'

'And what's Jimmy Duke been through that justifies beating up his own daughter?'

He sighs and flexes his fingers, as if straining to keep his patience in the face of my obduracy. 'When was the last time you read one of these?' he says, rapping his newspaper with his knuckles. 'Other than *The Times*? Or the *Daily Mail*? Or the *Express*?'

'Not for months, I have to say.'

'You should try this' – turning it over so I can see it's the *Daily Worker* – 'and then you might see what's really happening. There's a war on – has been for years. The government's trying to break the working class. Do you know how many are out of work?'

'No.' Even to me, my voice sounds small, and curdled with meanness.

'Getting on for three million.'

'I know, it's bad. But I can't see anyone's responsible for it. Certainly not the government. It's just this bloody depression. And at least they've got the dole.'

'And have you any idea how much that is?'

I shrug. 'Thirty bob a week?'

'For a widower like Jimmy, it'll be less than a quid. And do you know what he has to do qualify for it?'

I almost snap: *No, of course I fucking don't.* But I bite my lip, and content myself with a shake of the head instead.

'First he has to let the Means Test man into his house. The Means Test man can pry anywhere – open anything – to see if he's got a few shillings of savings tucked away. If he has: *no dole* until it's gone. Then he can go through every room, deciding unilaterally what Jimmy has to sell: a spare bed, a family picture, his grandfather's arm-chair – anything the old boy doesn't actually need just to survive from one day to the next. When that's all gone, and he's used up the proceeds on rent and coal and bread, Jimmy can sign on. But he has to do it twice a day –'

'Oh, come on! That's not true. My cleaning-woman's husband lost his job and I know he only goes in once a week. Spends most of the rest of the time in bed, according to her –'

He shakes his head. 'He's not a docker, then. Dockers are hired by the half-day. So if you don't turn up at the Labour Exchange every morning and every afternoon, the presumption is you're working. The whole system is organized to rub your nose in your own powerlessness, your own dependence on others . . .'

'I don't think that's entirely fair –'

'Oh, it's not the fault of the little despots who hand out the money; it's the fault of the well-fed, reasonable gentlemen who make the rules.'

Something reverberates in my head: an echo that I can't identify, but feel as a slight ear-achey pain.

'But why should they want to –?' I begin.

'To demoralize him. On the perfectly sound principle that a demoralized man is less likely to cause trouble. You can keep tossing him smaller and smaller scraps – and know he won't complain about it, for fear of ending up with sweet Fanny Adams.'

Sweet Fanny Adams. Three years ago, that wouldn't have been part of Christopher's vocabulary. But now it sounds completely unselfconscious, and when I catch his eye and smile, he doesn't smile back.

'The nub,' he says, 'is to make him feel responsible for his own misfortunes. Don't blame the government for the mess you're in. Or its capitalist masters. Or the economic crisis they've created. Blame yourself.'

There's a sudden eruption of noise from the table behind me: cup-clattering, newspaper-folding, someone clearing a phlegmy throat. Christopher stops abruptly, as if it's a comment on what he's been saying. Then he goes on, in little more than a whisper: 'And he does, Jimmy Duke. He does blame himself. He thinks it's his age. You hear him talking about it in meetings: he's too old for the job – or the employers think he's too old. Which of course makes him desperate to prove that he isn't. So every morning, seven-thirty sharp, you'll see him at the call-on, standing with three or four hundred other men, like bullocks at a cattle-market. When the foremen appear, he'll push forward, just like the rest of them – shouting and waving his arms, trying to get himself noticed. But it's the younger ones who generally manage to barge their way to the front and get selected. Jimmy hasn't worked for more than six months. He's already exhausted his insurance stamps, so he isn't getting full benefit any more. Pretty soon he'll be on Public Assistance. Twelve-and-six a week, if he's lucky. Could you live on twelve-and-six a week?'

A gush of sour anger spreads through my shoulders and down my arms. I clench my fists to hold it in. 'No.'

'It reduces you to an animal. Barely that. But an animal can't lose its self-respect. Jimmy can. That's the worst of it, from his point of view. It's made him' – so quiet now that I see the word, rather than hearing it – '*ashamed* of himself.'

Ashamed of himself. Ashamed of himself. Of course, *that*'s where the echo's from: Dr. Becker, talking about Irma Brücke.

'You meet him coming back from the docks or the Labour Exchange, he looks like this.' Christopher freezes his face into the glazed expression of a china figure: mouth pulled down, lips pressed together, unfocused gaze staring straight ahead. 'He won't look at you directly. He daren't, in case he breaks down altogether, and starts crying in public. That would be the end. The last scrap of dignity gone. After that –' He makes a cut-off-your-head swipe with his hand. 'So perhaps it isn't any wonder that when he gets home he lays into his daughter. It's the only outlet he's got – apart from hanging himself.'

'All right.' My eyes are stinging. Is he doing this deliberately, just to discomfit me? I wouldn't put it past him: he always had the surest instinct of anyone I knew for my weak points, and never hesitated to exploit it during the long rumbling undeclared war between us. I hope that's the answer, because then I can dismiss what he said simply as propaganda. But when I look into his face, I find he's close to tears himself. And whatever else may have changed about Christopher, I know he'll never be an actor.

'You don't want to believe me, do you?' he says.

'I believe you.'

'But you don't want to.'

'Well . . .' I begin. But a turncoat blush betrays me.

'*Nobody* wants to. I didn't want to myself. I'd probably never even have thought about it if it hadn't been for the crash. My parents were almost ruined. That's why they had to move: they couldn't afford the house any more. I was protected to some extent, because my allowance is paid by a family trust. But it was more than halved, even so. Overnight. One day I was comfortably ensconced in the life of a Cambridge dilettante. The next I woke up, just like that,' – snapping his fingers – 'to find it was completely beyond me.'

'I'm sorry.'

He shrugs. 'I've still got more than Jimmy Duke had, even when he was working.'

'I know. But –'

'But what?' He's lethally quick: a cat spiking a mouse. 'You think that's different, do you?'

I feel myself blushing again. 'Well, yes . . . Your whole background . . . The expectations you grew up with . . . I mean, Jimmy Duke would never have known anything but this. You always had wider horizons –'

He nods. 'I know. It's easy to think like that. Difficult not to. The working class are an entirely distinct species. They're used to privation. They don't feel it as we would. But' – mouthing it – '*it isn't true.*'

'Can I get you anything else, Chris?' says Syl.

Her voice is so loud it makes me jump. I jerk round, and find her standing six inches from my shoulder.

Christopher glances at the clock on the wall. 'No, thanks. I ought to be on my way.'

"Ow about you, love?'

'No, thank you.' But the moment I've said it, I realize I don't mean it. I don't want to leave: I want to stay in the smoky warm, and feel the presence of other people pressing in on me, and hear her call me *love* again. I start to form the words: *Actually, I'd like another cup of tea.* But it's too late: she's already gone.

'There was one awful night, I must admit,' says Christopher, 'when all I could think of doing was applying for a job in a prep school. But then I looked at the world around me, and thought: *I'm not just going to beat little boys and feel sorry for myself while Rome burns. What's the point in believing in the power of science to improve things, if you don't bring it to bear on your own time, your own situation?* Analyse: *that's what you were trained to do. Analyse.* So I did. And pretty soon saw that Jimmy Duke's life and mine aren't really separate at all. They're intimately connected. They always have been. Mine, in fact, depends entirely on his. So does yours. The pre-condition for being a Cambridge dilettante, or a film director, or any kind of bourgeois, is a hundred Jimmy Dukes – all labouring away in docks and mines and factories and railway engines and fishing-boats and fields. That's what people have to be made aware of. Otherwise, we're all sunk.' He starts folding his newspaper. 'Anyway –'

'But they're *not* all labouring away,' I say. 'That's the point.'

He pushes back his chair and stands up. 'Exactly. And look what's happened to me' – jabbing his chest with his thumb – 'as a result.'

It's more complex than that: it must be. But before I can organize my thoughts into a reply, he's started edging past me.

'Look, I'm sorry,' he says, 'I've got an N.M.U.W. meeting to go to. It was nice seeing you again, though. Just a pity we didn't have more time. You didn't tell me anything about you. Apart from your being married, that is.'

You didn't ask. Which a sudden spasm in my solar plexus tells me is just as well. It's not just Nicky: I'd rather he didn't know *anything* about my life.

'Everything all right?' he says, fumbling absently in his pocket for change.

'Yes, fine thanks.'

'Good. Well –'

'Please,' I say, reaching for my wallet. 'Let me do this. I'm the one with a job. The least I can do is stand you breakfast.'

He shakes his head. 'Thanks, but that'd be cheating. I allow myself so much a week, and have to try to live on that. Otherwise I wouldn't really know what I was talking about, would I?' He starts towards the counter.

'Hang on a second!' I say. 'Don't forget your book!'

He stops. As I hand it to him, I see what it is: a French novel called *Nadja*, by André Breton. He looks startled for a moment, then smiles as if a penny-dropping thought's just struck him.

'Perhaps it wasn't just a coincidence, our meeting again like this,' he says. He waves the book: Exhibit A. 'This chap'd call it *hasard objectif*. So – who knows?'

I watch him pay at the counter, then saunter easily to the door, stopping to greet a couple of men he knows on the way. As he passes the window he pauses for a second and peers in at me, grinning at the reversal of our rôles.

My pulse suddenly quickens. I find a blank page in my notebook and write: *Idea for a shot: face you haven't seen for some time appears unexpectedly at misted-up window. Or: face you've never seen before appears at window. Then much later on you meet the same face again, without any explanation of what it was doing there.*

When I look up again, Christopher's gone.

'Hello, darling!'

'Where are you?'

'In here.'

The only light is from the bathroom. I put my head round the half-open door. She's lying in the bath, her hair swathed in a towel. A little tidal wave sloshes up the side and over the edge as she turns to smile at me.

'Where's Mrs. G?' I say.

'Gone to see her son, I think. I told her she could have the afternoon off.' She stands up. 'Hand me that, would you?'

I take her towelling dressing-gown from the hook. She bows her head and dips her shoulders, as if she expects me to wrap it round her. But that would give the wrong signal: I don't want to go to bed with her. Not yet, at any rate. There's a gauzy shadow hovering behind my eyes. I won't feel entirely home again until I've dispelled it.

'Here you are.' Holding it out at arm's length.

'Thanks.' She gives a tiny shiver of disappointment as she puts it on. 'I thought it'd be nice for us to have a bit of time alone together.'

'Yes.'

'I feel so out of touch now. I actually think I used to see more of you before. I certainly knew more about what you were doing.' She steps on to the mat, and lifts her face. 'Mmm.'

I kiss her. Her skin's warm and clammy and smells of lavender. Moisture seeps through the front of my shirt. She puts her arms

187

round me, but gives me no more than a chappish pat on the back before pulling away again. If I don't want to make love to her, she isn't going to try to persuade me to change my mind. Always a good sport, Nicky.

'I'll make some tea, shall I?' she says, shuffling on her slippers. 'And then tonight I thought I'd do an omelette. I've put a bottle of Daddy's Pouilly Fouissé in the refrigerator.'

'That sounds lovely.'

She looks at herself in the mirror, then tugs the towel from her head, unpins her hair, and shakes it free. For a moment she's entirely absorbed with arranging it how she wants it: combing it with her fingers, and smoothing the feathery little curls at the base of her neck. For some reason, this abstracted practicality excites me far more than her nakedness did. I step forward and lightly touch her bum. She glances at my reflection in the looking-glass, and gives me an odd backwards half-smile, as if she'd momentarily forgotten I was there.

'Did you find what you wanted in the docks?' she says.

She's moved on already. I've missed my chance.

'Yes, I think so. It's very atmospheric. Though rather slummy, as you can imagine.'

She nods.

'A lot of the men are out of work. So it's hard for them to provide for their families. Most of the kids there look half-starved.'

'Poor things.' She turns to face me. 'Did you talk to anyone?'

'Not really.' Why did I say that? Why am I so reluctant to introduce her to Christopher, even vicariously?

'Well, you must tell me all about it.' She pinches my lapel and gives two little pulls: a conductor signalling that the bus is going. 'I shan't be long.'

I wait for the sound of the kitchen tap, then go back into the hall. I've got five minutes, at most. It takes me one of them to find North Woolwich Police Station in the 'phone-book, and another to reach the operator. By the time she's put me through, I can hear the clatter of cups and saucers.

'Yes, sir, can I help you?'

'I'm ringing up about an incident I witnessed this morning.'

He gives a sigh that makes the receiver rumble in my ear. 'What incident might that be?'

I explain as quickly as I can. He's so quiet while I'm doing it, I wonder if we've been cut off.

When I've finished, he says: 'Would you mind holding on a minute, sir? I'll go and ask.'

He obviously doesn't believe my story: my accent doesn't fit with it. Like the girl in Herman Street, he probably thinks I'm a reporter. I listen to every click and chitter and cough while he's gone, willing it to be him picking up the 'phone again, frustrated when it turns out not to be. When he does finally come back, I find I've ground a deep dent in the carpet with my shoe.

'I'm sorry, sir. We've no information at the moment.'

'I only want to know if she's all right –'

'I'm sorry, sir.'

'Know if who's all right?' says Nicky, as I ring off. She's standing in the kitchen doorway, holding a tray. I take it from her, and follow her into the sitting-room.

'No-one, really.'

I expect her to say: *It must have been someone*. But she doesn't: she just stands looking curiously at me for a moment, as if she thinks my face will tell her more than my words did. Does she suspect I've been unfaithful to her? – that I've got a mistress tucked away somewhere, and that's why I didn't want to go to bed with her when I came in? It's the first time the idea's ever occurred to me. An almost imperceptible eddy of cold air touches my cheek.

'It was just some poor woman I saw today. In a place called Berry Court. She'd had a bit of an accident, and I told a policeman about it. That's all.'

'Oh, dear.' She sits on the sofa and folds her legs up under her. 'What sort of accident?'

'I don't really know, to be honest. I think she'd probably fallen downstairs.'

'Why, had she been drinking?'

I shrug. 'I shouldn't be surprised.'

Her lips start to move, then stop again. She senses my evasiveness, but doesn't know how to deal with it. I don't understand it myself. It would be easy enough to get back to the straight and nar-row path, even now: I haven't strayed that far from it. *Actually, I think she'd been beaten up by her father.* But that would only make her wonder why I hadn't told her before.

'How about this tea?' I hear myself saying. And then, as she starts to pour: 'I had a wonderful idea for a shot today. Not for this film: something else. Our hero – or heroine – is in front of a building with a misted-up window. And suddenly a face seems to form itself on the glass . . .'

This feels strange. I'm just compounding my own dishonesty – inflating a small lapse into an act of betrayal.

I shouldn't have started writing again.

XIV

London
July 20

Yesterday I did it, finally: went back to the village. I didn't trust myself
to drive, so took the train and a taxi instead. It was stranger even than
I'd imagined. Me age five and me age seventeen and me now all
stuck in the same body, and not talking to each other. When I saw the
curve of the High Street and the row of cottages on the corner and
the church tower behind them, five-year-old me got a weird feeling in
her legs and wanted to go to the bathroom. Seventeen-year-old me
thought how small and suffocating it all looked. Me now just wanted
to run. As we passed the turning to our little house I had to pretend I
had a problem with my contact lenses. Just couldn't bear to set eyes
on it.

I'd tried Information but they didn't have a number for Torridge in
Gliston, and there wasn't a single mention of either June (who probably wouldn't be called Torridge now anyway) or Flo on the internet.
But Arkwright had managed to find them, with no more than their
names and a thirty-five-year-old address to go on, so I figured it could-
n't be too hard for me to do the same. My best bet, I thought, would
be to ask at the post office, so I told the driver to take me there. He
said he didn't know where it was. I told him it was part of the shop.
He said he didn't know where that was, either. I said I'd show him.

Why didn't it occur to me it might have closed down? It seemed
kind of eternal, I guess, part of the landscape: I never think or dream
about the place without seeing it and catching a glimpse of Mr.
Webster's moon-face through the glass door. The building's still
there, but the store-front's been replaced with a tasteful fake-
Regency window and a lot of recycled bricks. Next to the door there's
a cutesy oval china name-plate: "Webster's Cottage."

Makes me feel like a ghost.

I couldn't immediately think of an alternative plan, but I didn't want to
try and figure one out with the meter running, so I paid the driver, took

a card with his number on it to make sure I had a way out, and started walking along the street as if I knew what I was doing. A couple of doors down, an old man glowered at me through a dusty window. I guess he thought I was a city slicker or something, looking for a week-end hideaway. Seventeen-year-old me thought: That's typical: you're not back five minutes, and already they're getting you wrong.

The next half-hour I tried the Torridges' old house (nobody home), the rectory (not a rectory any more), and the last remaining pub (used to be the Plough; now for some reason the Pheasant). The landlord wanted to be helpful, but he'd only been there for eighteen months and had never heard the name Torridge. He tried calling an old regular he thought might know, but there was no answer. But the guy had been so nice, I thought the least I could do was have lunch there, so I bought myself a half of bitter and a sandwich. The beer wasn't such a good idea: it made me weepy. Not the alcohol so much, but the soapy bubbles and the licorice taste. Straight back to seventeen again.

When I got outside I was feeling so fuddled that I went into the phone-box on the other side of the road and started to dial for the taxi. Then, out of the corner of my eye, I saw the church again. I don't know why I hadn't made the connection before, but it suddenly struck me that Flo had been a regular church-goer, in a grumbling, dogged, English kind of way, and that I might find someone who remembered her there.

The place had always terrified me as a child, even though I scarcely ever set foot in it. Or maybe it terrified me *because* I scarcely ever set foot in it: it seemed completely alien, a distillation of death. Whatever, five-year-old me didn't want to go there at all. I had to force her through the gate and into the forest of tombstones – one of which, I knew, belonged to Joe Doughty, a boy about my age who'd been knocked off his bike and killed during his first year at secondary school. I'd used to stand in the road outside, and gawp at the freshly dug earth and the piles of flowers fading on top of it. Now (I couldn't help looking) it's just a hump in the grass, and the stone's rusty with lichen. Scary.

The door was locked, but I could hear something from the other side of the church: sounded like someone digging. I went round, blinkering my eyes with one hand to avoid seeing Mummy's head-stone. A well-built, neatly dressed woman was crouched over a new grave, planting a little rose bush. She took no notice of me until I was near enough to throw a shadow over her. Then she gasped and jumped up, dropping her trowel.

I apologized for making her jump. She put a hand over her heart and said: "Oh, God, sorry, I was a hundred miles away."

She had short tinted hair, and smelt of freesias. Her make-up was good, but streaked with tears. She tried to wipe them away, but her dirty fingers just smeared them into brown blotches. Then she stopped suddenly, her hand still hovering by her cheek.

She'd noticed something about me. I'd noticed something about her. The eyes. Everything else was different, but the colour of the eyes . . .

I glanced down at the headstone. It said: "In loving memory of Florence Torridge (Pledger)"; 1 May 1920 to five weeks ago.

The woman said: "Miranda? Miranda Whitaker?"

And I said: "June?"

We hugged, we cried, I told her I was sorry about her mother, she said, yes, it was a real shock, she'd been fine the day before. And then, at the same moment, the oddity of the situation suddenly hit us, and June pulled away, and asked me what I was doing here.

I told her I was hoping to discover something about *my* mother's death. She said was it anything to do with the guy from the university, Andrew Arkwright or whatever his name was? I said yes. Did she know what Flo had told him? She'd a sort of idea. What? That she didn't think my mother had meant to kill herself. Why? (Too prickly, too *how-dare-you?* – I could hear it in my own voice.) She blushed, and said if I came back to her place, she'd show me.

So we went. If nothing else had told me how much England's changed, I'd have known it when I saw her car: a black new-model Audi. While we were driving, she told me about her life: married at twenty; two kids, both grown-up and successful; divorce at forty-two ("Barry was a slob. Only interested in footie and beer"); now runs her own company, renting videos and DVDs.

She lives about ten minutes away, on the edge of the next village, in a development of five "executive homes." A stone-faced box, really, but a different world from the dumpy council house where she grew up. Inside, it has that *faux* New England smell of coffee and cinnamon and scented candles. The living-room wasn't what I'd have expected at all: minimal furniture, and bare wooden floors, and a bookcase full of titles like *Owning the Real You*.

But the past's not entirely dead. When I asked if I could use the toilet, she kind-of laughed and said: "Your Dad wouldn't like to hear you say that, would he?"

"Why not?"

"Well, you're meant to say *lavatory*, aren't you? That's what you always said. *Toilet*'s all right for a common little thing like me, but not for Miranda Whitaker."

I'd forgotten. All that linguistic bullying.

We sat in the kitchen, and had herbal tea and cookies. Only then did she ask what I'd been up to since we'd last met. Was I married? Were we still together? What about kids? But I couldn't help wondering if she was doing it because she'd read in a self-help book that you *should*: she had this fixed little smile, and kept nodding like a mechanical doll, and looking away before I'd finished what I was saying. The only thing that really seemed to rouse her interest was hearing that I'd worked on *Silowski and Sister* in the seventies.

"Are you having me on?"

"No, I promise."

"Well, that *is* funny. We always used to watch it – Barry and me. It was the one thing'd keep him out of the pub. But I'd never have guessed anyone I actually *knew* had anything to do with it. How'd you –? I mean, was it because of your dad?"

I managed to laugh. "No. I co-wrote the first few episodes with Hody. My husband. He was the producer."

She was smirking.

"It's a family name," I said. "His great-great-something-or-other was a hero of the Revolutionary War. Aaron Hody. Died fighting the British."

She blushed and gave a little shiver, as if I'd slapped her face. "Was he your husband before or after you worked together?" she said.

"Before. We met in Hollywood, not long after my father died. And fell in love, and got married, all ridiculously quickly. I was only eighteen, he was twenty-three. But it seems to have turned out O.K." I smiled and tapped on the table. "Knock on wood."

"So now you're really successful?" she said stiffly. "Living in Beverly Hills, and making movies?"

"No. I gave it all up."

"Why?"

I tried to explain. But when I started to talk about not wanting to manipulate people so that other people could sell them things, I could tell I'd lost her. She gave me a well-you-always-*were*-a-bit-strange-and-there's-no-point-trying-to-talk-to-you kind of look, then pushed her chair back from the table and said: "Anyway, you're here about your mum, aren't you?" With a sigh. Implying: *We belong in different worlds. I know you'd never have made the journey just for the pleasure of seeing someone like me.*

Awful.

"There's no hurry," I said. "This is really nice. A chance to catch up –"

She shook her head, said she'd got an appointment at four, and left the room. A minute later she came back holding a thick manilla envelope. Here, she said, this is why Mum thought your mother's death wasn't suicide. And *he* agreed. Who? The man who's writing the book. Alan Arkwright? Yes.

I could feel myself reddening, but I bit my tongue. The envelope was stamped "Davey Brooker University" and addressed to "Mrs. Florence Torridge." It was still sealed. I opened it, and found a little package, with a covering letter: *Dear Mrs. Torridge, Thank you so much for letting me borrow this. I have copied the relevant pages, and will be sure to acknowledge your invaluable assistance in my book. With best wishes to you and your daughter, Alan Arkwright.*

Or something like that.

Inside the package was a Letts diary for 1957. There was a little slip of paper sticking out of the top that obviously marked a place. I turned to it and found: Week beginning August 4th.

There was nothing for the day itself, Wednesday 7th. But Thursday 8th had: "Mrs. W. Cut and set. 11.00." Only the "11.00" had been crossed out, and "9.30" scribbled in underneath it.

June was watching me, to see if I'd got the significance. I said: "And Mrs. W was Mrs. Whitaker?"

She nodded.

"You're sure?"

"Yes."

"And, what – your mother thought a woman who was planning to kill herself wouldn't make an appointment to have her hair done?"

"No."

"But she could have arranged it weeks in advance."

"She could have. But she changed it. Just the day before. The day she –"

"How do you know?"

"I saw her."

And then she started to tell me a long story about how she'd just got home from school on the Wednesday when there was a knock on the door. Her mother was out shopping, so June answered it herself, and found my mother standing there, very flushed and voluble, and with a funny smell on her breath, which June later realized was probably brandy. Mummy said she'd had a call from my father, who was in London: he was going to be home earlier than expected the next day and she wanted to be ready for him. Could Flo come and do her hair some time before ten? June said she didn't know. At that moment Flo herself appeared, and a relieved June gratefully retreated upstairs. But not before she heard my mother saying: *Please, Flo: is very important. He love me. He say so, right out, like that. He say I am the one.*

She never saw my mother again.

He love me. He say I am the one.

I felt – I heard it, almost: a low subterranean rumbling – a tectonic shift in my sense of reality. But I didn't want to have to adjust to it here – to risk losing control and crying in front of June. So I told myself it wasn't conclusive – that when you're dealing with someone as changeable as Mummy, you can't rule out the possibility that something sent her tumbling back into despair again during the next twelve hours. And how, anyway, could I be certain it was true?

Irritation's easier to express than grief, I guess. I suddenly heard myself snapping: "So why did you never mention this to me before?"

She shrugged. "You never asked, did you?"

"But surely, you must have realized I *believed* it was suicide?"

196

She shrugged again. "We didn't know *what* you believed, till Dr. Arkwright got in touch, and showed us that interview you did after your father died."

There was a kind of sullen indifference in her voice that stung me – as if the Whitakers belonged to a completely alien species and it was self-evidently pointless for someone like her even to speculate about what might be going on in their heads. I'd always been aware, of course, that she'd felt a half-acknowledged gulf between us – but it had never occurred to me that it might have appeared as unbridgeable as that.

I was suddenly hit with a great surge of emotion. I couldn't have said what it was, exactly, but the effort to contain it made me tremble. If I didn't get out soon, I knew, it would finally breach the dam and overwhelm me completely.

I handed June back the diary, and asked if I could call a taxi.

I was in such a state that it wasn't until the car had arrived and I was about to leave that I thought to ask whether she had any other material that might help me.

No! she said, very emphatically. But she colored slightly, and quickly looked away, which made me suspect for a moment she was lying. But then I thought: why *would* she lie? What would she have to gain by keeping anything from me? Nothing, that I can think of.

Perhaps it was just that raking over our childhood again after such a long time made *her* uncomfortable, too.

I managed to distract myself on the way back to London with an inane game: how many words could I make out of the names of the places we passed through? But as I got back to the hotel, I could feel my defenses crumbling. I rushed up to my room, locked the door, threw myself on the bed, and howled.

No mistaking the emotion now. It was rage: with Flo and June, for not telling me sooner; with my arrogant younger self, for somehow giving them the impression I wouldn't be interested; with my mother, for leaving me so confused. And most of all – it had finally caught up with me – with Alan Arkwright, for dragging me back into all this. *You fucking little shithead!* I yelled. *Why couldn't you just leave us alone?* The thought that he was out of my reach – that I couldn't get at him in person – had me pummeling the pillow with my fists. After a couple of minutes it was beaten flat and sodden with angry tears.

I lay there, exhausted, wondering what I ought to do. The idea of having to admit defeat really riled me. Surely, with a bit of ingenuity, I might still be able to track him down and confront him?

I got up, and switched on my laptop.

Alan Arkwright isn't a very common name, at least: the only people he shares it with (according to the world-wide web) are an ice-hockey player in Vancouver and a drunk driver in Dunedin, New Zealand. But the twenty or so references to *my* Alan Arkwright just kept taking me back to Davey Brooker University: research awards, publications, last year's teaching schedule. There were a few bitchy comments from disgruntled colleagues that made me smile: one called him *a parody of academic self-importance*; another *a young fogey*. But there was absolutely nothing to suggest where he is now.

Then, just as I was about to give up, I found: *bfi/NFT/Special Events and Previews. Fri 28 July:* Finding the Human Thread: the Evolution of Henry Whitaker. *As part of our* Filming the Long Weekend *season, Dr. Alan Arkwright introduces three films charting the development of this quintessentially English documentary-maker of the 1930s and 1940s.*

Since Arkwright was meant to be abroad, I assumed at first it must be referring to an event last year. But when I checked the date, I saw it was the twenty-eighth of *this month*.

I couldn't believe my luck.

I read it again, just to be certain, then called up my e-mail account. There was a brief message from Hode, saying he was fine and hoped I was too. I clicked *Reply*, and began to tell him about my trip to Gliston. But after a few paragraphs I suddenly thought, *No, it's ridiculous to respond to a couple of lines with a blow-by-blow-account of my day.* So I saved what I'd done for my journal, and simply wrote instead: *Sorry, honey, but this is going to take longer than I thought. Another ten days, at least. Love you. M.*

XV

Shropshire – July 1934

Nobody takes a bath in his clothes. *Ergo*, I can't show the body.
And if I move it somewhere more decorous – his bedroom, say – the
murder method won't work. You can't electrocute someone in bed
and make it look like an accident. At least, I don't think you can.
And even if you could, it would make nonsense of the whole thing
– starting with the title. The whole point of calling it *The
Candlestick Maker* is that he's the third man in the nursery-rhyme
tub. *Rub a dub dub, three men in a bed* simply doesn't work. And
the censors would probably object, in any case. *The implicit reference to three men sharing a bed is altogether unacceptable.*

What if we heard the water overflowing – saw the manservant
running upstairs – caught a glimpse of the bath through the half-
open door – then got a close-up of his face as he pushed it wide and
discovered the corpse?

No: a ghost or a monster may be more frightening when you
can't see it too clearly, but a body's different. The audience would
be bound to feel cheated if they only saw the manservant's reaction
and not what provoked it.

A low shot, then, sideways on, so you just see the corpse's face in
profile, and nothing below the neck?

No, that wouldn't do, either. They'd still feel cheated, even if
the reason for it wasn't quite so obvious, because although they
were seeing the same thing as the manservant, they'd know intu-
itively it was from a different angle – which would jerk them
suddenly right out of the story and set them off wondering why.
By the time they'd worked out the answer, we'd already be on to
the next scene.

All right: what if the manservant tripped at the top of the stairs
and twisted his ankle, so that he had to *crawl* into the bathroom?
That at least would put him at the right level . . .

No, come on: this is getting ludicrous.

Just drop it. Go and talk to Max. Do it now.

I light a cigarette. And then – before I have time to change my mind again – hurry out into the corridor.

The door to the outer office is ajar. The first challenge will be to get past Cynthia Drew without being waylaid. I prepare my opening speech – *Any chance of seeing the Grand Panjandrum?* – and barge in, looking purposeful. Only to find Val Farrar sitting at the desk.

'Hello, old man. You after Max?'

I nod. 'It's just I'm meant to be leaving early today, and –'

'Ah, anywhere exciting?'

It sounds casual, but I know what he's thinking: *Trust him to be off on location somewhere.*

'No,' I say, pulling a face. 'Just Nicky's people. They're doing a pageant in the village this week-end, and we've been roped in to help.'

The corner of his mouth twitches. 'Well, that sounds like fun. And what part are you meant to be playing?'

'Oh, just third spear-carrier or something. But we're taking a couple of theatrical pals with us, who're going to be the stars of the show, so we need to get there in time for them to rehearse. And I was just hoping for a quick word before I went.'

'Well, he's not in, I'm afraid. I'm waiting for him myself. Cynthia had to pop out for a mo, so I told her I'd hold the fort.'

'Ah, right. I'll look back in a few minutes, then.'

I start to retreat.

He says: 'Haven't seen you for a while. How are things?'

'Oh, well, you know . . .'

'Strangely enough, I don't, old man. That's why I asked.' His colourless mouth buckles into a smile. But it's sad, not reproachful. One sufferer to another, encouraging confidence.

'Well,' I find myself saying, 'if you really want to know, I'm at the end of my tether.'

'Oh, I'm sorry to hear that.'

'I mean, I realize that must sound a bit thick, coming from me. But –'

He shakes his head, and kicks a chair towards me. 'Why don't you sit down and tell Uncle Val about it? Isn't always a good idea to keep these things to yourself.'

I ought to come up with an excuse and bolt. But my imagination's wrung dry and my legs suddenly feel too weak to make the effort. The chair looks irresistible. I subside on to it gratefully.

'You remember that time we met in the canteen? Before I went to Germany? And you talked about throwing it all up, and going off to run a pub somewhere?'

He nods. 'Oh, dear. As bad as that, is it?'

'Pretty much. The bloody *Candlestick Maker*'s driving me batty.'

'Hm. Always struck me as rather a cushy billet. What's the problem? The scenario, or –?'

'Everything. The characters – if you can call them characters, which you can't, really. They're not even puppets: at least a puppet gives an illusion of life when you pull the strings. The story – well, you know what that's like. Completely inane. Less genuine drama than an average game of Snakes and Ladders. And I can't even film *that* properly without falling foul of the censors.'

'Really? Why?'

I explain the problem about the body in the bath. He raises his eyebrows, and presses his lips into a comic-rueful grin. 'Well, you know – ours not to reason why.'

I shake my head. 'I can't help reasoning why.'

'The price you pay, I'm afraid, for being the sort of chap you are. I'm lucky, I suppose. I tend not to think about these things. Just get on with the job.'

Him lucky? An unexpected little barb of guilt pricks my chest. I cross my arms, trying to keep it out.

'Seems to me,' he says, 'that the whole thing's really pretty simple: a nice old boy called Sir Basil Hopkirk hands us a decent screw every month, and in return he expects us to entertain the great unwashed. Once we've done that to the best of our ability, we've fulfilled our side of the bargain, and earned our eight hours' dreamless sleep. The material we're given, and what the chaps at the Board allow us to do with it, aren't our department. So there's no point worrying about them.'

'And you don't ever wonder if your ability might be better employed doing something else?'

'I can't say I do, very much. To be honest, I'm not sure how much ability I've really got –'

'Oh, you mustn't –'

'No, no, it's all right, old man. I'm not under any illusions. I know I'll never be a Max, or even a Henry Whitaker.'

That *even* hurts. I try not to show it.

'I know *Tiddlywink* wasn't up to much,' he goes on. 'And I'm in no great hurry to have another go on my own. I'm happy enough just to trundle along, doing my lowly bit as an A.D., or whatever else they can find for me. All I ask is that it's in a good cause – and I really do think this is. I mean, you've only got to take a look at the papers, haven't you, to realize the poor old unwashed *need* entertainment? The pictures are probably the only respite they ever get from their lives. Which, let's face it, must be pretty awful at the moment. For a lot of them, anyway.'

I'm wilting with shame. And at the same time furious. I want to lean across, grab him by the throat, and scream: *So don't you think they deserve something better than* New Year's Eve *or* The Candlestick Maker? *Something that might actually nourish them, rather than just dulling the pangs of hunger?*

'Well,' I say. 'That's very admirable.'

'Not admirable. Just the kind of fellow I am. It's different for you, of course, I can see that. Not so easy.'

I shake my head. 'I'm probably just being self-indulgent.'

'No, it must be hard. There are so many other things you *could* be doing. Natural enough to wonder whether you've picked the right one.' He hesitates, looks away, swallows – then forces his gaze back to me, and says quietly: 'What does Nicky think?'

Something dark and unmanageable swims up from my belly and tries to push itself out as a sob. I get up and walk to the window, biting my lip to stop it. Behind me, I hear footsteps, and Val saying: '*Ah, buon giorno, Duce.*'

Then Max huffing: 'What have you done with Miss Drew? You chaps can't keep nabbing my secretaries and continuity girls like this.'

'Hard though you may find this to credit, Max,' says Val, 'even Miss Drew has certain physical needs that require her attention from time to time.'

'I don't believe you,' says Max. 'You've just got a dirty mind. I know for a fact that Miss Weedon never went to the lav. Not on her own, anyway. Henry'll bear me out on that, won't you, Henry?'

I've finally got my breathing under control again. I turn to face him.

'You're obviously better informed than I am,' I say. I mean it to sound light, but it comes out brittle. Two tiny spots of colour appear on his doughy cheeks.

'Well, I think that's probably true, old son. But I'm surprised she told you about it.'

Out of the corner of my eye, I can see Val wincing. Why is Max doing this? He must know how uncomfortable it is for both us. I clench my fists and start edging towards the door.

'What, going already?' says Max.

'Well, Val was here first. So –'

'That doesn't matter,' says Val. 'You're the one who has to leave early. I can wait.'

'You wanted to see me about something?' says Max.

'Yes, but I can come back another time –'

'Honestly,' says Val. 'And I shouldn't desert my post, anyway. Not after I promised I'd stay.'

'Well, if you're sure –'

'Come on,' says Max, touching my arm.

He leads me into his office and shuts the door. I'm suddenly hit by that odd sensation you get sometimes, when all the intervening associations are stripped away and a place looks just as it did when you saw it the first time. This isn't the shabby, smoky, compromised world of *New Year's Eve* and *Markheim* and *The Red Duster* (familiar blade-shaped scratch on the desk; venetian blind always drooping at the same angle): it's the virgin territory of February 1928, with an enigmatic stranger facing me and the just-glimpsed mysteries of film-production whirring in my head. And the consciousness of Nicky, still shiny from the chrysalis, sitting outside.

'So,' says Max as we sit down. He seems nervous for some reason, though I can't imagine it's anything to do with me. He's too fidgety even to go through the ritual of poking a hole in a cigar and lighting it, and instead plays with his new toy: one of those glass paperweights with a winter scene trapped inside it. This one shows a red-roofed Swiss chalet against a background of mountain peaks. The surface is smeared with his fingerprints.

He sees me glancing at it and says: 'Nice, isn't it? A gift from Greta. She said: *I think you feel at home here.* I said: *I would if I came in one day and found you rolling around on a bearskin rug in front of the fire.*' He shakes up a blizzard, then holds the paperweight in front of the Alpine poster on the wall. 'That'd make a good opening sequence, wouldn't it?' he says, watching the chalet reappear through the settling snow. 'First you're looking at this' – tapping the glass – 'and then, as you move closer, you find you're actually there. The place itself. Switzerland, or wherever it is. With a real cabin. Real mountains.'

'Ye-es.' Mustn't change the subject too abruptly. I count to three, then start tentatively: 'What I wanted to –'

'Corker of an idea, eh?' he says quickly. 'And yours for nothing, old son. You don't even have to give me a credit. You could soon work it up into something, couldn't you?'

I smile: he's changed it for me. 'That wasn't quite what I had in mind –'

'No? Well – that's a shame. Because it may be the best offer you're going to get.'

No hint of a twinkle as he says it. His face is at its fishiest: boggle-eyed and sulky. Somehow, he's guessed what I'm here for. It must be that that's making him uneasy – though I can't quite see why it should. But I'm determined to stick to my guns anyway.

'You've probably forgotten this,' I say, 'but the very first time we met – you know, when I'd sent you that outline for *The Binoculars Case*, and you suggested I should come and talk to you about it – you told me you liked the idea, but there was absolutely no chance of getting it made. But you did say it might be worth looking at it again in five or ten years –'

He nods. 'I haven't forgotten.'

'Well, it's been five-and-a-half . . . And I was just wondering . . .?'

I pause, waiting for him to help me. Easy enough for him to nod encouragingly and say: *What, if this was the right moment?* But he doesn't. He just stares, as if he's no idea what I'm driving at.

'I mean, I know I shouldn't complain – I've nothing to complain about – It's just *The Candlestick Maker* wasn't quite what I had in mind when I, you know . . . took the king's shilling.'

No answering smile. I've never known him like this. What the hell's bothering him? Could it be that he sees me as Mark Antony to his Caesar, and thinks that – having made it to director with his patronage – I'm now ungratefully trying to elbow my way in, and take the project from him?

I say: 'I wouldn't necessarily expect to direct it myself. I always thought you'd be the best man for the job. And I still do, if *you're* still interested. I'd be quite happy to do the scenario, and leave it at that. I just want to feel I'm putting my effort into something worthwhile.'

He shrugs, and juts his lower lip. I try to arrange my face into a complicit smile.

'I know things are a bit difficult at the moment. But I thought that maybe – if we approached Sir Basil together, in the right way – we might be able to rekindle his enthusiasm for Art?'

He doesn't laugh. He puts the weight down, flips it on to its domed top, then slides it across the blotter: a boat on a paper sea.

'There wouldn't be an icicle's chance in hell,' he says.

'Why?' I'm incensed at his dismissiveness. 'Look, don't misunderstand me, Max: I'm perfectly aware how much I owe the studio. But I think the studio owes me something, too, don't you? Enough, at least, to give serious consider–'

He looks up sharply, startling me into silence. 'Listen, old son. You could go and see Sir Basil –'

'I was talking about us *both* going –'

He appears not to have heard me. 'But I can save you the trouble. Because I know exactly what he'd say. *We've signed a contract to make so many pictures. We must a) deliver them on time; b) keep them within budget; and c) make sure they're acceptable not only to our American pay-masters but to the censors and the audience as well. The story of a neurotic young man who's morbidly obsessed*

205

with his father's killer and ends up fucking a half-starved German whore doesn't fit the bill. A fairy-tale about a body in the bath does. If you want to make the fairy-tale, splendid. If you don't, we'll find someone else to do it, and you can sling your hook.'

For a moment I'm too stung to speak. Then I hear myself drawling: 'So the plan to save British cinema has been indefinitely postponed, has it?'

'We're all in the same boat, Henry. Between you and me, I'm only hanging on by the skin of my teeth here myself. It's a case of one step forward, two back, if you're lucky. If you're not, it's just a case of three steps back.'

Well, fuck you. 'All right,' I say, getting up. 'Sorry to have taken up your time.'

He nods, and sucks his mouth into a salmony pout. As I reach the door he says: 'And how's Miss Weedon?'

It's meant to sound business-as-usual, but the edge of anxiety in his voice gives him away. He's afraid he's been too brutal, and now, before I leave, he's trying tentatively to re-animate the bond between us – starting with this one spider-web-thin filament.

I almost rupture it by snapping: *It isn't funny to keep calling her Miss Weedon, Max.* But some dim sense of self-preservation stops me in time.

'She's well, thanks,' I say.

'Give her my best.'

'I will.'

'And a bit of a wiggle.'

Cynthia Drew's back at her desk. Val's sitting opposite her, with the tooth-achey look you get when you're struggling to make conversation. It strikes me with a sudden pang how much he must miss Nicky.

'How did it go?' he asks, standing up, with a smile that says: *Thank God: help at last.*

'Fine.'

And then, all at once, the same dark unmanageable monster swims up in me again, and this time I know what it is: the suspicion that it might have been better if I hadn't walked in here five-and-a-half years ago, and Val had got the job and the girl, and I'd done something else entirely.

''Bye, then,' I say.

''Bye. Have a good week-end.'

'Thanks.'

I stumble into the corridor, my vision bleached and fuzzy with tears.

It's almost five by the time we get to Slip Hill. William's first out of the car. As his feet scrunch the gravel, he puts his head back and snuffs the air. It's sweet with the smell of roses and tobacco plants and freshly mown grass, but even in July the easterly breeze gives it an unexpected edge: a razor-blade hidden in cotton wool.

'What a lovely spot,' he says, nodding towards the jungle of rhododendrons.

Nicky smiles and squeezes his arm.

'Is that a tennis court through there?'

'Yes. Do you play?'

'I'm a demon. I'll show you, if you –' He breaks off suddenly, as Mrs. Weedon appears at the front door, with portly Jojo barging at her calves.

'Hullo, Mummy!' calls Nicky.

'Hullo, darling!' She's wearing a summery moss-green frock, and – for the first time I can remember – a daub of bright-red lipstick. Presumably it's meant to make her look sophisticated, but it only accentuates the vulpine curve of her mouth, and the hunger in her eyes.

'Mummy, I'd like you to meet William Malpert.'

I've been dreading this encounter for weeks: the collision between two completely different worlds in which I'm the only common element. All the way there, I've been preparing emollient little phrases (*Mrs. Weedon, may I introduce a fellow cat-enthusiast?*) to lubricate it. But I can immediately see that I needn't have worried: William's at his most boyishly charming, and from the moment they shake hands it's glaringly obvious poor Mrs. Weedon is smitten. She takes his arm as she leads us in to the drawing-room, and then sits gazing at him, pink-cheeked and sparkling-eyed with admiration, all the way through tea. Watching her, it strikes me I'm actually not required here at all: I could just slip back to London, and no-one would notice.

Afterwards, we go out into the garden to rehearse. The pageant, Mrs. Weedon explains, will consist of twenty scenes in all, but we're going to be involved in just one: the Battle of Slip Hill in 1642, when the Roundhead Captain Giles attacked the house of a local Royalist – only to discover it was being defended by his old Oxford friend Sir Richard Willoughby. Eventually the two men found themselves facing each other in single combat. After a desperate struggle, Sir Richard finally managed to disarm Giles – but then decided to spare him, saying: *A man cannot with honour serve his king, that hath betrayed his own heart.*

'That was very gentlemanly of him,' says William.

'Mm,' says Mrs. Weedon, squeezing his arm again, and blushing. 'That's why we thought it would be nice if *you* would play him, and Mr. Trayne could be Captain Giles. Nicky says you're both marvellous swordsmen, so we're hoping –'

'The foils are still in the car,' says Barrett. 'I'll go and get them, shall I?'

'What about me?' asks Nicky, mock-sulky. 'And Rex?'

'Rex won't be back till tonight. So he's just going to be a foot-soldier, like Henry. Is that all right, Henry? You did say you didn't want anything terribly big?'

'Yes, yes, of course. Fine.'

She turns to Nicky again. 'But you, darling, are Margaret Giles, which I think's rather thrilling. Captain Giles's sister. She was so overcome by Sir Richard's magnanimity that she came to thank him in person – and they ended up falling in love, and getting married.'

Nicky flushes.

'We'll need a bit of space, if we're going to be fencing,' says William, pointing at the croquet lawn. 'Would it be all right for us to set up shop over there. Or would shifting everything cause ructions?'

Mrs. Weedon laughs. 'Not at all. We can always find the holes again, can't we?'

We move across the grass in a line, harvesting hoops and sticks. As we're stacking them up on the terrace, Barrett appears at the corner of the house, holding the foils in one hand and the daggers in the other, and looking over his shoulder as if he's talking to somebody. A couple of seconds later Dr. Weedon trudges into view behind him, slouching under the weight of his medical bag.

'Daddy!' shouts Nicky.

'Hello, darling!'

She drops a hoop and runs towards him. William ambles after her at a discreet distance, then stops and hovers while she and her father hug each other.

As they separate, she turns and says: 'Daddy, I'd like you to meet . . .'

But she's too far away for me to hear the rest, and the next moment I'm back in the world of silent film, watching a dumbshow of smiles and nods and handshakes. Divorced from the familiar words, it seems as exotic and incomprehensible as the rituals of some primitive tribe. For a few seconds I have the dislocatory sense that I'm an ethnographic observer from another planet: I know, in theory, what the gestures mean; I can mimic them well enough; and yet I'm uncomfortably aware that they'll never come entirely naturally to me. If there's an outsider here, it suddenly strikes me, it isn't William or Barrett: it's me.

'Come along, chaps!' calls Mrs. Weedon, behind me. 'No slacking!' It's meant to sound playful, but the irritation in her voice is unmistakable. William certainly notices it – and guesses the reason for it, too; I see him glancing abruptly at her, then surreptitiously at Nicky and Doctor Weedon as they start strolling towards her, laughing and arm in arm. Did Nicky *explain* the situation to him before we left? The thought of it gives me a sour taste in my mouth: if she's not too embarrassed to say *I'm a Daddy's girl, and it makes Mummy dreadfully jealous*, what else might she be prepared to tell him?

'Henry!' says Doctor Weedon, limping up to me. 'Nice to see you.' He tries to unhitch Nicky's hand so he can shake mine, but she's so reluctant to let go that it's a few seconds before he can manage it.

No, I think. *She didn't tell William. She didn't have to. Any fool could see it.*

'How are you?' I say. But I can sense the answer from the lines on his face, and the slackness of his fingers.

'A wee bit weary, to tell you the truth,' he says. 'If you want a piece of advice from your father-in-law, Henry, it's: *Don't bother getting old.*'

'Oh, you're not old, Daddy!' squeals Nicky.

He bends his plasticine lips into a rueful smile. 'That's not what my aching limbs tell me. If we were living three thousand years ago, I'd be dead by now.' He points towards the faint smudge of hills beyond Wenlock Edge. 'The Iron Age chaps who built the earthworks up there would have considered themselves lucky to get to forty.'

'But you're not an Iron Age chap, are you?' says Nicky, hanging childishly on his arm again. 'You're a modern chap, who needs a bit of cheering up. We've just finished tea. Shall I bring you a cup – or ask Felicity to make you a fresh one? Then you can sit and watch us going through our scene for tomorrow while you drink it. It's' – laughing, and breathlessly parodying her own girlish enthusiasm – 'jolly exciting.'

'Aah!' he says. He turns his eyes up in mock-ecstasy. 'Sounds awfully tempting, I must say.'

'Right.' She slides one of the garden chairs behind him and gently coaxes him into it.

'Just as long as one of *you*', he says, subsiding with a sigh, 'will sit and keep me company.'

'Well, I can't.'

'Henry, then.' He says it casually, but there's an unexpected sharpness in his eye when he looks at me that makes me think he knew perfectly well Nicky wouldn't be able to join him, and he'd end up with me. I suddenly feel back at school again. *See me after prep, Whitaker.*

'I'm just not sure about the tea, though,' he says, with his best effort at a roguish twinkle.

'Beer?'

'I think so, don't you, Henry?'

Maybe it'll relax me. 'Yes, that'd be lovely. Thanks.'

'O.K. –' says Nicky.

'I wish you wouldn't say that,' groans Doctor Weedon.

She giggles. 'Sorry. All right. I'll be back in a sec.'

I draw up a chair next to him, and we watch William and Barrett going through the first moves of their fight. *Traitor!* shouts William, waggling his sword threateningly. *Villain!* returns Barrett, backing away. *Have at you!* cries William, launching himself forward – and all at once they're slashing and ducking and lunging at each other with frightening energy. But it's obvious they know what they're doing: five seconds is enough to give you that reassuring sense that you're in the hands of professionals and can sit back and enjoy the spectacle. Mrs. Weedon gapes open-mouthed.

Even her husband seems fascinated: he looks on raptly, as if we were at a cricket match, and acknowledges my presence only with the most anodyne comments: *My word!* or *They're awfully good, aren't they?* I begin to wonder if I was wrong in thinking he had an ulterior motive in asking me to sit with him: perhaps he meant what he said and was just hungry for company. But then Nicky reappears with two pint glasses of beer – and as she leaves to rejoin the others on the lawn he inclines his head towards me and murmurs: 'So, old chap, how are you?'

'Fine, thanks. How about –?'

'Work going well?'

'Mm . . . All right.' I say it equivocally enough to encourage further questioning if he's interested, but he isn't.

'Good, good,' he says abstractedly. And then, nodding after the retreating Nicky: 'And how's my girl? You treating her properly?'

My throat starts to burn. 'Well, I hope I am. I *think* I am. And she's flourishing, as far as I know. Why – doesn't she seem to be?'

'No, no, I didn't mean that. She *looks* flourishing. In the perfect bloom of youth.'

'Well, I'm glad to hear it,' I say.

We relapse into silence, watching the charade of Nicky trotting on as Miss Giles, and her mother sending her back and telling her to do it again more slowly.

Then, as she makes her second entrance, Doctor Weedon murmurs: 'I know it's hard to believe these things when you're young, Henry. But the trouble with blooms is, they fade eventually. And eventually's never as far away as you imagine.'

Oh, God, that's why: children.

'Something you learn, as a doctor, is that Nature may not be kind, but she's very wise. She allots a season to everything. And when that season comes, you can't afford to dawdle. Mm?'

I know what's coming and frantically try to think of some way of forestalling it. But I'm not quick enough.

'I mean, look at animals. Bitch comes on heat once every six months. You want a litter of pups, that's when you've got to get her covered – and the sooner the better, if they're going to be healthy. No good twiddling your thumbs and then introducing her to some frisky young brute the following week. Doesn't matter if he's a Cruft's champion; Nature'll just turn round and say: *Sorry, you missed your chance.*'

God, what a way to talk to your son-in-law about your daughter. I can't help it: I'm blushing. I say: '*But she's only twenty-six!*'

He shakes his head. 'Nature wouldn't like that *only*. You remember Mrs. Climthorne's daughter, Lally?'

'No, I don't think so.'

'You have met her, I know. She was at the staff Christmas party two years ago.'

'Oh, yes, yes, of course I did. Scrawny little thing.'

'Not any more. Breasts like melons, bursting with milk.'

'Really?' My gullet's so tight it's painful to speak. I stare at my feet, to avoid catching his eye. 'What, pregnant, you mean?'

He nods.

'But surely, she can't be more than twelve or –?'

'She's fifteen. It's a real scandal, as you can imagine. Poor Mrs. C didn't tell us for weeks. And she probably wouldn't have done, even then – only of course, what with my being the doctor here, she couldn't really avoid it. She was terrified, you see, that we might give her the sack. Needless to say, we didn't – but there are a lot of people in the village who think we should have done. Half of them won't even talk to her. And the vicar, naturally, can't resist making an example of the girl, without mentioning her name – you know: *Can we not see, even in our own small community, evidence of just how far the cancer of moral degradation has spread?*' He pauses a moment, then turns to me with a smile. 'A cancer, incidentally, you'll be glad to learn, for which the cinema is largely to blame.'

'Oh, dear.' For a moment, the tension between us dissolves: we've joined forces against someone else. 'Better not tell him what I do, then.'

He laughs. 'Ridiculous, isn't it? As if this sort of thing never happened before the war. Or before there were moving cameras. I mean, half the novels in the English language depend on little bundles left on doorsteps, don't they? *Tom Jones*. *Oliver Twist* –'

'Who's the father?'

'Oh, a farm labourer called Stanley Tibbets. I must say, he wouldn't be my first choice. Too many straws in his hair. Eyes a bit close together. Rumour has it that the mother was a good deal too fond of her brother, and there's actually only one pair of grandparents, instead of the customary two. But there: Nature won't be gainsaid. With the result that when Lally goes into the barn with Stanley, suddenly *He's touching me, Doctor Weedon, all over, and I'm getting these funny feelings, in places I never knew I had before, and then – I don't know – I just can't help myself.*' He laughs. 'It's heresy to say it, of course, especially in a place like this, but Nature actually knows better than the vicar. A lot of fifteen-year-old girls are perfectly capable of child-bearing. Sturdy. Vigorous. In their prime.'

He stops, and pretends to be absorbed in the pantomime romance being acted out on the croquet lawn. *Thank you*, says Nicky, swooningly clasping her hands together. *Nay, madam*, replies William, with a bow. *You paid that reckoning by coming here. The only thanks due now are mine to you.*

Is it just coincidence, or does my father-in-law think the sight of Nicky preparing to walk down an imaginary aisle with William Malpert will spur me to action?

'Look, I do understand,' I begin haltingly. 'And you mustn't think Nicky and I haven't talked about starting a family: we have. It's just a matter of picking the right moment. When my job's a bit more secure, and we can afford a bigger place . . .'

He sets his jaw.

Before he can say anything I hurry on: 'How about Rex? I mean, naturally you'd imagine that he'd be the one to have children first. You know, being the eldest. Has he shown any signs at all? Is there a girl in the off–?'

He shakes his head sulkily. 'Rex is a bit too interested in the theory to pay much attention to the practice, I'm afraid.'

'Really –?'

But at that moment Mrs. Weedon waves at us and calls out: 'Come on, you foot-soldiers! You can't expect the gentry to do all the work! You could at least look bellicose, and shout an insult or two.'

Doctor Weedon raises his glass. 'Filthy capitalists!' he roars.

Everybody howls with laughter. The tears are running down Nicky's face. I clench my fists, and stare at the white knuckles.

It's almost black: there's just a faint rim of light beneath a door that seems to be in the wrong position. No street lamps. No sound. Perhaps I'm in a coffin myself. Except that if I were, surely the crack of light would be above me, not over there to the left?

'Darling . . . Darling . . .' whispers Nicky.

'Where are we?'

'At Slip Hill.'

'Oh, yes, yes, of course. Sorry.'

'I heard you crying. Did you have the nightmare again?'

'I think I must have.' Yes, she's right: it *was* the nightmare. Only this time Christopher was in it. Or *near* it, rather: the image of his face on the steamed-up window seemed to flicker around the edges, a picture trying to find the right place to hang itself.

'Oh, poor you.' She pulls up her nightdress, so she can cradle my head on her bare breast. 'But it's all right. I'm here.'

She starts to stroke my forehead. Her fingers are hard and dry. Wipers on a wet windscreen.

'Sorry,' I say. 'I'm all sweaty.'

'Stop apologizing. I like your sweat.' She leans down and kisses it. 'Mm.'

'Thank you.'

I should say something more. Something reassuring. But I know it'd sound false.

'Are you O.K.?' she says finally.

'Yes.'

'Sure? Really?'

I don't trust my voice, so I try to nod. Hard to do when you're lying down. She laughs.

'Is that *yes*? It felt like a bird pecking.'

'Hm.'

She's quiet for a moment. Then she says: 'What is it, Henry? I'm so worried about you.'

'I'm fine.'

'No, you're not. You hardly said anything at dinner.'

I shrug.

'Ow!'

'Sorry. Well, it was hard to get a word in edgeways, wasn't it? Your father and William were chatting away so –'

'Mummy noticed. She asked if you weren't feeling well?'

'Well, I hope you told her I'm in the rudest of rude health.'

God: it sounds so hollow. Nicky hears it and sighs. Her soft wavery breath feathers my cheek.

'Please,' she says. 'Tell me.'

What should I tell her? That I'm a stranger in her parents' house? That food has lost its flavour? Flowers have lost their scent? That someone's put a spell on me, and I'm slowly freezing up, from the inside out?

'Henry?'

'I just . . . I just feel I'm in limbo.'

She tightens her arms round me. 'How can you be in limbo, when you've got me with you?'

'That isn't what I'm talking about.' But of course it is, partly. It's not that I doubt her love: it's just that it's lost its power to move me, for some reason. I'm conscious of warmth touching my skin, but it can't seem to penetrate to the ice beneath any more.

'What, then?'

'I saw Max yesterday.' I hadn't meant to tell her until I'd had a chance to think about it and come up with some sort of a plan: *Darling, I want to leave the studio;* or: *I'll give it one more film, and if things haven't improved by then, I'm going.* But it's less painful to talk about Max than about my feelings for her.

'What did he say?'

I tell her.

'He was probably just in a bad mood,' she says, when I've finished. 'Maybe his gut was bothering him again. Or – or else he was about to approach Sir Basil with one of his own pet projects and didn't want to queer his pitch by, you know, trying to push yours at the same time.'

'Yes, perhaps.' I mean it to sound animated – *Ah, I hadn't thought of that* – but somehow I can't find the energy. So it comes out sluggish instead: *That doesn't make any difference.*

'I'm sure . . . if you just quietly get on with *The Candlestick Maker* . . . and then go back to him, in a couple of months, things'll have changed.'

'Maybe. But I'm just so tired of having to skulk around . . . hiding what I *really* want to do . . . as if it's something to be ashamed of.'

'Oh, come on, you're no worse off than anyone else, are you? You're actually a lot better off, I'd say. Think about Max – everything *he's* had to contend with to get where he is. Or poor Val, having to watch *you* going from strength to strength, while he gets lumbered with *Tiddlywink*.' She runs her fingers over the washboard ripple of my ribs, as if she's going to tickle me – or jab me suddenly. 'Just count your blessings, darling. You've got an interesting job. A lovely wife. A nice flat. Friends. Talent.'

Why does that make me feel worse, rather than better?

'Yes, you're right, of course,' I say.

'You don't sound as if you think I am.'

'I'm just tired. Let's try and get some sleep.'

She doesn't believe me, of course. She knows that, for all her sweetness and patience, she's still failed to unlock the cell I'm trapped in. I can feel the acid burn of her misery on my back. It's not her fault, poor kid. Why can't I soothe her? All I'd have to do is let *her* soothe *me*.

It's impossible. I'm out of reach.

I breathe more slowly, trying to calm myself. She must misinterpret it as the sound of sleeping, because, after a while, I hear her crying, very softly.

Christ, this is breaking my heart.

*

Barrett wants a photograph of William and Nicky and me together in costume. He lines us up against a hedge and quickly takes five or six shots. Then he and the others go off to get ready for their scene, leaving me alone with Rex. Watching them crossing the field, laughing and mock-punching each other, gives me a strange first-day-at-school feeling of abandonment.

For God's sake, I tell myself. *Grow up.*

I turn to Rex.

'So, how was Germany?'

'Shouldn't you say: *And what news bring you of the Rhine country, friend?*'

'I don't think anyone can hear.'

Seeing I'm not going to respond to his joke, he laughs at it himself. 'Germany was fine,' he says.

'Whereabouts were you?'

'Oh, you know. All over the place.'

'Berlin?'

'Yes. I went to Berlin.'

'And –?'

He holds up a hand to silence me. There's a patter of applause from the crowd massed in front of us.

'Are we on,' he says. 'Or –?'

'The royal progress of Henry the Seventh,' announces the compère, as four or five cloaked horsemen trot into the field. They're followed by a woman riding side-saddle, who looks in imminent danger of slipping off, and a rabble of children dressed up as pages. 'At the entrance to the village, the King is greeted by Sir Oswald Amos.' A man in a tunic made out of an old sheet runs forward and drops to his knees in front of the leading horse.

'Henry the *Seventh*?' says Rex.

'Yes, still the Wars of the Roses.'

He rolls his eyes: *God, are we going to be here all day?*

'But the very end of the Wars of the Roses. We should be next, I think.'

'Really? I was always a bit of a duffer at history, but surely *something* happened between then and the Civil War? I mean, what about Henry the Eighth? The Reformation? Good Queen Bess?'

'Well, they obviously didn't have much impact here. So your mother and her friends must simply have decided to cut the whole period out.'

'Ah, yes, just zzt, zzt, zzt,' he says, laughing, and making a scissoring motion with his hand. 'Nothing to it.'

It's quite charming, in a whimsical way, but seems so completely out of character that for a second I wonder if he's been drinking. But no, that's ridiculous: it's far too early – and in any case, if he had, I'd be able to smell it on his breath. No, the truth is, it suddenly strikes me, that – after three years of marriage – I've still got only the haziest idea of what his character actually *is*. Apart from the wedding, I've met him only perhaps five times in my life. And whenever I have, he's been so taciturn, and slipped away so quickly, that it's been impossible to form a clear sense of him at all.

Right. This is your chance. You're going to pin him down.

'How did you find Berlin?' I ask.

'Oh, I just got off the train, and there it was.'

God, that old chestnut. I wait a second, then slam the ball back over the net: 'And did the train run on time?'

He blushes, and gives an idiot grin. 'Yes, it did, actually.' He's trying to make light of it, but his jaw's tight with embarrassment.

So *that*'s it. The idea never occurred to me before – at least, not consciously; but now it has, I find I'm not particularly surprised. Did I half-realize it all along? Is that why I didn't pry more, or ask Nicky about him: because I knew that, once I'd acknowledged it, it would inevitably define my relationship with him and the rest of the family? You can't sustain a state of uneasy neutrality with a Nazi sympathizer: you're either with him, or against him.

'There is one thing to be said, I suppose,' says Rex, lifting his pike, then thudding it back on the ground. 'At least we're on the right side. Just think about poor old Father over there. *He* has to endure all this in the name of the King. How *anyone* could have risked his life for *that* effete little runt –' He shakes his head and laughs. 'Just like one of his own spaniels. Fit only for lying around all day on a silk cushion.'

He's backing away from the edge: trying to find some common

ground where we can comfortably stand together. Should I go along with it: pretend I haven't noticed his pink face and fumbling manner, and add a contemptuous comment of my own about Charles I – to suggest that, yes, of course, I'm a fully paid-up member of the Roundhead Party, as any right-thinking young Englishman must be?

I can't: I'm too bloody angry. Not only that he thinks I'll fall for such an obvious diversionary tactic, but at his breezy assumption that – even if we don't see eye to eye about present-day politics – we still somehow belong to the same ideological club.

'So,' I say. 'Where else?'

'What?'

'Where else did you go in Germany?'

'Oh. Munich. Cologne.'

'And was it all as impressive as the *Daily Mail* says it is?'

He grins, but exasperatedly: it's a gibe he's heard before. 'You shouldn't rely on what you read,' he says. '*Wherever* it's printed. If you really want to know what's happening in Germany, you should go back and see for yourself.'

No, Rex: you can't sidestep it like that.

'But it meets with your approval?' I say. It sounds harder and more sullen than I meant it to.

He squirms, then mumbles: 'Well, I certainly think we could learn one or two things from what they're doing.'

'Such as?'

For a second he looks panicked: he casts about him, wide-eyed, as if he's trying to find some way of escape. Then sees the horsemen. The sight of them seems to calm him.

'Well, for a start,' he says, nodding in their direction, 'they wouldn't stand for any of *that* nonsense.'

'Really?'

'Absolutely. They'd see it for what it is. Backward-looking. Self-indulgent. Play-acting at history, rather than making it.'

'But surely – I mean, aren't *they* just a tiny bit smitten with their own history? The old dark pagan gods, and the Teutonic knights, and all that?'

'That's different, Henry,' he says softly. 'Ever since the war, the

Germans have been taught to despise themselves – to be ashamed of who they are. Now the Nazis are saying: *There's no reason to be ashamed. We are a great people. We have a great destiny. But in order to seize it, we must first understand where we came from. Not to distract us from the present, but to inspire us for the task ahead.*'

I try, but I can't resist the question any longer: 'You didn't go to Klosterfeld, did you, by any chance?'

He gives me an odd sidelong glance. 'No. Why?'

'Oh, it's only that I met somebody there once, who said pretty much word for word the same thing. And I was just wondering if it was coincidence, or whether you'd met him too?'

'You don't mean Dr. Becker, do you?'

God: I was right. 'Yes. So you have met him?'

'No, I . . . No.'

'But you've heard of him, obviously?'

'Yes. Yes, of course.'

'Why *of course*?'

He scans my face, frowning slightly, as if he can't believe my ignorance, and wonders if I'm affecting it just to provoke him. It's a response he's probably used to: *Hitler? Who's Hitler? Oh, that frightful little corporal chap* . . .

'Have they made him Minister of Health, or something?' I say. 'I wouldn't be altogether surprised. He was clearly a true believer.'

He doesn't answer at once, just goes on staring at me. After a few seconds he says quietly: 'Do you really not know?'

'No. What?'

'He was killed. Just before the election last year. By the Communists.'

'Oh, God!'

'Yes, I know. I'm sorry. But it's strange you hadn't heard about it before. It was a big story in Germany. Hitler called him *a martyr to the Reich*. And the people in Klosterfeld are putting up a memorial to him. I saw something in the paper about it, just last week.'

I don't know what to say. I don't even know what I *feel*. I can't unpick a clear thread from the tangle of emotions in my head: shock and pity and sadness and incredulity – and something sour and shameful, that might turn out to be a kind of vengeful satisfaction, if I could bring myself to look at it.

'Did you know him well?'

'No, we only met once.'

'What, just by chance, or –?'

He's genuinely curious. Has he misjudged me? Am I really a Nazi sympathizer, too? I can see the sudden flare of hope in his hungry eyes: perhaps, he imagines, instead of being distantly polite with each other, we could, after all, be friends. No – something closer than friends: co-conspirators, swaddled together in hot-house inti-macy by our shared allegiance.

I feel so short of air I almost panic.

'No,' I hear myself blurting. 'I knew his wife slightly.' Immediately, I know it's a mistake: he must realize what Irma Brücke did before her marriage. Snatching at the first lie I can think of, I blunder on: 'She was a friend of the family. Her parents knew my parents before the war. Since then, of course, she'd had an awful time of it. Her fiancé being killed, and so on. So when I went there in twenty-seven, I decided to look her up.'

He's staring at me, very strangely. He doesn't believe me. He's angry with me. No, not angry: something else . . .

'And now losing Becker, on top of it –' I say hurriedly.

'Oh, God,' he says. 'I am so sorry.'

Sorry?

'She was killed, too.' There are tears in his eyes. 'They all were. The criminals threw a petrol-bomb into the hall while the whole family was upstairs.'

My neck and fingers are numb. My head pulses with a nauseous anaesthetic hum. The only sensation I'm aware of is a fly-buzz annoyance at the margin of my attention: Nicky's brother is offer-ing me sympathy, and I don't want it from him.

Somewhere, there's another burst of applause. Then Mrs. Weedon's voice calling: 'Stir your stumps, foot-soldiers! Time to show what you're made of!'

'Come on, old man,' says Rex gently, laying a confidential hand on my arm. 'Brave face, just for half an hour. Then afterwards we can go off somewhere and have a *proper* talk. And a bloody good cry, if we feel like it.'

A distant trumpet blast summons us to war. Rex tweaks my cuff, then turns and starts towards the field.

I pick up my pike, and charge behind him: 'Yaaaaaaaaaaagh!'

XVI

My triumph at spotting Arkwright's upcoming event didn't last.

Take a brick away, and the whole wall starts to look shaky. At one level, of course, it was a relief to discover that seven-year-old me hadn't, probably, after all, unwittingly pushed my mother into killing herself by telling her about the other woman. But at another it was deeply unsettling. Mummy's suicide had always been a gloomy article of faith for me. If it turned out to be groundless, how much was I left with that I could really be certain about?

The truth – at least when it came to my parents – was: frighteningly little. I'd only the haziest idea how they met, and none at all why they got married. I was beginning to think perhaps I'd even fundamentally mis-read their relationship.

He love me. He say I am the one.

The *one*. The *one*.

And the worst of it was, it seemed too late to do anything very much about it. They were both dead. So was Granny. I'd even managed to miss Flo Torridge by a couple of months. The only person I could ask about it now (the idea was so humiliating it made me blush, even though I was sitting alone in my hotel room at the time) was Alan Arkwright.

Could you please –?

No: it was unthinkable.

I began casting around desperately for another lead. It was five minutes before I came up with one. I immediately dismissed it as being too far-fetched, and resumed the search for an alternative.

It took me another half-hour to acknowledge that there really wasn't one.

You'd think it'd be comparatively easy to get hold of an old BBC radio show – or at least to find out whether it still exists. But it isn't.

The eager kid at the BBC shop had never heard of *Niddle at Nine*, but thought I might like the complete *Hancock's Half-Hour* instead. When I convinced her it was *Niddle at Nine* or nothing, she referred me to the National Film and Television Archive. The National Film and Television Archive were nice enough, but – as the eager kid might have guessed from their name – didn't handle radio. *They* suggested the Sound Archive at the British Library. I called – made an appointment – and traipsed in the next morning full of excitement. Only to find that there are no surviving recordings whatever of *Niddle at Nine*.

What about scripts? Sorry, they don't have scripts. If anyone does, it'll be the BBC's Written Archive at Caversham.

By the time I called Caversham, I was beginning to lose hope. But the people there at least knew what I was talking about. Could I give them a date? No, but I figured it was most likely some time in 1955. They'd see what they could find, and let me know. If they *did* have something, it could be up to two weeks before they sent it to me.

I kicked around for the next couple of days, feeling more and more angry with myself. At first it was just because I was spending money I didn't have waiting for Arkwright's appearance at the National Film Theatre. Then I started to beat up on myself for waiting to see Arkwright at all. Wasn't I just being childish? What did I hope to gain from it, except an opportunity to vent my rage? which was caused, wasn't it, if I was honest, largely by the realization that his attack on me was more than half-justified?

I tried calling Hode. He wasn't home. I left a message, then waited in all evening for him to call back. He never did. The next day, I tried again. Same result.

It was as bad as trying to reach Arkwright. I felt I was being sucked into a black hole. It was getting to be a struggle to push myself out of bed in the morning.

Finally, I saw that the only way to break the vicious circle was to *do* something, however useless. So I went freelance again, and started to research Diddy Niddle on the internet.

No shortage of information there, at least. I found his dates (1920–91); pictures (eyes crossed, pointing a toy gun at his temple; wearing a mop-head instead of a hat; offering a giggling frizzy-haired girl a bouquet of leeks); tributes to his "ground-breaking style" and "anarchic humour" from other comedians. There was even a thirty-second audio clip of one of his shows: lots of silly voices and flatulent sound-effects. Listening to it, I couldn't imagine how I ever thought he was funny.

But as soon as I added "Omar" to the search, I drew a complete blank: there wasn't a single reference to "Omar" and "Diddy Niddle" together.

Perhaps, I thought, "Omar" and "Diddy Niddle" were actually the same person. "Omar" was a nickname. Daddy used it because they'd been friends at one point – which was why Niddle knew the story of how my parents had met.

I typed in "Henry Whitaker" plus "Diddy Niddle." Nothing.

Then, out of the blue, another possibility struck me: What if the connection wasn't with my father at all, but with my *mother*? What if Niddle had had an affair with her? Could "Omar" be *her* name for him? It had a kind of Germanic ring to it.

For a second or two, I couldn't get to grips with this idea at all. It wasn't possible to square the doting, weepy, holy-fool madonna I remembered with the act of infidelity: they just didn't belong in the same frame. Trying to force them together left me feeling like some-one paralyzed from the neck down, as if my mind had become suddenly completely divorced from the world of physical experience. Then, painfully, a nerve at a time, they started to fuse again, as I forced myself to confront the evidence.

To begin with: wasn't it pretty obvious by now that the doting, weepy, holy-fool madonna herself was just a childish idealization? Because Mummy had died when I was seven, I still had a seven-year-old's view of her. Flo, on the other hand, had looked at her through the eyes of another woman, and seen someone entirely different: a vain, skittish drunk, ravenous for love.

And, now I came to think of it, hadn't even the seven-year-old me suspected something? Wasn't that why the radio show had come back to me so powerfully? Even seven-year-olds know what jealousy looks like. And jealousy, surely, was the likeliest explanation of my father's rage?

I felt the way you do when you're inching your way into the ocean, getting ready to swim, and a big wave suddenly slaps you and sends you spinning: cold and dizzy and sick.

My hands were trembling as I typed in: "Diddy Niddle" plus "Romona Whitaker."

I held my breath. Then the message I was hoping for: *Your search – "Diddy Niddle" + "Romona Whitaker" – did not match any documents.*

I tried "Diddy Niddle" plus "Romona Stimpel." Same result. "Diddy Niddle" plus "Romona." Same again.

Not conclusive, of course. But still I almost cried with relief.

I could only think of one other line to follow: the chronology of Diddy Niddle's life. If there was any point where it seemed to coincide with either or both of my parents', then that would be a reasonable place to start looking for a clue to the link between them.

"Diddy Niddle" plus "biography" yielded a handful of results. Half of them weren't about him at all – and most of the rest only contained one or two references to him (*a new **biography** of Peter Sellers calls his appearance with **Diddy Niddle** "the low-point of his career,"* etc.). But there was one that looked promising: a "Diddy Niddle shrine," offering – among other things – "an humble account of the great man's doings and ditherings, from the cradle to the crematorium."

I quickly scrolled through it. It was all couched in the same arch style, but I did manage to extract a slender framework of facts. From which it appeared that Niddle's only venture into film had been a cameo rôle in a 1958 comedy called *Dr. Krazy*, that he had never set foot in Germany, and that he had only moved to London after my father had left. I was just about to quit when I saw a little rubric at the bottom of the screen: *This site is maintained by Herbie Wethered. To contact him with any queries or comments, click here.*

I clicked there, found the usual blank e-mail form, and fired off a quick message: *Can you help? I'm trying to find out whether Diddy Niddle knew my parents, Henry and Romona Whitaker. And/or somebody called "Omar."* Then, to bolster my flagging sense of moral superiority, I gave myself ten minutes off to surf a few Hollywood sites, and see what the Leviathan was up to.

When I checked my e-mails again, there was a reply waiting for me: *I cannot say I recognize any of the names. But mine humble abode is home to the world's largest collection of Diddyabilia, which may afford some pertinent information. If you would care to arrange a rendezvous, I should be happy to assist you in any way I can.*

At the end was a number. I picked up the phone and put it down half a dozen times. Then, before I had a chance to change my mind again, I gripped it tightly, and dialled.

Which is why, at 10.50 yesterday morning, I found myself getting off the tube at Edgware.

I'd already figured out the quickest route to his house and penciled it on to my *A to Z* map, so it took me less than five minutes to find Orchard Way. Which left me another five to check it out, and decide whether I was actually going to keep my appointment, or turn tail and run.

It looked respectable enough: a street of solid, orange-brick, between-the-wars houses set back from the road behind neat little front yards. A realtor would have called them "detached," but in fact they were so close together you got the impression they had to hunch their shoulders to fit into their separate lots. It was hard to imagine that anything very dreadful could happen in one of them without the neighbors hearing it.

I stopped in front of number 15. It was as well-cared-for and anonymous as all the others. The lawn was shaved and weedless; the white gable end with its fake Tudor beams freshly painted; there were lace curtains in the gleaming downstairs windows. Not a hint of menace, or even eccentricity, to be seen.

Just to be on the safe side, I switched on my cell-phone and folded it in my left hand, with the thumb positioned over the "9" key. Then I scrunched up the path and rang the bell. It made the kind of ding-dong chime you used to hear in sitcoms. Immediately there was a frantic scrabbling at the door-handle. Maybe it was deliberate: it sounded like a gag from *The Goon Show*. Then the door opened, and a guy about my age appeared, wearing a purple silk shirt and a shit-colored jacket covered in big red squares. He had parchmenty skin, and a ginger mustache so bright I think it must have been dyed.

"Ah," he said, showing me a lot of false teeth. "The weary traveler. Won't you please step inside?"

227

The hall was oppressively hot, and carpeted in a pink-and-white nylon shag pile that – by some weird synesthesia – suddenly brought the chemical-sweet taste of coconut ice back to my mouth for the first time in thirty years. A giant picture of Diddy Niddle, so grossly enlarged that the grain was as big as pigeons' eggs, grinned manically down from the half-landing. Everything else – pseudo-Chippendale chairs, reproduction mahogany table, airplane toilet whiff of air-freshener – was more or less what you'd have expected from the outside. It kind of reminded me of one of those "private hotels" we used to stay in (on the rare occasions we stayed anywhere) when I was a kid.

Wethered led me past the kitchen and into what he called the "ops room" (obviously a reference to something Niddle-related: he watched me closely to see if I got it and seemed a bit disappointed when I didn't) at the back of the house. The curtains were closed and the only light came from a couple of dim lamps in heavy red shades. It was probably a reasonable enough precaution: no different really, I suppose, than what art galleries do to protect their collections. But it did make me feel a bit like I'd blundered into Bluebeard's Castle. I kept a tight grip on my phone. It was slithery with sweat.

Originally, I guess, the "ops room" had been the dining-room; but now it was crammed with "Diddyabilia": pictures and bookcases and glass-topped display tables, and – really spooky, this – a tailor's dummy decked out in (I presume) one of the guy's suits. One wall was entirely taken up with filing-cabinets and index-card boxes. In the middle of the floor was a desk with a computer on it.

"Behold," said Wethered. "The dragon's lair."

He pulled out a chair for me, very formally, then sat down himself. He had, he said, more than two hundred letters to and from Diddy Niddle, and scores of articles, news stories and miscellaneous papers, all of them filed and cross-referenced, either on index cards or on the database on his computer. Since receiving my message, he'd been right through both, looking for the two names I'd sent him, but couldn't find a single mention of either of them. What was it that made me think Diddy Niddle had known them?

I'd promised myself that I wouldn't tell him. But now he confronted me with the question outright, I couldn't think of a convincing lie. And what, anyway, would have been the point? I couldn't expect him to help me if I didn't give him the only clue I had to go on. So I quickly sketched in what I remembered – though avoiding melodramatic words like "secret" and "mystery," and leaving out my father's reaction altogether. The impression I intended to give was that it was no big deal, really – just a funny little incident it'd be neat to be able to explain.

When I got to the end, he smiled, and jabbed a triumphant finger in the air: "Ah, yes, dear lady, I know the very one! 'The Curious Case of Horace Dogbiscuit and Lotte Schlossloss.'"

"Is that what it was called?"

He nodded, bright-eyed – and immediately started to recite the bits he could remember, switching between clippy English upper-class male (obviously Horace Dogbiscuit), and heavily accented German falsetto (Lotte Schlossloss). The effect was startling: a bit, I imagine, like being at a séance, and hearing the medium suddenly spout a parody of some dead loved one's voice – getting it near enough to be recognizable, but still not entirely right. The hairs on my neck prickled. I felt – in quick succession – shivery, faint and tearful.

But Wethered either didn't notice what he was doing to me, or didn't care. He just went on and on, obviously expecting me to love his performance to death, and puzzled that I couldn't respond with anything more than a fixed smile. The fixed smile cost me so much effort, in fact, that I missed most of what he was saying. But there were a few lines that I knew I had heard before – and they stayed with me:

Dogbiscuit: Meine liebe, will you marry me?
Lotte: Bot vee hartly know each other.
Dogbiscuit : It doesn't matter. I know you are the one.
Lotte : How to you know that?
Dogbiscuit : I saw your face in a puddle.
Lotte : A poodle? Vhat is this?
Dogbiscuit : A kind of French dog.

Eventually, thank God – just when I felt I really couldn't stand any more and was about to shriek *Shut up!* – he stopped, and sat there smirking and shaking his head. It was a second or two before I could trust myself to say anything. Then I asked him, pretty frostily, whether he knew where Niddle had got the story from. He said he supposed he'd made it up. Dogbiscuit and Lotte Schlossloss weren't based on real people? Not as far as he knew. And he didn't by any chance have a recording of the show? No.

I got up, shaking slightly, and thanked him for his time. He seemed surprised – dismayed, even – that I was leaving so soon. As I started towards the hall, he got between me and the door. He was so close I could smell the stale aluminum tang of his breath, and feel its warmth on my face. Had I been in touch with the BBC? he asked, laying a hand on my arm. I told him I had, and was waiting to hear whether they had the scripts.

"They won't have," he said. "All the *Niddle at Nine* scripts were destroyed."

"Really? That's a shame."

"Shame's one word for it."

"What word would you use?"

"I wouldn't be so indiscreet as to tell you," he said, with a man-of-the-world little smile. "But there are some people I know who'd say *convenient*." And promptly launched into a monologue about how there were certain individuals, naming no names, but not a million miles from here, most of them – *here* being close to central London, if I knew what he meant – who could sleep a lot easier at night knowing those scripts were no more . . .

"Well," I said, "that's very interesting."

I tried to sidestep him, but he tightened his grip. Perhaps he hadn't made himself clear: he was talking about *royal personages, members of the Establishment* and *well-connected foreign gentlemen*, who found Niddle's fearless ridicule a bit close to the bone. The sort of people who had *sold poor old England down the river*.

There was no way out. I pushed past him, and fled.

When I got back to the hotel, there was a letter waiting for me from the BBC. They were sorry, but the scripts no longer existed. They did, however, have the program logs, copies of which they enclosed.

I quickly flicked through them and found the one for "The Curious Case of Horace Dogbiscuit and Lotte Schlossloss." Most of it meant nothing to me: directed by X, original music by Y. But then I saw the cast list, and did a double-take.

The part of Algernon Stiffley-Duck was played by William Malpert.

XVII

London – April 1935

I clink my empty glass against hers. 'You want another one? While we can still afford it?'

Her eyes are bright and watchful. 'Do you?'

'Why not?'

'O.K.' She smiles. 'Sorry, Daddy.'

The smoke's so thick now it rasps my skin as I struggle to the bar. The only space is a narrow gap between the wall and an old man sitting on a stool.

'Excuse me,' I say, trying to squeeze in next to him.

He turns and scowls, as if I'm intruding on his personal property. His face has the sickly grey sheen of wet putty.

'Sorry,' I say. 'Can I just –?'

He looks away again, but doesn't move, so I'm forced to stand sideways. Even then, I can feel the spiky knob of his shoulder protruding into my chest, and smell the steamy fust of his rain-speckled coat. By the time our drinks appear, I'm light-headed from holding my breath.

'Excuse me –' I say, a second time.

He spins round, his lip wrinkled in a snarl. I think he's about to swear at me, but he doesn't. Instead, his teeth suddenly seem to detach themselves from his gums and jig up and down in his mouth. The effect's so surrealist I almost drop our glasses. My hands are still trembling as I reach the table. Beer slops on to the shiny surface.

'Damn, sorry; here you are.'

'Thanks. What did he say to you?'

'Who?'

She nods towards the bar. 'The old boy.'

'He didn't say anything.'

'Oh, really? I thought you seemed – I don't know – a bit taken aback.'

'I was.'

'Why?'

'Maybe I just imagined it. I don't want to put ideas in your head. But keep an eye on him. See what he does the next time someone goes and stands over there.'

'All right.' She's intrigued. This is fun: a kind of game.

'Anyway . . .' Raising my drink to her.

'Thank you.' She smiles and takes a sip of bitter, watching me over the rim of her glass. The skin crinkles around her eyes, and her whole face seems to soften, as if the artist's smudged the charcoal lines defining it. It's weeks since she's looked at me like that. The effect's immediate: all at once, the little boulder of ice in my stomach melts away.

This is my moment. '*Nay, madam, the only thanks due now are mine to you.*'

She flushes. She's flattered that I've remembered the line. She's flattered that I've used it. 'You don't have to thank *me* for anything,' she murmurs.

'Yes, I do. From the way I've been behaving, you probably think I don't realize just how difficult the last few months have been for you.' As I say it, I'm conscious that's selling her short. I could have said *last few years*. Ever since I first walked into the studio.

She shakes her head.

I reach out for her hand. 'But I do. And I know how marvellous you've been about it, too.'

I've taken her by surprise. She doesn't know how to respond. The easy thing would be to try to cover up her embarrassment: *Oh, come on, Henry, don't be such a silly.* But she doesn't. I watch the colour spreading over her face, and the slow throb of the vein in her forehead.

Finally, she swallows painfully and says: 'The only difficult thing has been seeing you so low.'

'I know. I'm sorry.'

'It's not your fault.'

I shrug.

'Of course it isn't,' she says. 'You're someone with very high standards, that's all. And it makes you miserable if you can't live up to them. That isn't something you should be ashamed of. Something you should *blame* yourself for. It just shows how much integrity you've got.'

'No, I'm afraid you were right. I probably *was* a bit arrogant. And impatient.'

'Well, you can't be patient for ever, can you? If British Imperial weren't giving you the opportunity to prove yourself, it was only sense to go somewhere else.'

I'm flabbergasted: after months of besieging the citadel, I suddenly find the defenders have slipped away in the middle of the night and reappeared waving my flag.

'I thought you thought I was being irresponsible? That I should have gritted my teeth and stuck it out? Until eventually Sir Basil called me in and said: *All right, my boy, I can see you're a genius. Name your price. Pick your own films to make. Just swear you will never leave us?*'

She laughs and shakes her head. She doesn't look the least bit shamefaced. I don't think she realizes she's contradicted herself. 'You shouldn't if it's torture for you. It isn't worth it.' She squeezes my hand, and half-whispers: 'I'd much rather have you like this again.'

'Even without a penny to my name?'

'That doesn't matter. Money's not the important thing.'

'Easy to say that, when you've always had oodles of the stuff. You may feel differently when you're trying to scrape by on twopence-halfpenny a week.' I mean it to be Bertie Wooster jocular, but it comes out sounding sour.

She looks at me for a moment, then says quietly: 'If you think that, you don't know me very well.'

'Sorry, I wasn't suggesting –'

She shakes her head: not hurt, but serious. 'I mean, we don't have to live in London, do we? We could give up the flat and rent a little cottage somewhere and keep chickens. I wouldn't mind. Honestly. My needs are simple: a roof over my head, a crust to eat, and a happy husband. Just give me those, and I'll be fine. The happy husband, especially.'

'I'll see what I can do.' I look down at the table to stop her seeing how close I am to crying.

234

'Come on,' she says. 'We'll start tonight. Let's forget about Luigi's. You can buy me fish and chips instead.'

'Oh, no, I'm not going to do that.'

'I'd prefer it. Really.'

'But this is meant to be –'

'It doesn't matter. I love fish and chips.'

'Don't you want to dance?'

'We can dance at home. I got a new record today. One the chap at Luigi's won't even have *heard* of yet.'

She gets up, and coaxes me to my feet. As we're making our way to the door, I hear her sucking in breath sharply. I turn to look at her. Her cheeks are puffed up, as if she's struggling to contain something. I raise an eyebrow. She shakes her head.

But as soon as we get outside, she explodes: 'Oh, my hat!'

'What?'

'That man at the bar. Either I've had too much to drink, or his teeth move. I distinctly saw him *wiggle* them at me as we went by.'

'It wasn't the drink. That's what he did to me.'

'What an awful old reprobate!' She rests her head on my shoulder for a few seconds, quaking with laughter. Then she pulls away, sniffing and wiping the tears from her eyes. 'I'm sure I'm going to have nightmares about him. If I wake up in the middle of the night screaming, you'll know it's because I've seen *the teeth*!'

The teeth. Already they're part of our private mythology: another thread in the invisible web of shared references that binds us together.

We start walking – me in the lead, her trailing slightly behind, humming 'I'm Hitching my Wagon to You', and gently tugging my hand first one way, then the other, in time to the music.

So that's it. All that anxiety, all those carefully prepared phrases for nothing. In the end, there was no need to fight her, or strew her path with petals, or whisk her away on a white horse. She's accepted everything: not with a sniffy little smile, but wholeheartedly. Generously. *Cheerfully*, even. She seems happier and more relaxed tonight than I've seen her for months.

We pick up our fish and chips in Pinsent Street, on our way home, and eat them on the sofa, giggling at the stories in the old bits of *Daily Mirror* they're wrapped in. Afterwards, she gets up and puts on her new record. It's a slow two-step called 'My Wonder of the World'.

'Come on.'

She turns off the lamps, so the only light's coming from the gas-fire and the milky wash of the street outside. As we dance, she sings the words in my ear:

> *The Pyramids have no appeal to me –*
> *Just piles of rocks in the sand.*
> *And Babylon ain't all it used to be –*
> *Those Hanging Gardens are just history.*
> *And as for the Colossus,*
> *I'm telling you wild hosses*
> *Wouldn't get me to go,*
> *'Cos I'm staying with my baby –*
> *She's the only wonder of the world I know.*

And then the 'phone goes.

'Damn it.' I blunder into the hall to pick it up.

'Henry? It's Christopher.'

'Hullo, Christopher.'

I glance at Nicky, who's watching me from the doorway. She rolls her eyes.

'Sorry to ring so late,' he says. 'I did try earlier, but –'

'Yes, we were out.'

'Is this a bad time?'

'Well . . .'

He doesn't seem to catch the reluctance in my voice.

'It's just I think I've got it.' The words gush unstoppably out of the receiver. Nicky can hear their excited tone, even if she can't make out what they're saying. She sighs. I wave my hand at her: *Wait. I shan't be long.*

'Yes,' I say. 'What?'

'Blood.'

'Blood? What, instead of ants?'

'Yes.'

236

'You were right about the ants – I can see that now.' His voice has a kind of febrile animation, as if he's been drinking. It's not going to be easy to get rid of him. 'Think about corpuscles instead.'

'Corpuscles?' I'm starting to feel giddy. Perhaps it's the beer. I slip the 'phone-book off the chair and sit down.

Nicky sighs again, more noisily this time.

'Yes. The way they carry oxygen – the stuff of life – to every part of the body. Isn't that exactly what seamen and dockers and steve-dores do? The body in this case, of course, being the Empire?'

'Ah.'

'I'm going to have a bath,' murmurs Nicky. She brushes past me without catching my eye.

'And I love all those circulation *words*, don't you?' says Christopher. 'That *dee* dee *dee* dee *dee* dee cadence: *Beating. Thudding. Throbbing. Pulsing.* I've got a few phrases already. *London, the unsleeping head and heart. Lifeblood pumping round the world.*' He pauses, waiting for me to respond. When I don't, he says: 'Well, naturally they're still a bit rough. But –'

'They're fine. But could we maybe talk about this tomorrow, after I've had a chance to clarify my thoughts a bit? You know I'm meeting K.-M. first thing, and we're going down to Woolwich together –?'

'Mm. The problem is, I'm meant to be having dinner with Clumber on Thursday, and I've *got* to have something pretty definite by then.' He hesitates, then mumbles awkwardly: 'No chance *you* could be there too, I suppose?'

'Afraid not.' I don't mention we're having dinner with Max instead. He might suspect I was backsliding.

'That's a pity.' But he sounds relieved rather than disappointed. I don't think he wants me to meet Clumber, for some reason. If he *had*, then surely he'd have asked me sooner?

'Anyway,' he says. 'I'm going to have to stay up all night, working on it. And before I start, I've got to make sure we at least agree about the general principles.'

Oh, God. I can't just abandon him, then. I listen to the sploosh of the bath. At least five minutes before Nicky will reappear.

'O.K.,' I say. 'Well, to begin with, I can't see how you'd *film* it. I mean, what images would you use to suggest the human pulse? Or –'

'That's easy. A ship's funnel belching smoke. Or – or – or – the driving rods on an engine. Anything, really, that's regular and mechanical.'

I try to imagine it. He's right: it's possible. You could post-synchronize the sound track, so that the words kept time with the rhythm of what you were seeing. Not subtle, but effective.

'And how about corpuscles?' I say.

'Well –' There's a muffled crackle: he must have put his hand over the receiver. It's not enough, though, to stop me hearing a faint trickling sound.

'What are you drinking?'

He sniggers. 'Brandy. It's something Barrett Trayne told me. He said when he had to stay up finishing a scene, he kept himself going by drinking brandy till three in the morning, and then switching to black coffee for the rest of the night.'

'Sounds like spectacularly bad advice.'

'Yes, well . . .' His voice is unsteady with laughter. 'It's starting to feel like rather bad advice, actually. Anyway. Corpuscles. How about a whole crowd of men scurrying from ship to warehouse, laden with boxes?'

'We-ell . . .'

'What's wrong with that?'

'Not very specific, is it? It'd actually fit better with the ants.'

'All right. We'll commission some graphic sequences, then. We shouldn't be afraid of being *avant-garde*, should we?'

I don't know what to say. Or, rather, I don't know how to say it.

After a couple of seconds he prompts me: 'What?'

It's no good: I can't shirk it. I'll just have to try to be as diplomatic as I can.

'Look,' I say, 'I know you think I've been hopelessly corrupted by the movies. But I really do feel we need to follow some kind of a personal story. To draw people in. Keep them interested.'

There's a sharp *huff* at the other end of the 'phone.

I hurry on, before he has time to fire an answering salvo. 'I'm not saying we shouldn't use the circulation idea. I think it's very good. Very powerful. But if that's all we use, if we just make this for members of the Film Society, we'll simply end up preaching to the converted. What you've got to do is move people like, oh, I don't know – Nicky's parents. Solid citizens who read the *Daily Mail* and have never set foot in an industrial town. And you'll only do that by showing them that the working classes are real human beings, just like them –'

'You know, you're quite wrong, Henry,' says Christopher. His voice is lethally quiet and deliberate. 'I don't think you've been corrupted by the movies. I think you were corrupted years before you even *saw* a movie, by the sainted Mr. D. In fact, it suddenly strikes me that's the reason you went *into* British Imperial. Secretly, you were hoping they'd let you make *Oliver Twist* or *Great Expectations*. Only they wouldn't. So you thought maybe you could do it with me instead.'

Hard to say what staggers me most: his rudeness, his ingratitude – or how close he is to the truth. I start rehearsing a reply in my head: *I think you forget: it was you who asked me to do this film. And it's only because I said 'yes' that you got the money, if you recall – because I'm Clumber's sole guarantee that it will at least be competently made.*

But if I say that, there'll be no retreat.

I open my mouth. Shut it again.

I think he must sense that we're tottering on the brink, too, because for a couple of seconds he doesn't speak either. And when he finally does, his tone's much more conciliatory. Apologetic, even.

'I'm sorry, look, I know that sounded a bit harsh. Must be this bloody brandy. They only had the cooking variety.' He pauses. I can hear his fingers drumming on the telephone.

Then he clears his throat and goes on: 'Do you know who I saw the other day?'

'No.'

'Guess.'

'Gandhi? The Prince of Wales? Gracie Fields?'

'William.' It's meant to sound casual, but I'm not deceived for an instant. He's still a hopeless actor. I'm astonished he hasn't realized it by now.

'Where?'

'In West Ham.'

'*William*? In *West Ham*?'

'I know. I thought it was a bit funny, too.'

'What was he doing?'

'Coming out of the station, just as I was going in.'

'No, I mean, why was he there?'

'Haven't a clue. He cut me dead.'

'He was probably looking for a sailor. And mortified that you'd spotted him doing it.'

It may well be true, but it's a cheap gibe, nonetheless. Christopher laughs. I laugh back. We're still as far apart as ever, but the no-man's-land between us is suddenly less hostile. There's a palpable slackening of the barbed wire. Why does it take sneering at someone else to have that effect?

Sometimes I think being human is irredeemably unpleasant.

'Maybe he was worried I'd run off and tell Barrett,' says Christopher.

'I doubt it. They've split up.'

'Oh, I didn't know –'

'Yes. It must have been, oh, a good couple of months ago now. Barrett left. Just couldn't stand the temperaments any more.'

'Ah, well, that might account for it then. Sexual frustration.'

It hovers awkwardly between a joke and an observation. Your *turn to laugh at* my *snideness, if you want.*

I resist the temptation. 'He seems to have taken it rather badly,' I say. 'Become a bit of a recluse. We invited him over to dinner a couple of times, but he always said no. So . . .'

'You haven't seen much of him, then?' he asks eagerly, as if the answer really matters to him. Could he be secretly jealous of my friendship with William?

'No,' I say. 'We haven't seen him at all. I suspect *Mr. Ribbon's Holiday* may still rankle a bit. He thinks I'm to blame for what happened. The *still-birth of his film career*, as he puts it.'

'Ah.' Christopher sounds relieved.

'Why?'

'It's just . . . It occurred to me . . . You might have mentioned, you know . . .'

'What? – what we're doing, you mean?'

'Yes.'

'Well, I might have, but I didn't have the chance. And even if I had, I can't imagine he'd have been terribly interested. Certainly not interested enough to go and take a look at the docks himself, if that's what you were thinking.'

'No, no, you're right.'

It's too hasty: a tortoise ducking back into its shell. And all at once it finally hits me what's bothering him: the fear that I might have really wanted to do this as fiction rather than documentary, and started talking to actors behind his back. I'm so outraged that, tired as I am, I feel I can't just let it pass. I'll have to have it out with him.

'Look, Christopher –' I begin.

But at that moment Nicky emerges dramatically from the bathroom, draped in a towel, her pink shoulders fringed with foam. She positions herself directly in front of me, and – when she can see she's got my attention – lets the towel drop to the floor.

'What?' says Christopher.

Nicky watches me steadily, but she doesn't smile. This isn't coquettishness: it never is, with Nicky. It's a straightforward challenge: him, or me?

I hesitate less than a second. 'I'm sorry,' I say into the 'phone. 'I've got to go.'

'But, hang on a second, what am I going to tell Clumber?' he says, breathy with panic.

'Tell him about the circulation idea. See what he thinks. I'll ring you tomorrow night, all right?'

I'll have it out with him another time.

It takes us ten minutes or so to find the right vantage-point. It's K.-M. who finally spots it: the entrance to a builder's yard in a side-street, fifty feet or so from where it intersects with Albert Road. When you stand with your back to it, the two terraces of houses meet at an oblique angle in the top right-hand corner of your field of view, making a satisfyingly geometrical frame for the torrent of men pouring towards the docks. Above the dark line of the roofs there's a ragged scarlet-and-gold bruise where the rising sun is trying to break through the cloud.

K.-M. nods towards it.

'There, you see?'

I nod back. Max is right: he's got the best eye in the business.

I lean against the gate-post, make a square with my fingers, and watch the procession moving in and out of shot: a manager crawling along in a little black car; a trickle of sober-suited permanent staff on bicycles; and the throng of casual labourers trudging past – one or two of them weaving between the others at a faster pace, as if they think getting there early will guarantee them a job.

After a couple of minutes I've seen enough. I scribble a few quick sketches, then turn to K.-M. and say: 'Ready?'

He's scribbling, too, and holds up a finger to tell me to wait. It takes him another minute to finish. What's he seen that I haven't?

We join the crowd, trying to make ourselves as inconspicuous as possible by keeping to the edge of the road. We get two or three odd glances, but most of the men don't seem to notice us at all. Perhaps, with our hats and overcoats and notebooks, they just assume we're a couple of the functionaries who check and weigh and sample cargoes, on the way to work ourselves.

We turn right, and I suddenly find myself in a place that seems to have an odd negative-image familiarity about it. It's a second before I realize why: this is the street where I met Christopher the last time I was here – only we're approaching it from the other end, so that the pub and the shop opposite have swapped sides. As we pass the café, I can't resist peering in through the misted-up window where I saw his face. Some childish part of me half-expects to be amazed again – to see a sign or a miracle. Or a revelation, even, of how to make this film.

Needless to say, I'm disappointed. Apart from Christopher's not being there, it all looks pretty much the same. Just inside the glass sit an elderly couple I've never set eyes on before, who immediately sense my presence and glare up at me. Most of the other tables are empty. The woman stands at the counter, refilling a sugar-bowl. A little girl kneels on the floor next to her, haranguing a marmalade cat. The cat obviously doesn't like it: it cowers under her hand, ears flat against its head, frantically looking round for an escape. As I watch, it manages to twitch out of her grasp and leap towards the door, but she grabs it by the ruff of fur around its neck and presses it down again, wagging a scolding finger in its face.

I'm about to turn away when it suddenly hits me that *this* must be the same child Christopher bounced on his knee two and a half years ago. God, what a sobering thought: something that feels like recent history for me must be *pre*-history for her.

I hear myself saying: 'Your Mr. Einstein's right.'

K.-M. manoeuvres himself next to me. 'Einstein?'

'Time *is* relative. It speeds up as you get older. When we're eighty, if we last that long, the world will be rushing by in a blur.'

'You are Jewish, Henry?'

I spin round to face him.

He smiles. 'This is Jewish science you talk about. It is not true for Aryans, like me. So if –'

'Oh, fuck off,' I say under my breath, laughing.

He takes the optic from his pocket, and squints in through the window. 'You think to film in here?'

I almost say: *I don't know.* But I can't afford to undermine his confidence. It's the director's *job* to know, and if he actually realized just how few of my ideas have survived last night's conversation with Christopher intact, he'd probably get up and leave.

'Let's go,' I say, pulling away abruptly and looking at my watch, 'or we'll be late.'

'Smells good,' says K.-M. morosely, as we rejoin the stream of men. 'We should have breakfast there.'

I shrug. 'Too late now.' But he's right: you learn a lot just from sitting in a place like that, and a plate of sausage, egg and fried bread apiece would have set us up for the day. Why hadn't it even occurred to me that we might go in without Christopher to protect us? I shouldn't need him as an intermediary any more: I've got to start making my own way. I'll never feel I belong here, but at least I can justify my presence now, if people ask. I'm not doing this for Sir Basil, after all: I'm doing it for *them*.

We turn towards the docks. A bad-tempered wind is gusting in from the Thames, throwing angry little handfuls of rain against our faces. It smells of oil and coal-smoke and dirty river. But mixed up in it is a tantalizing hint of something else, that makes me shiver with pleasure. I slowly fill my lungs, trying to identify it. No, not one thing, but two: a kind of warm drowsy sweetness (tobacco, perhaps?), and the hard, exhilarating edge of salt water. We must be at least twenty miles from the sea, but the Atlantic and the Pacific are still sluicing through the ships' bilges. All at once, I feel oddly hungry, and there's a scratched-metal brightness behind my eyes: the shimmer of a tropical horizon.

Damn it: this isn't good. I'm meant to be thinking about working conditions and rates of pay, and the only thing that really excites me is a whiff of *Treasure Island*.

Perhaps Nicky was right, after all: I'm simply not cut out for documentary.

I must concentrate.

The dock gates are already open. A policeman stands in front of them, watching the stream of men pressing past. It seems to gather momentum as it reaches the entrance, as if it's being drawn towards a vortex. Might you be able to suggest that, I wonder, by inserting a shot of draining bath-water?

No. It'd be too tricksy. Too confusing.

'I don't think he likes us very much,' mutters K.-M. suddenly in my ear.

I glance towards him. He's stiff with apprehension, padding along beside me with soft, big-cat steps so quiet you can barely hear them.

'Who?' I say.

He nods towards the policeman, who's spotted us, and is tracking our approach with a puzzled frown.

'He's just never seen us before, and is wondering what we're doing here.'

K.-M. nods, but his eyes are wide and he swallows noisily. For a moment I can't understand why he's so nervous: in the past, he's always struck me as being almost cowishly placid. And then I realize: after everything he went through during his last few weeks in Germany, attracting a policeman's attention must feel rather more dangerous for him than it does for me.

'Don't worry,' I say, taking the letter from my breast pocket. 'I've got this. And if that doesn't work, the worst he can do is tell us we can't come in.'

In fact, though he continues to stare at us, the man shows no sign of saying anything at all. Perhaps it's not his job to challenge people. But rather than chancing it, and risking a bellowed *'Ere, where do you think you're going?* as we pass the gate, I decide to take the initiative myself.

'Morning,' I say.

The policeman nods, still frowning.

'We're doing some research for a film. I've got a letter here from the studio . . .'

He takes it and reads it slowly, silently mouthing the words. When he's finished, he pinches his chin, then starts again. He obviously doesn't know what to make of it. I'm terrified he's going to refer it to a superior – or, worse still, ring British Imperial.

'So,' I say, reaching out my hand for the letter. 'Is that all right? Can we go in?'

He reads it a third time, nibbling his lip. I hold my breath. Then he touches the peak of his helmet, and hands it back to me.

I breathe again. 'Thank you.' My shirt's clammy with sweat. God, how could I have been so irresponsible? If he *had* rung British Imperial, it could easily have cost Cynthia her job. Vowing to be more careful in future, I re-fold the letter – but not quickly enough to stop K.-M. noticing the address at the top.

He laughs softly. 'How did you get that?'

'Trade secret.' I just hope Cynthia doesn't offer him a chocolate the next time he's in the office.

The men are lining up, nine or ten deep, at the edge of a wide cobbled road crazed with railway tracks that runs the length of the dock. Some of the smaller ones – worried, presumably, that they won't be seen otherwise – are frantically trying to butt and push their way to the front. A couple of them are too successful, and spill off the pavement altogether. Instantly an angry voice (I can't see whose) orders them 'back on the stones'.

K.-M. and I hang well back, to make it absolutely clear we're only here as observers – but as the crowd grows, we have to keep shifting our position. It induces the same sense of powerlessness in me that you get from a force of nature: we're just a couple of kids on the beach, retreating before the incoming tide. Eventually, we end up penned in the angle between two buildings, with a swelling sea of cloth caps stretching away in front of us – its surface broken only very occasionally by a non-conformist hat or bare head. There's one figure I find particularly intriguing: a tall, scarecrow-gaunt man of about fifty, wearing a tattered black bowler and a bright-red scarf, who looks as if he'd be more at home in a fairground than a port. While the other men shift and stir around him, he holds himself bolt upright and stares straight ahead, as rigid as a guardsman.

I turn to K.-M. 'You're bigger than I am. Can you see what that chap's gawping at?'

He stands on tiptoe and cranes his neck. 'No. Sorry.'

I poke round, and find an empty crate stuck in the corner behind us. It's just high enough to let me see the other side of the road. A group of bull-shouldered men are huddled in the lee of a giant warehouse, talking and laughing. At first sight, they don't look very different from the people in front of me. But as soon as they begin to move, you see they carry themselves with the ease and arrogance of farmers at a cattle-market. These must be the foremen and gang-masters – the bosses who'll decide who works today, and who doesn't.

I glance back at the scarecrow. What he's looking at, I see now, is the nearest foreman. And what he's trying to do (it seems incredible, but I can't think of another explanation) is hypnotize him, in hope of catching his eye when he turns.

All at once, one of the foremen bows his head, and they all look at their wrists, or reach into their pockets. They must be synchronizing their watches.

I check my own watch: 7.40. Only five minutes to go.

'The action's all going to be over there,' I say, getting down again, and jabbing a finger towards the warehouse. 'We'd better move, pretty sharpish, or we'll miss it.'

We can't fight our way to the front: people would think we were a couple of strangely dressed johnny-come-latelys trying to get an unfair advantage and refuse to let us through. And the building to our left prevents us from going further into the dock and getting round the end of the crowd that way. So we edge slowly back towards the entrance, until eventually we find a place where the dense forest of bodies starts to thin. The men here look glumly at us as we squeeze between them, but they don't try stop us: they're obviously the runts and stragglers, too old or weak or broken-spirited to put up any resistance, and mournfully aware that – barring a miracle – they won't be selected. Among them I recognize the pale jowly face of the man who beat up his daughter the last time I was here.

What was his name? Jimmy – I remember that: like the camera-man on *Markheim*. But what else?

No: it's completely gone. Awful.

As we reach the front, the crowd suddenly goes quiet. There's a palpable change in the atmosphere: a sudden surge in barometric pressure, as if we're about to have a thunderstorm. The hairs on my arm prickle.

I look for the foremen. They've left the shelter of the warehouse and are crossing the road. I feel, for a moment, as if I'm watching a scene from *The Battleship Potemkin*: a confrontation between the people and the forces of tyranny. If the crowd used its superior numbers against them, they'd be completely overwhelmed.

I'm frightened even to clear my throat, in case I somehow snap the tension and set off a burst of gunfire.

Then, all of a sudden, the foremen are yelling: 'Freddie's gang!' 'Barney's gang!' 'Marsom's gang! Four men pro rata on frozen meat!' And the men are eddying towards them in little spurts, spar-rows descending on a crumb: jumping on each others' backs; jostling each other out of the way; frantically waving their registra-tion cards, and shouting: 'Here I am!' 'Here I am, Barney!' 'Over here!'

It's a pitiful sight; but for some reason it's that *Here I am. Here I am* I find most heart-breaking. As if they actually thought Barney (or Freddie, or Marsom) was looking specifically for them: wanted some quality only *they* could bring to the business of shifting crates or sacks or slabs of meat. How could you convey the poignancy of that: men continuing to assert their individual human worth, in a system designed to reduce them to beasts of burden?

The answer is: you couldn't. Not, at least, if you followed

Christopher's plan. No-one would deny that corpuscles are useful. With the help of a good graphic artist, you might be able to make them seem awe-inspiring – even beautiful, in an abstract, geometric kind of way. But the only way of creating *sympathy* for corpuscles, so that the audience actually cared about their fate, would be by anthropomorphizing them: *plucky little Colin Corpuscle and his lisping younger sister Carol*. And that's Disney's territory, not ours.

Men are shouting and swearing at each other now, and here and there a few fights are breaking out: you'll see the sea of people suddenly bubble and part, and catch a surprised *ooph!* and a shocking flash of bright-red blood, before it settles down and closes again. But it's too late to make a difference now: the foremen have chosen their teams, and the successful men have already got their tickets and started to gather into gangs. The rest – including, I notice, Jimmy Whatever-his-name-is and the man in the bowler hat – are trudging slowly back towards the gates. Instinct tells me to follow them, see where they live, start to find the elements of a *story*. But that's wrong, I know: I've got to find a different approach here.

So I turn to K.-M. instead, and say: 'So. Where would you shoot this from?'

He points to the top of a flat-roofed warehouse. 'Or maybe a crane, if we could get the equipment on to it.'

He's right again: from above, you'd be able to see everything. And when the men put their hands up, it would have the effect of a flower suddenly opening. Yes, forget about story: just look for striking images, and hope that – when you've got enough of them – they'll dictate their own relationship to each other.

So that, for the rest of the morning, is what we do, sauntering as unobtrusively as we can from one end of the huge dock to the other, avoiding trains and trolleys and work-gangs, and only making frames with our fingers or using K.-M.'s optic when we're sure no-one's watching us. Even with these restrictions, there's no shortage of likely candidates: the cormorant cranes lined up along the quayside, waiting for food; a shipful of frozen carcasses – transformed by the pollarding of heads and legs into lumpy abstract sculptures – being loaded on to a refrigerated railway wagon; the sweaty 'hatcher' guiding the crane-driver, his upturned face crossed by shadow as the jib swings above him; men who seem to have hooks for hands jabbing and hoisting bags of wool, while in the background a whole army of barrels advances slowly across the cobbles towards them. At the end of three hours we've got a catalogue of fifty or more shots and short sequences: enough for ten minutes of film, if we used them all.

'All right,' I say. 'Good. How about lunch?'

K.-M. nods and pats his stomach.

'Pub? Or do you want to go back to that café?'

He hesitates, debating between grease and beer. It still strikes him as an unaccountable flaw in the national character that there are so few places where you can get both.

'Well, we don't have to decide now,' I say. 'There's a pub almost opposite the café. So we can pop our heads in there – and if we don't like the look of it, just slip across the road.'

But I can't help hoping we *do* like the look of it. After the knuckle-rapping I gave myself this morning, I shouldn't still be uneasy about seeing the woman in the café again (God, what was *her* name? Can't remember that, either), but I am. And the prospect of the alternative – a snug bar with a coal fire, probably, and a warming bottle of stout or barley wine, and no need to talk to anyone except K.-M. – is irresistibly seductive.

It takes us twenty minutes to get out of the dock. On the way, we barely speak: K.-M. is still discreetly scouting for new shots with his optic, and I'm going over and over the ones we've already got, trying to find some organic structure for them. *Cranes; crane-driver; hatcher; sacks; men with hooks* . . . No, fine up to that point, but then it just peters out. Start with ship, rather than shore, then: *sacks in the hold; stevedores unloading them; hatcher; men with hooks* . . . That won't work either: the approach is different, but you still end up hitting the same brick wall. Where to go after that?

All right: begin with the call-on – pick out the men selected for the sack-hooking gang and follow them to the quay . . .

No . . .

And so on and so on. God knows how many times I reshuffle the sequences in my head: it must be at least fifty. But try as I may, I can never find an order that gives me that authentic, thrilling tingle in the solar plexus: *Ah, yes, of course! It has to be this way, and no other*. Without a story, there's simply no internal logic connecting them: they're as inert as pictures in a photo album. We could cut them to fit Christopher's poem or commentary, of course, but that wouldn't be much better: they'd merely be a series of illustrations, related not to each other, but to the words they're serving.

The thought of it makes me want to burrow into a dark corner somewhere and go to sleep . . .

'He still doesn't like us, I think,' says K.-M. suddenly.

I look up. We're passing the gate. The same policeman's on duty. He's looking at us suspiciously – not our faces, this time, but our pockets, as though he thinks a foreign sailor's slipped us some precious jewels and we're trying to smuggle them into the country.

'Thank you,' I say. 'Goodbye.'

He doesn't smile or say anything, but draws himself up stiffly and touches his helmet again. There's something about the way the line of his uniform straightens as he does it that suggests a piece of thread being pulled taut by a needle.

I don't know why, but that image sends a throb of excitement through me. An idea's beginning to form, I can feel it: it's as if an ice-dam's suddenly melted, and the river's gurgling back to life. I mustn't look too closely, or it may freeze up again: all I can do is avert my gaze, and let it reveal itself when it's ready. But it's good to know it's there.

There's a little crowd of five or six people gathered in the road in front of the Rising Sun. Most of them I've never seen before, but there are two figures I recognize: the scarecrow-man in the bowler hat, and the little girl we saw in the café this morning. They're all staring into a narrow alley running between the pub and the next house. As we approach them, the little girl glances towards us. Her face is blotched and stained with slug-trails of snot. K.-M. stops and looks at her through his optic. As conscious of the attention as any actress, she responds by sobbing, and thrusting her fists into her eyes, as if she's trying to grind the tears back in.

'What's the matter?' I ask her.

She shakes her head, and starts to wail.

The scarecrow says: 'Lost 'er cat, ain't she? 'E's only gone and got 'i'self stuck in there, and now 'e can't get out again.'

I peer into the alley. About five yards in, a young man in a battered felt hat and a long scarf is kneeling on the ground with his back to us. He's holding the hindquarters of the cat, and trying to pull the rest of it out through what looks like a broken ventilator grille. But it's jammed fast, and every tug provokes a new storm of howls and hisses from the cat, and a chorus of sympathetic *ooohs* from the crowd.

'Hm,' says K.-M., as if he's pondering the problem. He glances at me, eyebrow raised: *Why don't we do something?*

I'd like to, but I don't want to look as if I'm meddling. And why, anyway, should we assume that our efforts would be any more successful than the other chap's?

'My cat-extricating experience is pretty limited,' I say.

'Well, mine isn't,' says K.-M., to my surprise. 'Let me have a look.'

He swaggers into the alley, and squats down next to the young man. I can't hear what either of them's saying, but I can tell from K.-M.'s nods that the young man's explaining what's happened.

The little girl starts to cry again, with big noisy sobs that convulse her whole body. Perhaps she reasons that if two men are needed to deal with it, it must be a bigger problem than she'd thought. A plump woman in a flour-spattered green dress reaches down and tousles her hair:

'There, love, it's all right. Don't you take on so.'

God, I wish I could film this. There's something so touching about it: men and women worn down to the bare threads by poverty and unemployment, who've still got enough human feeling to be concerned for a child and her pet cat. *That*'s what you show the middle classes, Christopher, if you want to change their minds.

The cat-rescuers have agreed a new strategy: K.-M. tries to widen the opening, while the young man gingerly works the animal from side to side, hoping to ease it through. I move to get a better view, and frame a little sequence: the two figures hunched together; then a close-up of their gentle, patient fingers. In my head, a commentary voice says: *It is easier for a camel to go through the eye of a needle than for a rich man to enter into the kingdom of God.*

There: *needle* again. The new idea's gathering strength: I can almost see it, churning away at the very edge of my vision. Any moment now, and it'll make itself known to me.

There's an *aah!* from the little crowd and the young man scrambles up, clutching a squirming mass of orange fur. Still with his back to us, he holds it out towards K.-M., acknowledging his contribution. K.-M. smiles, and lightly strokes the cat with the back of his fingers.

The young man turns. *God*, I think, *he looks just like William.* And then, with that odd, vertiginous sense that the wall between two worlds has suddenly crumbled: *It is William.*

He catches sight of me at the same moment and instantly looks away again, nearly colliding with K.-M. Then he realizes it's too late, and turns back with a shamefaced grin: *All right, it's a fair cop, guv.*

I've seen him angry before, upset, even apologetic – but never sheepish. I can only assume that there must be some truth in the nasty little crack I made to Christopher: he's found a sailor-friend, and doesn't want anyone to know about it.

He emerges from the alley, avoiding my gaze, and hands the cat back to the girl. It's reluctant to go to her: it *meows*, and struggles in her arms, and she's too preoccupied with trying to hold on to it to acknowledge William, or say *thank you*. But he doesn't go unrecognized: the man in the bowler pats his shoulder, muttering, 'Well done, mate,' and the rest of the people murmur their approval as they shuffle away. Something in their manner puzzles me: a kind of friendly, taking-it-for-granted casualness that suggests familiarity and respect – which doesn't seem quite to fit with the sailor-friend theory.

He waits till they've gone, then turns to me: 'Hello, Henry.' He sounds weary and resigned: a prisoner who's just been found guilty and is waiting to hear his sentence.

'Good God,' says K.-M., standing just behind him. 'You know each other?'

'We were at university together,' I say. 'Heavens! Just what is the allure of this place for old Cantabrigians? First I meet Christopher here, and now you.'

'It must be its uncanny resemblance to the backs at King's. All the *jeunesse dorée* drifting past in punts.'

K.-M. laughs admiringly: this is the drawling irony he likes to think is typically English. But I can tell William's heart isn't in it: his smile's too quick, his eyes too uncertain. He's trying to reprise a rôle he's no longer comfortable with.

'No, really,' I say. 'What are you doing here?'

He hesitates – then, forcing himself to meet my gaze, says: 'I'm helping to run a soup kitchen.'

It sounds too matter-of-fact to be a joke – but then, unlike Christopher, he's a very good actor.

'Are you pulling my leg?'

He shakes his head.

'I think this is wonderful,' says K.-M. 'You are a very kind man.' To my astonishment, he seems close to crying.

'*Why?*' I ask.

'People are hungry.'

'No, I know, but . . .'

'I'm working with a priest –'

'A *priest?*'

He nods. 'A saint. Called Father Noyce.'

'I see.'

I don't, of course: I'm hopelessly confused. A seismic shift has occurred in the earth's crust, but I can't make sense of the changed landscape it's produced. All I'm aware of is a chaos of competing thoughts: *William's no longer an actor. He's gone back to the Church. He'll be here while we're filming. He and Christopher are a problem. He and my cameraman – to judge by the flush on K.-M.'s cheek and the unmistakable hunger in his eyes – may turn out to be another problem. God –*

And then, all at once, I'm not aware of them any more. The cat suddenly breaks free of the little girl again, and as I watch her running down the street after it – *Come back, Tiger! Come back!* – my new idea for the film finally crystallizes in my head, and everything else is swept out of the way.

'Here we are,' says the cabby. He stops in front of a big painted sign

253

saying 'Cholmley Gardens'. Beyond it stretches a long low block of flats.

'Thank you.' I give him five bob and tell him to keep the change. Perhaps if I'm generous the gods will look kindly on me tonight.

'You're a gentleman,' he mumbles, then drives off quickly before I have a chance to change my mind.

'So,' I say, joining Nicky on the pavement. 'Is this the sort of place you'd expect him to live?'

She smiles and shakes her head. 'But then I never know quite what to expect with Max.'

It's a fairly new building, but resolutely old-fashioned, with beef-red brick walls, and Tudorish mullioned windows. There's no central hall, so it takes us a few minutes to find the right staircase. By the time we struggle up to the top floor, we're both a bit sweaty and breathless. I wait a moment or two before ringing the bell: I need to be at my best for this.

Max opens the door himself. I'd always thought he might let his hair down a bit at home, so I was all ready for tartan slippers or a canary-yellow cardigan. Instead, he's wearing a sober grey suit and a maroon tie. More like an undertaker than a film director.

'Henry. Miss Weedon. Come in.'

The flat's a surprise, too. No piles of papers; no dark corners fuggy with cigar smoke; no leather-bound volumes of erotica poking out from under chairs: the whole place is as bland and anonymous as his office, with pale nondescript wallpaper and flaw-less modern furniture. He leads us through into a sitting-room that might be a Heal's show-room, full of glass and pale oak and geo-metric blocks of colour: plain green curtains, and rust-red cushions, and a bright red-and-yellow abstract painting on the wall. A small woman is sitting in an arm-chair by the empty fireplace. She smiles and gets up when she sees us.

'This is my wife, Vera,' says Max.

'How do you do?'

'How do you do?' Her voice is as neutral and backgroundless as the décor. 'Please, won't you sit down?'

We settle ourselves on a pristine sofa that still smells faintly of the shop.

'Sherry?' says Max.

'Thanks.'

He opens the bottom half of a fake Hepplewhite cabinet-bookcase, takes out a bottle of Tio Pepe and pours us a thimbleful apiece.

'Well, cheers.'

'Cheers.'

I'm beginning to think I've made a mistake. The reason he's never invited me here before isn't that he was trying to conceal a life of secret depravity, but simply that he feels it doesn't show him to best advantage. His natural element is the studio: away from sets and actors and cameras, he's a beached seal. And he's broken with that tradition now not so he can humiliate me in the privacy of his own Bluebeard's Castle, but as a rite of passage, to mark our transition from colleagues to friends. Far from being apprehensive, I should feel honoured.

He chats affably with Nicky, while I exchange platitudes with his wife: *beautiful weather; nice flat; convenient position; yes, isn't it?* She's pleasant enough, but not really there. She probably thinks the same about me. She and Max seem a strangely ill-assorted couple: she's half his size, with tiny delicate bones and a wan little mannequin's face too perfect to be pretty. I can't help imagining them in bed together: his belly swagging saddle-like over her slim waist, and squeezing the breath out of her.

After a few minutes, she excuses herself and goes out to the kitchen. Max is recounting an anecdote about Val Farrar, which has Nicky weeping with laughter. I don't want to butt in, so I get up and stroll over to the window. In the middle of the grounds is a tennis-court, where a couple of young women are getting in one last match in the gold-dust glow of the setting sun. As I look down at them, a cold draught seems to touch my skin. I'd come here armoured against criticism, and this is what I find instead: a glimpse of an enchanted England of secret gardens and wholesome girls and long summer evenings that could have been mine, if I'd stayed at British Imperial. No, an England that *was* mine: its fuzzy radiance reaches far back into the past, touching Nicky and Clapham Common and Cambridge and my parents with a kind of numinous brilliance. Why the hell am I cutting myself off from it? Why am I cutting

Nicky off from it? It's her world, after all; and who knows whether she can really be happy – whether our marriage can survive, even – in any other setting?

'Dinner's ready,' says Vera Maxted behind me.

There's a provincial-hotel feel to the dining-room: the table covered with a starched white cloth, and napkins folded into neat little pyramids, and rolls in a basket, and fluted curls of butter. But my first whiff of the soup is enough to tell me that the meal's going to be in a different class altogether. It's served by a maid in a prim uniform that looks as new as everything else, but I can't believe she cooked it. I glance across at Vera Maxted, who's looking inquiringly at Max. He puts his spoon to his lips, then nods slowly. She smiles, and looks away again. Perhaps *that*'s why he married her: for her culinary skill. There'd be a certain logic to it, for a *gourmand* like him: whatever else may fade and fail, *haute cuisine*'s a pleasure you can pretty much always depend on.

For an hour or so, as we progress through perfectly grilled lamb chops and salad and mint-speckled new potatoes and a buttery *tarte tatin*, the conversation continues in the same anodyne vein. By the time the maid comes in to clear away our pudding plates, I'm convinced that I really must have made a mistake. If Max was going to attack me, he'd have done it before now – so I can dismantle the defences in my head and start to relax. Politeness only demands that we stay another forty minutes or so, and then we can leave without a stain on our characters.

And then, as the girl closes the door behind her, Max leans across to Nicky and says: 'Just give Henry's pockets a pat, will you, Miss Weedon?'

It's such a violent change of tack that for a moment she's completely bewildered. '*What*?'

'See if there are any spoons in there. I always knew it'd be a bit chancy, letting him in here. With his passion for pilfering things.'

She darts a startled glance in my direction.

'He means you,' I say.

'Oh, oh, I see –'

'Not *just* her. I gather you're planning to take my cameraman now, as well.'

He's starting his third glass of burgundy. His cheeks are beginning to look flushed, and one of his gleamy eyes is a bit bloodshot.

'I'm only borrowing him, Max. You can have him back again.'

'Oh, really? Can I have Miss Weedon back again, too?'

Nicky laughs. Vera gives Max a *behave yourself* stare. I suddenly wonder if she imagined they might have been having an affair before I came along.

'That's up to Miss Weedon,' I say.

'I should be careful, Henry. You could say something you'll regret. I mean, given the choice, she might just decide that coming to the *Atlas* première with me next week and seeing all the stars was a more tempting prospect than sitting at home all day, waiting for you to stumble in with *The News of the Slums*. Eh, Miss Weedon?'

Nicky's non-plussed. She looks to me for guidance, smiling uncertainly, all gums and lips. I wish that smile didn't embarrass me.

The maid brings the cheese in. I wait till she's gone again, then say: 'Actually, the slums are pretty interesting. You'd be surprised.'

'I would. Very surprised indeed.' His voice is dangerously quiet, and he isn't smiling. I can feel a palpable drop in the temperature, as if someone's just opened the door of a refrigerator.

While I'm still trying to decide how to respond – laugh? let it go? stand my ground? – Vera Maxted turns to Nicky and says brightly: 'Talking of the première, I was hoping I might consult you about what I ought to wear?'

Nicky blushes with surprise. 'Really? Well, I'm not that much of an expert, I'm afraid –'

'More than I am, I'm sure. I've got the dress. It's just a matter of picking the right jewellery to go with it.'

'Well, I'd be happy to have a look, if –'

'Would you? That's very kind.' She glances quickly at Max, then back at Nicky. 'I don't know about you, but I'm not very fond of cheese. So maybe we could slip out now and leave the gentlemen to their Cheddar?'

Nicky giggles. 'Like Victorian ladies. Yes, yes, of course.'

And they're gone. It was effortlessly done. Either Max must have given her a pre-arranged signal, or she's an old hand at getting the women and children into the boats before the ship goes down.

257

Max refills our glasses, making odd little huffing sounds as he ponderously trickles the wine. I know he's trying to intimidate me – but for some reason I don't feel intimidated at all. In fact, I'm rather excited.

As he puts down the bottle again, I say: 'I know you think what I'm doing's perverse. You probably think it's priggish, too. But I honestly believe it's an important project. And I won't be wasting everything I've learned from you. I'll be incorporating it – *all* of it. Making words and pictures work against each other. Finding ways to thread a human story through the facts . . .'

He holds up his hand to stop me – shaking his head so hard his double chin wobbles. However much he may disapprove of my apostasy, he obviously doesn't want to debate it tonight. He takes a sip of wine, then reaches into his breast pocket and takes out a thick envelope.

'There,' he says, slapping it down in front of me.

Inside are a dozen or so photographs. For a fraction of a second, I can't make head or tail of them: they just appear to show a man and a woman talking in a garden. Then I realize who the man and the woman are: me and Irma Brücke.

'How the . . . *fuck* did you get these?'

He shrugs. He seems totally unrepentant. 'I paid a man to take them. I thought it'd be interesting to see what your Miss Mayer looked like.'

I can't imagine what he's doing. Is going to try to *blackmail* me? Threaten to show them to Nicky if I don't change my mind?

He sweeps the pictures up suddenly and drops them back in his pocket. 'Just don't forget,' he says, fingering the bulge they make in his coat. '*That*'s what you came into this business for.'

XVIII

It made me nervy, hanging around the hotel room waiting for a phone-call from Hode that I knew wasn't going to come at that hour in the morning, so I got to the National Film Theatre stupidly early. I picked up my ticket, then bought myself a coffee – which was a mistake, because I was already zinging with adrenalin so much I couldn't keep still. Then I hung around the foyer, looking at all the faces of the other people, wondering if one of them was Arkwright. I'd never even seen a picture of him, but for some reason I still felt pretty sure I'd know him. It was just as well I didn't spot any likely contenders, because I'd have probably hit them.

When they announced "Finding the Human Thread: the Evolution of Henry Whitaker," I hurried to the door, hoping to beat the crowd. But there wasn't a crowd – in fact, I was the only person there. I went in, settled myself in an end-of-the-row seat near the back, and tried to keep my legs from jittering too much while I waited. I was just beginning to wonder if I'd somehow got the wrong cinema when an old man with a walking-stick came in. He looked round, noticed me, and mumbled something about *Is this the right place for the Henry Whitaker thing?* I nodded, and said: *I hope so.* I don't think he heard me, but he saw the nod. He smiled back, then sat down at the other end of the row I was in, hooking his stick over the seat in front. It seemed strange for him to sit so close to me, when he had the whole theater to choose from. But then I guessed maybe he was lonely and it gave him a spuri-ous sense of human contact. Either that, or he was just too tired to hobble any further.

A slow trickle of people followed him. Except for a group of five studenty-looking kids who strutted straight to the front, laughing and jostling each other, they were mostly elderly, and seemed weirdly diffi-dent – talking in whispers, and settling themselves in out-of-the-way seats, like mourners at a funeral trying not to get in the family's hair.

The whole atmosphere, in fact, was more crematorium than movie theater – right down to the curtain and the lectern at the front.

As they closed the doors, I did a quick head-count: thirty-two. It made me a bit nervous: it's hard to hide in a crowd that small. But it was also a relief, because I'd been half-expecting to find myself surrounded by a mob of Whitaker fans howling for my blood. Obviously Arkwright's efforts to interest the world in England's quiet genius and his bitch daughter hadn't been very successful.

A gray-haired guy in a sport jacket and an open-necked shirt walked out in front of the screen. He wasn't my idea of Arkwright – too old, and not weaselly enough – but he was carrying a folder, so I figured it must be him. At least he didn't seem too intimidating: he was craning his neck and blinking at us, as if he weren't used to the lights, and when he pulled his notes out his hand was shaking visibly. If it came to a fight, it didn't look like I'd have too much trouble with him.

It took him a few seconds of tapping the microphone and glancing imploringly up at the projection-box to get the PA system working. Then he cleared his throat and said: *Good afternoon, and welcome to this special screening of three films by Henry Whitaker.*

In that split second I think I knew, from his hang-dog expression, what was coming next.

As some of the er . . . sharper-eyed among you may have noticed already, I'm not Alan Arkwright. Alan, unfortunately, isn't very well at the moment, and won't be able to be with us today. So you're stuck with me, I'm afraid. My name's Dave Burton, and I work in the archive here. I can't claim to be a Henry Whitaker expert like Alan, but I have managed to pull out a few interesting facts . . .

I felt a kind of earthquake of rage. The guy had eluded me again. Maybe he really was sick, but I doubted it. More likely, his secretary had told him I was in the country, and – knowing this was the one place I could actually get at him – he decided not to turn up. Either way, I wasn't going to stand for it. I grabbed my coat and my bag and started to leave.

Then I saw the old man, and realized I'd have to ask him to move. And suddenly, every therapist I ever met was whispering in my ear: *Why are you behaving like an angry child?*

The answer, of course, is something I've spent most of the last thirty years trying to avoid. But standing there now, in a cinema where they were about to show three of Henry Whitaker's films, it was inescapable: *Because my father still makes me feel just as I did when I was four. All the same symptoms are there: the sense that someone stronger than I am has got me cornered, and squeezed the breath out of me, and is scraping a comb across my skin.*

I forced myself to sit down again. I'd missed a lot of what the gray-haired guy was saying, but I caught the tail-end of his introduction to the first film. It was called *Mr. Ribbon's Holiday*. It was one of the few surviving quota quickies that Henry Whitaker made during his apprentice years at British Imperial Pictures. Did everyone know what quota quickies were? Well, for the benefit of any philistines who *didn't*, snigger snigger: they were short, cheap films that cinemas had to show alongside Hollywood movies to fulfill the legal requirement for a percentage of every program to be British. The quality was pretty much what you'd expect from a picture made in six days on a shoestring budget. Its main interest for a modern audience was the few early glimpses it gave of Whitaker's unusual sensitivity, and the clues it offered to his future career – as we'd see when we came to the second film, where he revisited some of the same material in a different form.

I guess that – having made the more or less conscious decision as a kid that I wanted to know as little about my father's life as possible – I should have realized I'd be hearing a lot of stuff that was unfamiliar to me. But all of this was *so* new that I couldn't link it up with the man I remembered at all. For a wild moment, I found myself wondering whether the guy Burton had been talking about actually *was* the man I remembered: maybe there'd been another film-maker called Henry Whitaker, and Arkwright had somehow confused them, and I'd been answering questions about the wrong person all along, hence the misunderstandings . . . Then reason kicked in: *Another man of the same name who knew Arthur Maxted? Who made documentaries? Who married a woman he met in a displaced-persons camp in Germany?* No: this wasn't mistaken identity, it was escapology – the dour sadistic loser wriggling out of his chains before my eyes and reappearing as a bright-eyed young director of *unusual sensitivity*.

261

Burton sat down. The house lights dimmed. The curtain parted. I was suddenly terrified that the silence and the blank gray screen were going to fill with something so overwhelming that I'd cry out or faint. Then I saw that unmistakable dots-in-front-of-your-eyes flicker, and heard the click and hiss of the sound-track, and breathed again. This was O.K.: old-movie-land. Nothing to do with me at all. When the title – *Mr. Ribbon's Holiday*, in thick white letters – wobbled up, accompanied by a distorted fanfare, I was so relieved I started to laugh.

And I wasn't alone. It really *is* a pretty funny movie – though clearly it wasn't meant to be. Mr. Ribbon (an astonishingly camp performance from a gone-to-seed matinée idol called Hugh O'Donnell) is a mild-mannered English butler, working for some big industrialist in an unnamed eastern-European country. One evening he overhears his employer's sicko son conspiring with an anarchist – at least, I assume he's meant to be an anarchist: he has crazed Rasputin eyes, and an obviously false beard – to assassinate the boy's father and make it look like the popular young heir to the throne, Crown Prince Rudolf, did it. That way, the kid – whose dad is threatening to disown him if he doesn't stop holding wild parties and abusing the servants – will inherit the family fortune, and the liberal, pro-British Rudolf will be discredited, destabilizing the fragile political situation and pushing the country into chaos.

Ribbon's horrified, of course, and slumps in a chair, gasping like a fish, to prove it. Realizing that not only a man's life is at stake but also *British interests*, he tries to call the British embassy, but the conspirators discover him, and he has to go on the run. The continuity's so bad – one minute he's in a car, the next he's hiding in the back of a truck – that you have no idea where he's going, but he ends up getting to a port and stowing away on a liner. Pretty much the only scene that wasn't shot in the studio is the one showing the ship's arrival in London. You're looking down a little street of terraced houses towards the river, and suddenly this huge black shape drifts silently into view, towering above the roofline and blocking out the light. You get a brief glimpse of Mr. Ribbon peering through a fake porthole with a yearning expression. Then, without warning, he's on shore, being welcomed in one of the little terraced houses by a family of warm-hearted cockneys. The end. The *end*? Yup: credits.

I was still laughing. I'd come through. All my fears of being swept away by emotion were groundless. The shot of the ship gliding in had been good, but anyone could have done that – and otherwise it was a lousy film. I looked round at the other people in the audience. They didn't seem impressed, either: they were twitching and coughing, or glancing surreptitiously at their watches. My version of my father was still intact.

Then Burton bobbed up again to introduce the next film: a documentary, this one, called *The Call-On*. It was the first of a series Henry Whitaker made in the 1930s with his Cambridge friend Christopher Morton Hunt. They were funded by an industrialist called Charles Clumber, who'd made a fortune in detergent and wanted to spend some of it helping "the different classes of our nation to know and understand one another." At his best, said Burton – shifting responsibility for what he was saying by making it obvious he was reading it from a book – "Whitaker was the supreme lyricist of English documentary. In his mature work – particularly *Autumn Poppies* and *Better than Magic*, which showed the same community in two very different moods – he elevated the form to the dignity and complexity of art."

God, I thought, bracing myself, *that's quite an endorsement. Maybe this time Houdini will manage to break free.*

For the first couple of minutes I was fine. The photography was a whole lot better, no question: there were some beautiful shots of ships and cranes and warehouses silhouetted against the dawn, and an atmospheric sequence showing a whole crowd of men leaving their homes and surging into the docks in search of work. And it was also edited properly, so that you got the sense the director knew where he was going, and how he was going to get there. But there was something so remote about the sooty back-streets, and the swarm of ant-like figures in their cloth caps, that you might as well have been watching a natural-history film, or images sent back from the surface of Mars. And the commentary was from another world, too: a long free-verse poem, full of metaphors about circulation (the dockers are *corpuscles*; trade is the *life-blood of the nation*, etc.), and declaimed in one of those impossibly clipped thirties English voices that sound like self-parody today. When it told us that *the min are leaving their families, hoping to earn a crust of brid by the swit of their brows,* I thought: O.K., I'm safe.

But then, without warning, there's an abrupt change of scene: we break from the four dockers we've been following and find ourselves inside one of the houses, looking at a little girl playing with her cat. The commentary stops: all we hear is a few simple notes on the violin, and the girl saying *Don't you run away again, Tiger. Please please please.*

The mood is so different – we're eavesdropping on a tiny personal drama, rather than listening to a public lecture – that at first I wondered if it might just be the result of clumsy cutting, like the jump from car to truck in *Mr. Ribbon's Holiday*. But in that case, you'd expect the sound-track to be ragged, and it isn't: it's exactly synchronized. And there's a kind of mini-short-story perfection about the whole scene that makes you think it's intentional: at the end of fifteen seconds or so, the cat suddenly jumps up and makes a dash for the door, with the child running after it and calling its name. Immediately afterwards the film cuts back to the docks, and – with military precision – the commentary starts again. You're not sure what the purpose of showing you the girl-and-cat episode was, but you know there had to have been one. It lingers puzzlingly at the edge of your mind, like the echo of a dream that won't quite go away, though you've no idea why.

I was starting to feel uneasy. Just as I'd managed to convince myself that I was comfortably out of reach, Daddy had stretched across the divide separating us and touched me. I couldn't understand the appearance of the little girl – but I couldn't simply dismiss it as predictable or irrelevant or inept, either. I wanted to see her again, and find out what happened to her and her cat. And at the same time, I *didn't* want to, because I was frightened of the power she had – the power *my father* had – to surprise me, and draw me into her story.

The next section of the film shows the four men we've already met being selected for work at the *call-on* – an impressive set-piece, this, I have to admit, shot from above, like a crowd scene from Eistenstein – and going to their various jobs unloading tea, wool, wine and frozen meat. You've almost forgotten about the little girl – or concluded that she's just an unaccountable anomaly – when suddenly she's there again, standing at the entrance to an alley and asking a scrawny-looking man in a bowler hat whether he's seen the cat. He shakes his head, and she hurries on down the alley, and disappears round the corner at the end.

Six times you see her, in all: peering into a Dickensian court, or talking to a woman outside a shop, or searching a soup kitchen in a church – where, for an instant, the two strands of the story meet, as the camera moves up from a pair of shoes she sees under the table and you discover that they belong to a floppy young man in a Fair Isle sweater and a long scarf who's serving some of the rejects from the call-on. Her scenes develop a kind of rhythm: you start to be able to anticipate them, like the return of a theme in a piece of music – and you get the same sense of satisfaction when they appear. By the end, you're quite desperate for her to find Tiger. There's an awful moment, as the commentary finishes and the music sweeps towards a climax, when you think she isn't going to. And then, just at the last moment, the camera pans away from our four dockers tramping homewards to the little girl, squatting on the ground in the shadow of a crane, and cradling the cat in her arms. Why it's so effective I still haven't figured out: it somehow makes you feel that all the human effort you've witnessed – not just hers, but the men's, as well – wasn't in vain. The instant I saw it – I couldn't help myself – I started to sob.

I was so embarrassed, I stayed in my seat, pretending to read the program, as the lights came up and people filed out for their interval coffee and cookies. After a minute or so, I thought I'd calmed down enough to follow them. But just as I reached the foyer, I noticed the old man with the stick, standing by himself close to the door. I tried to edge past him, but he sensed my approach and turned towards me. He'd been crying, too. And he could obviously tell that I had, because he immediately gave me that kind of *I know how you feel* smile you see at funerals. Tears jabbed my eyes again, and I had to bite my lip.

"What was it?" he said. "The little girl and the cat?"

I nodded.

"Yes," he said. "He was a clever chap, old Whitaker. Knew how to play on the heart-strings."

"So it had the same effect on you, did it?" I asked.

265

I was just trying to be friendly, but for some reason the question seemed to make him uncomfortable.

He went pink, and looked away. "Well, not so much this time," he said. "I'd seen it before, you see. Knew what was coming."

I wanted to know *where* he'd seen it before, of course, but before I could ask him he said *would I like a coffee?* and I said *yes, but I could get it myself*, and he said *no, wait here*, and hobbled off to buy it. I doubted he'd actually be able to carry a full cup, but he seemed so pleased that I didn't have the heart to refuse: he was lonely, I guess, and knew that it would at least guarantee him ten minutes of human company. And I *might* be able to find out who he was, and whether he knew something about my father.

"Here we are," he said. He'd dangled his stick over his wrist and was holding the saucer in both hands, but he'd still managed to spill half the coffee into it. "Sorry about the . . ."

"That's O.K. Aren't you having one?"

He shook his head. "Better not, if I'm going to sit through another film, I'm afraid. I've reached that sort of age, you know." He smiled. "Anyway," – he said, hastily changing the subject – "it's an awful pity young Arkwright isn't here. He'd have been able –"

"Why *isn't* he here? Do you know?"

"Well, he's ill, isn't he, poor chap?" he said brusquely. "The other fellow told us. I just wish he'd been equally well informed about Henry Whitaker."

I said it wasn't really Dave Burton's fault, if he'd had to stand in at the last moment. The old guy shook his head again, and went into a long spiel about how anyone remotely acquainted with Whitaker's work would have known that the little girl and the cat was *the great man's big idea* for *The Call-On* – and one that he continued to use, in one form or another, in his later documentaries. If they hadn't got anyone else sufficiently *au fait* to be able to point even *that* out, then they should have asked *him* to do it instead.

Very interesting, I said, oh-so-casual. And how did *he* know about it? Had he worked with Whitaker? Or known him personally?

"I was a friend of a friend," he said quickly. "A dear friend of a dear friend, you might say."

Ah, now you're talking, I thought. I shot him what I hoped was a butter-wouldn't-melt-in-my-mouth smile and said: "Am I allowed to know who, or –"

"I'm afraid I'm going to have to sit down," he said abruptly. He was starting to sway, and had to steady himself with his stick. I found us a couple of empty seats against the wall, and helped him into one of them. He thanked me, then slumped back with a sigh, fluttering his eyes. I thought I'd better give him a moment to recover before repeating my question. But once again he beat me to the draw.

"And what, may I ask," he said, sitting up suddenly, "is your interest in this, exactly?"

I was so surprised I couldn't think of an answer. I blushed and mumbled *Mm, well* a couple of times, then looked round desperately for inspiration and spotted the open door to the cinema. "Just that, I suppose," I said, hitching a ride towards it with my thumb. "I find it all fascinating."

"But I couldn't help noticing," he said, "that you didn't ask what the big idea was. Only how I knew about it."

I remember thinking: *A guy as old and frail as he was shouldn't be this smart.*

"Maybe I find the man more intriguing than his work," I said. But it sounded really tacky. I could tell he wasn't convinced: he didn't even bother to say anything, but just went on X-raying me with his eyes.

I didn't know what to do. His prickliness when I'd asked him about Arkwright made me think they might well be friends, which meant it would be pretty stupid to take him into my confidence. But once I'd committed myself to a lie, there'd be no way I could retreat from it later on.

I almost turned round and walked away. Then I thought: *That wouldn't just be rude, it'd be self-destructive*, because I'd never have this opportunity again.

I pulled out the other chair, and sat down. "I'm Henry Whitaker's daughter," I said.

You'd think he'd heard a car back-firing or something. He twitched and blinked involuntarily. "Are you, indeed?"

I suddenly decided I had nothing to lose by being honest: if it turned out he and Arkwright were friends, he must have a negative opinion of me already, so the worst that could happen was that I'd just end up confirming it. And there was a chance, if I played my cards right, that I might convince him the negative opinion was *wrong* and shift the balance of power a teeny bit in my favour. So I told him the facts, but in a more-in-sorrow-than-in-anger kind of a way. All I said about Arkwright was that I felt he was misrepresenting me and my mother – and that since he hadn't replied to my last e-mails, I'd come over hoping to see him in person, but hadn't had much luck so far.

Come over from where? asked the old man. I told him. He nodded and smiled.

"Well," he said, "I can't say I'm awfully surprised. He's a knowledge-able chap, of course, and tremendously *keen*: you really can't fault him on that. Always makes me think of an eager young dog, bounding about all over the place and sticking his cold wet nose into every-thing. But he does have rather decided views, and he isn't frightfully enthusiastic about people who don't quite, you know, share them. He, er . . . I hope you won't mind my saying this, but I can't help thinking *his* Henry Whitaker is just a little bit of a plaster saint . . ."

I felt crazy with relief. No, I said (though careful still to keep my voice down), I didn't mind at all. In fact, I quite agreed with him.

He smiled again: not just a flash of false teeth, this time, but a soft-ening of his whole face. My gamble had paid off, I could tell: he appreciated my openness with him. Far from turning him against me, it had made him feel he could lower his defenses and be a bit more open with *me*.

"I'm Tommy Ryder," he said. He watched me closely as I took his hand. "Means nothing to you, evidently?"

"No – my father and I didn't talk much, I'm afraid."

"I didn't mean that." He drew a little frame round his face with his finger. "I meant *this*."

I shook my head. "Sorry."

"I was an actor. Well, still *am* an actor, every once in a while, when they need an old fusspot to get bumped off after the first fifteen min-utes of a detective show. But in the fifties and sixties, I used to do quite a lot. *Carry Ons*, and *Bridges over this and that*, and the occa-sional bit of kitchen sinkery. That kind of thing."

What could I say? I just shook my head again, and smiled sympa-thetically.

"Ah, well, vanity of vanities, saith the Preacher, all is vanity. You're just too young, I suppose, that's what it is. Frightening thing, the fourth dimension." He gazed past me wistfully, as if he could see Time trashing the place behind my back and knew he was powerless to do anything about it. Then he turned back suddenly. "You probably won't even remember my friend, then."

He meant it to sound like a throwaway line, but his eyes contra-dicted him: I could feel them on me like a limpet.

I laughed, but my heart was thumping in my ears. "O.K.," I said. "Try me."

"His name was William Malpert."

At exactly that moment the PA system huffled: *Please take your seats, as the program will continue in three minutes*. He must have seen from my expression that he had me, though, because he asked: *Do you want to go back in?* with a smile that said he knew the answer already.

"I'd actually rather hear about William Malpert," I said. "But I don't want to stop you, if *you*'d like to –"

"I've seen *Better than Magic* before," he said. "And you could always pick up a copy there" – nodding towards a little table in the corner, where a sad-looking silver-haired lady was selling merchan-dise – "if you wanted one."

"Well, O.K., if you're quite sure . . ."

"No disrespect to your father," he said. "But really, the only reason I came today was to see William. Which I've done. So –"

"Why?" I said. "Was he in *Mr. Ribbon's Holiday*?"

He laughed. "Ah, well, thereby hangs a tale. He was supposed to be. Your father got him a small part as one of the government chaps welcoming Mr. Ribbon home. You know: *Well done, Ribbon. Your timely action has averted war. The nation owes you a great debt of gratitude*. They even went so far as to shoot the scene. But then the picture turned out to be over-length, so they simply cut it out again, and ended with Mr. R's arrival at the docks."

"*Over-length*? It wasn't more than an hour, was it?"

"That's all quota quickies were meant to be. Well, all they were

269

required to be, anyway. And, of course, the assumption was that no-one would choose to sit through a second more than they had to of a film like that, when they could be watching the Hollywood variety instead. So most of the time the law was followed to the absolute letter – didn't matter what you hacked out of a quota quickie, or whether what was left made any sense, just as long as the end result came in at exactly an hour long. Which naturally suited the American studios that were paying for them down to the ground, because it only made their movies look even better in comparison."

"That's outrageous!" I said. "The poor guy! He must've been furious!"

Tommy Ryder laughed again. "Oh, he was at the time, I'm sure. But he ended up actually being quite grateful. His performance was pretty wooden, by all accounts. It wouldn't have done his reputation much good if it had ever been shown. He just wasn't a film actor, that's the truth of it. He needed a live audience. Which is why he came into his own with radio and television."

"So, hold on," I said. "If he wasn't in the movie after all, how come you said you came to see –?"

"Ah, well, that's the irony." He looked round, as if he didn't want anyone else to hear him. The last few stragglers were trooping back into the cinema. He kept his voice low, even so. "He didn't appear in the film he *should* have been in. But strangely enough there was a glimpse of him in the other one."

"What, *The Call-On*?"

"Yes." He was almost whispering now. "The chap in the long scarf at the soup kitchen."

"*Really*?"

He nodded.

"He worked there for a few months, during one of his heroic episodes."

The way he said it, it sounded as if I must know what William Malpert's heroic episodes were. I suddenly felt breathless with panic. It was like snorkeling for the first time: you peer through your mask and realize that beneath the glittery surface there's a whole world of alien creatures, and you don't have the least idea what most of them are, or how they live, or which ones might be dangerous. What made it even worse was that *this* was a world I should have been familiar with. Tommy Ryder, reasonably enough, took it for granted that I knew the basic terms of reference already. Without them, how on earth could I hope to assimilate what he told me?

"Well," I said finally, trying to come across as cool and unfazed. "That'll make an intriguing little footnote for some future film historian."

"Not future," he said, waggling a finger at me. "Young Arkwright's planning to make quite a thing of it in his book. Or so he tells me." He paused, scrunching up his spiders-webby old eyes and squinting at me.

Maybe he saw how confused I was, because after a couple of seconds he said: "Look, tell you what – why don't you come back to my flat? It's only just round the corner. And it'd be easier to explain things there. There are pictures I could show you, and so on."

Maybe I was crazy, after what happened with Herbie Wethered, but I didn't hesitate.

"O.K., thank you, I'd like that."

I did as he suggested, and bought a copy of *Better than Magic* from the sad-faced lady. Then we picked up a cab, and the old guy gave the driver an address in Kennington. On the way there he didn't once look out of the window, or make any comment about where we were going: modern London, evidently, was too scary and depressing for him even to acknowledge it. Instead, he stayed luxuriously in the past, enjoying the (pretty unusual, I imagine) experience of being able to share his reminiscences of William Malpert with someone who actually wanted to hear them. So I learned how William had once reduced Gilbert Harding to tears with one of his famous put-downs; how his appearance at a Royal Command Performance had had the Queen Mother (bless her) *in stitches*; and how – to the astonishment of people who only knew his acerbic public persona – he couldn't hear a Christmas carol without weeping. Though Tommy Ryder never actually said so, it was quite obvious, by the time we arrived, that William had been not just a friend, but the love of his life.

That was something else I should have known, or at least been able to guess: William Malpert was gay.

"You'll have to forgive a bit of a muddle," said the old guy, as we drew up in front of a dingy Victorian building with dirty walls and scabbed paintwork. "It's the curse of the bachelor life, I'm afraid. When you're on your own a good deal, you tend not to make the effort."

He led me through a damp-smelling little hallway into a small one-bedroom apartment on the first floor. The air was clammy and cold and hazy with dust, so you felt more like you were walking into a store-room than a living-room. There were a couple of chairs in front of the gas-fire, and a too-big square table in the middle of the floor, but more or less all you could see otherwise were trunks and boxes crammed into corners or piled up against the wall.

He glanced at me anxiously, trying to gauge my reaction. It must have been pretty obvious, I guess, because after a couple of seconds he said: "I know: it looks as if I've only just moved in."

"Either that, or you're getting ready to move out again."

He giggled, and bent down to light the fire. "Actually, I've been here fifteen years. And have no intention of going anywhere else – unless some kind person offers to whisk me away to the Riviera. There just wasn't enough room, you see, so I never really bothered to unpack. I know where everything is if I need it. Well, almost everything. And from time to time I carry out a cull, to stop my life being taken over by paper. Now. What can I offer you? Tea?"

The thought of the germs and the bugs made me gag. "No, I'm just fine, thanks."

"Right . . . Well, in that case . . ."

He glanced round, didn't see what he was looking for, then nodded to himself, and headed for the bedroom. As he went in, I got a quick glimpse of an unmade bed strewn with dirty clothes. Then the door shut behind him, and I heard muffled grunts as he struggled with something.

"You O.K.?" I called. I didn't want him having a heart attack. "Can I give you a hand?"

"No. Thank you. I'll be out in a moment. Please. Have a seat." He was so wheezy, he had to pause between each word. But he obviously didn't want me to see the mess in there, so I left him to it and sat down by the fire. A cloud of dust blew up from the chair as I hit it. It smelt kind of spicy, and made me sneeze, like snuff. I wondered whether he had a vacuum cleaner, and would let me use it. Then I thought: *No, it would be rude to ask – and it's none of my business, anyway.*

"Here we are," he gasped, opening the door again, and dragging an old canvas trunk behind him. "The William archive." He slid it into the space between the two chairs, then flopped down opposite me. When he'd gotten his breath back, he flipped up the latches and opened it. It was stuffed with photograph albums, letters, postcards, loose pictures. Lying on top was a neat little black box. "And this," he said, handing it to me, "is what you must admire first."

Inside was a medal: a curvy white cross with a crown at the centre, lying on a bed of velvet.

"What is it?" I asked.

The old guy's face was shiny with pride. "William's DSO. The second highest award for gallantry, I believe, after the VC."

"How did he get it?"

"The most heroic of his heroic episodes. His unit was coming under fire from a German machine-gun post in Normandy. So he went round behind it, crawling and dodging the whole way – then burst in suddenly, shouting: 'Your only hope is to surrender!' And the poor old Jerries did."

"Why? I mean, if it was just him, surely –?"

"Exactly. He did it by sheer force of personality. His German was pretty good, of course." He hesitated. Then, blushing, he murmured: "Thanks to K.-M."

K.-M. rang a very faint bell, but I couldn't think why. I nodded anyway. The old guy wasn't deceived.

"You must have heard of K.-M.? He was your father's cameraman for years."

"Oh, yeah, yeah, of course."

"So that helped. Gave it the authentic air of an order. And then there was the element of surprise. Instead of his battle-dress blouse, William was wearing a woman's frock he'd found in an abandoned farm-house. It was less constricting, he said. So his appearance must have been rather startling."

I started to laugh. "You haven't got a picture, have you?"

"Sadly, there were no photographers present. Much to William's chagrin: his most spectacular performance ever lost to posterity. We've pretty much everything else, though." He started to riffle

273

through the pictures like a card-sharp, pausing every now and then to hand one to me: William on vacation in the south of France, sipping a drink under a café umbrella; William on a TV panel show called *Mince my Words* with a couple of other faces I vaguely remembered from my childhood, but couldn't name any more; twinkle-eyed William talking to the Queen Mother after the famous Royal Command Performance. I tried to seem interested, but Tommy must have pretty soon sensed that I wasn't: when you're old and lonely, I guess, you know from experience that *Oh, really? How fascinating* is usually the prelude to *Well, I have to be going now*, and that your only chance of averting it is to change direction fast.

"Anyway," he said, snatching the Queen Mum back, "you don't want to see all this, do you?" And before I had time to reply, he started pulling things out of the trunk and stacking them in wobbly piles on the floor. About three-fourths of the way down was a piece of striped wallpaper, stretched along the entire length like a false bottom. It was so brittle with age that it crackled as he picked it up. Underneath were three manilla envelopes.

"*This* is what you're after," he said, taking them out and laying them on his knee. "The early years. Not an awful lot left, I'm afraid."

He peered into the first envelope, then shook his head and put it down again. But when he looked in the second one, something caught his eye. He slipped it out and handed it to me.

"This is only the runt of the litter. There were two sturdier siblings, taken at the same time – but I gave them to young Mr. Arkwright, along with most of the other things you'd probably be interested in. If only you'd come a few months ago . . ."

I'd already seen one of the sturdier siblings, on the wall in Arkwright's office: the picture of my father with a young woman and another young man, all of them wearing period costume, standing in a country garden. Tommy Ryder was right: this one *wasn't* so good – the other guy was looking away, and Daddy was blinking. But the image of the woman – sandwiched between the two men, with an arm round each of them, and smiling directly at the camera – was, if anything, even clearer. It still gave me the sense that I might have seen her before somewhere. But not, I was almost certain, in a normal social context: her face had the strange numinous tug of something

274

glimpsed in a dream or a work of art. Which seemed odd, given how utterly ordinary and down-to-earth she looked.

"That's William with my father, is it?" I said.

He nodded.

"And –?"

"And, yes – what was her name? Awful, I don't remember. But they were all very close – as you can tell, from the photo. William absolutely adored her, of course. Quite often used to go away with her and Henry for the weekend." He twisted his head so as to see the picture right-way-up. "I've a feeling that was taken during a pageant at her parents' house. Would that be right, do you think?"

"I'm sorry . . . I don't who you're talking about –"

"Your father's first wife. You know. What *was* she called? Damn, it's on the tip of my tongue. N– N–"

It was a good thing I was sitting down: if I hadn't been, I'd have fainted. The room went dark at the edges and started to merry-go-round. For a second I thought I was going to throw up. The next moment I was fighting tears.

"Come on, help me," said Tommy Ryder. "I'm an old man. Nora? No. Nancy? Oh" – as he noticed what was happening to me – "I'm sorry. I should have thought, shouldn't I? This must be very difficult for you. The predecessor problem. I do understand, believe me." He waved the envelope he was holding, then started to scrabble inside it. "Why do you think I keep all this stuff safely tucked away? It's to avoid this chap." He slid out another photograph and laid it on his outstretched hand. "Here he is, look: K.-M. Just after William managed to get him released from internment in 1941."

It was a portrait of a fair-haired, big-shouldered man with a stat-uesquely perfect face. I took one look at it, and suddenly heard myself making that noise people make when they're in shock: sob after sob heaving up from the pit of the stomach and ending in a dreadful *er-er-er-er-er*. It was as much of a surprise for me as it must have been for Tommy Ryder. I'm still trying to figure out why a picture of some guy I'd barely heard of should have made me do it. Maybe it was a delayed reaction. Or else just the last straw – the final tiny detail that told me I was defeated. There was just too much I didn't know – had never known – for me ever to catch up. Even if I accumulated all the facts, it was too late now for me to re-adjust my understanding of the world to accommodate them.

"Oh, dear," said the old guy, slapping his own hand. "Do *please* forgive me. I feel an absolute swine. Anyone – apart from that prize chump, Tommy Ryder, of course – would have realized what was likely to happen if you were presented with a picture of your father and his – *Nicky*, that was her name, wasn't it? – just like that, completely out of the blue. I mean, it's bound to stir up all kinds of old feelings towards her that you'd much rather forget about."

I know: I should have put him out of his misery by explaining that wasn't the problem. But I was still crying so much I didn't think I'd be able to get the words out. And if I *did* manage to say it, I'd have to tell him the reason: that I didn't *have* any old feelings towards her, because until three minutes ago I hadn't been aware of her existence. That seemed such a crazy confession, I just couldn't bring myself to make it. I mean, how could a daughter possibly *not* know something like that about her own father? He'd have to think I was either incredibly stupid, or incredibly uninterested in my parents, or both. And at that instant, all I wanted to do was get out of there, without him having a worse opinion of me than he did already.

"Oh, I know, tell you what," he said, getting up: "why don't we both have a little something, to make us feel better?" He went out into the kitchen, and came back with a couple of glasses and a bottle gray with dust. "I'm not much of a toper," he said, pulling the stopper out. "Haven't had a whiff of this stuff since the Christmas before last. But brandy can't go off, really, can it?"

He poured us a half-inch apiece, and handed me mine.

"Here we are. Purely medicinal purposes, as the old joke goes. Well, cheers."

I didn't trust myself to reply. I just took the glass, and nodded.

"The curious thing is," he said, "that it had quite an effect on me, too, indirectly. If it hadn't been for that German business after the war, I should probably never have er . . . ended up with William. So I suppose I'm rather in your debt, really – or your father's debt, at any rate – for the best thirty years of my life." He laughed. "It *was* in Germany, wasn't it? – that your father met your mother? When he was making the film about the refugees?"

I just nodded again.

"I thought so. Well – don't worry, the secret's safe with me, for the simple reason that I never heard it."

The little hairs on my arms prickled. "What secret?" I said.

"You know." He tapped his nose. "The *mysterious incident*. All *I* know about it is that it happened in Germany. And had something" – leaning across and pointing at my National Film Theatre carrier bag – "to do with *that*. But –"

"What – *Better than Magic*, you mean?"

He nodded. "William wouldn't tell me any more. Except that it was a moral to us all, because it showed the danger of exposing an impressionable mind to a cock-eyed theory." He saw my bemusement, and gave me a discreet prompt by raising his eyebrows and mouthing: "*Surrealism*."

"*Surrealism* was the cock-eyed theory?"

He mistook my ignorance for outrage.

"Yes, though I hasten to add, that was *his* view of it, not mine, just in case you're a fervent Max Ernstophile. Anyway, the point is, K.-M. told *him* what had happened in Germany, and William always thought he shouldn't have done. He had an odd code of honour – William: you could gossip and back-bite to your heart's content about anything you saw or overheard. But something a friend told you in confidence was absolutely sacrosanct. He could be a *little* bit paranoid, sometimes, poor fellow, and I expect he thought: *If K.-M.'s prepared to do this to Henry, what would he be prepared to do to me?* So that was the beginning of the end of the relationship, I think. Neither of them really admitted it at the time, but after that K.-M. started going back to Germany more and more, with William's blessing. They preserved the fiction, of course, that it was just to work, but both of them knew that wasn't the whole story, so it wasn't much of a surprise when K.-M. eventually wrote to say he'd found someone else and wasn't coming back." He blushed. "Which opened the way for a breezy young chap called Tommy Ryder to appear on the scene. So it's an ill wind, and all that. Let me top you up."

I did. The alcohol was already having an effect: not reducing my misery, but sealing it off, so it felt like it was in the next room.

I managed to find my voice again: "Thank you." It sounded almost normal.

He smiled. Relieved I'd stopped wailing, I guess.

"I never had the pleasure of meeting the authors of my happiness," he said. "William wouldn't have anything to do with your father, I'm afraid. Not after he left Nicky. I'm sorry to say he always bore a bit of a grudge. I did meet *her* once, though. She came to see William, oh, years later – some time in the seventies, I should think it was."

I heard myself saying: "And what was she like?"

"Oh, well, you know. Perfectly pleasant, I think. I can't really remember. She and William went into his study, so I don't know what they talked about. She took some things with her when she left, a whole bag of stuff – I do remember that." He hesitated a moment, then started to rootle around in the trunk. "Actually, you should be able to judge for yourself, because I'm pretty sure I've got a picture of her somewhere . . ."

"I know," I said, wondering if his memory was starting to go, and waggling the photo of the three young people under his nose. "You've shown me already –"

"No, no, one that I took, that day. William was very keen to have a picture of them together, for some reason. So I dusted down the old Brownie, and – Ah. Here we are."

It was a five-by-seven print with a yellowing white border and curled-up corners. The two of them were posing side by side in front of a French window. William, obviously, was one of those lucky guys whose looks improve as they get older: his hair was white, but still thick and well groomed, and set off by a handsome vacation tan, and his thin foxy face had filled out, giving him the comfortable, nothing-left-to-prove air of an aging film star. The woman, by contrast, appeared edgier and more tentative, as if the intervening years had sapped *her* confidence rather than strengthening it. Her eyes were warier and more watchful; the sharp contours of her face had been blurred by a thickening of the flesh and a loosening of the skin, and the pristine forehead had been invaded by worry-lines. But her features were still quite recognizably the same – and gave me, even more strongly than the earlier pictures, an odd unplaceable sense of familiarity.

"She used to write to William quite a lot, too," said Tommy Ryder. "I think they kept in touch till the end of his life, though I never saw her again."

"Have you still got any of her letters?"

He shook his head. "I'm afraid I destroyed them all in an earlier cull. Young Arkwright was furious when he found out. He thought I'd been very naughty."

"Might she still be alive, do you think?"

"It's possible, I suppose, but I wouldn't have thought so: she'd be getting on for a hundred now."

"And you don't know how I could find out?"

He shook his head again. "Sorry. Haven't even got an address, or anything."

"Did she remarry?"

He hesitated, frowning with concentration. "I think so. But I'm afraid I don't know the name."

"Well, thank you," I said, draining my glass, and putting it down. "That's been very interesting." As I held out the picture of the three young people I noticed something written on the back: "Slip Hill, Shropshire. July 1934." Without thinking I said: "May I keep this for the time being?"

"Of course. Keep both of them, if you like." He seemed pleased. I might bring them back in person and give him another twenty minutes of company.

He tried to persuade me not to leave, saying *Why didn't I wait till I was feeling a bit stronger?* etc. etc., but I lied shamelessly, saying I had some place to go and didn't want to be late. It was only as we reached the door that my fuddled brain finally made a connection it should have seen much earlier.

"Tell me," I said: "does the name *Omar* mean anything to you?"

"Of course," he said. "It was William's nickname for K.-M." He laughed. "Like the poem, you know: 'The Rubaiyat of Omar Khayyam.'"

XIX

London – June 1936

There's a traffic jam in Piccadilly. As you cross the road, eyes screwed up against the sun, you can feel the heat pulsing off the cars and the warm breath of their exhausts. The pavement on the other side's so packed with people that it's hard to find a space.

'Heavens,' says Nicky. 'It's like trying to get on an escalator. I'd no idea Surrealism was so popular.'

We all laugh, except Christopher, who bridles and says: 'Well, I've a feeling you could be quite surprised, actually.'

Nicky blushes, and pulls an *oops-what-have-I-done?* face.

It's a struggle not to hit him. Why is he always so sour with her? 'It was a joke, Christopher,' I say. 'I know you find that a difficult concept to grasp, but you could at least try to understand. She doesn't really imagine this whole crowd's on its way to the New Burlington Galleries. Perhaps it'd be easier if you thought of it as a kind of dramatic irony. She *pretends* to believe something that the audience knows isn't actually true, and the humour's in the –'

'Yes, well, the point is, I think it *is* true. I'll bet you a good half of these people are going to the exhibition.'

I shrug despairingly. He doesn't see. But William does, and murmurs in my ear: 'Q.E.D.'

But Christopher's right, in the event: when we try to make our escape into Bolton Street, it turns out that everyone else seems to have the same idea and we find ourselves caught in a sluggish human stream that eventually spills out into Curzon Street and settles in an eddying pool of people in front of number 65. It's a surrealist enough image in its own right: a bizarre road-accident between a Mayfair cocktail party, an art school, a C.P. meeting and a theatre queue. There are little knots of society women in slinky dresses and fashionably wide-brimmed hats chatting and laughing together, while their bored-seeming men smoke and gaze desultorily off into the distance; stately old Chelsea bohemians decked out in beads and bow-ties; respectable couples who look as if they've just got off the train from Dorking or Amersham to go to a matinée of *Follow the Sun*; a chubby-cheeked don or two. And a lot of scruffy young Fitzrovians, who stand around in groups of four or five talking earnestly to one another – clearly enjoying the novel experience of being the priesthood for once, rather than the heretics. One of them recognizes Christopher and comes over to speak to him. I can't hear what he's saying above the buzz of the crowd – but from the eager expression on his face, I've a feeling I wouldn't find it terribly sympathetic. Then I notice his baggy trousers and crumpled coat, which are so like mine that for a moment I have the odd illusion I'm looking into a mirror. It's a bit of a shock to realize *my* get-up's as much a uniform as everyone else's. An outsider as given to categorizing as I am would instantly put me and this chap in the same camp.

Moral: don't categorize so much.

There's a welter of *hullo, darling!*s as the people just ahead of us stop to greet some friends. We edge past them to the door and pay our one-and-threepences. William picks up a copy of the catalogue and gingerly starts to leaf through it.

'I shouldn't bother with that, if I were you,' says Christopher, gently taking it from his hand and putting it down again. 'I'm told it doesn't bear much relation to where things actually are.' He's smiling, and his face has the glow of a schoolboy who's just been publicly acknowledged by the Captain of the First Eleven, and let in on its secrets. 'Breton breezed in at the last minute, apparently, and insisted that everything had to be rehung.' He makes it sound like a triumph rather than a fiasco.

Inside, it's smotheringly hot: the air stuffy with sweat and scent and the clubby smell of Jermyn Street barbers and expensive suits haunted by cigar-smoke. Apart from a pair of giant lips hung above one of the doorways, you can really only catch tantalizing glimpses of the exhibition, as the shifting crowd briefly opens a temporary avenue and then closes it again.

'I don't think we're going to be able to do this *en masse*,' I say.

To my surprise, Christopher agrees. 'No, you're right,' he says, glancing round. 'There isn't room for a party of five traipsing about together.'

'So it's every man for himself,' murmurs Omar.

Christopher nods, then plunges into the throng without looking back.

'What about every woman?' says William. He touches Nicky's arm. 'I hope *you're* going to stick with me and Omar, my dear. We can be embarrassed together.'

God, he's changed. For a second I can see what he'll be like in twenty-five years: a witty, well-loved bachelor uncle, comfortable with his queerness, queenily guying the *Daily Mail* prejudices of the middle class – while managing to make it absolutely clear that he shares them himself.

Nicky looks at me uncertainly, then giggles and squeezes his arm. 'All right.'

It's quite understandable that she'd prefer his company to mine – but I can't help feeling stung by it, nonetheless. Then I tell myself to stop being so perverse: I wanted to be alone, and I am. No seminars from Christopher; no sniggers from William: I'll be free to react spontaneously, without having to tailor my response to anybody else.

But it isn't easy. The first impression, when you've fought your way to the edge of the room, isn't of individual pictures, but just of generalized chaos: bright shards of colour jagging out at you, and tangles of barbed-wire lines, and strange blobby shapes that look as if they'd turn into something if you stared at them long enough – only you *can't* stare at them long enough, because someone is always gliding in front of you, or nudging you from behind. I eventually manage to station myself with my back to an abstract sculpture – a kind of rough round obelisk, with a long sausagey object balanced on the point – so that at least I'm protected from the rear. But even then it's hard to concentrate on the picture in front of me: a mutilated one-armed figure, half statue and half (or so it seems) decomposing flesh, standing on one amputated leg on a black ball. On either side of it are highly stylized ruins: behind, receding geometrically to the horizon, what looks like a harbour wall, which passes a mysterious conical object in the water and a line of little islands before finally vanishing into a huge glaring sky. All over the figure and the buildings are strange serpentine forms that seem on the point of disclosing some secret to me – but before they can do it, a woman's voice six inches from my elbow says: 'Is it a Dali?'

I turn towards her. She isn't talking to me, thank God, but to a grey-faced man on the other side of her.

He sucks in his cheeks, then slowly shakes his head. 'The visual puns are too crude.'

'Mm?'

'Look.'

And the next moment they've moved past me, and are peering at the canvas. I could change my position so as to see over their shoulders, but short of stuffing my fingers in my ears I couldn't avoid hearing his exegesis on the painting – which would destroy the whole point of looking at it in the first place. If Christopher's right, and Surrealism's really going to help me out of my predicament, I can't simply ingest it second-hand. I've got to discover it for myself – or let *it* discover *me*.

But obviously it isn't going to be easy. Most of the crowd behave as if they're at a fairground freak show rather than an exhibition: they gawp and snigger and point discreetly, shaking their heads and murmuring, *Oh, my dear!* You'd think the organizers would have tried to break down their misconceptions, but instead they seem hell-bent on reinforcing them. A man in a green suit, smoking a green pipe and accompanied by a woman with green hair, is attracting as many raised eyebrows and surreptitious smiles as any of the exhibits. Another – a sullen cherub with curly dark hair – walks about offering people cups of boiled string, politely asking if they'd like it *weak or strong?* The idea, presumably, is to evoke the world of dream – but the result is more like a Varsity rag day. The only genuine *frisson* comes from a woman in a white satin gown with a cage of roses on her head, who drifts ghostlily by holding a rose-filled model of a human leg in one hand and a pork chop in the other – and even that rather loses its effect when you get close to her and your nose tells you that the chop is starting to go off in the heat.

As I try to get out of her way, I'm pushed up against a tight-knit little group of people who are trembling with collective laughter. At first I assume it's the pork-chop phantom that's got them going, but then I notice they're all looking the other way, towards a picture of a female bust with the belly broken open and a cloth spilling out of the hole to cover the genitals. Immediately in front of it stand William and Nicky. It's obvious at a glance that he's the cause of all the hilarity: his face is contorted into the *What, me?* expression of a wag who's just set the table on a roar, and doesn't want to be seen laughing at his own *mot*. The next moment, he puts one hand over his own eyes and the other over Nicky's, in a parody of outraged modesty – sending her into giggles, and sparking off another wave of merriment from the onlookers. I look round quickly for Omar, and find him standing a little way off, watching the curious antics of the English with a fixed smile that says he knows he's meant to be amused but can't for the life of him see why.

I don't want to catch his eye: I don't want to be implicated. I move on, before any of them has a chance to notice I'm there. The next room, thank God, is quieter, for some reason – the crowd so thin in places that two or three of the pictures are clearly visible even from the doorway. One of them, in particular, instantly grabs my attention. It's like nothing else I've seen so far: compositionally simpler, and – except for a small red-orange blaze in the bottom left-hand corner – more sombrely coloured. In the middle of a dark rectangle is a huge ragged blue-and-grey hole, with three splayed yellow arrows descending from it into the surrounding darkness. Only as you get closer do you see that the arrows aren't really arrows at all but the legs of an easel, standing on the rocky floor of a cave. You couldn't *tell* it was an easel, from a distance, because the painting standing on it blends so perfectly with the hazy mountain view behind it. And then you see why: the painting on the easel doesn't just *represent* the centre of the scene: *it is the centre of the scene itself*. Its colours and contours seamlessly connect with the colours and contours beyond its own borders – so that if the artist hadn't marked the edges of the canvas, you wouldn't know they were there at all. At its very heart, clinging to the side of the mountain, is a romantic little castle, which seems totally inaccessible and yet makes you long to find a way to get to it.

I am enchanted. This really does work like a dream: not bellowing its oddness at you but slipping it unobtrusively under the door, so you're not sure if what you're looking at is real or not. For a minute or two I stand staring at it, struggling to grasp what it's trying to tell me. The red-orange glow to the left of the easel is a fire: the cave is home, perhaps – Plato's cave – and the landscape we see outside it completely beyond our reach. The castle may not even be there at all, in fact, but just an invention of the invisible artist, to make the landscape appear less alien and give us the illusion of a distant goal. If you could take the canvas away, all you'd see is a bare mountain . . .

No, this is banal: I'm trying to rationalize the meaning, rather than letting it seep in subliminally, as I should. I need to see the picture afresh. I shut my eyes, and try to think of nothing. After a few seconds, I'm aware that someone is edging in alongside me: I can feel the quiver of the floorboards as he settles himself and the warmth of another body radiating against my shoulder. Surely, I think, he doesn't have to be that near? I struggle to ignore it – but then the unpleasant thought strikes me that it may be William, fresh from his triumph in the other room, and bent on delighting his admirers with a bit more fun, this time at my expense. I tell myself I'm being paranoid, but – try as I may – I can't eradicate this idea: as soon as I succeed in half-emptying my mind, it's promptly invaded by a vivid image of him smirking archly, and pressing a mocking finger to his lips, as he rolls his eyes in my direction. Then all at once there's a loud sniff six inches from my ear, and my resolve crumbles altogether.

I turn and look. I was being paranoid: it's not William. But oddly enough (how Dali would love this), it *is* someone connected with him.

Barrett Trayne.

'Oh, God!' he says. 'Henry Whitaker!'

His breath is sour with last night's beer, and he looks awful: gaunt and saggy at the same time, as if the skin across his face has been drawn so tight it's lost its elasticity. His forehead's creased with slack grey lines. His jaw's a mess of scabs where he's cut himself shaving, and little black tufts which he hasn't managed to shave at all.

'How are you?'

He doesn't even try to pretend: just shrugs, and murmurs: 'Oh, well, you know. Things have been better.'

'I'm sorry.'

He nods. 'Can't seem to get much of a grip on anything any more.' He splays his fingers and studies them for a moment. 'Anyway . . .'

'Still writing?'

'Trying.'

'I haven't seen anything for a while.'

'No. No-one has. There's not much demand for my sort of stuff these days, it seems. Musical shows, costume plays – that's what people want, apparently. If I could just come up with something light and frothy about the life of Alfred, Lord Tennyson.'

You can tell from his tired little smile and pat delivery that it's an old joke – veteran of God knows how many embarrassing conversations when he's tried to lessen the pain of his humiliation by making light of it. I laugh. He gives me a quick grateful glance, as if I'd picked up his SOS signal and flashed a message back through the fog. His eyes are wet and pink-rimmed.

'Unfortunately, it seems to be beyond me,' he says. 'Like pretty much everything else at the moment.' He hesitates, then clears his throat awkwardly. 'I have actually got something, though, that I think, er, might do as a film. Would you be at all, um – I mean, would it be worth –?'

Oh, God. 'I'm not with British Imperial any more, Barrett. I'm not working in features at all –'

'No, no, I know that. But still, I'd love to know what you make of it. I really think it could strike a bit of a chord with people. It's about a young man and his mother . . .'

Well, fancy that: just like the last one. And the one before that. I don't say it, of course, but he can obviously read the thought in my face.

'No, this is different, Henry! Very much a play of the moment. A play that tackles the big questions. You know: class. The rôle of the artist in a capitalist society. The young man's a poet, you see. He feels he's above politics – that his gift exempts him from having to respond to the historical crisis brewing all around him. But then, one day, an old tramp comes to their door. Or, at least, they *assume* he's just an old tramp –'

'Well, it does sound interesting, Barrett. But I'm afraid the cinema's even more of a lost cause these days than the theatre. That's why I left –'

He winces, but it's not enough to stop him.

'If you just *read* it, Henry, I honestly think you'd see: it . . . it really does take the scalpel to this sick old country. Pretty unflinchingly, though I says it myself as shouldn't. And lays bare its rotten bourgeois soul. Not *obliquely*, like Auden, and all those clever poet chaps, but *directly*. You know?'

It's a dismal spectacle: watching a little boy trying to inflate a punctured tyre that loses air as quickly as he can pump it in. He knows it isn't working, but he's so desperate, he can't think of anything else to do and keeps going anyway, working faster and faster, vainly hoping for a miracle.

'What my piece does is hold a mirror up to the audience and force them to look at themselves. Even when they're . . . picking their noses. Or –'

I can't stand any more: it's squeezing the breath out of me. 'All right,' I say. 'I'll take a look at it.'

'Thanks.'

'But please don't get your hopes up.'

He nods. The muscles tighten in his throat. He looks as if he's going to burst into tears.

I pat his shoulder, then turn quickly towards the picture. 'What do you think of that?'

He still can't speak. He gulps, and makes an odd reedy noise.

'It's the one thing here I really like. So far, anyway.'

'Yes,' he says, croaky with phlegm. 'Me too. *La Condition Humaine.*'

'Is that what it's called?'

He nods again. 'Magritte.'

We stand looking silently at it together for a few seconds. Learning the title and the artist has cost me my innocence, so that – instead of approaching it entirely unencumbered, as I'd hoped – I find I'm seeing it through a kind of sediment, made up of what I know about Magritte already. But it still has the power to transport me and fill me with mute longing.

'Certainly seems like *my* condition, all right,' says Barrett: 'stuck in a cave, with everything worth having out of reach. You probably think I've only myself to blame, but . . .'

'No, of course I don't.'

He lets out a sob, tries to strangle it, and ends up turning it into a falsetto whimper. The man standing next to him – a frightening figure in a blue blazer, with a thin silvery scar buckling one side of his face – glances sharply towards him, scowling sourly. I nudge Barrett out of range of his disapproval.

'I know exactly what you mean,' I say. 'My condition, too.'

'You've got a wife, at least.' He's still staring at the picture. 'And a job.'

'Well, yes, of a sort, I suppose. But that doesn't stop me feeling I shouldn't really be here at all, but somewhere else – somewhere I can just catch a glimpse of, occasionally, but never get to.'

He turns and looks curiously at me, unsure if I'm serious. He's never heard me talking like that before. He's probably never heard *anyone* talking like that before – or not, anyway, in a place like this, in the middle of the day, in front of a lot of strangers. It suddenly strikes him that his behaviour has brought us to the brink of a social precipice and we're in danger of tumbling over the edge into an embarrassingly public exchange of maudlin confidences.

His upbringing reasserts itself, and jerks him back. 'Sorry,' he mumbles finally. 'Not a pretty thing, self-pity. I shouldn't be inflicting it on you, should I?'

'That's O.K. –'

He stops me with a shake of his head. 'How's Nicky?'

'Oh, fine, thanks.' I glance round quickly: no sign of her, or any of the others, yet. But it's only fair to warn him. 'She's here, actually.'

'Oh, really?'

'Yes. With William.'

A red bruise appears on his face. He tries to hide it by turning away, but I can see it spidering along the broken veins at the edge of his cheek. Thirty-year-old men don't normally have broken veins. He must be drinking more heavily than ever.

'I don't think I could . . .' he mutters, doggedly facing the wall. 'I mean, we haven't seen each other for a couple of years. Perhaps it'd be better if I just popped off . . .'

Yes, it probably would: particularly given that Omar's here, too. 'Shall I go and see if the coast's clear?'

'Would you mind?'

'No, of course not.'

I make my way back to the door and peer into the first room. They're still there, standing in front of another picture – but so hemmed in by other people that they'd be unlikely to notice us unless they happened to turn round at the exact moment we passed them.

It's an unavoidable risk. I catch Barrett's eye and beckon to him. 'See them?'

He nods.

'If they spot us together, you're sunk. So I think the best thing'd be for you to go ahead on your own – and then I'll follow at a safe distance, and intercept them if it looks as if they've seen you.'

'Thanks.' His eyes are flooded with tears. He takes a couple of steps, then comes back and awkwardly kneads my shoulder. 'Funny, isn't it, the people who turn out to be your friends in the end?'

'Yes.' I'm conscious that the scar-faced man's staring at us again. Out of the corner of my eye I see him muttering something to his wan little bush-baby wife: *Couple of pansies*, probably. I push Barrett gently away. 'Go on.'

'All right. Just wanted you to know.'

I give him a ten-pace start, then begin strolling after him. But when he reaches the middle of the room he stops again and calls: 'By the way, where shall I send it?'

'What?'

'The play?'

I make a shooing gesture that I hope conveys: *Keep going, we'll talk about it outside.* He hesitates for a second, then turns and hurries out into the street. I'm almost at the door myself when Christopher suddenly looms out of the crowd and plunges towards me. He's with one of his Fitzrovian friends: a lanky, fastidious-looking young man with a thick caul of fair hair swept back from a patrician forehead.

'Was that Barrett Trayne I just saw leaving?' says Christopher.

'Yes.'

'Did you know he was going to be here?'

I shake my head.

'Hm, that's a bit of a coincidence, isn't it?'

His sudden credulousness about clairvoyance and apparitions and strange goings-on still astounds me: despite his efforts to explain, I still can't quite fathom how he squares it with being a Marxist materialist.

'Well,' I say, laughing, 'it's a rather low-grade kind of coincidence, if it is. I don't think destiny's really pulling out all the stops.'

His companion smiles. He looks frighteningly assured. 'Ghosts don't always appear on moonlit towers,' he says. 'The marvellous, the *hasard objectif*, can erupt anywhere – in railway stations, Lyons Corner Houses, cinema queues: the drabbest, most mundane places. Perhaps *especially* in the drabbest, most mundane places – and to the most unexpected people.'

'Henry,' says Christopher. 'I don't think you know Edmund Pelling, do you?'

'No –'

'We must've been up at Cambridge at the same time,' says Pelling. 'I can't imagine how we managed not to bump into one another.'

Because I was skulking in my rooms, guiltily reading Dickens, and shadow-boxing with my own psyche. 'I knew you by repute, of course. Nobody could have failed to.'

'Oh.' He makes a self-deprecating whistling noise through his nose, but I think he's pleased. 'Anyway – ten years or whatever it is too late: how do you do?'

'How do you do?'

His fingers are hard but sinuous. They give me the odd sense that a bony octopus is wrapping itself around me.

'Edmund's one of the committee.'

'What, for – for this, you mean?'

Pelling smiles. 'Mm.'

'Oh, congratulations. I think it's a tremendous achievement.'

'You're enjoying it?'

'Very much.'

'I'm glad.' And he seems to be. But there's a kind of silky detachment in the way he says it that suggests he probably wouldn't have been terribly put out if I'd said I wasn't. 'Anything in particular strike you?'

'*La Condition Humaine.*'

He nods. 'Yes, magnificent, isn't it?'

I nod back. Sweat suddenly prickles my neck: I mustn't forget poor Barrett. When I look through the window I can just see him, hovering at the edge of the stir of people in front of the gallery, waiting for me.

'Look –' I begin.

'I don't know if you saw any of Edmund's own work?' says Christopher. 'He's got a few pieces here.'

Yes, of course: he's a painter, isn't he? How rude of me. 'No, I'm sorry, I don't think –'

'It doesn't matter,' says Pelling. And again I get the impression that it really doesn't. What must it feel like to be so indifferent to other people's opinions?

'Listen,' I say, 'I've just got to nip outside for a minute or two. But then I'll come back, if I may, and search them out.'

'There's really no need,' says smiling Pelling.

'No, I'm looking forward to it,' I say, starting towards the door.

'Before you go, though,' he calls after me, 'I did just want to say how much I admired *The Call-On.*'

I stop dead. 'Really?'

'Yes, I've been telling Christopher, I thought it was a marvellous piece of work.' The angles of his mouth and jaw soften. 'I especially liked the little girl and the cat. A lovely effect.'

'Thanks. Thanks very much.'

My face is on fire. I make a bolt for the door. God, what a relief: even the heat of the afternoon feels soothing after the atmosphere inside.

But Barrett's gone.

*

'Well, I don't know about anyone else,' says William, wiping his forehead, 'but I am in urgent need of a drink.'

Guilt about Barrett's made me snappish. I hear myself saying: 'Too much for your Anglo-Catholic soul, was it?'

A beer-lorry judders past just as I get to the *Anglo-*, so I can't tell if he's heard or not. But Christopher smirks, and Nicky gives me a sharp glance.

'How about this?' says Omar, pointing to a pub on the corner. He's still confused about the licensing laws. 'Shall we go here?'

'I don't think it's open yet,' I tell him.

'Even if it were,' says William, shaking his head, 'it'd be full of people drinking sausages out of ashtrays.' And then, catching sight of the name-board: 'Besides, I think we've seen enough green men for one day already.'

We retrace our steps down Half Moon Street and into Piccadilly. But then, instead of heading east again towards the circus in hope of finding an early-opening pub, William leads us across the road into Green Park. 'We'll fare better, I feel,' he murmurs, 'if we put a bit of fresh air between ourselves and Monsieur Breton.'

It's an odd decision for a man in urgent need of a drink, but nobody seems to mind, not even Christopher – probably because it means he can monopolize my company, leaving the three frivolous lost souls to go on ahead, laughing and horse-playing among themselves.

'So,' he says, falling in beside me, 'tell me what you *really* thought?'

'It was very interesting.'

He waits for me to go on.

When I don't, he says: 'It's good to have Edmund Pelling on our side, at any rate. He's done a couple of films himself, you know?'

'What – documentaries, you mean?'

'Yes. Nothing very grand. Little things for the G.P.O. But he says *The Call-On*'s inspired him to be more ambitious. He really – well, he told you, didn't he? How much he liked little Cath and the cat?' He pauses, then goes on awkwardly, without looking at me: 'I must say, by the way, you were absolutely right about that. And I was wrong. I realize that now, after talking to Edmund.'

'Well, that's good,' I say, as magnanimously as I can. 'Thank you.'

Christopher nods. 'He pointed out, which I really hadn't seen, that it's an authentically surrealist *motif* – a living limb, as he put it, grafted into the core of a machine.'

'Yes,' I hear myself saying. 'That's an interesting way of looking at it.'

'*Interesting* again,' says Christopher. 'I thought it was brilliant. Anyway, the point is that he thinks we can build on the idea together. Develop an entirely new form – as radical, in its way, as what the Russians were doing in the twenties.'

'Mm.' Why can't I sound more enthusiastic? Why can't I *be* more enthusiastic? I try the phrase in my head: *Henry Whitaker: the father of surrealist documentary film.* That, surely, wouldn't be a bad epitaph? But for some reason it has me twitching and thrashing in panic.

'He suggested we might even start a new organization,' says Christopher. 'A new *movement*. Just the three of us, to begin with. Then later, if we wanted, we could ask a few like-minded people to join us.'

'To do what, exactly?'

'What we're doing now – only much more systematically. Instead of making films piecemeal, for, you know, Clumber, or the G.P.O., or the Milk Marketing Board, or whoever it might be, we'd be studying and recording the life of the whole country – in just the same way that an ethnographer studies and records the life of a primitive tribe. In fact that's what we'd be: auto-ethnographers. The job would be to describe and explain our society to itself.'

'But you couldn't do *everything*.'

'No, no, of course not. But we'd choose our own subjects, to make them as representative as possible. I mean, you could have, oh, I don't know – London clubs. Pigeon-racing. The temperance movement – what's left of it. Bargees. The list's endless.'

'And who'd pay for it?'

'Well, I'm going to be talking to Clumber about it, to see if he might be interested. Provided you agree, of course. And Edmund seems convinced there are others like him, who might be willing to help. Other *rich men with a vision*, as he calls them – self-made businessmen, most of them, needless to say, who are capable of seeing beyond their narrow class interests and realizing that without revolutionary change the whole bloody country's done for.'

I can feel the rake of his gaze on my face as he waits for me to say more. But what *can* I say that won't just end up leaving him more dissatisfied than he is now? *I'd like time to think about it?* It's true, but he'd naturally press me to say why. And if I told him *that* – that I'm still not certain this is what I should be doing at all – I know from experience what the response would be. It's already playing, now, on a private little screen in my brain: the sulky-boy red cheeks; the shake of the head; the hurt pout as he says, *Christ, Henry, what more do you bloody want?*

I'm saved by William, who's stopped suddenly at the edge of the park and is staring at a pretty little early Victorian pub on the far side of the road.

'Yes,' he says. 'That'll do, I think, don't you?'

'I'd say it'll do very nicely indeed,' says Nicky.

After the brilliant sunshine outside, we're not prepared for the gloom of the saloon bar. At first all I can make out is a few cardboard-cutout figures looming through a haze of smoke and muted light from the window. Even when we find a table and sit down, the people next to us are no more than a couple of ghostly silhouettes. It isn't until the waiter appears to take our order that my vision's finally cleared enough for me to see who they are: the scar-faced man who glared at Barrett, and his timid wife. Obviously they must have been as eager as William for a change of scene and equally confident that they'd find it here. I can tell he recognizes me, too – but instead of nodding or smiling to one another, we both go through the ludicrous English pretence that we've never set eyes on each other before in our lives.

But there's no immediate danger of a border incident, because Christopher and Omar are sitting next to him, and I manage to position myself between Nicky and William at the other end of the table.

'Ah,' sighs William, when our drinks have arrived and he's taken his first sip of beer. 'This is a distinct improvement, isn't it? I have to say I found *Monsieur Breton et compagnie* something of a trial.

And no, it's nothing to do with my Anglo-Catholic soul, Henry.'

Oh, shit. I make a stab at a devil-may-care grin, but I can feel myself blushing.

He goes on: 'I haven't *got* an Anglo-Catholic soul. Anglo-Catholicism was a *phase*. Everyone has phases they grow out of, don't they? Even – heaven forfend – Henry Whitaker.' He turns towards me, with a smile that's just under control. 'Some people, I believe, even grow out of being *queer*.'

Nicky squawks, then glances at me to see if she should be amused or outraged.

'Fair enough,' I say, laughing.

The boil's lanced: William relaxes, and starts opening a bag of potato crisps. 'No, what I really objected to,' he says, offering them round, 'was how ugly and meaningless and *badly done* it all was. You got the impression of a lot of sniggering little kids doing rude scribbles to shock the grown-ups. *Look: I've done a breast.* Mine *looks a bit like a willie. Tee-hee-hee.*'

Nicky guffaws.

He goes on: 'Do you think it's too late to enter something myself?' He takes a pen from his pocket, then reaches for my Player's packet. 'May I? Thank you.' He flicks open the flap, pulls out the inner sleeve and scrawls a gape-mouthed little face on it, with ink tears dripping from the eyes. Then he bores open the hole between the lips, and sticks a fag in it. 'There, now. *L'esprit de* something. They're very keen on their *esprits*, aren't they? *L'esprit de la tristesse.*'

Nicky squeals. Christopher glances at us, wondering what the joke is – and when he sees it, to my surprise, starts laughing himself.

'Yes,' he says. 'You should smuggle it in there. I'm sure they'd accept it as an authentic surrealist act.'

I know William's baiting me, and I oughtn't to rise to it, but I can't help it: he's being such a bloody *bully*. I'm not even certain who the victim is – the struggling surrealist artist seems to have merged, in my head, with poor Barrett Trayne, to create a distillation of bruised, misunderstood humanity – but I know I have to go to his defence.

'I actually think you're being a bit unfair,' I say.

'Oh, really – un*fair*?' says William, with the triumphant little wrist-flourish of a toreador who's goaded the bull into charging. 'Can you be a bit more particular? Tell us which pieces you *didn't* think were ugly and meaningless and badly done?'

'Well, I liked one of the Magrittes. I don't know if you saw it. *La Condition Humaine.*'

'You'll have to remind me.'

I remind him. He shrugs. 'More competent than most of them, I suppose. And the joke was clever enough. But I promise you, you'd see better in a second-year art school show.'

'I didn't think it was a joke.'

'What did you think it was, then?'

I tell him. Christopher listens too, I notice.

When I've finished, William says: 'Mm, well, it's a lovely idea.' He stretches his mouth and eyebrows into a comic mask of surprise, adding the unspoken coda: *And completely mad.*

I know it's a mistake, but the words just force themselves out before I can stop them: 'Well, Barrett agreed with me.'

For a second his face has that sea-sick look: am I telling the truth? Am I obscurely mocking him? What can he grab on to, to hold himself steady? Then the shutter closes again, and he murmurs: '*Barrett?*'

'Yes.'

'I didn't see him there.'

I hesitate for a fraction of a second, to give it some emphasis. 'No.'

He frowns at me, uncertain what I'm trying to convey. Surely I don't have to spell it out?

'You mean,' he says finally, 'my not seeing him wasn't an accident?'

'No.'

'Well, I suppose I can understand he might feel a bit embarrassed at bumping into me, after what he did.'

God, the injustice of it. I want to yell: *After what he did? You drove him to it, by being so bloody impossible. And if you could see what it's reduced him to now* . . . But I know it would only have the perverse effect of making him more self-righteous.

296

'And as for his reaction to the picture,' he drawls, 'I can't say I'm terribly surprised. I always did think you and he were rather similar in some respects. Particularly your pronounced tendency to see what's behind your eyes, rather than what's in front of them.'

Nicky giggles – then catches my expression and stops.

I clench my fists under the table. 'So what's your interpretation of it, then?'

He shakes his head, as if he thinks it's too trivial to interpret at all, then takes a leisurely sip of beer, to signal that he's dropping the subject. But Christopher, sniffing the opportunity for a lecture, suddenly rushes in and snatches it up himself: a hyena grabbing the lion's carrion.

'I think what Magritte's telling us,' he says, 'is that representation and reality are the same thing. Because, from a Surrealist perspective, the dichotomy that we're brought up to believe in, you know, between *ob*jective and *sub*jective, is ultimately false.'

William delicately dabs froth from his lip with the tip of his tongue. 'Mm,' he murmurs, 'well, I'm glad someone's put me straight on *that*.'

Christopher doesn't hear. But Nicky does, and squeals again – attracting a vicious glare from the scar-faced man at the next table.

I wish she'd stop squealing.

'We *have* to be brought up to believe in it, of course,' says Christopher, 'because it's essential to the survival of capitalism.'

William gazes towards the window, and starts drumming his fingers lightly on a beer-mat.

'No, really,' Christopher goes on. 'I mean, the objective is the realm of the *ego*, isn't it? – the rational self, if you like – which bourgeois society sees as the highest part of the psyche, and invests with its own power and its own ghastly values. Whereas the *subjective* corresponds to the unconscious *id*, which we're taught to see as something inferior – something dangerous and unruly, that has to be ruthlessly subordinated to the ego, in exactly the same way that the workers and native people have to be subordinated to the ruling class.'

William mimes a yawn. Nicky laughs. The scar-faced man's lips quiver. I can't hear the sound that comes out, but I can see it: *Tch tch*.

'That', says Christopher, sensing he's losing the others, and latching desperately on to me to avoid being shut out altogether, 'is why Breton called his review: *Le Surréalisme au Service de la Révolution*. It's no good simply overturning the bourgeois state, and seizing control of the means of production and distribution. Man cannot be *truly* free until he has thrown off the tyranny of the bourgeois-conditioned *ego* in himself –'

He stops suddenly, as the man at the next table finally snaps – tutting and sighing, and then noisily clearing his throat. Christopher jerks round to face him, grateful for any response – even a hostile one. They glower at each other.

Christopher says: 'Was that a comment on what I was saying?'

The man swallows uncomfortably. His cheek is flushed red, except for the scaly white furrow of the scar. He shifts in his seat and mutters something. All I can make out is *clever young men*.

'England must be the only country in the world where *clever* is a pejorative term,' says Christopher.

I can't catch the man's reply, because at that moment William sticks the empty crisp-packet on his head and says: '*L'esprit de pomme frite très très mince*.'

Nicky struggles to keep a straight face. Her shoulders shake; her mouth contorts into a succession of odd shapes – then she loses the battle, and erupts with a noise that startles the whole bar, turning heads and stopping conversations in their tracks. It's frightening to see her like this: her face blotched with heat and tears and alcohol, the vein on her forehead throbbing furiously, a dribble of mucus hanging from her nose, so long and thin you expect to see a spider dangling on the end of it. Normally she'd be reaching for her handkerchief to clean herself up, but now she doesn't seem to care about her appearance, and just sits there helplessly, hiccoughing as she fights for breath.

God, I'm going to start hating her in a minute. I look away quickly – but it's too late. The sea-wall's been breached and I can't plug it up again: every face I settle on now – sly William, flushed Christopher, the blazered man at the next table bubbling with mean-spirited rage – is tainted with the same contagion. The only exception is Omar, who sits quite detached from it all, as pale and unruffled as if he were being cooled by an invisible electric fan, watching the burlesque being played out around him with impenetrable serenity. It's hard to know what he's thinking. He's probably wondering how he managed to end up in a nation of overgrown children.

'If you'd seen what I did, in the war,' the scar-faced man is saying, 'you'd be singing a different tune.'

'And who was it that benefited from the war?' says Christopher. 'Arms manufacturers. International bankers –'

The man shakes his head angrily. But it's impossible to hear what he says, because at that moment William crumples the crisp-packet and stuffs it in his mouth, sending Nicky into another seizure.

I can't stand it any more. I touch her wrist, and whisper: 'I'm going.'

She looks at me, startled, as if, without explanation, I'd suddenly slapped her face. 'Hm?'

'I'm leaving,' I say, getting up.

'Why?'

I shake my head quickly: *Tell you later.*

Her forehead runkles with bafflement. 'Where are you going?'

I've no definite plan: just a vague hunger that's tugging me towards the river. If we walked down past Victoria, we'd be at Vauxhall Bridge in less than half an hour. After the feverish artificiality of the afternoon, it'd be a relief to stroll along the Embankment, feel the breeze on our faces, the sense of light and space, and the odd solace that comes from seeing something formed by geological time rather than the mayfly life-cycle of human beings. And perhaps if we lingered long enough we'd see the lights coming on on the bridge, and suddenly find ourselves swingboated back to our first journey across it together six years ago (the awkward intimacy of the cab; the driver with his religious tract; the memory of William in Barrett's play still printed on our minds), and begin to discover each other again, as we did that night.

'I don't know,' I say. 'Somewhere. Are you coming?'

She paws my sleeve. 'Oh! Do we have to? This is fun.'

'Well, I'm going now.'

Instead of getting up, she turns to William with a *can't-you-do-anything?* expression.

'Henry can go off and be miserable by himself, if that's what he wants,' he says. 'You stay and have another drink with us. We'll pop you into a taxi later on.'

She smiles up at me, and lays a hand on mine. 'Would that be O.K.?'

'Yes, of course.'

I feel quite lost when I get outside: an empty car waiting for a driver. I start walking more or less aimlessly for a hundred yards or so, then for no particular reason take the first side street I come to. At the far end is a 'phone-box. It suddenly strikes me that's what I should do: ring Barrett, explain what happened at the gallery, and make sure he has my address. He might even like to meet me for a drink. He seemed lonely enough to be glad of some company.

I'm half-way there when I realize I haven't got his number. I could go back to the pub and ask William for it, but I can't really face the idea. All at once, in fact, I'm aware that I haven't got the energy to face anything. Leaden-legged, I stumble into the park, and find a shady spot to lie down.

When I wake up again, it's already dusk. Nicky must be wondering where the hell I am.

I hurry home. But when I get there, she still isn't back.

XX

Shropshire
August 1

Slip Hill's a big place. The entrance is guarded by an electric gate. It's too high to see over, but if you peer round one of the pillars you can just catch a distant glimpse of red brick. Impossible to imagine what it must have looked like in the thirties.

I tried buzzing the intercom twice. There was no reply, but the second time I noticed a quick prick of light from somewhere inside the grounds, like the sudden dazzle from an opening window or a moving car. I waited another minute or so but didn't see or hear anything else.

I pulled the hire-car on to the verge, then walked further along the road, searching for another way in. But there was nothing but a continuous wall of neatly trimmed hazel running the entire length of the garden. I bent down at one point to look through a narrow gap – not because I was seriously thinking of trying to crawl through it but simply in order to find out if the owners were genuinely as obsessive about intruders as the gate suggested.

They were. Behind the pleasant rustic façade was a discreet flash of iron fist: the dense mesh of a security fence.

The sight of it, for some reason, almost derailed me. All the feelings of helplessness and despair I'd been keeping penned up since my visit to Tommy Ryder suddenly broke free again. Why was I reduced to this? I could just about understand why my father would have wanted to keep Nicky's existence from me when I was little: it must, after all, have been a painful subject for Mummy even at the best of times, and he was probably frightened I'd unwittingly say something that would push her right over the edge. But surely he could have told me later? Or Granny could have mentioned it? Or Arthur Maxted, even, might have said something, on one of the rare occasions I'd actually seen him when I was staying in his house in Hollywood?

The truth was, I'd been the victim of a massive conspiracy. And the worst of it was that I'd connived at my own deception. I'd accepted the hedge at face value and never dreamed of looking to see what was behind it. It was wishful thinking to imagine I could do anything about it now: my faulty map of the world was so deeply etched into my brain that nothing would ever erase it. I should just give up and go home.

I rootled around in my head for a counter-argument. I couldn't find one. I levered myself up and started walking back towards the car. Then I was pole-axed by an even worse thought: perhaps I don't even *have* a home. Perhaps I'd *never* had one. What if the deception hadn't stopped when I got to America? What if Hode's *You have to do it, honey, go ahead, I'll be fine* was just a convenient way of getting rid of me so he could cheat on me with someone else? Which would explain why I'd only had two short e-mails from him, and one rushed call.

I leaned on the car-roof, huffing like an old woman, my pulse thumping so loud that for a moment I thought I was going to have a heart-attack. I soon realized I wasn't – but those few seconds of panic were enough to jolt me back into myself. I was still alive, thank God. It might be late, but it wasn't *too* late. *Whatever* the truth was, I could face it. The only unforgivable thing – the thing that would make it impossible to go on without losing my mind – would be to flinch from going on trying to find it.

I took a few deep breaths to steady myself, then resumed my search for another way into Slip Hill.

There wasn't one. But twenty yards beyond the edge of the grounds I saw the entrance to a field. The only barrier was a token strand of orange string. I stepped over it and started following the line of the garden as it dropped away from the road.

There was a pleasant soporific smell of grass and wild flowers in the air, but the breeze carrying it felt oddly sharp, as if it couldn't decide whether to be summer or fall. In the distance was a hazy ridge of wooded hills that seemed sort of familiar to me, though I was certain this was the first time I'd ever been here in my life. It wasn't until I'd gone fifty paces or so that it suddenly occurred to me where I could have seen them before. I stopped, and took out the photos

Tommy Ryder had given me. Yes, that was it: I was looking at the backdrop to the picture of Nicky and Daddy and William. This must have been the exact spot it was taken.

"Can I help you?" said a voice behind me.

I turned round. There was a woman standing in the garden, staring out at me over the top of the hazel hedge. She was about forty, I guess, with short, well-styled hair, and wearing a high-necked blouse and a mannish jacket that looked like it had been tailor-made for her. There was a lot of make-up on her face. I found myself wondering who she'd put it on for.

"Are you looking for something?" she asked. I couldn't tell whether she was genuinely trying to be helpful, or it was just an icily polite way of saying *What the hell are you doing here?* And from her manner, I'm not sure that she knew herself. She kept tugging nervously at something below the level of the hedge that was hanging on a worn leather strap round her neck, and her expression – wide eyes, pouty tremulous mouth – appeared tentative and curious and protective all at the same time.

"Well, in a way," I said, holding out the photograph. "I'm looking for her."

She frowned with concentration, but obviously still couldn't see properly, so I took a couple of steps towards her. She flinched and backed away. For a second I saw what was on the end of the leather strap: a battered pair of binoculars. So that, presumably, explained the odd flash of light at the gate: she must have been spying on me ever since I got here.

"May I see?" she said, forcing herself forward to the hedge again.

I gave it to her. She stared at it for a couple of seconds, then squinted into my face, searching for a resemblance.

"Who is she? A relative of yours?"

"Kind of an *honorary* relative, I guess you could say. Her name was Nicky. At some point in her life she'd have been Nicky Whitaker. She lived here during the 1930s. Or, at least, her parents did."

"The 1930s?"

I nodded.

"But she won't – I mean, you can't be expecting –?"

"No, I know; she probably died years ago –"

"Well, there must be a more recent address for her than this."

I showed her the writing on the back of the picture. "That's all I have."

She gawped at me suspiciously. She probably thought I was a criminal, trying to bullshit her way out of trouble after being surprised casing the joint. I couldn't blame her, really: it must have sounded a pretty flimsy explanation.

While I was trying to figure out how much more I should tell her, she said: "And how did you find the house, anyway, if that's really all you had to go on?"

"Oh, that was easy. I searched for *Slip Hill* and *Shropshire* on Google, and came up with a local-history site that had some old pictures on it. One of them had obviously been taken at the same time as this one, and in almost exactly the same place. So I knew I had the right Slip Hill." I wagged a finger at the ridge of hills in the picture. "Did you recognize the view?"

"Oh, yes, yes," she said quickly. But I don't think she had: I could see the tension leaving her neck and shoulders as she realized there might be some truth in my story after all.

"Do you know anything about the history of the house?" I said, quickly following up my advantage.

"Not really. Well, not that far back, anyway. We only bought it five years ago."

"What about the previous owners? Might they know, do you think?"

She shook her head. "I'm pretty sure they weren't here terribly long, either. You could try asking them, I suppose. But they retired to Spain somewhere." She grimaced. "And they're not very good at answering letters."

"O.K." I thought about asking whether I could come in and look round anyway, just out of curiosity. But she didn't seem like she'd be very comfortable with the idea, and I didn't want to embarrass either of us. So I just nodded, and started back towards the road.

"There was one thing, though," she called after me.

I stopped. She was hurrying to keep up with me on the other side of the hedge, weighing the binoculars in her hand.

"We did find these," she said. "They were up in the roof. They'd managed to get stuck, somehow, behind the old water-tank. We

304

only discovered them when we had a new one put in. I think they must have been there for years. They're old – First World War, apparently."

"Well, that is kind of interesting." I lingered for a second or two, for politeness' sake, trying to look as if I meant it.

Just as I was about to move on again, she said: "What really freaked me out was that there was something else inside the case. Well, two things, actually: a photograph and a letter." She shivered. "I found it a little bit spooky, to tell you the truth."

"And do you still have them?"

"Not the letter." She must have seen my disappointment, because she went on defensively: "Well, we couldn't read it, you see. It was in German. But we did keep the photograph."

"It isn't of Nicky, presumably?" I said. "Or either of these two?"

She peered at my picture again. "No. It is a woman. But not her."

"Is there anything written on the back?"

"There was. But that was in German, too. And you can't see it now. Neil – my husband – had it framed." She hesitated, then smiled and said softly, mouthing the words as much as speaking them: "He likes to pretend she's an ancestor, I think. Neil feels a bit short of ancestors." She glanced sharply towards the house, as if she was frightened that despite her precautions he might have heard her anyway. "He'll be back any minute."

"O.K.," I said. "Well, thank you."

As I was getting into the car, a red-faced man in a big blue 4x4 drew up in front of the gate. Neil, presumably. He half-opened the door, and for a moment I thought he was going to run after me. But instead he just sat there, scowling, until I was out of sight.

I'd already decided that if I drew a blank at Slip Hill, I'd drive back into the village, and ask at the shop or the pub. I was half-way there before it struck me that this had actually been a non-idea – just a little piece of candy, in reality, that I'd promised myself as a bribe to get me through the ordeal of going to the house. It was the state of my stomach that gave the game away: after being in knots all day, it all at once felt relaxed, as if it knew the danger was past and there was no risk of encountering anything disturbing or unexpected. And of course – I quickly realized – there wasn't, really. I might be able to discover what Nicky's family were called or what they did or whether or not they were well liked in the village, but none of that would add much to what I knew already. It was obvious just from seeing where they lived that they must have been wealthy, or at least very well-off. What I needed now wasn't more information about the privileged world Nicky had grown up in, but an explanation of why my father had abandoned it.

The more I churned it over in my mind, the less graspable it seemed. It might just about make sense as a kind of Zen gesture: a serene, deliberate renunciation of wealth and fame by someone who'd found spiritual enlightenment. But that wouldn't square with the man I knew at all. He wasn't serene: he was angry. And – though he pretended sometimes to be above such base considerations – it was quite obvious that he minded not having money. Being rich might not have been the most important thing in the world to him, but I'm certain he'd have preferred it to being poor: I can remember how much he hated being *trapped* (as he put it) in a small house, and having to go *cap in hand* to Granny for my school-fees.

I went through it again and again, trying to superimpose the Henry Whitaker who'd married Nicky and known William Malpert over the father I'd experienced as a child. It was useless: the gap between them was unbridgeable. I couldn't think how I might even begin to narrow it.

Until, quite suddenly, I had to swerve to avoid a rabbit. For a second my mind went into suspension. When it started up again, something that had been nibbling at the edge of my consciousness for days had managed to break through my defenses and force itself on my attention: Tommy Ryder had said that his "secret" had something to do with *Better than Magic*. And I had a copy of *Better than Magic* in my bag.

I still don't know why I'd been so resistant to looking at it before. I was frightened to expose myself to more of his work, I guess, in case it ambushed my feelings the same way *The Call-On* had. Even now, the thought of it gave me a sharp jab in the solar plexus, as my tummy-muscles clenched again.

A good sign. I drove straight back to the B&B and asked the land-lady if I could borrow a VCR.

She was very sweet about it – said I could use the one in their living-room, as long as I didn't mind her husband being there too. I obviously couldn't object – the old guy was an invalid, and didn't have any place else to go – but I wasn't crazy about seeing it with some-one else. What if I broke down and started to howl? Or he began making unkind comments about the movie?

In the event, I needn't have worried. For most of the time the old guy just sat and dozed in his chair. And *Better than Magic* – though I found it strangely mesmerizing – didn't catch me off-guard the way *The Call-On* had done. Not only did I have a better idea of what to expect, but the film itself, made three years later, was subtler and more oblique, with more seamlessly integrated effects – so that where the *The Call-On* was clearly divided into the straightforward (the dock scenes) and the mysterious (the little girl and the cat), this presented you with both strands simultaneously, making it impossible to see the boundary between them.

The narrative – in so far as there is one – follows the lives of five people in a northern industrial town during a single week. You see an unemployed man collecting the dole; a seventeen-year-old girl with a pale, touchingly optimistic face that you know will look old before she's thirty, who's been lucky enough (the Depression isn't over yet, and work's still scarce) to get a job in a cotton mill; a young couple preparing for their wedding, and debating whether, once they're mar-ried, they should emigrate to Canada or Australia or New Zealand in search of better prospects. The common thread running through all these stories is the importance of *cinema*: those precious few hours every week when – however hard and depressing your life the rest of the time – you can simply throw it off, and plunge naked into a glori-ous rush of fantasy that carries you irresistibly toward glamour and happiness and love. It's the mill-girl who encapsulates the thrill of it, and gives us the title: *Fellas is all right, I suppose. But going to the pictures – well, that's better than magic, in't it?*

There are some wonderful juxtapositions: a scene of the young couple dancing together like Fred Astaire and Ginger Rogers, with the rhythm provided by the clack of the mills; another of the girl working at her giant loom, accompanied by a big band on the sound-track, that gradually dwindles to a single violin when we close in on her face, and see her ecstatic expression – drooping eyelids, half-open mouth – as she thinks about the movie she's going to that night. The sense of yearning for something you can see but can't grasp is palpable. In my favourite moment, right at the end (which *did* make my eyes prickle), the same girl is watching a dramatic sunset over the hills behind the town. As the camera turns, to show it from her point of view, the mill-chimneys and back-to-back houses in the foreground seem to dissolve away, and we see what appears to be the same landscape (presumably a craftily painted flat) with only one barely visible building in it: a romantic little castle clinging to a dis-tant slope. Although he doesn't spell it out, my father leaves you with the strange (particularly for a documentary) impression that the imaginary world is actually more powerful than the real one – capa-ble, if we'll only let it, of erupting into and transforming even the most ordinary lives.

I was so completely absorbed that it was only when the credits started, and I saw the name *Karl-Maria Glocke* come up under *Camera*, that I remembered why I'd been watching *Better than Magic* in the first place, and realized it hadn't told me what I'd hoped it would. If there was any clue in it as to why Daddy had left Nicky and married my mother, it had completely passed me by.

I glanced across at the landlady's husband. His eyes were closed, and he was snoring softly.

I re-wound the tape, and pressed *play* again. If there *is* anything there, I told myself, *this* time I'll get it.

I really concentrated, pausing every few minutes to assimilate what I'd just seen, but I only found one thing that hadn't struck me before. About half-way through, there's a shot of the queue outside a cinema on a Saturday night. The overall effect is incredibly drab: slate-coloured sky, a steady drizzling rain, pinched bodies in cheap gray Sunday-best clothes. But one figure stands out: a fashionably dressed woman in a neat little hat and a fur stole who wouldn't look out of place sitting in a West End theater or a café on the Champs-Elysées. My immediate thought, from her fish-out-of-water appearance, is that it must be Nicky. It certainly *could* be her – but the quality just isn't good enough for me to be sure. As we watch, though, she does something that I *do* recognize: turns and smiles at the camera, as if – alone of all the people there – she's aware of it, and wants to acknowledge its presence.

And that, of course, was what the extra did in the rushes Daddy was viewing the last time I saw him. It was *that* gesture he wanted the film editor to re-run again and again, before finally giving me his last, tremulous thumbs-up. I've no idea what it meant to him – but to have excited him that much, it must have been something pretty significant.

The old man was still asleep. I ejected the cassette, and tiptoed up to my room.

For the next half hour I lay on my bed, trying to come up with a theory. Perhaps while my father was making *Better than Magic* Nicky turned up out of the blue and – without telling him – infiltrated the cinema queue. She meant it as a practical joke, but when he saw her there he was so incensed at the way she'd compromised the film he walked out on her.

But even a man as irascible as Daddy, surely, wouldn't have left his wife for quite such a trivial offence?

He might, if it hadn't just been an isolated incident. What if she'd been having an affair with someone on the shoot? K.-M., say? Hence "fucking Omar"?

No – K.-M. was gay. And anyway, if that were the case, why would my father have left the shot in the finished film? Or given me the thumbs-up, when he saw the same thing again in the movie he was working on at the end of his life?

No. Better admit it: I'm still at a complete loss.

I'm writing this in my bedroom at the B&B. From the window I can just make out a distant wooded slope, which must be part of the same ridge I saw from the field at Slip Hill. Maybe it's just the impact of *Better than Magic*, but I can't suppress a trembly childish sense that if I could just reach it, I'd find the answer there. I know perfectly well, of course, that I wouldn't – that if I *did* drive out there, I'd feel that whatever it was had magically migrated again and was now winking at me from the next shimmery horizon.

But it's a potent enough longing to make me close the curtains.

XXI

Shropshire – December 1937

'Well, thank you,' says Percy.

'No, thank *you*, for coming.'

He shakes his head. His eyes are sparkly. 'Shame our Betty couldn't be 'ere, too. She'd 'ave given 'er eye-teeth to see that. But you know 'ow it is. If she'd a' taken two days off work, she'd 'ave been out of a job.'

'Yes, it's very hard.'

'But it were proper decent of you, anyroad. I appreciate it. There's not many, I dare say, would have done the same.'

'Oh, I don't know about that.' But I do: he's right. Even Christopher, I suspect, if he were here, would have been puzzled. I can hear him whispering peevishly in my head: *Of course, we'll arrange a screening for them when it's finished. But is it really strictly necessary for them to see work-in-progress? I mean, we're the film-makers, aren't we? I wouldn't expect them to consult me about cotton-carding or loom-maintenance.*

'And what's it to be called?' he says. 'Do you know yet?'

'*Autumn Poppies.*'

He nods. His jaw starts to work, as if he's trying the title out in his mouth before delivering a judgement. Then he blinks suddenly, and turns away, biting his lip.

I touch his arm. 'Would you like a drink?'

He gulps, and nods again.

We go into the saloon bar of the Wheatsheaf and tack our way through the lunch-time crowd to an empty table in the corner. A spotty waitress trails after us, then stands staring at Percy's contorted face with the unselfconscious curiosity of a child. I don't want to add to his mortification by making him speak, so I quickly order for both of us: Mackeson for him, bitter for me, and a couple of sandwiches.

As she leaves, he clears his throat and mutters: 'Sorry.'

'No. You can't help it. It's bound to be upsetting.'

'Ah, but you'd 'a' thought we'd be used to it by now, wouldn't you? It's more'n twenty year since the Somme, in't it?'

I almost reply: *Getting used to it's not the same as getting over it, is it?* but that might seem presumptuous and intrusive. So instead I say: 'Well, I don't know. I'm not sure we do these things awfully well in this country.'

He shrugs. 'Mebbe. But still, there's nowt to be gained by skriking, is there? That won't put baby back in the cradle, as my grandma used to say.'

'No, but it might –'

I pause. I'm not going to corner him. If he wants to know *what* it might do, he can ask. If not – if the feeling it's indecent to talk explicitly about these things is too deeply ingrained to be shifted – then I must take a more oblique approach.

He says nothing, but picks up the ashtray and starts wiping a thin coat of dust from one of the notches with his finger, as carefully as if he were cleaning a gun.

'Did you know my father was killed?' I say. 'At Ypres?'

He nods.

'It's not the same as losing a son, of course, I realize that. But still . . .'

'Bad enough, I dare say.'

'I was nine at the time. You'd have thought at that age I should have been able to grasp what it meant. But I couldn't. My mother told me he wasn't coming back, but I didn't really believe it. I just didn't see how you could snip off one bit of reality like that, and still leave the rest of it intact. If he were *really* dead, everything else would have changed, as well.'

I pause, wondering if I've lost him. I haven't: after a second, he nods again.

'What made it harder was, they never found the body. So you could always cling to the hope they'd made a mistake – confused him with another man. Or else reported him killed when in fact he'd only been wounded. Every morning, during the school holidays, I'd stand for hours looking out of the landing window, thinking at any moment I'd see him hobbling up the path.' I hesitate, then take a chance: 'Probably, you know, with a bandage round his head, and an old crutch given him by the kindly Belgian family who'd taken him in and nursed him back to health.'

It's all right: he's not offended. His mouth twitches into a rueful little grin of recognition.

'My mother must have realized what I was doing, I think – otherwise I know she'd have asked me. But she never said a word. And I had no idea what she was thinking at all. She never even mentioned my father – except in passing, when she was talking about our life before the war. Did I remember one summer Daddy found a starfish on the beach at Littlehampton? – that kind of thing.'

A bad choice, I know as soon as I've said it: he probably hasn't heard of Littlehampton – and if he has, it'll simply be as a place where people like me go on holiday, and people like him don't. I try to think of an example closer to his own experience.

But before I can find one, he surprises me by muttering: 'Aye, it were like that wi' our Peg, and Georgy. She'd see a spider, she'd say, *Ooh, that's as big as th' attercoop frickened the lad, thi mind that?* But never: *My 'eart's broke.*'

The invisible wasteland of flints and thistles between us has magically dissolved. I want to reach across and touch his hand, but I'm frightened it'd only break the spell and send him scuttling back for cover. The effort to restrain myself makes my arm ache.

'The only time the subject ever came up,' I said, 'was afterwards, when they were bringing the body of the Unknown Warrior home. My mother took me to watch the train carrying it to London. It was quite an adventure for a thirteen-year-old. We stood on the station platform in the middle of the night – or, at least, it felt like the middle of the night to me. It was pitch-black, and rainy. All around us were women in deep mourning. And then suddenly it appeared in a cloud of smoke, all lit up like an ocean liner. Everybody fell silent. As it was passing us, my mother whispered: *Perhaps that's Daddy in there.*'

'Aye.' His voice is bubbly with phlegm.

'And that's what did for me –'

''Ere you are,' says the waitress. She slides a wobbly tray on to the table, dodgeming the ashtray and scattering beer-mats in every direction. Percy splutters with laughter. The girl stops dead, glass in hand, and gawps at him again. She's so rapt that I can only get rid of her by finishing unloading the tray myself, and thrusting it back at her.

'Well, cheers,' I say.

'Cheers.'

He's still heaving and snuffling: a boy who's heard a fart in church and can't stop sniggering. Useless to try and resuscitate the conversation at this point: the mood's punctured. I push the sand-wiches towards him.

'Ta.' He takes one, chews the corner off it – and almost chokes as another fit of giggles hits him. He thumps his chest, coughs hoarsely, then looks up at me, red-faced: 'Sorry. You were sayin'?'

'Hm?' I'm half-laughing myself now, though I've no idea why.

'About your dad?'

Does he really want to know, all of a sudden – or is he just embar-rassed by his own behaviour, and anxious to change the subject? I wait a moment. He prompts me with a jerk of the chin.

'Well,' I say, 'it's just that I was haunted by the idea – you know: that my father *was* the Unknown Warrior. Probably half the people in the country were thinking the same thing, about their husband or their father or their son. But because no-one ever really talked about it, we didn't realize how common a feeling it was. Everyone thought it was just *them*. Well, I did, anyway.'

He's staring at me. I can't tell if he thinks I'm mad, or is just astonished to hear anyone actually saying these things. But the beer's starting to insulate my nerve endings and make me reckless. I hear myself going on:

'I began to have dreams about it. Or rather, one dream in partic-ular.'

He nods encouragingly.

'Well, a nightmare, really.'

And suddenly I find I'm describing it to him. I don't know why: I hadn't *meant* to do more than mention its existence – just to let him know that I wasn't simply an observer but had a private succubus of my own that would help me to understand the monsters (*How*

314

did the lad die? Was he in much pain? Was he thinking of his mam
and me, and wondering why we couldn't help him?) which must
haunt his inner world, and which he could never acknowledge to
anyone else. But now I've started, it seems curiously easy. No, more
than easy: an immense, unimaginable release.

He's puzzled, I think, but he hears me out. When I've finished, he
nods, and screws a finger into his temple. 'Well, you 'ave to 'ave a
bit goin' on in 'ere, don't you?' he says. 'Fert 'ave a dream like
that.'

His accent sounds stronger than before, and more alien. Is he
making fun of me? Or has my openness embarrassed him so much
that he's retreated into the persona of the bluff, no-nonsense north-
erner?

But it's too late to back down now, in any case. I fortify myself
with another gulp of bitter, and go on: 'That's why I wanted to
make *Autumn Poppies*. I mean, you know, Armistice Day's starting
to lose its significance now, isn't it? It's turning into just another
date on the calendar. Another ceremony. You know exactly what's
going to happen even before it's begun. The Last Post. Someone
reciting: *They shall grow not old, as we that are left grow old –*'

'What, not clever enough for you, that, is it?' There are little pan-
tomime-dame spots of colour on his cheeks. This is getting
dangerous.

'Not *clever*. It's only that I think, for a lot of people, it's increas-
ingly becoming just a kind of going through the motions. And
especially *younger* people, of course, who can barely remember the
war – or perhaps don't remember it at all. That's why I thought – if
they could really see the *personal* significance it still has, for you,
and Ada, and all the thousands of people like you, up and down the
country –'

I pause, waiting for a signal: a nod, or a word, or merely a soft-
ening of the face to encourage me. Nothing: he just glowers at me.
I start to panic.

'I mean, that's the essence of art, isn't it? To take someone's experience, and make it – not universal, you can't do that, but something
that touches other people directly, through *their* experience.'

God, why am I saying this? He's looking stonier by the second.

315

'So that's what I was trying to do . . . You know . . . With you. And Georgy . . .'

Still not a twitch of understanding. I can't go on. He's frozen me into silence.

For God knows how long, we just look at each other. Everything around us suddenly seems slowed and magnified, so that I'm agonizingly conscious of the *whoom* of a motor-bike in the street and the chime of cutlery on crockery at the next table and the dreary drone of a man's voice at the bar.

Finally, Percy drains his glass and pushes back his chair. 'What you can do for Georgy . . . an' your old fella . . . an' the 'ole lot of them', he says, getting up, 'is stop the next one. So the young folk don't 'ave to find out for theirselves. It were meant to be the war to end war, you mind that?' He holds his hand out. 'Anyroad, I best be goin' now. So' – fluttering his fingers at the table – 'thanks for that.'

I can't fathom his mood: he doesn't seem angry, exactly – just withdrawn behind a barricade where I can't reach him.

I follow him to the door. I don't want to leave him like this. I can't think of anything else light and inconsequential to say, so when we get outside I ask: 'Can I give you a lift to the station?'

He flushes suddenly, and shakes his head. 'I'm stoppin' wi' my niece tonight, ta anyway. She got us a ticket for the openin' o' that new picture-'ouse: Gaumont State in Kilburn.' He smiles, looking sheepish and proud at the same time. 'That Gracie Fields'll be there. You wait till I tell our Betty about that. She won't scarcely credit it.'

I end up having to make a dash for the train. The beer's loaded my legs with weights, and I'm struggling with my luggage, so for a few seconds I feel I'm trapped in one of those dreams where, however hard you run, you never seem to get any closer to where you're going. I wrench the door open and throw my cases in just as the whistle blows. Mercifully, it's not as packed as I'd feared: the Christmas rush obviously hasn't started yet. I find a compartment with only two other people in it, squeeze my bags on to the racks, and settle myself in a window seat.

As we jerk and hiccough into motion, I arrange my coat over my knees as a blanket, then slip out *The Face on the Cutting-Room*

Floor and open it. This is the moment I've been promising myself for days: a chance to get swept up in someone else's story, with no responsibility for how it turns out. But I'm so tired that after the first short chapter I find I'm having to re-read every sentence two or three times to make sense of it. Then even that doesn't work: whole pages seem to be detaching themselves from the book and drifting away beyond my grasp. By the time we reach Watford the battle's lost. I ball my scarf into a pillow, and go to sleep.

Except it's more like delirium than sleep. I'm spared the nightmare, at least: no Daddy rising from the tomb. But he's in there, nonetheless, as a kind of obscure off-stage presence. I can still feel the lurch of the carriage and the steady *de-de-de-DE* of the wheels, but I'm not on my way to Shropshire: I'm being whisked through the Kent countryside with the body of the Unknown Warrior. And, at the same time, I'm on a different journey altogether, rattling towards Klosterfeld to find Irma Brücke and give her the binoculars. But the two trains are moving in completely opposite directions, of course, so I'm being slowly spun from one to the other, drawn into a longer and longer thread that I know at some point is going to snap.

And then suddenly the coach begins to sway more violently and I hear the groan of the brakes. I open my eyes again: we're slowing down for a station. One strand of the dream evaporates instantly: there's no coffin to be seen; the young couple opposite me aren't in uniform; and the line of lamp-lit faces I can see on the platform are smiling and laughing. But the other part lingers for a few seconds: I've already jumped up, groping in my pocket to make sure the binoculars are still there and mumbling *Ist hier Klosterfeld?* before I realize that this isn't Germany either.

Mercifully, the young couple don't seem to have noticed my eccentric behaviour: they're much too interested in each other. But I'm sweating with embarrassment, nonetheless. For years I've managed to masquerade, if not as normal, then at least as more or less socially acceptable. But today, all at once, the hobgoblins seem to have begun tugging at the curtain and showing their ugly little faces to the world. First I tell Percy about the nightmare, then I catch myself doing this. If I'm not careful, I'm in danger of turning into

317

one of those people you instinctively cross the street to avoid. I'm probably more than half-way there already.

Why now? There must be a reason. One occurs to me just as the train starts to pull out again, and I watch the station lights shrinking into a fuzzy bracelet of yellow beads through the rain-spattered window: it's ten years, almost to the day, since my first *real* trip to Klosterfeld. Then I was on the eve of my twenty-first birthday; now I'm approaching my thirty-first. Perhaps the trickery with time is an attempt by my subconscious to make me look back at the way I've come since then – contrast my still-adolescent longings with what I've actually achieved.

I take down the bag with the stop-start volumes of the book – *this* book – in it. That, it strikes me, as I open it, is another hobgoblin in itself: how would I explain to my fellow-passengers, if they asked, that I always carry an intermittent record of my life with me wherever I go – not to mention a pair of German field-glasses with a picture and a letter stuffed inside the case? I glance across at them, wondering if they've noticed. They haven't: they're only worried that *I* might have noticed them. The man snatches his hand guiltily away from the girl's thigh, and she blushes and smoothes her skirt with a sheepish little smirk.

There's a sick pang in my stomach before I start. I hate re-reading old letters and diary entries, even at the best of times: hindsight always gives you the dismal sense that you're watching the *Titanic*, lights blazing and dance-band playing, drifting towards the iceberg, and are powerless to do anything about it. So it's no surprise to discover that re-encountering my younger self like this is a melancholy business. There's a phrase or a detail that has me wincing on almost every page, and some passages – my night with Irma Brücke; my cocky conversation about film with Christopher – expose my blindness and naïveté so mercilessly I have to skip them altogether.

But what I'm *not* prepared for is the cumulative effect of seeing the whole story together. I expected to find (naturally enough) what I remember writing: a fractured, disconnected catalogue of false starts, frustrations, wrong turnings, thwarted efforts, half-fulfilled ambitions. What emerges instead is something very different: an unmistakable pattern that integrates all the episodes into a coherent

318

whole. But the common threads holding this web together have nothing to do with me – or, at least, nothing to do with my *intentions*. I'm not the spider; I'm the fly.

Here I am, in December 1937, sitting on a train that's taking me to Christmas with Nicky's family. Let's rewind the film to the beginning: to that other train, in December 1927. If I can just find Irma Brücke, give her the binoculars, reach some kind of shared understanding with her, in which each of us is able to acknowledge the other's loss, then that will finally tourniquet our wounds and conclude my unfinished business with my father's ghost. Only when I *do* find her, it's beyond me: I end up making things worse for both of us. Wounds untourniqueted. Business unresolved. Unable to think of anything else to do, I write to Max.

Six weeks earlier, and he probably wouldn't have seen me. But he's just moved to British Imperial, and been given a modicum of power. And a new secretary called Nicky Weedon . . .

You could say, of course, that seen from this vantage-point, any life would look the same. We make our destiny with the materials to hand. Possibilities are closed off every second. We start off on a thick trunk, and then find we've taken one fork rather than the other, and then a particular branch, and then a series of smaller and smaller twigs, until the only choice left to us is whether we die lying on our back or on our side.

But something else seems to be at work here: something we don't have a term for, except the question-begging catch-all *coincidence*. It wasn't enough for Fate to throw Nicky and me together: it had to clinch the matter by making William her neighbour, and dispatching me upstairs to complain about the noise he was making (if she'd done it herself, they'd never have realized the connection), and then sending us to see him at the theatre on the very evening he couldn't accept her invitation to come back to her flat afterwards and drink malmsey, thereby forcing me to go on my own. Would I have married her if it hadn't been for that?

I honestly don't know.

And what about Christopher? Suppose I'd gone to the docks to find locations for *Mr. Ribbon's Holiday* and hadn't happened to look in at the window of the café just as he was looking out? Would

319

it still have occurred to me to try my hand at documentary? Would it still have occurred to him to ask me?

Again: I don't know. But something – or someone – seems to have marked out my path so clearly that I couldn't miss it. Leaving nothing, as it were, to chance.

My path to what, though?

I'm suddenly aware that the train's started to slow again, and the couple opposite have stood up and are putting on their coats. As she fiddles with her top button, the girl's craning her neck, trying to see inside my bag. Without thinking, I lay my arm protectively over the opening.

'What's that?' she giggles, as they bustle to the door. 'Family secrets?'

It so incenses me, for some reason, that I clench my jaw and mutter: 'I don't fucking know!' I'm just in control enough to wait till they're in the corridor, so with luck they won't have heard. But I can't go on acting like this. There's Christmas at Slip Hill to get through.

I stuff the books back, and close the bag. As I'm pushing it on to the rack again, a red-faced couple and their two children come into the compartment and colonize the empty seats. For the rest of the journey I listen politely as the parents chat to me about the weather and the extraordinary musical gifts of their little girl.

Nicky's waiting at the station with the Daimler. She hugs and kisses me, but her smile's strained and there are little bruise-coloured pouches under her eyes, as if she's been crying. As we're driving away, she asks me how the film's going, but I get the sense it's more out of duty than genuine interest, and she's really thinking about something else completely.

Finally, after a long silence, I say: 'What's the matter?'

She shakes her head.

'Are you angry with me?'

'No, why should I be?'

'You seem a bit upset about something.'

'Why do you always assume everything's to do with you?'

I've never heard her so snappish with me. She's very close to tears.

After a second she shakes her head again and says: 'Oh, I just wish we could go off and be on our own together somewhere!'

'Why? What's happened?'

She sighs unsteadily.

'Is your father nagging you about children again?'

'No, I think he's given up on that.' She sniffs, teetering between laughter and crying. 'Realizes it's a lost cause, probably. And, anyway, he's far too furious with Rex at the moment to bother much about me.'

'What's Rex done?'

She sucks breath through her teeth. 'Said he won't fight, if there's a war with Germany.'

'God!'

'I know. There was an awful row about it at lunch today. Daddy was apoplectic, and poor Mummy was in floods. And Rex just sat there, with that wounded-martyr little smile of his, refusing to justify himself – as if, you know, he thought we were all just so far gone it wasn't worth trying to convince us. I think that's what really got Daddy's goat. At one point, I honestly thought he was going to hit him. And I wouldn't have blamed him if he had. I felt like giving him a sharp kick under the table myself.'

She sounds more animated, and even manages a smile: it's obviously a relief to her to be talking about it. But I still get the impression it's a distraction from her misery, rather than the real cause of it.

'Here we are,' she says, turning into the drive. The house is dark, except for a dim glow from the kitchen and a solitary light in one of the servants' bedrooms.

'Where is everyone?' I say.

'Mummy and Daddy have gone out. They're having dinner at the Moorgates'.'

'And Rex?'

She shrugs. 'I haven't seen him. He's lying low somewhere, I expect, skulking and sulking.'

Well, that's something, anyway: at least I won't have to face anybody tonight.

*

There are a couple of letters addressed to me lying on the dressing-table. One of them, in a too-big brown envelope postmarked Barcelona, is a post-card from Christopher. On the front is a picture of a wounded rifleman, his head clamped between the initials P.S.U. on the left, and U.G.T. on the right. He's pointing directly at the viewer (you can't see it without thinking of Lord Kitchener telling you that your country needs you), and saying: *I tú – que has fet per la victoria?* Catalan, not Spanish, but the meaning's clear enough: *What are you doing for victory?*

On the back, Christopher's written:

You remember Breton telling us that Surrealism would call forth, from 'exterior reality', or whatever his phrase was, something to correspond to its own bizarre images? He was right. When you've seen the juxtapositions created by war – a baby's head on the body of a dog; two severed hands still clutching the steering-wheel of a burnt-out taxi – you never want to look at a Dali again.

Anyway, happy whatever-you're-celebrating. How's the Armistice Day film going?

Needless to say – not much chance of an Armistice Day here.

Christopher

So, I think, lowering myself gingerly into the bath, and *ooh*ing and *aah*ing as the heat starts to coax the aches from my body, *What am I doing for victory?* The inescapable answer is: *Not very much.* There's a war coming, no doubt about that: everybody feels it. Christopher's fighting it already, in Spain. Rex, somewhere in this very house, is preparing to join the enemy. It's going to be an even greater horror than the last one. Percy's right: I should be doing everything in my power to avert it.

Instead of which, I'm lying here, agonizing about art and whether or not I'm fulfilling my destiny.

When I get back to our room, Nicky's brought up a tray with half a cold steak-and-kidney pie on it, and some left-over vegetables. There are two plates.

I say: 'Oh, you shouldn't have waited for me. Why didn't you have something earlier?'

'I wasn't hungry.'

She still isn't, apparently. Neither am I. We have two or three mouthfuls apiece, then admit defeat. I take the tray back down to the kitchen in my dressing-gown, and put the remains of the pie in the larder.

By the time I get upstairs again, she's in bed. But despite our five-day separation, she doesn't want to make love. She lies turned away from me, gripping a pillow, wound into her own private world. She waits till she thinks I'm asleep. Then she starts to cry: huge half-strangled sobs that clench her whole body as if she were suffering a fit.

I prop myself on one elbow, and stroke her shoulder. 'Darling, what is it?'

She rolls over and clutches me, nuzzling her wet face against my neck. 'I didn't want to tell you,' she whispers.

'What?'

She hesitates a second, then tightens her hold till her nails are gouging my flesh. 'William rang. He's . . . he's had some awful news. About Barrett.'

'What – you mean he's had an accident, or something?'

'Oh, God!' She starts to convulse, thrashing the bedclothes with her feet. 'He's put his head in a gas oven!'

For a moment I lose the power to breathe. Even when it comes back to me, I can't say anything: there's simply no connection between what I'm feeling and words. All I can do is rock Nicky in my arms. After a few minutes the butterfly flutter of her breath on my chest tells me – to my surprise – that I've soothed her to sleep.

It's not your fault, I tell myself.

But a furious lynch-mob howls me down: *You didn't get his number. You didn't 'phone him. You didn't send him a card saying: 'Good to see you again. Don't forget to let me have that play.' If you had – who knows? It might just have made enough of a chink in the wall to save him.*

Human beings are neglectful. Anyone might have done – or failed to do – the same thing.

Ah, but you're not like anyone, *are you? There's something special about you. Didn't you spend three hours on the train today, tracing how some mysterious force keeps intervening to shape your life? All those coincidences, just to bring you here. It doesn't matter that the same coincidences drove Barrett to gas himself. I mean, take the night at the theatre. If Omar had come with you then, William would have met him before the affair with Barrett got under way and Barrett might have found someone else, who didn't systematically snip away at his confidence until it was in threads. But that would have prevented you and Nicky being alone together, so of course it couldn't happen . . .*

All right, all right, it's madness. And I'm a monster.

Enough.

I carefully extricate myself from Nicky, and roll out of bed on to my knees, so as not to disturb her. It takes me a minute or two of groping around in the dark to find the book-bag. Then I edge to the door, and tiptoe out on to the landing.

The whole house is still. I creep up the stairs and prod open the hatch to the attic. There's no light up there, but a thin sliver of moon through the grimy skylight shows me the bulk of the water-tank. I feel my way towards it, lean over the open top, and drop the bag behind it.

I'm half-way downstairs again when it occurs to me what I've done. Anyone could find it, at any time. The things I've written about Nicky . . .

It's a struggle to retrieve it. And as soon as I've done it I start berating myself again. *Typical back-sliding: you decide on a dramatic gesture, and then repent of it. The whole thing's meaningless. Tomorrow you'll have forgotten all about it and be back to your old solipsistic ways.*

I open the bag, take out the binoculars, and hide them behind the tank. It's not everything, but it's a token of good faith. I won't be able to retrieve *them* even if I want to: they're too small for me to reach. If someone else comes across them, they won't be able to connect them to me. But *I* know what they mean to me, and the significance of what I've done.

The book I'll deal with later.

XXII

Shropshire
August 2

It was the least likely place: a gas station. I'd decided to go take a look at the hills I could see from my window. Not that I was dumb enough to think I'd find anything there; I just wanted to give myself a break before heading back to London, and thought they looked pretty. But when I got in the car, I noticed the fuel gauge was showing almost empty. I figured I might not find anywhere to buy gas once I was out in the country, so I stopped at the first place I came to: a supermarket on the edge of town.

There was a mud-spattered Volvo estate filling up on the other side of the island, with three noisy young kids bouncing up and down in the back. I didn't pay much attention to them until after the driver had gone to pay, when the rambunctiousness started to get a bit out of control: lots of flailing limbs, and squeals, and *Give it backs*. Finally, as I was hooking the hose back, I heard a shriek like a dog-whistle. I looked round, and saw the oldest boy had wrestled something from one of the others and was throwing it out of the open window.

I bent down to pick it up. It was a half-eaten candy-bar.

"It's mine! It's mine!" screamed a little girl with a chocolate-smeared face, thrusting her hand out for it.

"Sorry," I said, "I don't think your mommy would like you to have this now. It's all covered in dirt."

"No," said a voice at my shoulder. "Thank you. She wouldn't."

I turned, and did a double-take.

It wasn't her. It couldn't be: this woman was no more than early fifties. But – aside from the hair, which was short and wavy – the resemblance was remarkable: the same wide mouth, and prominent nose, and direct gaze. If you saw her alongside the later picture Tommy Ryder had given me, you'd have thought you were looking at sisters.

325

"Sorry," she said. "Did I make you jump? Here, let me get rid of that."

I watched as she took the remains of the candy-bar and dropped it in a trash-can, then tore a length of paper towel from a dispenser next to the pump and fastidiously wiped her fingers with it. It was all effortlessly ladylike – her arms and hands moving with a kind of sinuous grace, like a ballerina's. Seeing it immediately sparked another connection, which I realized I should have made much sooner: the strange woman I'd found talking to my father in the sitting-room, the week before my mother died.

"Yuuugh!" she said, chucking the towel. "It looked absolutely disgusting, didn't it? You've probably spared us all botulism." She opened her door. "Well, thanks again."

"Excuse me," I said. "Was your mother's name Nicky, by any chance?"

She jolted, as if I'd hit her. Then, very slowly, her face softened into a smile. "Yes. How on earth did you know that?"

"I've seen pictures of her. At least, I think I have. She isn't still –?"

She shook her head. "She died ten years ago. But where did you see the pictures?"

I hesitated. I ought to tell her the truth. But I'd no idea what her feelings were about my father. And I wasn't sure I was ready for the emotional discharge of trying to figure out *my* feelings about *her*.

"I'm over from the States," I said, "doing some research on Henry Whitaker."

"Oh, are you indeed?" The first hint of frost. "Something to do with the centenary, is it?"

"In a way."

"What – you're writing a book?"

"It's more just personal interest. For the moment, anyway."

She nodded. "Well, yes, Nicky Whitaker was my mother. Except she wasn't Nicky Whitaker by that point, of course. She and Henry didn't have any children. I mean, not together. As I expect you know."

"Yes," I said. Though I hadn't: it had just never occurred to me, for some reason, that they might have done. "And your father? If it isn't a rude question?"

"Oh, he was a chap called Val Farrar."

"What, the film director?"

326

She nodded.

"*The Scallywag Gang* man?"

She flushed with pleasure. "Yes, that's right." She reached a hand across the car. "I'm Sally Davenant."

"Bbbbbbb," I mumbled.

"Sorry?"

"Miranda Bbb."

She looked oddly at me, sucking her lip. I could tell what she was thinking: should she be polite and English and leave it, or risk asking me to repeat it yet again? Before she could decide, the kids suddenly started bawling again, and she stuck her head inside the car and shouted: "Oh, for heaven's sake, you lot, do shut up!"

When she emerged again, I plucked up my courage and said: "Look, I can see this isn't the right time, but later on, this afternoon, maybe, could we have coffee or something? It'd be really helpful to talk to you. If you wouldn't mind."

She wrinkled her eyes. "No-o," she said, in a slow, stoned-sounding kind of voice I couldn't quite interpret. "I wouldn't mind. Why don't you come to lunch?"

"Oh, no, you don't have to do that. I could just –"

"No, lunch would be nice. My husband's away at the moment, and I'm on my own. Let me give you directions." She reached into the car again, rummaged in the glove compartment, and pulled out a crumpled sheet of paper and a pencil. It took her a couple of goes, interspersed with a lot of *Oh, damn, damn, no, that's not it*, to draw a map she was satisfied with.

"Here. Oneish all right?"

"Yeah, yeah, fine. Thank you." I looked at what she'd given me: a mess of wavery lines and arrows, with a childish picture of a house in one corner, and the address – *The Stumps, Aston Orrell* – scrawled above it.

"All right," she said. "I'll see you then."

It was only after she'd gone and I saw the clerk glaring at me through his window that I realized I still hadn't paid for my gas.

I abandoned the hills: they were too far away, and I was too nervous. When you're feeling the way I was, I knew from experience, peace and solitude are the last things you need: they just create a sounding-board for your anxieties. And my anxieties were querulous enough as it was: any louder, and they'd paralyze me altogether. Had I blown it already, by not explaining that I was Henry Whitaker's daughter up-front? Should I say: *Look, I'm sorry, there's something I should have told you* as soon as I walked through the door? That would look pretty creepy, like I'd deliberately wheedled my way into her home under false pretences – and if she had a problem with Daddy (which was quite likely, given her situation), she might even say: *Well, I'm sorry, that rather changes things*, and ask me to leave again at once. But if I waited, and then sprung it on her in the middle of lunch, it'd be creepier still. It was right away, or never. If I missed my chance, I'd end up having to lie for two or three hours. Leaving aside how uncom-fortable that would make me feel, I wasn't sure I could come up with a cover story that would convince her.

And then there was the practical question of what, if anything, I ought to take. I didn't want either to embarrass her or to look like a cheapskate. After a lot of existential agonizing I finally settled for flow-ers, and a couple of bottles of wine which I stowed in my shoulder-bag: I could leave them there when I first went in, and then – if it seemed like I needed to up my ante – produce them with a flourish.

For all their messiness, the directions she'd given me were actu-ally pretty straightforward – with the result that I got to Aston Orrell far too early. As I turned into her lane, I almost collided with a man on a bicycle coming towards me. For a split-second a pale, wide-eyed face stared at me through the windshield. It was much too close and looked terrified. No, more than terrified: *hunted*. I stamped on the brake: he swerved and wobbled; the computer bag hanging awkwardly over his shoulder suddenly swung out and pulled him half-off, so that he ended up hopping along on one foot and drag-ging the bike between his legs like a child's hobby-horse. I rolled the window down to ask if he was O.K., but by the time I'd got my head out he'd already remounted and was pedaling furiously along the main road.

I went on till I was past her driveway, then stopped the car and peeked in through a hedge. No security fence this time, at least. The Stumps was a square, red-brick house with a clutter of out-buildings, standing in a big garden at the edge of the village, so that beyond it all you could see was fields and woodland. There was no sign of the Volvo, or the children – or of anything else, really, that would give you the least idea who lived there, or what they were like. I passed the time counting the slats in the shutters: a total of two hundred and forty. At five after one I started the car again and drove in the entrance.

A strong smell of baking bread was leaking out of the half-open front door. I tried yanking on the old bell-pull, but it didn't seem to work, so I put my head inside and called: "Hello!" From somewhere in back I could hear a thin strain of classical music and the *clunk clunk* of an oven door shutting. The next second she appeared in the hall, patting her hands on a striped butcher's apron she'd put on over her shirt and blue jeans.

"Come in! Come in!"

"Thank you." I handed her the flowers. "These are for you."

"Oh, how sweet of you! Let's get them straight into some water, shall we?"

As she took me back, she noticed a door standing ajar on the other side of the hall, and made a little detour to close it.

"Kids' room?" I said.

She shook her head. "The kids are back with their mother, thank heavens. My daughter Jenny. I was just looking after them for her this morning, while she went for an interview."

"*Grand*children!" I said. "You don't look old enough."

"Oh, well that's very kind of you. I certainly *feel* old enough, I can tell you." As she led me into the kitchen, she bent down to pick up a boggle-eyed wooden train lying on the floor. "Three hours is about as much as I can manage now." She tossed the train into a toy basket in the corner. "It's lovely, actually. You can *play* at being Mummy for a little while, and then when you're tired of it hand everything back to the grown-ups. Have *you* got children?"

"One. A boy. Well, a young man, now."

She nodded. She was too polite to ask if *I* had grandchildren, too. "Do sit down, won't you?" she said, pulling out a chair at the big pine table on her way to the sink.

I hesitated. "Is there anything I can do to help?"

329

"I don't think so, thanks. Just as long as you don't mind me putting things out round you."

I sat down and watched her rattling around in a cupboard for a vase. When she found it, she filled it with water and dropped the flowers in, lightly flicking the stems like a harpist fingering the strings. In less than half a minute they were perfectly arranged.

"There," she said. "Aren't they pretty?" She put them down in the middle of the table, fine-tuning the leaves, then glanced back at the huddle of dishes standing next to the Aga stove. "Actually, you know, there is one thing. How are you at salad?"

"Pretty good, I think."

"In that case . . ."

She brought me what looked like a freshly cut lettuce, still wet from the tap, and a cucumber, and radishes, and a knife and a chopping-board, and a big wooden bowl.

"How about a glass of wine while you work?"

"O.K. Thanks. Which reminds me" – fumbling in my bag – "I brought these."

"Oh, that's very sweet of you, but you really didn't have to." She looked at the label on the red, and nodded. "I think I'll join you. I don't at lunch-time, as a rule. But it's nice, isn't it, just once in a while?"

There were big French windows at the end of the room, overlooking a terrace dotted with white chairs and bordered by a box hedge. Bright sunlight was coming in through them at an angle, turning the steamy atmosphere into a golden haze. As the wine and the regular rhythm of cutting and slicing started to take effect, I began to feel as if I'd walked into some kind of benign fairy-tale, where nothing could harm me and everything would somehow be magically resolved. I knew, of course, this was a dangerous deception: the underlying situation hadn't changed, and one misjudged word could reveal that I wasn't what I seemed and rupture the enchantment. But, try as I might, I couldn't force my mind back to the problem of what I should tell her, and when. It was just too blissful sitting here, sensing her working companionably around me – taking a loaf from the oven; adding herbs to a glugging saucepan; setting out knives and forks – and enjoying the odd illusion that we were old friends who'd known each other all our lives.

She added hard-boiled egg and olives to the salad, dressed it, put bread and an earthenware tureen of soup on the table, then glanced round for anything she might have missed.

"No," she said after a moment, sitting down, "I think that's it."

"It all looks wonderful."

"A bit pot luck, I'm afraid. I'm doing you the honor of treating you like one of the family."

Family? Could she have somehow figured out who I was, after all? I feverishly re-ran in my head the half hour or so we'd spent together. Might she have seen something in my car at the gas station? Or peeked in my bag while I wasn't looking?

She poured some soup into my bowl, then held the ladle suspended above it. "And do you know why?"

I shook my head. My tongue seemed stuck to the roof of my mouth.

"Because you knew who my father was."

"Don't most people?'

"He's not as well known as he should be." She finished serving the soup, then cut a slice of bread and offered it to me on the point of the knife. "So when you mentioned *The Scallywag Gang*, it put you straight into my good books."

"Oh, yeah, well, it's a great movie."

She laughed. "You've actually seen it?"

"Sure. Five or six times. Maybe more. They were always showing it on TV when my son was little, and he just adored it."

"How extraordinary." She shook her head, marveling at it. This, it suddenly struck me, when she was feeling flattered and well disposed towards me, would be the moment to tell her. The way in would be easy enough: *Michael always loved old English films – you know: all those village greens, and eccentric spinsters, and black-marketeers in trilby hats. They were an idealized picture of his own lost world: the place I'd left, and he'd never seen. I was born here, you see . . .* But I couldn't quite get the tone of voice right in my head.

I was still struggling with it when she went on: "Well, I agree: it is a lovely film. You may think I'm being ridiculously partial, but I'd put it among the great British pictures – alongside, you know, *Passport to Pimlico*, and *Kind Hearts and Coronets*, and *Lawrence of Arabia*. I honestly believe that's the kind of reputation it would have now, if only Daddy had behaved like any other director and used it as a ticket to Hollywood and gone on to make a name for himself. But he wouldn't. He was too modest. '*Oh, well, that's awfully nice of you, but I really didn't have very much to do with it. I was just terrifically lucky. I had marvelous actors. A marvelous writer. Marvelous cameraman. They're the chaps who deserve all the credit.*'"

I laughed. "He sounds sweet."

"He *was* sweet. *Lucky* was his word. He was lucky to have my mother – even though she'd been married to someone else for fifteen years, and was still –" She stopped abruptly, as if she'd taken the wrong turning and suddenly found herself on the edge of a precipice. "He was lucky to have me, bless him," she went on, after a second, "even though I'm sure he'd have really liked a son, to play cricket with him, and tinker around with old cars. He was lucky to have this house –"

An electric buzz prickled my fingers. "Oh, so *they* lived here, did they? Nicky – your mother – and –?"

She nodded. "But it wasn't his idea; it was hers. So they could be near her parents at Slip Hill. And then finally, when Gramfer died, take Granny in. Never mind that it meant moving away from *his* family, and his friends. That was the story of his life, I'm afraid." She started refilling our glasses. "I never heard him complain about it. He always maintained, to his dying day, that he felt he'd been extraordinarily blessed."

"Well, then, he had, hadn't he?"

She paused, bottle in mid-air, and stared at me with a little frown. "Do you know, I find myself thinking that sometimes, too? More and more, actually. I mean, it all still seems terribly unfair to me – but if, in the end, he genuinely didn't *feel* hard-done-by, who am I to say he was?"

I nodded.

"The problem is, though, how can I ever really know what he felt? It's too late to ask him. You grow up with this fixed idea about your parents, and by the time you start to question it, they've gone. Sorry, sorry; I'm just assuming we're in the same boat, aren't I? Are yours still –?"

I shook my head. Another chance to tell her. They kept coming, but it was like playing one of those crazy-driver computer games: I could never figure out how to respond quickly enough.

"Oh, look here, I'm being an appalling hostess, aren't I?" she said, prodding the salad bowl. "Please: have some of the fruits of your own labor."

"Thank you. Mm, this is all delicious." I took a couple of spoonfuls, then nudged it back towards her. "I suppose what really matters is whether they were happy together. I mean, sorry if I'm being too personal here, but do you think your mother loved him?"

She waggled her fingers to say no, I wasn't being too personal. She thought for a moment, then said: "Ye-es. No. Yes. Well, it depends what you mean by love. She liked him, I think. Enjoyed his company. And was always a dutiful wife – no, that makes it seem too grudging: a *good* wife. Very loyal."

"Sounds O.K."

"Yeah, except that – God, I don't know why I'm telling you all this; you must have a sympathetic face or something – she never stopped loving Henry Whitaker, too." Her eyes were suddenly full of tears. "And that – poor Daddy – was something else entirely."

"When – did she and Whitaker get divorced?"

"Nineteen forty-six. But I think things had been pretty difficult before that."

I took a shot in the dark. "Because of *Better than Magic*?"

"Why do you say that?"

"I don't know – I just thought . . ."

"Well, it's the first I've heard of it, if it was. Not that that necessarily means anything. I realize now, there was an awful lot my mother didn't tell me. And, again, I didn't have the gumption to ask: I always just assumed it had something to do with their having been apart so much during the war. Maybe Whitaker had some wild affair and couldn't settle down again afterwards. That's what happened with a lot of people, wasn't it? I'm pretty sure my mother wouldn't have been unfaithful to *him* – she was much too besotted with the man, though I've never really understood why." Her mouth tugged into a disturbingly Nickyish smile. "You're a fan, of course, so perhaps you can explain it."

333

I panicked for a second. Then, before she could pursue it, I quickly asked: "And what actually caused the final break-up, do you know?"

She took a sip of wine, then put the glass down slowly and started fiddling with it, running her finger distractedly up and down the stem. She was obviously trying to decide how much more she should say.

After a few seconds, she began uncertainly: "Well, my mother, you can imagine, hardly ever spoke about it. It wasn't just painful for her – it was agonizingly embarrassing, because she felt it reflected appallingly both on her and on him. So I only got a pretty watered-down version. But what I heard, for what it's worth – this is still sort of between ourselves – was that he'd gone to Germany after the war, to make a film about the refugee problem. You know, all those millions of people who'd been shunted around during the fighting, or forced into slave labor, and ended up homeless – or even stateless, some of them. He was incredibly depressed, apparently, by what he saw there: the sheer scale of the destruction and the suffering. And of course they'd found the concentration camps by that point. Anyway, he got so bad eventually, he stopped talking. He stopped eating. And then one morning he wouldn't even get up. His cameraman –"

"K.-M. Glocke?"

She nodded. "Though my mother usually called him 'Omar', for some reason. Anyway, he had to lift Whitaker out of bed, and half-carry him to the car, and push him out again the other end. He was *just like a ventriloquist's dummy*, he said – I always remember that; I couldn't believe that someone whose first language wasn't English would be able to come up with such a perfect image. But my mother said, no, Omar spoke English better than most English people."

She took another quick swig of wine: fortifying herself for the dénouement.

"So eventually, after they'd traipsed round for an hour or so achieving nothing, Omar got really angry with him. They were standing outside the dining-room, or the mess hall, or whatever the place was called, at the time. Omar shook his shoulder, and pointed to the queue of inmates waiting to go inside. 'Look at those poor people!' he said. 'We are here to help them!' Whitaker didn't reply. When Omar

334

turned back to him, Whitaker was just staring, like this" – gaping, and widening her eyes – "at one of the women. Just absolutely, you know, love at first sight."

I had to screw up my face and bite my finger to stop myself crying.

"I know, I know," said Sally Davenant, half-giggling. "It does seem awful to laugh, but it is rather funny, isn't it? I mean, the idea of this English chap standing there, looking into a crowd of emaciated, lice-ridden European refugees, and suddenly being struck by a *coup de foudre*. But Omar swore that's what happened. Whitaker was absolutely transformed by it, he said. Instead of being depressed, he seemed almost manically elated."

I tried to strangle a sob. It came out as a choking sound instead.

Sally Davenant laid a hand on my arm and said: "Are you all right? Do you want some water?"

I managed to say no, I was O.K.

She went on: "There was obviously more to it than that. For one thing, Omar refused ever to work with Whitaker again, and spent the rest of his life hinting that he knew some dark secret about him which he wasn't at liberty to divulge. I'm pretty certain my *mother* knew what it was: she and Uncle William were very close, and I always had the impression *he*'d told her. But whenever I quizzed her about it, she just clammed up. All very mysterious." She laughed. "And, needless to say, terribly frustrating for me."

"Yes, it must have been."

"In any event, a couple of weeks later, they started shooting. Originally, Whitaker planned to use the woman's story in the film, but it turned out she couldn't remember what had happened to her clearly enough. She'd been just too traumatized, I suppose. But he went to see her every day while they were there, and at the end of the shoot he told Omar that as soon as he could get a divorce, he intended to marry her and bring her to England." She shrugged helplessly. "So, there you have it. My mother was abandoned for a chimera."

I couldn't control myself any more. From the reediness of her voice, I think she was close to tears herself. But my vision was so blurry, all I could make out was the puzzled tilt of her head as she watched me.

After a few seconds, she pushed her chair back and got up. "I'm going to make some coffee," she said.

335

I hid my face in my hands and listened to the ordinary domestic noise of a tap splooshing and metal grating against the Aga and water starting to thrum in the bottom of a kettle. I should have found it reassuring, but it was too remote: the soundtrack to another universe. The one I was in didn't have those kinds of physical details. It was black and featureless: not a place so much as a state of endless, spiraling, sea-sicky motion, where there was nothing solid to hold on to at all.

I heard the clink of china, and then soft footsteps as she moved towards the door. I didn't bother to look up: I guessed she just had to go to the bathroom. She must have been gone a while, though, because the kettle had been boiling for two or three minutes by the time she got back.

She didn't speak again until she was putting the cups out on the table. Her voice was so quiet that I missed the first few words, but they were obviously about my mother, because when I came in she was saying: " . . . there was a daughter, too, I believe, who went to America. I often used to think about her when I was growing up, wondered what she was like. Did you ever read *The Amulet*?"

I shook my head. There was a gurgle of pouring coffee.

She went on: "I loved that book as a child. I was always nagging Mummy to read it to me. There are two halves to the amulet. The children have one, and they have to find the other to make it whole. I thought that was like that poor woman's daughter and me. Do you want milk?"

I just managed to nod.

"Each of us had – each of us *was* – one half of the child my mother would have had if she'd stayed with the man she loved."

I sat up and looked at her. She looked back.

"And here we are, Miranda," she said.

She pushed the cups and plates out of the way, and leaned over and hugged me.

We carried our coffees out on to the terrace, and sat half-facing each other in a couple of the white chairs. We were so close our feet almost touched. For a while we didn't say much: just the occasional little flurry of small-talk about the smell of the roses and the beauty of the view. It could have been uncomfortable, but it wasn't: rather than retreating from our conversation at lunch, it just felt like we were building on it, by taking our new-found intimacy for granted. I couldn't help wondering how she'd worked out who I was, and feeling embarrassed that I hadn't told her; but most of all I was relieved that she knew, and that it had drawn us together rather than pushing us apart.

So it seemed quite natural when, after muttering something about a plague of greenfly they'd been having, she bent down, and scratched her ankle, and said: "You're not really what I expected."

"What did you expect?"

"Well, when I was young, I used to picture you as romantic and gipsyish – you know: raven hair, and big gold earrings. I suppose I thought the result of such a bizarre story was bound to be pretty exotic."

"You were right about the hair, at any rate." I twisted round and touched the middle of my spine. "I used to have it down to here. Some of the girls at school used to call me *Ruth*, and whisper *Jewess* behind my back. And when I first went to the States, a lot of people thought I was Mexican."

"*Was* your mother Jewish?"

"I don't know. She didn't like to talk about it. To be honest, I'm not sure she knew for certain: she'd been just too traumatized."

She nodded. There were tears in her eyes. "It must have been very difficult for your father. If he imagined he'd found his ideal woman, and then it turned out she wasn't even clear who she was herself."

"Yes. Though it's funny, I don't remember that being a problem, really. I mean, he might get slightly frustrated with her when she couldn't recall some simple fact about the house she'd lived in, or where she'd gone to school, or whatever, but that didn't happen very often. It wasn't the lack of a past that bugged him, but the way she acted around him. I think what he wanted was a fiery, soulful European. And she just wasn't that way at all. All *she* wanted, you know, was a kind of John and Mary life with a nice home, and maybe a trailer they could take to the beach."

Sally Davenant smiled. "And did he ever tell you how they met?"

I shook my head. "I never heard the story before today. Well,

337

except once, kind of. But I'd no idea what it was back then." And I told her about "The Curious Case of Horace Dogbiscuit and Lotte Schlossloss."

"How extraordinary!" she said. "We listened to that, too."

"*Everyone* listened to *Niddle at Nine*, didn't they?"

"Yes, I know, but this was special, because Uncle William was in it."

"William Malpert?"

She nodded. "Not that he was my *real* uncle, of course. Just a friend of Mummy's. But that's why I remember it so clearly. And exactly the same thing happened, only for us it was the other way round. Daddy sat there puffing on his pipe and chuckling, and Mummy said she had a headache, and rushed out of the room. And she was someone who *never* had headaches. Afterwards I heard her crying in their bedroom. And she almost never cried." She tugged at a blade of grass growing up between two paving stones, tickled her lip with it, then gave me her most Nickyish grin. "So there, you see. It's true. We're mirror images of each other."

Maybe the wine and the confessional atmosphere had made me suggestible, but as I looked at her I suddenly saw my features swimming on to her face and laying themselves over hers. The effect was so disturbing that I had to turn away sharply. A flock of birds was stippling the sky above the distant woods, as remote and serene as a Japanese print. I calmed myself by watching them, and rewound the last ten minutes' conversation in my head, looking for a way back on to safer ground. Finally I found one.

"So," I said. "And how did you see me later on?"

"Mm?"

"You visualized me with raven hair and earrings when you were young. What about when you got older?"

She laughed. "Oh, the raven hair and earrings survived until about a year ago, I think. And then suddenly you turned into an Amazon, more or less overnight."

I hesitated for a second. Then I said: "Did that have anything to do with Alan Arkwright, by any chance?"

She blushed and smiled, as if I'd surprised her in some discreditable act. "Yes, that's right. How did you know?"

"I don't think anyone else thinks of me like that."

"No, I can't imagine they do." She paused, winding the bit of grass round her finger. Then, without looking at me, she said: "It is a bit awkward, actually. The thing is, you see, he's working here."

"What – *Alan Arkwright*?"

She nodded. "He has been, for a few weeks."

I couldn't assimilate this information at all. "Where . . . I mean, why . . .?"

"Here," she said, suddenly getting up and starting towards the house. "I'll show you."

Oh, God, I thought. *I'm not ready for this.* "He isn't here now, is he?"

"Oh, no. He bolted when I told him you were coming to lunch."

I grimaced. "I'll bet he did. He's been systematically avoiding me."

"When I say *you*, I don't mean *you* you. I just said an American woman I'd met, who was interested in Henry Whitaker. But he did look pretty shocked, I must say, so perhaps that was enough for him to work it out." She stopped and turned at the French door, waiting for me to catch up with her. "I didn't guess it myself till later, when I saw your reaction to the Germany story. Then I popped out and checked his notes. Your age was right. Your not-quite-American, not-quite-English accent was right. And in the *Family photos* file I even found an old picture of you – taken in the seventies, I'd say, but still quite recognizable."

She led me back through the kitchen and into the hall, then stopped in front of the door she'd closed when I came in. "I don't know if you know anything about the state of the British university system these days?" she said, with one hand on the knob. "It's publish or be damned. So Arkwright made me promise I wouldn't let any other scholars near this till he's finished, in case they stole his exclusive and produced their *own* Henry Whitaker book, and he found himself out of a job. But you're not another scholar, are you? So I think I'm in the clear."

She turned the handle and pushed open the door. The first thing I saw was a long dining-table, running almost the whole length of the room and draped with blankets to protect the surface. Strewn across them was a chaos of pens, opened and closed notebooks, index cards, old photographs, and stray sheets of paper. In the middle was a printer, surrounded by a tangle of computer wires. But the computer itself was gone.

"It's all my mother's fault," said Sally. "She collected everything she could that had any sort of connection with Henry Whitaker. Pictures. Copies of his films. Things he'd written, or that had been written about him. She was completely obsessive about it."

So many emotional currents started to eddy through me that all I was conscious of was a kind of shivery turbulence where they collided. I wasn't cold, but I began to tremble.

"*Why?*" I said.

"Well, she didn't talk about it much. It was just sort of a given, when I was growing up. But I think she felt she'd failed him, and was trying in some way to make up for it."

"*She*'d failed *him*?"

She nodded. "He was a genius, you see – that's what she thought. And geniuses need understanding. And she hadn't given him enough of it, which is why he'd gone off the rails and ended up dying more or less in obscurity. So she felt the least she could do was to make sure that when people rediscovered him, and wanted to know more, there'd be something for them to work with. No-one else at the time was doing anything about it, so she took the job on herself. '*Just you wait, my girl*', she'd say. '*One day, people will be beating a path to our door.*'"

I was still having trouble figuring out my feelings. All I could do was nod, and murmur: "Wow."

"And she was half-right, I suppose. One minor academic doesn't really qualify as *people*. But it's some vindication of her faith, isn't it? Pity she didn't live long enough to see it." She hesitated, then laughed. "Though I'm not sure, to be honest, just how thrilled she'd be, if she knew the effect it's had on him."

"Why? What's –?"

"I think he's close to a nervous breakdown, poor chap." But the smile, I noticed, still hadn't completely faded from her face. For some reason, the mix of pathos and low comedy in her manner made me think of the man I'd almost run into in the lane.

"Does he ride a bicycle, by any chance?" I asked.

"Yes. Why, did you see him?"

"I think I nearly killed him."

"Oh, dear." She swallowed a guffaw, turning it into a hiccough. "What happened?"

I told her.

When I'd finished, she said: "Well, it might have been a mercy, actually. You'd have put him out of his misery."

I couldn't suppress a *frisson* of pleasure – mingled with a completely contradictory stab of outrage that he was finding my father difficult. "Why is he having such a hard time of it?" I said.

She shook her head. "He's terribly cagey about it. Doesn't want to give any hostages to fortune, I suppose, by saying something he might regret later. But a few days ago, in an unguarded moment, I did hear him say he thought Henry Whitaker was quite mad."

"*Mad? Daddy?* How *dare* he?"

I glanced at her. I could tell from her smile that she'd caught the irony of the situation. I smiled back. We both began to giggle, like two schoolgirls tittering at a *double entendre*.

To distract myself, I started looking through a pile of photographs on the table. There were a few I recognized from Granny's collection, and one of the pageant that had obviously come from Tommy Ryder, but otherwise they were all new to me. Most of them were from the 1930s: Daddy gazing wistfully away from the camera, with a cigarette in his hand; Daddy in a foreign-looking garden, talking to a woman I didn't recognize; Daddy directing a crowd of people in front of a war memorial; several of Daddy with William, and with another man I thought might have been Christopher Morton Hunt. But there was one very obvious omission.

"There don't seem to be any of your mother," I said.

"No." Her throat tightened. "It was a concession to my father, I think – a way of trying to spare his feelings. Not that she ever said so – or, at least, never to me. But I suspect the idea was that if she airbrushed herself out, she could just about maintain the fiction that this was a purely academic exercise. She wasn't doing it because Henry Whitaker had been her husband – oh, no, nothing to do with that at all. It was simply that he'd been a great man, whose memory ought to be preserved, you know, in the national interest or something."

"God," I said. "Your poor father."

She nodded. "But he even went along with it – that's the strange

341

thing. In public, anyway. '*I knew Henry Whitaker, and he was an extraordinary chap, no doubt about it. So I think it's marvelous what Nicky's doing. Really marvelous.*'"

I couldn't speak for a moment. Then I managed to squeeze out: "And poor you, too."

She nodded again. She was close to tears.

After a second she said: "It *was* difficult. For years I couldn't even bear to hear Henry Whitaker's name. It just made me feel too awful about Daddy. I hated Mummy for liking him best – and at the same time, I hated him for leaving her, and making her unhappy. It was all very complicated."

"It must have been."

"But just because of that, of course, I was completely fascinated by him. I used to have fantasies that he was really *my* father, too, and that one day he'd come and take me away to live with him. The thought of it really terrified me. But it was also terribly exciting, in an odd way. I kept thinking I saw him, peering in at the window, or flitting through the bushes in a big black coat, and I didn't know whether or not I should tell." She smiled, but she was quietly crying.

I held back a second, then reached out and touched her hand. "Hm, well, one way and another," I said, "he seems to have screwed up both our lives pretty successfully, doesn't he?"

She shrugged. I could see she was about to say something, but at that moment the telephone started to ring. She resisted for a moment, but the tone was so bossy she couldn't ignore it. She mouthed *sorry*, then went out into the hall to answer it.

I waited till I heard the murmur of her voice, then sat down and began riffling through the pictures again. After all the emotional bloodletting we'd been through, there was actually something rather soothing about these glimpses of a lost black-and-white world, which – now I'd got over the surprise of discovering its existence – seemed safely remote from me. I could try to guess names and dates and places, then turn over and look at what was on the back without fear of finding anything too disturbing.

And then, at the very bottom, I came across one that gave me an almost physical jolt, like touching a live wire: a colour print of a sick old man, red-eyed from the flash, sitting glumly in a cutting-room in

342

front of a Moviola film-viewer. No question about names and dates and places here: it must have been taken in Hollywood, within a few days of the last time I'd seen him. What threw me wasn't just the shock of recognition, and his ghastly appearance, but the sudden breaching of the barrier between Nicky's Henry Whitaker and mine.

"That was Alan Arkwright," said Sally, re-entering the room, "wanting to know if the coast was clear. I told him it wasn't. So he won't be coming back today."

I didn't know if I was sorry or not. For the first time in weeks, I'd started to lower my guard – and at the thought of having to gird up my loins again and prepare myself for a fight, I could feel the energy hemorrhaging from me. On the other hand, having pursued the man so relentlessly and finally got him cornered, I couldn't just let him escape again.

My confusion must have shown, because after a moment Sally went on: "Sorry, was that the wrong thing to do?"

"No, it's fine."

But I could hear the flatness in my own voice. Sally heard it, too.

She frowned and said: "I got the impression you didn't particularly want to meet him."

"I don't. But I guess I feel I ought to be strong, and force myself. I mean, that's what I came here for, really. And so far he's managed to elude me."

"Oh, dear. Well, I suppose I could ring him back."

"Did you tell him who I was, this time?"

She shook her head. "I wasn't sure if you'd want me to. And I didn't know what effect it'd have on him."

I nodded. "Thank you."

"But still, he'd be bound to smell a rat, wouldn't he?"

She sat down next to me. Her lips moved, and she drew in her breath to say something else, then she changed her mind. I gave her a moment to change it again.

When she didn't, I said: "How did your mother get this?"

I held up the picture.

She leaned forward, squinting at it. "Oh, Max must've given it to her, I think."

343

Of course – she'd known Maxted too. It was perfectly obvious: I'd just been so busy trying to absorb everything else, it simply hadn't occurred to me. But for some reason the idea of it still gave me an odd, nauseous twinge.

"I expect it was when she went over to get the film," said Sally.

"What film?"

"You know. The one he was working on when he died."

"Excuse me?"

"The one about your mother. *The Great Disaster*, as Arkwright calls it."

"But it was never finished."

"No, but they'd shot over two hours of footage. When she got it back here, my father ran through the whole thing, gamely trying to piece it together, or at least find some logic in it. But it was beyond him. '*A bit too deep for me, I'm afraid.*'"

I smiled. "Yes. I could never understand how Daddy was allowed to do it."

"Oh, well, that's easy. It was Maxted, wasn't it? I mean, he was the most powerful director in Hollywood by that point. And he pulled strings. Said this was the cinema of the future. Even put up some of his own money, I believe –"

"I know," I said. "But what I mean is, *why*? It can't have done his reputation any good. And it must have left a huge hole in his bank balance. You begin to wonder if my father had something on him, and was blackmailing him."

She laughed. "I don't think it was that. Or not according to Mummy, anyway. She told me Max always said" – slipping into a passable imitation of Maxted's voice – "*that he knew Whitaker had a great film in him*. And that he felt personally responsible, somehow, for the fact he'd never made it. So when your father approached him with his big idea, and told him how ill he was, Max realized it was his last chance to help him." She hesitated a moment. Then, carefully watching to see my reaction, she went on: "My father was hardly ever horrible about anyone. But even he said, after he'd seen it: 'Well, if Henry had a great film in him, I'm afraid it's still in there.'"

I smiled. She smiled back, relieved that I wasn't offended.

"Listen," she said. "What are your plans?"

"Well, I have to get back to London at some point. But –"

"Because I was just thinking: if you could spare the time, why don't you stay for a couple of days? Then you could go through this stuff at your leisure. And tomorrow, of course, Arkwright will be here – so if you want to see him, you can just burst in and take him unawares."

Most of the rest of the day we talked. A lot of it was just the usual magpie chatter about families and work and homes and vacations that always gets traded at social occasions. But there were moments, too, when I had the strange sensation that we'd managed to migrate inside each other's heads, the way twins are supposed to sometimes. When I told her how my TV career had gone on the rocks and left me unable to write anything longer than a shopping-list for twenty years, for example, she said, totally out of the blue: "Well, at least you're able to write again *now*, aren't you?" Or, weirder still: while *she* was telling *me* how she sat by her mother's bed when she was dying, I suddenly had the inexplicable sensation of something pressing against my fingers. The next second, Sally said: "I asked her to let me know if she could hear me. She didn't open her eyes or say anything, but she managed to give my hand a little squeeze."

It was nearly one in the morning when we finally hauled ourselves upstairs. I was so shot that – after saying a bleary goodnight on the landing – I went straight into my room and, without even getting undressed, lay down on the bed and passed out.

But my brain had too much to process to allow me to sleep peace-fully. I woke again suddenly, sticky with sweat, and completely disorientated. Then – *flip, flip, flip*, like a sequence of cards in a game of solitaire – the events of the last twenty-four hours came back to me, and I remembered where I was. I fumbled for the light-switch, took my clothes off, then crept out and showered as quietly as I could. By the time I'd finished, my mind was humming so much that I realized it was pointless to go back to bed. I was too nervous about meeting Arkwright; too jittered by everything Sally Davenant had told me; too curious about what else I might discover in the chaos on the dining-room table.

I put on my dressing-gown, and tiptoed downstairs.

There was something uneasy about sitting there, all alone, at three in the morning. Even though, if Sally heard something, or noticed the light and came down to investigate, I could probably explain myself, I was haunted by the sense that I was intruding: on her, on Nicky, on Arkwright – above all, on my father. Once, when I was five or six, I'd spied on him through the bathroom keyhole to find out how men peed. I'd known it was wrong, but I couldn't help myself. Now, looking at notes and letters he'd never intended me to read, I had the same queasy feeling. I could sense his disapproval, even after more than thirty years.

But as it turned out, I didn't find anything very sensational. There were a few anodyne post-cards to Nicky from places where he was filming; some ideas for documentaries that never, in the event, got made; jokey little exchanges with William Malpert and K.-M. Glocke. Nothing about Mummy at all – except a cryptic note to Arthur Maxted written when Daddy was working on his final movie: *How about calling it* An Ordinary Woman? *Or even just* Ordinary? *Because that's the point, really. Romona (and I wish I'd realized this earlier, while she was still alive) was a profoundly* ordinary *person.*

It wasn't much, but it was something. I put it on one side, assuming I'd soon have more to add to it. But after half an hour it was still on its own.

It was only then that it occurred to me how incredibly stupid I was being. Arkwright, obviously, must have sifted through the material before me – so if there were any other gems there, the chances were he'd removed them already. I immediately switched my attention to his own papers. But they proved even more disappointing: just pages and pages of mundane facts – date of birth; education; brief biographies of family, friends and colleagues – together with files of unexceptional photos – including the one that Sally had found of me. If he *had* discovered anything more interesting, he must have taken it with him when he bolted.

But could he have done? The more I thought about it, the less likely it seemed. When I saw him on his bike, all he was carrying was his computer case. The most you could squeeze into that, in addition to a laptop, was a few sheets. I simply couldn't believe that several weeks' work had failed to produce a more substantial haul than that.

I looked around for a cabinet or a bookcase where he might have stowed it. There was nothing but an old sideboard – and when I got up and examined that, all I found was cutlery and place-mats and a set of glasses. But as I turned to go back again, I noticed an odd crease in the blanket covering the table, as if something angular was pressing against it. It was the wrong shape, and in the wrong place, to be a leg. I knelt down, and lifted the blanket.

What confronted me was an image from my childhood: the words *Anchor Butter*, in faded red and green, stamped on the side of a battered carton. I groped for the edge of the box and tried to pull it towards me, but all that happened was that the cardboard started to tear. So I stood up, and gradually nudged it out with my foot.

It wasn't surprising it was so heavy: inside were twenty or so notebooks, most of them in hard covers. As I squatted down again to examine them, I noticed someone had scribbled something on the lid of the box, then crossed it out again. I peered closely at it, lifting the flap to catch the light, trying to decipher the obliterated word. When I succeeded, I had to clutch the table to stop myself wobbling over. It was: *Miranda?* I couldn't tell whether the question mark was original, or had been added later.

I grabbed a notebook at random, and opened it at the first page. It was lined, and covered in handwriting – unmistakably my father's, but younger and less crabbed than I remembered. I scanned it quickly, looking for a phrase or a name that might tell me what it was. The first sentence that caught my eye was: "When William ambles on with a wheelbarrow, I want to scream: *Hurry up, for Christ's sake!*"

I hurried on, jumping over paragraphs of dialogue, until another line tripped me up: "I hear Nicky sniffing, and look towards her."

William. Nicky. My mouth was dry, and my pulse was trampolining in my throat. Somewhere in here there must be *Romona*.

I pulled out the rest of the notebooks and started riffling through them, looking for dates. The earliest was December 1927. Then, in rapid succession, I found February 1928, April 1930, and October 1932. I went on, more and more frenetically: July 1934; June 1936; December 1937.

But no 1946.

At first I thought I must just have missed it, somehow. I immediately started over again, flipping the pages more carefully.

347

But I hadn't missed it. It wasn't there. The last entry was headed *September 1939*.

I sat there for the longest time, feeling so sick and muzzy with disappointment that I couldn't move. Then, slowly, I managed to rouse myself enough to start putting the books back in the box. I'd almost finished when I suddenly remembered *Better than Magic*.

It was made in 1938. So there should at least be something about that.

It took me a couple of minutes to find the right notebook again. Then I carried it upstairs with me, got into bed, turned to the first page, and read:

XXIII

Burnley – November 1938

I change trains at Preston. Just as the whistle blows a boy wrenches open the door and hurls himself into my compartment. Three others follow him. They sprawl panting on the seats, laughing at the muffled curses of the guard on the platform. Their wan malnourished faces are spotted with colour from the effort of running. Two of them are coughing and wheezing with bronchitis. They're too busy sniggering and elbowing each other and making *fuck off* signs at the invisible guard to take any notice of me, but I know I've seen them before, though I can't place where. Not surprising: I must've seen a thousand emaciated boys with the same sick-bed pallor and *sod you* expressions over the last three months.

As we emerge from the shelter of the station, a bead curtain of rain rattles against the window. I peer through it at the untidy progression of warehouses and grubby commercial hotels and advertisement hoardings and soot-covered villas, waiting for the magic moment. I know exactly when it's coming and how it's done, but the old sleight-of-hand still thrills me, even now: with a quick *hey presto!* the black industrial landscape is whisked away, and we're in a different century. No more than fifty yards from the track there are sheep grazing, their dirty wool sodden and pearled with rain; beyond them, the land undulates down into a wooded valley, and then rises again to a sloping ridge, where the first lights are starting to appear in the windows of a stone farm-house. And – here it is, that sudden merry-go-round *whoosh* in the belly – in the distance, through the mizzle, you can just make out the dove-feather grey of the Pennines, shimmering faintly in a patch of watery sunshine that we're too low down to see.

'Eh, look, that's the fella as did them films.'

It's said in a stage-whisper, but too loud for me to be able to pretend not to hear it. I turn quickly. The furthest boy is staring at me.

349

He's bigger than the others, and almost film-star handsome when you see him full-face, with sensuous lips and a flinty Western-hero gaze. He flinches for a second as our eyes meet, but doesn't look away. I know why I recognize him now: he was one of the crowd coming out of the matinée of *Wallaby Jim of the Islands* at the Grand.

'What you doin' now, then?' he says. 'I thought you was finished?' His tone's poised between insolence and genuine curiosity. Which way it tips depends on me.

I smile. 'I thought I was too.'

'So why you comin' back?'

First rule when you're cornered: ask for assistance. 'I need a bit of help.'

'Oh, aye?'

His neighbour – a button-eyed little weasel with a pink rash on his throat where he's scraped himself shaving – whispers something in his ear.

''Ey, shurrup, you!' says the first boy, jabbing him in the ribs and grinning. I'm shocked to see that half his teeth have gone already. So much for his good looks.

'Yes,' I say. 'I'm trying to clear up a mystery.'

'Oooh, a mystery!'

The others laugh. I click open my bag and slip my hand inside. All I can feel is my notebook. *Jesus!* I think. *They've disappeared!* I scrabble around wildly, trying to find them. *I knew it! There really is something strange about all this. I'm dreaming, or under a spell . . .*

And then I have them: the stiffness of the sheets, the warm stickiness of the glazed surface.

I shut my eyes. Stupid, stupid: how *could* I have imagined they'd disappeared? Nicky's right: if I'm not careful I'm going to go off the rails altogether.

I take a deep breath, and start to slide the first photo out.

'I know,' says the weasel suddenly. ''E's got a girl 'ere.'

More laughter. I stop sliding.

'Is tha' right, then, mister?' asks the first boy. 'You soft on a Burnley lass?'

I hesitate for a moment, then discreetly drop the picture back. 'All the Burnley girls are nice,' I say.

'Aw,' says the weasel, 'you should see my sister.'

I laugh with them. 'But I'm a married man,' I say. And then, before they have a chance to push me even further into a corner: 'And where have you lot been?'

'Preston,' says the first boy. 'Lookin' for work. There's nowt to be 'ad in the mills. It's that Gandhi fella, me dad says – tellin' the natives not to buy our stuff.'

'And did you have any luck?'

He shrugs. ''E' – nodding at his neighbour – 'got took on at Perrins. You know, the engine-makers. On account of 'e's proper 'andy, see?'

The weasel gives the self-conscious comic grimace of a small boy at his own birthday party.

'But I don't reckon there'll be owt for the rest of us, not till the war come. *Then* we'll be wanted, right enough.'

He's right, of course. It's all too easy to imagine: stick them in khaki and put them in a trench, and you could be looking at a picture of the Somme.

'You think it's inevitable, do you?'

He frowns. I can't tell if it's because he doesn't know what *inevitable* means, or just isn't used to someone like me asking him that sort of question.

He hesitates, then throws the ball back at me: 'What do you think, then?'

'Well, I'd like to think it could still be avoided. But if I'm honest, I can't really see how, short of a miracle. Hitler becoming a Quaker, or something.'

He flashes me his mangled smile. 'Me dad says we should've told 'im what's what when 'e went in the Rhineland. If you let 'im get away wi' that, 'e'll reckon 'e can get away with anythin'.' Perhaps I don't look encouraging enough: he suddenly seems to lose confidence. 'Tha's wha' me dad says, anyroad.'

'Yes, well, I'm afraid he's right. The trouble is, we expect people to be rational. Reasonable. And they're not, most of the time.'

That puzzles him. His eyes drift away while he thinks about it.

Finally he looks at me again and nods. His lips move; but before he can speak, the weasel says: 'You know what? Up at Colne, they're burnin' a 'ouse at Guy Fawkes, 'stead of a bonfire. To show what'll 'appen when a bomb 'its. I don' rightly reckon I wants to know, meself.'

Everyone laughs. And suddenly it becomes a general conversation: about the new A.R.P. centre being built at Throstle Mill; and the Corporation's plan to use cellars as air-raid shelters (*They can 'ave ours*, says the weasel, *if they don' mind sharin' it wi' a rat as big as their yeds*); and how the operators at the telephone exchange have been practising saying *Number, please* with gas masks on. It's still bubbling away when I see the familiar fish-bone pattern of the grey-roofed little terraces on the hillside, and realize we're pulling into Bank Top station.

I say goodbye, then quickly gather my bags and slip out of the train ahead of them.

Well, if nothing else, I think, *I succeeded in distracting them from the question of why I'm here.*

But then, as I'm walking along the platform, a surge of laughter erupts from the clatter of footsteps behind me, and above it I can hear the weasel's voice saying: 'An' I bet I knows who it is, an' all. Betty Minton.'

At least they can't see my blushes.

It's still only 4.30. Percy won't be back for another couple of hours or so. I'd planned to get my hair cut in the morning, but it suddenly occurs to me it might be a good idea to do it now. If Percy sees me shaggy this evening, and then miraculously spruced up in time for my meeting with Betty tomorrow, he might draw the wrong conclusion.

I leave my suitcase at the Sparrow Hawk, then make my way to the Croft. Maison Hugill's still open. As I'm trying to see if there's a queue, Mr. Hugill recognizes me through the window and beckons me inside. He's embarrassingly friendly – gestures me to the chair with a big smile and a courtly flourish, and immediately starts asking about the film. *How are we getting on with it? When will it be finished? Am I going* – a phlegmy little chuckle here, to show he's only joking – *to make Betty Minton a Hollywood star?*

I manage to fend him off with a lot of *oh, fine, fine*s and a few jokes of my own. But it's a warning: I can't expect to be anonymous here any more. Pretty soon the whole town will be aware that I'm back. And if I do or say anything the least bit eccentric, it'll be common knowledge within twenty-four hours.

Afterwards, I go to the Co-op in Hammerton Street, buy a bag full of the plainest groceries – even butter or dried fruit might give the impression I was trying to sweeten someone up – then walk down the path towards Tisker Street. It's quite dark now, and the shallow valley on the other side of the canal is layered with pale strands of light from the living-room gas-lamps, giving you the odd illusion that you're looking at an ocean liner. Here and there in the spaces between them you can see the dim smudge of a candle-flame flickering in a bedroom window.

Percy answers the door himself, wearing a collarless shirt and his Sunday-best braces.

'Oh, 'ow do, 'Enry.' Still looking at me, he jerks his chin over his shoulder and calls: 'It's 'Enry, luv.'

'O-o-o-o-o-oh!' shrills Ada, from somewhere inside, as if I've turned up at the wrong time, and she's panicking.

'Hello, Percy,' I say. 'Did you get my telegram?'

'Oh, aye.'

And the next moment, as he moves out of the way to let me in, I see it there, laid out on the table: *Returning unexpectedly. May I come and see you tonight? Henry W.*

'We reckoned mebbe it were bad news,' he says. 'The only other one we ever 'ad, see, it were about Georgy.'

'Sorry. I couldn't think of any other way to reach you quickly enough.'

'Oh, it don' matter,' says Ada, suddenly appearing from behind him. 'It were nice 'avin' the little fella knock and say: *Telegram, miss.*' She stops, wiping her red hands on her apron, and smiles at me. 'So you 'aven't 'ad enough of us, then?'

'I'll never have enough of you, Ada.'

She blushes. 'Oh, get on wi' you, you daft ha'perth!'

I slide the Co-op bag on to the table, as inconspicuously as I can. 'Though I imagine you must be pretty sick of *me* by now.'

She shakes her head.

'Come on, lad,' says Percy, touching my arm. 'Come an' rest your pegs, while she's makin' the tea.'

We sit facing each other in the two tattered arm-chairs, leaving a wide enough gap for Ada to be able to get to and from the stove. The atmosphere's heavy with that characteristic sour fuggy smell of gas fumes and cooking and tobacco-smoke and unbathed bodies and dirty work-clothes and burning coal, all spiced with a faint whiff of washing-soap. Even after only a few days I seem to have lost my immunity to it. For a second, I'm terrified I'm going to retch.

'So how are you, Percy?'

He nods, slowly lowering his eyelids, then raising them again. 'Oh, not so different from a week ago.'

'What happened in the election?'

'Oh, aye, that. Well, the socialists tek a beatin'. Lost five seats.'

I show my sympathy by clicking my tongue. But he dismisses it with a quick shake of the head. Politics, obviously, isn't uppermost in his mind at the moment.

'An' 'ow's about you?' he says. He studies me closely, trying to read something in my face I haven't told him.

'Oh, fine, thanks.'

'Glad to 'ear it.' He taps the mouthpiece of his pipe against his teeth. ''Ad yer mallet powed, 'ave yer?'

'Oh, come on, Dad,' says Ada, edging between us to fetch the kettle. 'Tha knows 'e won' know what tha's on about.'

Of course he knows. That's the point. It's a way of demonstrating his power over me: he understands how things work here, and – despite the time I've spent in Burnley – I still don't. He makes sure I'm watching him, then forms a pair of scissors with his fingers and snips along his hair-line.

'Tryin' to impress someone – is that it?'

Oh, God. I'm fifteen again, up before the Headmaster. *Perhaps you'd be good enough to empty your pockets, Whitaker.*

'No,' I say. 'It was just getting a bit long, that's all.' But I can feel the heat surging to my cheeks. I hope he thinks it's just the effect of the fire – but I suspect he doesn't, because he keeps staring at me,

354

which only makes me go redder still. I desperately want to break the tension by saying something more, but every idea I come up with just seems like a blatant attempt to change the subject.

In the end it's Ada who saves me. 'Ooh, 'eck,' she says, rooting around in the cupboard by the sink. 'Where'd that sugar go, then?'

'You'll find some in there,' I say, jabbing an elbow at the Co-op bag on the table.

'Mm?' She peers inside it, then laughs uncomfortably. 'Oh, there weren't no call for you to do that, 'Enry. This 'ouse in't a model. You don't 'ave to bring your own jackbit.'

'No, but you're always feeding me. I never get a chance to feed you.'

She looks at her father. He nods. Obviously pride isn't uppermost in his mind at the moment, either.

He waits for her to start unpacking the groceries, then says quietly: 'So, then, what were so unexpected?'

I still haven't worked out quite how to put it. But the longer I delay, the more suspicious it'll make him – so I snap open my bag, and take out the first print of Frame 278.

'It's not very clear, I'm afraid,' I say, handing it to him. 'It was taken from the film. You know – the scene outside the Empire, when people were waiting to go in. Two weeks ago today, it was, wasn't it?'

He examines it silently for ten or fifteen seconds. Then he looks up, his forehead runkled with puzzlement. 'Aye,' he says. 'Very nice.'

'Is there anyone there you don't recognize?'

He frowns at it again. 'Well, aye, o' course, there's bound to be some, in't there? I mean, I know most of the faces, like, but I couldn't put a name to all o' them. Nobody could.'

I stand next to him, and point to the woman in the fur stole. 'Who's that?'

He brings the picture nearer and squints at it.

'Where's she reckon *she's* goin', then, dressed like that?' He ponders for a second or two, then shakes his head. 'No, I've no idea. I never saw 'er before in me life.'

'Let's 'ave a sken, then,' says Ada, stationing herself behind him.

355

'Oh – that's – that's wossername, in't it? – that posh girl married young Pickerin', you know: Pickerin's Engines?' She leans closer, pursing her lips with concentration. 'No, it in't,' she says finally. 'Dunno *who* it is.'

'There must be somebody could tell you,' says Percy. 'Let's see' – marking the figure immediately to the right with the stub of his finger – 'who's yon fella be'ind 'er?'

Ada shakes her head.

'All right, then' – moving to the right again – 'well, you know this 'un, at any rate, don't you?'

She laughs. 'I should say I do.' She turns towards me, jerking her thumb at the door. ''E lives right over there, see, does Jacky Andrews – 'as done since he were a babe. So 'e were always under my feet when 'e were a lad, moitherin' me.'

'Well, then,' says Percy. 'An' what about 'er?'

'Oh, aye: Glad Mulligan.'

'So one of 'em's goin' to know 'er, in't they? Mebbe they was all together.'

I'm surprised how much he seems to be enjoying himself: I'd expected him to quiz me about *why* I wanted to discover the woman's identity, and thought I was going to have to coax him into helping me do it. Instead he's taken up the challenge himself with childlike enthusiasm. It's a second or two before I guess the reason: he's *relieved*. Ever since he got the telegram, he must have been worrying that my real motive for coming here was to see Betty again. Now, at a stroke, the spotlight's shifted on to somebody else entirely – and a complete stranger, at that.

'What 'appened, then?' says Ada, edging her way back to the table. 'You lend 'er ten shillin' or summat, and she never paid you back?'

I laugh. 'That's it, yes. So: do you think maybe you could ask them for me? See if you can come up with a name?'

'Well, I don' see why not,' says Percy. He waggles the picture. 'You can spare this, can you?'

'Yes, I've got more copies of it. I . . . I was thinking I might ask Betty about it, too.'

His shoulders stiffen, and I think he's going to try to deter me. But then he nods and says: 'Oh, aye, well 'appen she might know.'

I hesitate a second, then decide to take a chance: 'The thing is, you see, Percy, I don't want to make a big fuss about this and get everybody talking. You know what they're like. Mention that I'm looking for her, and the next thing you know it'll be all round the town that I think she's my long-lost sister. Or else that I fell in love with her at first sight and want to elope with her to Gretna Green. So I think it would be best if we could just keep it as a kind of *by the way, do you happen to know* kind of thing.' I take out the packet of production stills, and hand it to him. 'To make it easier, I brought these along, too. They give a pretty good idea of what the film's going to look like. And no-one'll think it's strange I gave them to you, will they? I mean, they all know we're friends. And that you were interested enough in the process to come down and see us editing *Autumn Poppies*. So –'

He stiffens again. I hesitate, to give him a chance to speak. But he just *harumphs*, and settles himself heavily in his chair.

'I'm not asking you to lie, Percy. Just to be a bit discreet about it, that's all.'

'Hm.' He examines his pipe, then meticulously rubs at a little medallion of ash on the bowl until it's gone. 'An' *is* she your long-lost sister?'

'No, of course not!'

''Ow's about th'other thing, then? Gretna Green, an' all tha'?'

'No!'

He sighs, and crosses his arms, and glares mulishly at me: *Come on, I wasn't born yesterday.*

'I'm just curious about her. Honestly. I'd really like to know where she came from, and how she got there.'

'On 'er own pegs, I 'spect. Same as everyone else.'

I can feel myself starting to slither. If I miss my footing now, I'll slide straight into the abyss. I've got to find a way of explaining that doesn't simply make him think I'm mad, or deceitful, or both.

'The thing is, Percy, we were outside that cinema for two hours. If she was there, I'm certain I'd have noticed her –'

'What do you mean, *if*? She were there. This' – holding up the picture – 'proves it, don't it?'

'All right. But it's strange, isn't it? I mean, I remember the people

357

all around her, but I don't remember seeing her. Neither does Omar. Nor do any of the crew.'

He sighs again. I'm trying his patience.

''Ow many was there in tha' crowd, do you reckon? Two 'undred? Three 'undred?'

'Something like that.'

'Well, you can't expect to remember 'em all, can you?'

'No, but she really stands out, doesn't she?'

'Why? 'Coz she's dressed like a lady, you mean, and not like a mill-girl?'

'That's partly it. Not too many fur stoles in Burnley. But –'

He rolls his eyes. 'Nay, but there's rich folks 'ere too, you know.'

'I know. But most of them don't queue up for the Saturday matinée at the Empire.'

He starts to reply. I can see I'm in danger of getting bogged down in an endless debate about social class in Burnley, so I hurry on.

'And anyway, she's looking straight into the camera. When I specifically asked everybody not to. I simply can't see how we could *all* have missed that. I mean, it's just conceivable that Omar and I might have both happened to turn away at exactly the same moment. But the assistant cameraman must have been watching.'

Percy shrugs. 'Per'aps 'e were day-dreamin' about 'is missus, or some such. Funny what you don' see when yer mind's on summat else. Or mebbe 'e did see 'er, an' didn' say so, case you made 'im stop an' do it again, like. 'E wouldn't be the first fella to keep 'is mouth shut so 'e can get 'ome for 'is tea. Then after, when you ask 'im, *What's this, then?* – 'e'd 'ave to lie about it, wouldn't 'e?'

I can tell from the flat tone of his voice that it's a final judgement. If I go on arguing, I won't get him to retreat from it: I'll just make him angry, and humiliate myself. And what, in any case, could I say? He's right: that *is* the most plausible explanation. Pointless to deny it.

So I just murmur, as tentatively as I can: 'Still, if you wouldn't mind asking . . .'

He nods. And then, before I even have time to say thank you, Ada's calling: 'Ey, tea's up.'

'Tha's good,' says Percy, abruptly pulling himself to his feet. 'I'm right clemped.'

Tea is the usual stew-with-a-crust-on-top – though in my honour, presumably, Ada's used neck of mutton rather than corned beef and made an apple pie for pudding. We talk about their family, and mine, and the Munich agreement, and what the people in London think about the film, and what it's going to be called (when I tell him, Percy repeats it a couple of times, then gives it his seal of approval by nodding and muttering: *Aye, aye,* Better than Magic, *tha's gradely*); but – though she remains a shadowy, unacknowledged presence – nobody refers to the woman in the picture again. Percy, I'm sure, thinks he's doing me a kindness by giving the subject a wide berth: he has the stolid, slightly embarrassed look of an old duke whose son is making a fool of himself with a chorus girl – and who knows that the less he says about it now, the sooner the infatuation will pass and the less tortured by self-reproach the boy will be afterwards. I can't tell what Ada feels, because – as always – she's anxiously attuned to his mood and quick to adapt herself to it. After casually mentioning Jacky Andrews again only once, and seeing her father's response (shoulders braced; a hurried twitch of the head), she steers clear of Frame 278 for the rest of the meal.

Only at the very end, when she's cleared away, and I'm just getting up to go, does Percy suddenly murmur: 'You remember tha' time we went to the pub, 'Enry, you an' me? When I were down in London, afore Christmas?' He's fiddling with his pipe again, and scrupulously avoiding my gaze. Obviously this is important.

'Yes, of course.'

'An' you tol' me about tha' dream o' yourn? About yer dad, an' the tomb o' the Unknown Soldier?'

My heart starts to thump. I hold on to the back of my chair.

'Well, there were summat I always meant to say to you after, an' I never rightly 'ad the chance. What it is, see, is I don' reckon you're right about 'im – the Unknown Soldier, I mean. What meks 'im special is that 'e *in't* special. They never give 'im the VC for bein' a 'ero. They give it 'im for bein' *ordinary*. For standin' in for all them ordinary fellas who *weren't* 'eroes. An' never wanted to fight. An' did it anyway.' He suddenly looks up at me. There are tears in his eyes, and his jaw's so tight he can barely get the words out: 'Like our Georgy.'

*

Fate led me to Irma Brücke; maybe it'll lead me to the woman in the fur stole. The next morning I get up early, and scour the town centre, keeping my eyes peeled for her. There's no Bar Alfred in Burnley, of course – but then a smoky basement frequented by whores isn't the kind of place you'd expect to find someone like that, anyway: *she*'ll be here to buy a birthday present or a new hat, or to meet her friends somewhere *chic* (or as close to *chic* as Burnley can manage) for morning coffee. So I start with the better shops, and then move on to the markets, without encountering a single even faintly plausible candidate. Finally, around eleven o'clock, I descend – in hasty succession – on the Waverley, the Black and White Café and the Savoy, flitting between the tables with an abstracted *Where's-the-person-I'm-meant-to-be-meeting?* expression that I hope will make me inconspicuous. It seems to work: no-one challenges me, or even gives me a second glance. But I still see nobody remotely like the woman in Frame 278.

At 12.30 I give up, and make my way to Brad Street Mill. I've been waiting by the gates for less than five minutes when the first girls start spilling out. I'm startled to see that quite a number of them seem to recognize me: a tall blonde with a boyish strut makes her friends laugh by saying '*Ow do?* as she swaggers past; a few give me shy waves; and five or six of the younger ones huddle together in a little group, whispering and giggling, all the while watching me out of the corners of their eyes. I begin to wonder if this was a mistake: by making such a public appearance I'm almost certainly condemning poor Betty to a barrage of teasing when she goes back to work on Monday. But on balance, I still think I'm right. Seeing me here, people are bound to assume (I hope) that Betty and I have nothing to hide; and – since gossip thrives on secrecy – the whole thing should be forgotten by the end of the week. If I'd followed my original plan and gone to her house last night, I'd probably only have been spotted by two or three neighbours – but, precisely because of that, it might have looked as if I were trying to sneak in to see her under cover of darkness, and the malicious tittle-tattle could have gone on for months.

Betty's one of the last to emerge. The reason, I suspect, is that she thought I might be waiting for her and took a few minutes to smarten herself up. Her hair's freshly brushed, and she's as perfectly made-up as a model. Under her old coat she's got on a grey cardigan and a grey-and-pink Viyella dress and a necklace of coral-coloured glass beads. The individual components aren't noticeably different from what the other women are wearing; it's the sense of colour and design with which she's put them together that make her stand out. If it weren't for the apron and the workbelt she's carrying over her arm, you wouldn't guess she was a mill-girl at all.

She blushes and smiles as she sees me. ''Ullo.'

'Hello, Betty. How are you?'

'All right, thanks.' It's a struggle for her to hold my gaze, but she manages it. ''Ow about you?'

I nod. 'Were you expecting me?'

Her blush deepens. 'Me grandad said you were coming back.'

I nod again. 'I almost looked in on you yesterday, and then thought maybe this would be better. Could I buy you lunch somewhere?'

'Ooh, yes, I'd love that. Thank you.'

'I was thinking of the Savoy Café. You're pretty much dressed for it.'

'Aye, that'd be grand.' She says it quietly, but her voice is wavery with excitement. She turns to the girl next to her, who's gawping at us open-mouthed. 'Would tha be a luv, Win,' she says, holding out her belt and apron, 'an' tek of care of tha' for me, 'til Monday?'

It sounds so like Percy talking to Ada that it's almost as if she's slipped into a trance and been possessed by someone else. Win hesitates, then nods hurriedly, and takes the bundle into her arms.

'Ta,' says Betty.

As we start to walk, I ask: 'So which one is the real you?'

'Pardon?'

'The Betty who talks like that? Or the one who speaks the way you do to me?'

She goes redder than ever, and laughs. 'I dunno. I didn't know they were different. They're both me, I s'pose.' She ponders for a moment, then gives me a sidelong look and asks: 'Are you always the same with everyone, then?'

I can't answer at once: it's a question I've never been asked before. 'No,' I say finally. 'But thinking about it, I can see it might be better if I were a bit more like you.'

She's pleased, but puzzled. 'Like *me?*'

'Yes – you know: just naturally adapt myself to whoever I'm with.'

'Oh, but I think you do do that.' She hesitates. Then, staring at her feet, she mutters: 'I'll bet there in't a lot of Cambridge fellas who could just come up 'ere, like you did, and, you know . . .'

I shake my head.

'No, but it must be 'ard for you, after what you're used to, 'avin' to go in all the little 'ouses, and talk to folks like me grandad and me aunty Ada. Well,' – suddenly so quiet I can barely hear it – 'and folks like me, too, if it come to that.'

I nearly say: *I find it easier talking to you than to almost anyone in the world.* But I stop myself in time. That, at least, is one burden I can spare her.

'*That* isn't hard,' I say. 'It's a privilege.'

She pulls a face, as if she thinks maybe I'm joking.

'No, honestly, I mean it. But I can never entirely, you know, *lose* myself. I'm not just talking about here. Anywhere. I always feel where I *really* belong is somewhere else. And I have to sort of keep faith with it by holding myself back.'

'Well, where is it, then? The place you *do* belong?'

I swore I wasn't going to confide in her. And now here I am, starting to do it. Why does she have this effect on me?

I force myself to shrug. 'I've no idea. Just inside my head, probably.'

We walk on in silence. We seem incapable of small-talk with each other: we both seem to feel that if we're not going to say what we're really thinking, there's no point saying anything at all.

It isn't till we're settled in a corner table in the Savoy Café and we've ordered our meals that she turns to me and says: 'I'm that way sometimes, too.'

Odd: despite the hiatus, I know exactly what she's talking about.

'Yes,' I say smiling. 'I can imagine you are.'

'When I were a nipper, I didn't believe I were me mam an' dad's daughter at all. A lot of little 'uns are like that, I s'pose, in't they, sometimes? But me, I felt it the 'ole time. I 'ad this story I used to tell meself: about 'ow I come from a really posh family, an' they really loved me an' all – you know, I were their little princess. But then one time the nanny left me in me pram in the park, while she were, you know, carryin' on with 'er fella, and the gypsies come and snatched me away, an' sold me to me mam an' dad. But me *real* parents were still lookin' for me, and some day they'd see me, playin' in the street, an' they'd say: *Ooh, look, there's our Betty!*' She laughs. 'Funny, in't it? I always thought they'd 'a' give me the same name. But o' course they'd 'a' prob'ly called me Cecily or somethin' like tha', wouldn't they? Anyroad, they'd know who I was. An' they'd take me off in a big car, and I'd live 'appily ever after.'

The waitress brings our mixed grills. I'm still feeling extraordinarily jumpy, and as she puts the tray down, I glance round surreptitiously to see if we seem to be attracting any attention. I tell myself we should be all right: even in a place like this, extra-marital eating isn't a sin. But you can never be quite certain that some lynx-eyed busybody won't spot us anyway, and put the worst possible construction on what we're doing. Sure enough, a middle-aged chap sitting in the window *is* looking at us. From his appearance – trim grey hair, dark heavy suit, gold-rimmed glasses – he could be a newspaper editor. I can imagine the headline already: *Married film director in lunch scandal with mill-girl.*

And then, as he catches my eye, his face breaks into the most beatific, Mr. Cheeryble smile. I'm so relieved, I start laughing.

'What?' asks Betty, when the waitress has gone.

'You never know,' I say. 'It might still happen.'

'Pardon?'

'The big car, and the living happily ever after.'

She gives me a startled-rabbit stare. Her lip starts to quiver.

I say: 'Over there. By the window. Look at the way he's beaming at us. Got *long-lost father* written all over him.'

She flushes, and tries to smile, but can't manage it. 'Oh, aye.'

Fuck, why did I do that? I kick my own ankle under the table, hard enough to make myself wince. I should have known she'd mis-interpret it. I half *did* know, if I'm honest. I was leading her on, simply for the gratification of glimpsing the strength of her feelings for me. It was inexcusable. And if I apologize, it'll only make things worse. So I say nothing, and concentrate on eating, though it's a struggle to get the food down. Betty goes on staring out of the window.

Finally, when I'm half-way through a sausage, she turns back to me and says: 'I s'pose tha's why I like the pictures so much, really. I mean, it's like getting' on a train, in't it, and just *knowin'*, whatever 'appens, it'll end up takin' you where you want to go? You know: the parents'll find their baby. The fella'll get the girl. The girl –' She pauses, sniffing and swallowing hard. 'But tha's not life, is it? It's somethin' else. There's stories. An' then' – looking down at her plate suddenly – 'there's this. An' the trouble wi' me, me mam says, is I muddle 'em up. Can' seem to tell the difference between the picture world, and the real one. So I'm a reg'lar ol' barmpot. That's what she says, anyroad.'

'Well, in that case I must be one, too. Because I do the same thing.'

'Oh, but it's different for you, in't it? You make films. So o' course you can't 'elp getting' 'em all muddled up wi' your life. It's only natural.'

God, she's given me the perfect cue. It's almost irresistible. The phrases are already forming themselves in my head: *Well, it's odd you should say that, because that's why I came back. I'm beginning to think we may not be barmpots, after all, you see. That perhaps the two worlds actually are connected . . .*

It'd be wonderful to be able to be absolutely explicit about it, for once, and see another human being's response. But I vowed I wouldn't do it to her. Convincing her, after all, wouldn't be much of a test: she's young, and impressionable, and more than half-infatuated with me, and wouldn't have the knowledge of psychology or surrealism to be able to evaluate my ideas properly. And her imagination's wildly overactive as it is – so once I'd planted the seed in her head, it'd be impossible to uproot it again. That's not a legacy I want to leave her with.

So in the end I nod at her plate and say: 'Are you going to eat something?'

364

'I'm not that 'ungry, all of a sudden.'

Oh, God. My stomach cramps with guilt. 'Come on,' – trying to sound cajoling elder-brotherly – 'you've got to keep your strength up.'

She smiles, and starts poking at her food. I'm anxious not to distract her, so I wait while she hacks a few little scraps from her chop and dutifully chews them.

Then, as she pushes her plate away, I slip a print of Frame 278 out of my bag, and say, as off-handedly as I can: 'Can I show you something?'

She dabs the corner of her mouth with her napkin. 'Course.'

I give her the photograph, and prepare to go through the same routine. But she's quicker than Percy, or Omar, or the crew. Before I can ask if there's anyone she doesn't recognize, she's found the woman in the fur stole herself.

'Who's that, then?'

'I don't know. I was hoping you'd be able to tell me.'

She frowns and sucks her lips – looking, for a moment, eerily like her aunt, as if time's suddenly got impatient with her and middle-aged her at a stroke.

Finally she shakes her head and says: 'No. An' I don' remember seein' 'er there, neither. An' I'd 'a' thought I would 'ave, what with 'er nice clothes, an' all.' She hesitates. Then, forcing herself to meet my eye, she says: 'Pretty, in't she?'

'Yes.'

She looks so hopeless and wistful and vulnerable that, without thinking, I go on: 'That isn't why I want to find her, though.'

It's a mistake: I know as soon as I've said it. I try to head her off by flourishing the menu at her. But I've barely opened my mouth to ask if she'd like anything else when she says: 'So why *do* you, then?'

'Well . . .' I struggle to think of something that'll seem plausible, but all that comes to me is the phrase I used to Percy yesterday: 'I'm just curious about her, that's all.' It sounds even more threadbare this time.

'But I don' get it. I mean, if it in't tha' you like the look of 'er, why does it matter so much?'

'I . . . I . . .' I feel myself blushing. I can't bring myself even to face her. Instead I fiddle desperately with my knife, putting a bit of bacon-rind round the edge of my plate – as if occupying myself with something so inane somehow excuses me from answering her.

'You think' – dropping her voice to a whisper – 'she's a *ghost* or something?'

I shake my head. 'Not a ghost, exactly.'

'What, then?' And, when I don't say anything: 'You're givin' me the shivers.'

I make myself sit up and look at her. 'It'll probably turn out that she's just a perfectly ordinary woman who decided to go to the cinema that afternoon. And the only reason none of us remembers seeing her is that we all happened to be doing something else at the exact moment when, you know, she crossed our field of view. But I'd still like to find someone who *does* remember seeing her and can tell me who she really is. And I was hoping maybe you'd help me.'

She obviously feels cheated: I can tell it from the dissatisfied way she scans my face, looking for a clue to what I'm keeping from her, and wondering if she dare ask me outright again what it is. But in the end, she simply nods and says: 'OK. I'll call round some o' me friends this afternoon, an' see what I can find out.'

'That'd be terrific, Betty. But please –'

'Don' worry, I'll be careful. I shan' let on why I'm askin'.'

'Thank you.'

'You want to come over ours later? Then I'll tell you 'ow I got on.'

'I . . . I think it might be better if we could meet somewhere else, if that's all right with you. I just don't really want to have to explain to your mother what I'm doing here. Or to anyone else, for that matter.'

She nods.

'How about the Sparrow Hawk at seven?'

The peachy tinge of her cheeks deepens to pink. 'O.K.'

'I'd be very happy to buy you dinner there, if you'd like.'

Pink turns to crimson. 'Mebbe. Anyroad, I'll see you then.'

I feel flat and lethargic after we say goodbye, but I know that if I go back to the hotel I won't be able to sleep. The critical voices are too insistent: *Why the fuck did you do that? Why not arrange to meet her somewhere else? You're just teasing her, and yourself – still dangling the possibility of a relationship you know would be destructive for you, and a disaster for her. In addition to which, she must now be convinced you're certifiably insane. So you're not just prolonging the turmoil for her, are you, by turning up again like this and twitching her strings? No, you're making it worse – because now she'll realize the man she's been in thrall to is a lunatic.*

I could resort to Scotch – but that would only bind and gag my tormentors for a couple of hours, and their rage when they broke free again would be awful. The only alternative, I know from experience, is strenuous exercise – so I set out for Towneley Park, half-walking and half-running. My shoes slither and pinch my feet; my bag tugs at my shoulder, turning me into a grotesque lop-sided hunchback; the air's cool, but so sozzled with damp that in less than ten minutes my shirt's glued to my back and the lining of my jacket's chilly with sweat. When I arrive, I stand admiring the house for thirty seconds – then immediately start the return journey, hobbling along at the same frenetic pace. It's uncomfortable, but that's the point: when you're shivering and in pain, you can't think.

Promising myself the luxury of a bath and a change of clothes, I limp back into the Sparrow Hawk. A podgy, respectable-looking couple with a preposterous amount of luggage are standing in the hall, complaining to the unfortunate boy behind the desk about being put in room 11, when they'd expressly asked for room 4. I wait till they've finally capitulated and begun their trek into the interior, tutting and grumbling. Then I dart in behind them before anyone else has a chance to arrive. The boy, sulky and red-faced after his recent mauling, frowns at me.

'I know,' I say, smiling. 'I look a fright. Can I have the key to number ten, please?'

He looks round at the rack. 'It in't there.'

'It must be. I handed it in this morning before I went out.'

''Ang on,' he says, and disappears into the office. I can hear the muffled drone of his voice, and then a woman's, but not what they're saying. Perhaps, it suddenly occurs to me, I really *have* gone crazy. What if I *remember* handing it in, but didn't actually *do* it?

I shake my pocket. There's no answering jangle.

The boy reappears, gingerly touching his jaw as if he's got toothache. 'Seems like your wife tek it,' he says.

'My *wife?*'

He nods. ''Bout an hour ago.'

I hurry up the steps, my heart thumping. Has Betty finally got sick of our shadow-boxing, and decided to force my hand by letting herself into my room? Will I find her stretched out naked under the eiderdown, her clothes neatly folded on the chair?

I push open the door.

'Hullo, darling,' says Nicky. She's sitting on the corner of the bed, her hands demurely folded in front of her. She glances quickly past me into the corridor, as if she expects to see someone else there.

'God!' I say. 'What's happened?'

'Nothing's happened. I just thought I'd come up and see you, that's all.'

'Why didn't you 'phone?'

'I wanted it to be a surprise.' She gets up and walks towards me, holding out her arms.

'I'm all sweaty,' I say, backing away.

'So I see. But I told you before: I like your sweat.'

She hugs me, pressing her hands against the back of my head and running her tongue lightly over my lips. Her skin's dewy and smells faintly of soap. I let out a little moan.

'Aren't you going to close the door?' she whispers.

I reverse a couple of steps, and barge it shut. She pushes me against it and kisses me, clamping her mouth over mine and murmuring hungrily. When she pulls away again, she's panting. She half-turns, and – crooking her hand behind her – impatiently drums her fingers on the row of buttons at her neck. I undo them and help her lift the dress over her head. Underneath, she's wearing nothing. She pirouettes round to face me again, slips off my jacket, then begins yanking at my shirt.

'I really need a bath,' I groan.

'Oh, bugger baths.'

She licks my chest, then moves down towards my belly. Her hands start fiddling with my waistband and flies. She half-gets up, drags me towards the bed, then drops back on to it. As I spread-eagle on top of her, she winds her arms and legs round mine, as if she's trying to plait our bodies together. Then, as she pulls me into her, she lets out a strange gruff sound so primitive that it isn't even pleasure or pain yet, but just the raw, undifferentiated protoplasm of sensation.

I've never known her like this before. I've never known either of us like this. We're pummelling the bed so violently and making so much noise that for a moment I can't help wondering what the respectable-looking couple next door must be thinking.

And then, as she shrieks, and arches her back, and digs her nails into my shoulders, and I feel myself starting to dissolve, I don't care what they think any more.

For a long time afterwards, we lie on our backs, saying nothing – as if, having divested ourselves so shockingly of our individual selves, we feel awkward about trying to put them on again.

Then, very gingerly, Nicky rolls over, and lays her arm across my torso, and murmurs: 'Oh, God, I've been so frightened.'

I stroke her hair. 'Why?'

'I thought I was going to lose you. I haven't lost you, have I?'

'Of course not.'

'Mmm.' She snuggles into the crook of my shoulder. I twist my neck, and just manage to see my watch on the bedside table. It's almost five: two hours before I have to go down to meet Betty.

Nicky shifts her head so she can look up at me. 'You're not going to leave me for Betty Minton, then?'

'Whatever gave you that idea?'

She shrugs. 'Christopher rang me last night. And that set off alarm bells, because you know normally he'd rather have his teeth pulled than speak to me. So I asked him what was wrong? And he said, did I know why you'd come back here? And I said, well, you hadn't told me the details, but I gathered it was something technical to do with the film. And he said it was nothing technical to do with the film at all. In fact, it was a completely unnecessary trip: all that had happened was that while you were looking at the rushes, the figure of a mysterious woman had shown up in a crowd scene, and you'd got a bee in your bonnet about her and wouldn't rest until you'd managed to find out who she was. And he was seriously worried about your sanity.'

I'm cold suddenly. I retrieve the eiderdown from the floor, and arrange it over our legs. 'I'm sorry,' I say. 'He shouldn't have done that.'

'Well, you can imagine what I thought, can't you?'

I nod.

'Poor old Christopher: he can never see anything beyond the end of his nose. But anyone else would have immediately realized that was just an excuse. So I decided to get on a train, and try to . . .' Her voice wavers. 'Try to . . .'

'Yes,' I murmur, hoping if she knows I understand, she won't feel the need to go on.

But she goes on anyway: 'Try to win you back.'

Jesus. I don't trust myself to speak for a moment. Then, very gently, I say: 'It wasn't an excuse, Nicky.'

'Promise?'

'Promise.'

She shivers. I pull the eiderdown round her shoulders. She clutches it to her, taking childish comfort from the warmth.

'Why didn't you tell me about it, then?'

'I was frightened you'd think I'd finally gone off my rocker,' I say, trying to make it sound like a joke rather than a vote of no confidence in her. 'If I found out who she was, you'd never need to know anything about it all. If not – well, I'd cross that bridge when I came to it.'

'And *have* you found out?'

'Not yet.'

She sighs. 'May I see her?'

I get out of bed and bring her a print from my bag. She stares at it for a long time. I'm ready for another comment on the woman's looks, or the stylishness of her clothes. But in the end she frowns up at me and says: 'You told *Christopher*.'

'Yes, well, I thought he'd . . . I thought it wouldn't seem so strange to him. I mean, I know he doesn't like to be reminded of it, but *he* was the one who introduced me to Surrealism.'

370

'Mm.' She's suddenly fascinated by the hairs on my chest, and starts combing through them with her fingers, as if she's searching for a particular one. I know what that means: she's got something delicate to say to me, and doesn't want to look me in the eye while she's saying it.

'Well, what he told me', she murmurs, 'is that you hadn't really understood it.'

'What – Surrealism?'

She nods.

'Well, that's a bit rich, isn't it, coming from him? Given that he seems to have decided now the whole thing's nonsense, anyway. I think I've understood it perfectly. *"The marvellous, the* hasard objectif, *can erupt in the drabbest, most mundane places. Perhaps especially the drabbest, most mundane places."* That's what his friend Pelling said, when we met him at the exhibition. He even – I distinctly remember it – used *cinema queue* as one example of the *kind* of place it *might* happen. You could see that as an *hasard objectif* in itself.'

She's found the hair of her dreams, and is examining it minutely.

'Christopher says *hasard objectif* doesn't work like that.'

'Well, I don't recall his taking issue with Pelling about it. And anyway, how the hell does he know how it works? Breton's defini-tion – I looked it up – is something like: *Objective chance is the form of exterior reality which opens a path for itself in the human unconscious.* I mean, that's pretty general, isn't it? He doesn't pro-vide a diagram with it, and operating instructions.'

She starts to laugh, then quickly stops herself.

'And do you . . . do you really believe that's what she is? – the mysterious woman?'

'At the moment I'm just trying to find out if anyone knows who she is. If they do, well, then fine. That'll be the end of it . . .'

'And if they don't?'

I don't want to do this. Even the *thought* of doing it turns my muscles to jelly and leaves me with only one overwhelming urge: to pull the blinds down, and hide inside the darkness of my own head. But then it *always* makes me feel like that, which is why I've never done it before. I'm just too terrified, that's the truth of it. I can't help imagining her face as I tell her: the wrinkled forehead, the big white teeth nervously nibbling at her lower lip, the bright lost smile. And then, at the end, the sense that I've tugged and stretched the threads of our relationship so violently that they've finally snapped alto-gether – collapsing us into a couple of disconnected marionettes staring sightlessly at each other across an unbridgeable divide.

But I know I'm being unfair. Years ago, I swore I wouldn't under-estimate her again – and here I am, still doing it. I *must* give her a chance now. Otherwise – whatever happens – I'll never forgive myself.

'You remember my dream?' I say.

'The one about your father?'

I nod.

'Yes, of course I do.'

'Well, there have been times – ever since I first had it – when I've felt it was a . . .' I hesitate, almost say *sort of*, then tell myself this is the moment I have to throw away my crutches. 'A *sign*. That I'm called to do something.'

'What?'

'I don't know, exactly. The problem – I told you, didn't I? – is I can never understand what he's trying to tell me.'

'But you must have some idea. I mean, if –'

'I've got some idea, yes. There've been other signs, too.' I hesitate, then brace myself, and take a run at it. 'I suppose what it is is that I have to try to *redeem* something through art.'

'Redeem what?'

'Suffering. No, that's not quite it. Not just suffering. *Experience*.'

'Well, that *is* what you do, isn't it? With the documentaries?'

I shake my head. 'I've done my damnedest to convince myself. But I know, really, that documentary isn't art: it's just a collage of cut-out shapes stuck together. The only skill involved is in deciding which shapes to use, and how to juxtapose them. What an *artist* has to do is snatch at the little tufts and wisps of individual lives – indi-vidual deaths, even – and use his *imagination* to transform them into something that resonates with *other* individual lives. You know, like a perfectly tuned string on a guitar, or something. Because that, ultimately, is the only way to save them – to rescue them from meaninglessness and oblivion.'

372

She breathes heavily, and fiddles with her chosen hair as she thinks about it. Finally, she says: 'Well, that does sound very noble.'

Oh, Christ, this is what I dreaded. It could be her mother talking. But I force myself to go on: 'And then I start off . . . writing to Max . . . or figuring out how to do that shot on *Markheim* . . . or working the story of the little girl and the cat into *The Call-On*. And I think: *This is it. This is it. At last, you're on your way.* But somehow I always get deflected, and end up doing something . . . something less than that. Or *other* than that, anyway. And bit by bit I allow myself to be persuaded that the whole thing was a delusion, and I must just accommodate myself to the life I've got. And then all of a sudden, *bang*: there's *another* sign.'

She gazes up at me. 'Like this woman?'

'Well . . . If it turns out . . . Oh, God, I don't know, Nicky. I didn't want to say anything about this until I was certain.'

Or ever, probably, if I'm honest.

She keeps on staring at me. It's a look she's learned from Jojo: trusting, imploring, poised hopefully on the edge of laughter. Any moment, she thinks, I'm going to break into a smile and say *Just kidding*. And she'll be able to mock-beat me with her fists, and squeal: *Oh, how* could *you be so rotten?*

But then, as it dawns on her I'm serious, she suddenly pincers me in her arms, and nuzzles my chest, and starts – almost silently – to cry.

'It's all right,' I say, stroking her shoulder.

'Is it? I hope it is.' She sniffs. 'Oh, God, please, please, just promise me.'

'What?'

'That you won't go mad.'

I say nothing. How the hell can anyone promise that, unless they're mad already?

After a few seconds she prompts me: 'Please?'

I sigh. 'All right. I promise.'

She tightens her grip on me, and burrows her head deeper into my flesh. And in no more than a couple of minutes is asleep.

I lie there, rigid, for what seems like hours. But I must doze off myself at some point, because I suddenly find myself coming to with a jolt, and looking frantically for my watch.

Seven minutes to seven.

I extricate myself as gently as I can, put on a clean shirt and trousers, and tiptoe out to face Betty.

Unbearable. It's all just unbearable.

XXIV

I woke finally to find the notebook still open on my bed, my hand splayed out across the last two pages. The air in my room was already warm from the sun, and through the open window I could smell toast and coffee. My head felt hot and groggy. I'd obviously overslept.

For a second I thought the world of Burnley and Nicky and the woman in the stole must have been a dream. Then, just above my index finger, I caught the words *tiptoe out to face Betty*, and realized it hadn't. But it still had the *atmosphere* of a powerful dream – lingering at the edge of my vision like a numinous mist, as if it contained the secret of the universe, and then suddenly evaporating when I tried to grab hold of it. I knew that once I *had* grabbed hold of it, it would change my understanding of my own life more fundamentally than anything else I'd discovered. But I couldn't force it: I was going to have to wait for it to disclose its meaning to me bit by bit.

At the moment, only one clear thought penetrated the smog: that I needed to get the notebook back again, before Sally became aware I'd taken it. I wasn't sure if she even knew of its existence – but if she didn't, she'd want to know what it was, and if she did, she'd be bound to ask me what I made of it. And I didn't relish the thought either of telling her the sneaky way I'd found it, or of having to explain that it contained a graphic sex scene between my father and her mother.

I got dressed, draped my jacket over my arm, hid the notebook behind it, and went downstairs. The dining-room door was half-open. I crept up to it and peered in. No Arkwright. No anyone, thank God: it was exactly as I'd left it. I hurriedly returned the notebook to the box, then crossed the hall to the kitchen. Sally was stooped in front of the Aga, taking a tray of croissants out of the oven. As she turned to slide it on to the table, she saw me and smiled.

"Oh, hullo."

"Hi."

"How did you sleep?"

"Oh, fine, thanks."

But I could tell from the way she was looking at me that she knew I hadn't. You can't fool your twin.

"Well, not that well, actually," I said. "It wasn't the bed or anything. I was really comfortable. I just had too much to think about."

She nodded. "Me too. Your turning up like this, it's a bit like" – hesitating for a second, and staring out of the window, as if she thought she might find the image she was looking for there – "it's a bit like walking into the house you've lived in all your life, and suddenly discovering there's another room in it, that must have been there all along, but you never even noticed before."

"Yeah, I know. Except in my case, it's more like I was living in the *room* all this time, and now I've discovered the rest of the house." *Including, last night*, I suddenly thought, *a whole new floor.*

She laughed. "Shall we take this outside? Or are you sick of the terrace?"

"No, outside would be great."

We piled mugs and toast and croissants and coffee and juice on to a couple of trays, and carried them out through the French door. As we emerged into the open, I stopped for a second to enjoy the luxurious feeling of the sunshine wrapping itself round me, and to snuff the hot perfumey scent of roses and drying grass.

"You seem quite at home here," said Sally, when we'd finished clunking everything on to the table and sat down. "Would you ever think about coming back? Permanently, I mean? To live?"

I turned and gazed at the view. It was tremulous with heat-haze, through which you could see shimmery little bursts of pink and white and yellow from the pergolas and flower-beds. The distant hills looked clearer and more real in the morning light, but they were still beautiful – the trees along the top the colour of beetle-wings, and the softer green of the slopes below mottled with shadows. And this evening, if the weather held, they'd get their magic back and promise you access to another world.

"It is lovely," I said.

"I sense a *but.*"

I smiled. "Well, when I was young, it was awfully tantalizing. I saw all this" – waving my hand towards the horizon – "and I *longed* to belong in it, to feel it was really mine, but I never did. It was always just out of reach. And now, I'm afraid, it's much too late. Perhaps in my next life. Or a parallel universe. The one where Henry and Nicky stay together."

Her eyes filled suddenly with tears. She blinked them away, then steadied herself by glancing towards the kitchen and saying: "I wonder where Alan Arkwright's got to?"

"What time does he normally get here?"

"Nine-thirty, ten."

I looked at my watch: almost 10.15.

"Perhaps he saw my car, and realized I must still be here, and decided to scurry home again."

She shook her head sceptically. "Oh, I can't believe he'd go to that much trouble to avoid you."

"I can."

"Goodness." She poured two mugs of coffee, and handed one to me. "Whatever have you done to the poor man?"

It suddenly struck me I'd never really asked myself that question: I'd been too obsessed with what *he* had done to *me*. I took a sip of coffee and thought about it for a moment.

"I don't know, to tell you the truth," I said finally. "I honestly can't think of anything that would make him that mad at me. But I guess he just feels I rained on his parade."

"What?"

"Sorry. American expression. I mean, he thought Henry Whitaker was really going to put him on the map, didn't he? He'd be able to take the credit for rediscovering this long-lost figure, and showing the world what a wonderful director he was, and making everyone tut and sigh over how much more he might have achieved if his own niceness hadn't betrayed him into marrying my mother."

Sally blushed and gave a guilty little smirk of recognition: this probably wasn't that far from Nicky's view, either.

"Only I really undermined the whole thing, by saying my father *wasn't* nice, and I wasn't interested in his work, and I didn't want anything to do with the celebration, which I suppose was probably a big disap-

377

pointment to him. Well, more than a disappointment: a real danger. Because he must have figured that *both* our versions couldn't be true, and if mine turned out to be right, he'd have lost his ticket to fame and fortune, wouldn't he? So he had to do everything he could to discredit me."

I stopped, listening to the harsh echo of my own sarcasm – *tut and sigh, fame and fortune* – reverberating in my ears. Why was I being so aggressive?

"And do you still believe your version *is* right?"

Disconcerting, having a twin. She said it at the precise instant that the notebook yielded up part of its significance to me. I suddenly saw that the man who'd written it didn't square with Arkwright's ideas – but didn't entirely fit with mine, either.

"I don't know," I said. "I'm thinking about it."

"So what made you change your mind?"

I felt myself coloring. "I didn't say I *had* changed my mind, did I? I said I was *thinking* about it."

I tried to put her off by making it sound mock-angry: *Hey, just kidding.*

She smiled, but I knew she wasn't deceived, and she knew I knew.

"What did for *Arkwright*, I think," said Sally, tactfully busying herself with a bit of croissant to avoid having to look me in the eye, "was the book."

I took a sip of coffee. "Mm?"

"You know, your father's – well, it was a sort of diary, I suppose, really, only he didn't call it that. He called it his *book*. And he didn't write it continuously, only at critical moments. And not at all after the beginning of the war." She nibbled at the croissant, giving me time to say something. When I didn't, she asked: "He never mentioned it to you?"

"No."

"Well, I remember Mummy telling me about it. She thought it was very important and wanted to add it to her collection, so after he died she looked for it everywhere she could think of. But it never turned up, and eventually she assumed he must have destroyed it." She looked up at me. "Only evidently he hadn't. A couple of months ago, Alan Arkwright found it."

"Where?"

"He refused to tell me. He won't even let me look at it. Not that I want to, really. Your father used it, I gather, to record his most private thoughts and feelings – all the things he could never *say* to anyone. And apparently there's quite a lot about Mummy in it, so . . ." She tore off another piece of croissant and smoothed jam over it. "I was curious, of course. But I knew it'd just make me feel angry, and dreadfully sad."

Thank God she was delicate enough not to look at me as she said it. I silently took a deep Yoga breath, and tried to will the embarrassment from my face.

"Anyway," said Sally, "it was reading that that seemed to persuade Arkwright that Henry Whitaker was mad. Not just at the end of his life. Pretty much from the start."

Henry Whitaker was mad.

Immediately, a whole peal of answering phrases started to chime in my head: *I mustn't make him think I'm mad. Promise me you won't go mad. How can anyone promise that, unless they're mad already? All right, I promise . . .* The notebook wasn't being coy any more. It was suddenly screaming the connections at me.

"Listen," I said, "can I ask you a *huge* favour?"

"Yes, of course."

"Do you still have *Ordinary*?"

"I'm sorry? Oh, oh, I know what you mean." She couldn't help smiling. "The unfinished film. Yes."

"Would there be any chance of taking a look at it, do you think?" She pulled a face. "Well . . ."

"I mean, not if it's a problem –"

"It's not a problem. I just don't know what kind of condition it'll be in. The cans haven't been opened for thirty years, probably."

"Hasn't Arkwright seen it?"

She shook her head. "He knows it's a write-off. It has to be, doesn't it, to bear out his theory? He's only interested in the early documentaries. Or, at least, he was. Now I'm really not sure *what* he's interested in."

I'd pictured myself having to go through it by hand, or – at the very best – on a film-viewer. So I was quite surprised when Sally took me

379

across to one of the out-buildings after breakfast, threw open the door, and led me into a miniature cinema. It was dusty and smelt of damp, but she still beamed with pride as she flicked on the light, and I saw the curtained screen, and the tiny projection-box, and two rows of battered flip-up seats that looked as if they'd been snaffled from a pre-war flea-pit.

"My father had it converted when they first moved here," she said. "It was supposed to be for his work, but really I think he did it mostly for me. You can imagine the effect it had on my social life. They'd get in a Marx Brothers or something, and he'd be the projectionist, and my mother would dress up as an usherette, you know, with a torch and everything, and say *Would you like to come this way?*, and hand out ices in the interval. It was wonderful. Kids'd do anything to get an invitation to my birthday parties." She laughed. "It was a bit of a rude shock when I grew up and realized I wasn't actually the most popular person in the universe, after all. Anyway" – patting the nearest seat and sending up a white puff of dust – "why don't you sit down, and I'll go and see if I can find it."

"Sure I can't give you a hand?"

She shook her head. "No, that's fine. There really isn't room for two people."

I sat down. She opened a door next to the screen, letting in a current of cool musty air, then quickly slipped through and closed it behind her. After a few seconds a pencil of light appeared underneath it and I could hear the familiar clatter and grate of film-cans being pushed around. In less than a minute she was back, holding four large cans.

"Sorry," she said, hastily shutting the place up again. "I wasn't being secretive. It's just something Daddy always drilled into me: you've got to keep the film-store cool. Now, let's have a look."

She put the cans down on the seat in front of me and started to untape the top one.

"Are you sure that's it?" I said.

She squinted at the label, then nodded. "Why?"

"I was expecting a lot of little reels, not four big ones."

She shrugged. "Perhaps they were spliced together, to make them easier to transport." She pulled out a tongue of film, blew a few bright-orange specks off the surface, then held it up to the light. "Mmm, doesn't seems too bad. We'll probably find there's been some deterioration – you can't avoid it; but it should be viewable. Are you looking for anything in particular?"

"A crowd scene."

She quickly checked the other labels. "Have you any idea what number it was?"

"I don't have a clue."

"Then we're just going to have go through the whole thing till we find it." She gathered up the cans and started towards the projection-cubicle. "I'm quite excited about it, actually. I've never seen it before."

"Are you O.K. lacing it up?" I said. "It can be kind of fiddly, if you're not used to it."

She smiled. "I'm used to it."

And she must have been, because less than three minutes later the room went dark and the curtains whirred magically open and the screen suddenly filled with the familiar migrainey storm of scratches and pricking lights.

To begin with, I couldn't make sense of it. Or rather, I could make too much sense of it. What I remembered was a chaotic, meaningless jumble. This was jerky, and full of gaps, and damaged in places, but a lot of it seemed to have been tentatively arranged in almost-coherent sequences, and there was even the odd tantalizing hint – recurring *motifs* of a station clock, always set at 11.05; or a long black car, driven by a sinister, half-seen man – that they might somehow be connected. It was obvious now, at least, why there were only four cans: someone must have made a serious stab at editing *Ordinary* before the whole project was finally abandoned.

The first reel starts with a woman sitting at a table. In front of her is an open photograph album. Occasionally she'll glance down at a picture, or turn a page, and then look up again, thinking (you imagine) about the image she's just seen. You can't tell whether you're in town or country, a house or an apartment, and the light from the window behind her keeps her more or less in silhouette, so you never get a clear look at her face. From the little you *can* see, she doesn't seem particularly like Mummy. But suddenly, after twenty seconds or so, she reaches purposefully for her coffee cup, presses it between her hands, then looks down at it as if she can't imagine what it's doing there, and puts it back again. The next moment, for no apparent reason, she starts to shake and flex her shoulders. It's all so eerily familiar that, when I saw it, I had to clamp my lips between my teeth to stop myself crying.

God, I thought, *this is going to be bad.*

There's no sound-track. Maybe my father intended to leave it like that, as a kind of tribute to silent cinema – but watching it I found myself waiting for someone to tell me what was going on, which made me think he was probably going to use a voice-over narrative but never got round to recording it. Certainly, without it, the structure's terribly confusing. In the next few sequences you keep seeing the same woman again, as her younger self in (to judge by the clothes) the 1930s. Only there isn't just *one* younger self: there are three. One's a fashionable Viennese; the second a bourgeois Jewish girl in Budapest; the third the daughter of the butcher in a poor, out-of-the-way eastern-European provincial town. (The various locations are suggested by huge, very obviously painted flats – whether as an artistic statement or an economy measure, it isn't clear.) What the three characters share, though, for all their differences, is a kind of relish for the details of life: a cup of coffee; a new pair of shoes; a band playing in a café or a park, which – even if they just come upon it by chance – invariably sets them moving in time to some tune we can't hear.

For most of the first three reels, the trio of stories weave in and out of each other, and back to the woman at the table, like ribbons on a maypole. Each has its own emotional dynamic, which produces some wonderfully touching moments: the butcher's daughter playing with her dog in an orchard, rolling among the fallen apples until her clothes are stained with juice; the Jewish girl's little skip for joy when she sees her musician boyfriend arriving at the station. But as they go on, the links between them steadily get more and more insistent and ominous. The black car drives out of frame in Vienna, and then – in the next shot – into frame in Budapest. A menacing flight of bombers, in strict formation, appears on the horizon, and as it grows relentlessly bigger you see its shadow passing over all of their faces in turn. Each of them witnesses a gang of thugs murdering an old man – the same thugs? the same old man? – in the street outside her home.

And then, at the start of reel four, everything changes. You see the Viennese girl looking at herself in a mirror – perching a little hat on her neat curls, and wrapping a fur stole round her shoulders, as a prelude (you guess) to going out. After a few seconds, she pouts with satis-faction, nods, and then turns away – only to stop at the last second, and swivel back again. The camera follows her, and we see what's caught her eye: a cloud of moths is settling on her head. Or rather, on the *image* of her head – because when her hand flies up to brush them off her, there's nothing there. She gasps, and lunges towards the glass. Not there, either. They're in the mirror world, but not this one.

The woman watches helpless – you can see the anguish in her gaping mouth, though you can't hear what comes out of it – as the fluttering blizzard covers her reflected self, and then begins to con-sume it. First her mirror clothes are corroded to holes and tatters – giving us a glimpse of breast, and even the dark hint of a nipple, that must have been unimaginably daring at the time. Then her mirror face is slowly picked and torn and plucked away – revealing, not the bones and empty sockets you expected, but a rapid succession of other faces, like the layers of a Russian doll: first the butcher's daugh-ter; then the Jewish girl; and finally a ghastly, sunken-eyed, shaven-headed travesty – who might be the ghost of any of them, deprived of her beauty and personality.

That shot finally undid me. I heard what sounded like someone else's voice whimpering *Mummy*, and then I was shuddering and howling and pummeling my knees with my fists. The film became mobile wallpaper: a shifting blur of unrecognizable black-and-white shapes. I wanted to ask Sally to stop it, but I couldn't even lift my hand to signal to her, let alone speak.

I heard the squeak of the seat next to me. "Are you OK?"

I tried to nod, but the effect was lost in another paroxysm of sob-bing.

Sally put her arm round me. I don't know how long she sat there, holding me. But it must have been a while, because I'd already almost

383

cried myself out when she suddenly squeezed my shoulder and whispered: "Crowd scene."

I opened my eyes, and rubbed the tears away with my fingers. On the screen, a cordon of men in S.S. uniform was pushing a huddle of frightened people toward a railway station. An old man who tried to escape was whipped back, then knocked to the ground and kicked. His wife screamed, and was hit in the face with a pistol. Her glasses shattered, and she collapsed on top of her husband. Guards swarmed in on them, jabbing at them furiously with sticks and rifle-butts.

The camera pulled back and up, to give us a long shot of the whole scene. My stomach tightened: this, I was pretty sure, was it. And then I *knew* it was – because, all at once, I spotted her. She was standing, just as I remembered her, in the middle of the frame, wearing a fur coat and with expensively cut hair – a startling island of elegance in a sea of shabby clothes and hung heads.

Sally must have sensed my tension. "What is it?" she said.

I nodded at the screen. "Watch."

The next second, the woman in the fur coat turned towards the camera and smiled.

"Is that it?" said Sally.

"Yes. Just try and remember it, will you?"

"Why?"

"If you have a VCR, there's something else I'd like to show you."

She re-wound the film, switched off the projector, and then – saying she'd put everything away later, when it had had a chance to cool – took me back into the house. On my way upstairs to collect the cassette I glanced into the dining-room, but there was still no sign of Arkwright.

By the time I got down to the living-room, Sally had already switched on the TV and the video. I slipped in the tape and told her not to look while I was finding the right place.

When I called her over finally, she said: "O.K., what is this?"

"It's a film he made in 1938. *Better than Magic*. Do you know it?"

She shook her head.

I pressed *play*. She bent forward, hands on knees, and peered at the television. To begin with, as the camera panned slowly across the cinema queue, she seemed puzzled: obviously it hadn't struck her immediately that there was any similarity between this scene and the one we'd just been watching. But as we started to close in on individual faces, and the woman in the fur stole seemed to detach herself more and more from her surroundings, as if she was being faded in from some completely different film, I saw Sally twitch and stiffen. She inched nearer to the screen, frowning with concentration.

And then – as the woman in the stole suddenly turned and smiled – she burst out: "Oh, my God! She's doing exactly the same thing, isn't she?"

"Yes."

"Let me see it again."

I whizzed the tape back and replayed it.

"Strange. But it isn't the same woman, is it?"

"No."

"Though they are dressed very much alike."

"Yes."

"Hm." She gave a little shudder – then saw a straw, and grasped at it gratefully: "Well, it was probably deliberate, wasn't it? He directed them to do it. Or the second one, anyway. I mean, maybe that time" – nodding at the TV – "it was simply an accident, but he liked the effect so much that when he was making *Ordinary* he got that woman to repeat it."

I shook my head. "He'd never met her. She was just an anonymous extra. He'd never met either of them. He didn't even know who they were."

"Well, must just be a coincidence, then, mustn't it? It isn't really that unlikely, is it, if you think about it? I mean, if you shoot enough crowd scenes, however careful you are, you're bound to get a few where people are looking at the camera."

"I don't think my father thought it was a coincidence."

She didn't answer at once. She hunched her shoulders and pressed her hands together, as if she had to tense her muscles to prevent herself shriveling with embarrassment.

Finally, she said quietly: "What *did* he think, then?"

"I think . . . I think he thought it meant something."

"Meant what? Something *odd*, you mean?" And then, when I didn't reply: "Come on, you have to explain."

"I will, I promise. Or, at least, I'll try. Just as soon as I've got it straight in my own head."

It sounded O.K. at the time, but a few minutes later, while Sally was fixing lunch and I was getting things ready to set the table, that phrase kept repeating on me. Why had I said it? How could I really explain? How could I ever be sure that I *had* it straight in my own head? Over the last couple of weeks I'd taken it more and more for granted that I was going to try to make sense of it by writing about it. But what, honestly, could I actually say? That my father was crazy? That he was a weird misunderstood visionary? The truth was I didn't know, and I never would. I couldn't even be certain I'd drawn the right conclusions about what had – or he *thought* had – happened to him.

And then – just as I'd slapped down one place-mat and was about to put down the other – it hit me: I didn't *have* to explain his side of the story, because (insofar, at least, as anyone could now) he'd already done it for himself. All I had to do was provide my own, and set it against his.

By the time we started to eat it had more or less sorted itself out in my mind, with almost no conscious effort on my part – leaving me feeling strangely breathless and light-headed, as if some benign alien had seized control of my thought-processes. What added to the sense of unreality was the sudden realization that – after my months-long obsession with Alan Arkwright – he had now, at a stroke, become irrelevant. It sounded, from what Sally had said, as if his project was in complete disarray. But if he did go ahead with it, and was reckless enough to repeat his attacks on Mummy and me, it actually didn't matter too much now, because my book would refute them, and he'd end up with egg on his face. And unless he showed up within the next few hours (which, given his behaviour to this point, seemed almost unimaginable) he wasn't even in a position to make life difficult for me over my father's notebooks. Sally couldn't really refuse to let me have them: I was Henry Whitaker's daughter, after all. He'd even written my name on the box.

"You're very quiet," said Sally. "Penny for your thoughts."

The perfect opportunity: I should ask her about it now. "Sorry," I began. "I was thinking about Arkwright."

She laughed. "Oh, dear. *What* were you thinking?"

"Well, I was just wondering –"

I stopped. I knew, suddenly, that I couldn't do it – or, at least, not without having made one last effort to see him. It'd be shabby and spiteful. And it would leave me with that odd, cheated sense you get when you've walked downstairs expecting fourteen steps – and after thirteen, suddenly find you're at the bottom.

"I was wondering where he lived," I said.

"Slough, somewhere, I think –"

"No, I mean here."

"Oh, that's easy: in a caravan. On Jury's Farm."

"How far is it?"

"Oh, only a couple of miles." She hesitated. "But I don't know what he'd feel . . . I mean, I don't think he's keen on visitors. It's probably a bit of a pig-sty. And if the whole reason he's hiding there is he doesn't want to see you . . ."

I shrugged. "I think I'll give it a try anyway, if that's O.K."

She stared at me for a second, then nodded. "All right. Let me give you one of my famous maps."

Caravan wasn't a word I'd used much since moving to America, and unused words tend to get fossilized, so – without even thinking about it – I just assumed I was looking for one of those curvaceous little Wendy Houses on two wheels that I'd seen wobbling around behind Rover cars when I was a kid. What I actually found was a kind of junior mobile home: long, and slab-sided, and supported on concrete blocks. It stood about fifty yards from the half-timbered farm-house, in a patch of green, boxed in by hedges, that might have been an orchard once. Beyond it stretched a muddy yard, surrounded on three sides by big modern farm-buildings.

I pulled the car off the road, and got out. I could just see a segment of bicycle-wheel sticking out beyond the end wall. That made it more likely he was there, presumably. I felt a surge of relief and a tingle of fear, which met somewhere in the pit of my stomach, almost cancel-ing each other out. I told myself that neither of them was really

387

appropriate, now: whatever happened, this simply wasn't that big a deal any more.

I strolled through the narrow opening in the hedge, trying to look as relaxed as I could. But it was difficult: the ground was corrugated with hard dry ruts, overgrown with thick grass that made them impossible to see. Twice I stumbled and almost twisted my ankle. The second time, a dog at the farm heard me and started yapping.

I knocked on the glass panel in the top of the door. Nothing. I knocked again, and held my breath, praying that the dog hadn't alerted him and made him lock himself in the bathroom. After fifteen seconds or so there was a muffled shuffling sound from the depths of the caravan. I breathed again. A moment later, a man appeared.

It was hard to believe this was Alan Arkwright. Tommy Ryder had described him as an *eager young dog, bounding about all over the place*, and that was pretty much the way he'd come across in his letters. This guy looked more like an old bloodhound. He was stooped and shabbily dressed, with dirty hair and bloodshot eyes. He hadn't shaved, and the stubble on his chin was flecked with white.

He peered out. When he saw me, he stood quite still, blinking at me for a few seconds. Then he fumbled uncertainly with the handle for a moment or two, and finally pushed open the door.

"Mr. Arkwright?"

He nodded wearily, and started retreating slowly. He didn't ask me to come in: just seemed to assume that I would, whether he invited me or not. So I did.

I was hit by a warm, bitter smell of mildew and dirty clothes and stale toast that almost made me gag. *God*, I thought, *this is how Daddy felt when he walked into that house in Burnley nearly seventy years ago.* That, I realized, was something else the notebook had done: opened a kind of short-cut through time, so that for a moment his experience could spark across the gap between us and connect directly with mine. And that was just one volume. How many similar worm-holes would I find, when I read the rest?

The venetian blinds on the windows were half-closed, but there was enough light for me to see a long table set into a dining recess. The surface was covered with crumbs, unwashed plates and cups, a

388

lidless jar of Marmite smeared with butter, bits of newspaper, a dog-eared book held open by a bag of sugar. The only sign of order was a pile of stapled documents in one corner: dissertations, maybe, though I couldn't imagine anyone marking anything here.

Arkwright was already slumped on the bench-seat at the far end. I sat down facing him. He didn't say anything, but fingered his neck apprehensively, like a child awaiting punishment.

"You know who I am?" I said.

He nodded.

"Why didn't you answer my messages?"

He raised his eyebrows and shook his head, as if he were at a loss to understand it himself.

"I've been dreading this," he mumbled finally, staring at a ring-mark on the table. "I'm not going to try to make excuses. I know I've behaved appallingly. You probably want to kick me." He looked up at me with doggy eyes. "You can, if you want to. I deserve it."

My rage was ebbing away. I tried to hold on to it: I needed the energy it gave me. But it just trickled through my fingers.

"I don't want to kick you," I said.

He relaxed slightly, as if he'd really thought I might. "The thing is, I was always intending to, the minute I was back on an even keel again. Only I never did get back on an even keel again. Everything just went on getting worse and worse."

"With your book, you mean?"

He nodded.

"Yes," I said. "That's what Sally Davenant told me."

He nodded again. His hands were shaking. He glanced round desperately, like an alcoholic looking for a drink.

Then he forced his gaze back to me, and said: "And now I'm in a real hole. I've got a publisher waiting. The university breathing down my neck. The conference coming up. For which I'm being inundated with submissions." He slid a document from the pile and dangled it in front of me: Exhibit A. I just had time to read: *Whitaker's first documentary,* The Call-On *[1935], is a multi-layered palimpsest, establishing and erasing meanings,* before he smacked it down again with a despairing flick of the wrist. "And all I want to do is forget about the whole thing."

I couldn't not feel sorry for him. But that didn't stop an exultant voice in my head hissing: *Serves you damn well right.*

"The problem is, you see, I've rather publicly nailed my colors to a particular mast." He suddenly saw the irony of saying this to me, of all people, and gave the ghostliest wisp of a smile. "As you know. And once you've done that – in my world, anyway – you can't really take them down again, and nail them to another one."

It was rubbing his nose in it, but I couldn't help asking: "And what one would you nail them to now, if you could?"

I regretted it the instant I said it. I didn't actually want to hear his assessment of my father. Whatever it was, it must be the sober, take-it-or-leave-it judgment of an academic. Mine – if I could ever resolve my own feelings enough to have one – would be the messed-up, you're-stuck-with-this response of a daughter. There was no point grappling with each other's views. We'd be trading moves on different chess-boards.

"Henry Whitaker the –" he began, then stopped and shook his head. "I don't know. I don't like to say it. There was just something . . . *wrong* with him, that's all."

This was what I'd been hoping to avoid. I felt I couldn't let it go without trying to say something in Daddy's defense – but nothing I did say would have the slightest chance of making him change his mind.

I opened my mouth – shut it – opened it again.

"Yes, yes, I know," he muttered. "You've every right to scream *I told you so.*" He hesitated a fraction of a second. "Even though it's all your fault, really."

My *fault?* I thought. *Right, that does it.* But then I saw his pathetic lop-sided grin, and realized: he was just trying to defuse the situation by teasing me.

He said: "You're the one who put me in touch with Flo Torridge." He hesitated. "Did you know your father kept a kind of diary?"

"Oh, it was Flo who gave you that, was it?"

He flinched, and started to go pink. "You found it, then?"

He seemed genuinely surprised. I almost said: *It wasn't that difficult. Underneath a table isn't the greatest place to hide something.* But I didn't have the heart. He was squirming like a puppy that's just taken a shit on the carpet. Hard to believe that this was the guy I'd come half-way round the world to find.

"You probably think she shouldn't have let me have it," he mumbled sheepishly. "But she said she'd been keeping it for you for more than thirty years and you'd never shown the slightest interest in it, so if I wanted it she'd sell it to me. She used to watch those *have-you-got-a-fortune-in-your-attic?* programmes on television, and I think the idea that something she had might be valuable really tickled her. I gave her two hundred and fifty quid for it. She seemed quite satisfied with that – and I squared it with my conscience by telling myself it wasn't hers to sell anyway, and all I was doing was paying rent for the years she'd had it up in her roof." He managed a tiny laugh. "But it was like, you know, the curse of the mogul's eye or something. I'd come by it dishonestly, and it destroyed me."

"You don't really believe that?"

"Well, not *literally*, of course." He paused, and scrutinized me. I could tell what was going on in his head: perhaps with Henry Whitaker's daughter, that *of course* was taking too much for granted.

For a moment I thought he was going to come out and say it. But in the end he didn't have the nerve to be that aggressive, and just muttered: "I certainly wish I hadn't done it, though. If I'd never seen those notebooks, I'd have been able to finish *my* book without a qualm. The worst that could have happened would have been, you know, that someone else found them later on, and said I'd been wrong about a few things. Well, all right, quite a lot of things. But at least the book would have been out by then, and I'd have moved on to something else, and I could have said, O.K., fair enough, but I wrote what I did in good faith, on the basis of the material that was available to me at the time. That sort of thing's always happening in academe. It's a bit wounding, but people survive it. They don't necessarily lose their jobs over it, anyway."

"Are you in danger of losing your job?"

"Not immediately. I'll be edged out. They just won't renew my contract. Or they'll renew it for another year – but make it clear I needn't ever bother applying for promotion."

"Why don't you just write a different book? Not *Henry Whitaker, Quiet Genius*, but *Henry Whitaker, whatever you think he is now*? I bet you hardly anyone would notice, if you didn't point out you were doing it. And so what, even if they did? The academic world has a long and distinguished tradition of people flatly contradicting themselves, doesn't it?"

He nodded. "I know, I know, but that's just what I've always hated about it: the lack of integrity; the shifting sands of relativism. I've got myself a bit of a reputation, actually, for standing up against all that – for daring to say, you know, *no, hang on, there really is such a thing as the truth, and it's our job to find it*. Which of course isn't a very fashionable view these days, especially in my field. So I've managed to make quite a few enemies among the post-modern mafia who run most of the Cultural Studies departments. All of whom would be rubbing their hands in glee to see me hoist with my own petard."

I couldn't decide if that was the way he expressed himself naturally, or he was trying to be mildly humorous about it. I smiled, just to be on the safe side. But he'd already turned away.

"There was a few days' honeymoon, when I started to read: I was even quite excited about it, despite the strange beginning. And then I thought: *Well, this isn't quite what I'd have expected, but I can still incorporate it, if I just trim my sails a bit.*" He paused. When he went on again, the resonance had suddenly gone from his voice, making it sound dull and far-away. "But then . . . when I got to the end . . . you know, to the bit about . . ."

I suddenly couldn't bear to hear it from him: this was our secret, not his.

"What – the woman in the picture, you mean?"

He nodded. "It was at that point I knew, really, that the game was up. I should have thrown in the towel then, I suppose, but I didn't have the guts. So I've just let things drag on and on, I'm afraid. And on. And . . ."

The words petered out, as if he was slowly losing interest in his own predicament.

"So what are you going to do?" I said.

He sighed, blowing the air out noisily through his nose. "Oh, I don't know. I've been looking for new jobs. There's one here" – listlessly tapping the newspaper on the table – "in Australia. I wouldn't get it, but . . ." He moved the bag of sugar, and flipped up the cover of the book so I could see the title: *J. B. Priestley: Portrait of an Author*. "And I'm vaguely considering trying to do something about him. He's about due for a reappraisal, I think."

I couldn't resist it. I said: "He did have very weird ideas about Time."

Arkwright had the grace to grin. But then, suddenly – like a rolling ball reaching the end of its trajectory – he appeared to run out of steam. His shoulders sagged, his head fell back against the seat, and he half-closed his eyes. I waited a minute or so for him to shake himself out of it and resume the conversation, but he didn't. He seemed totally impervious to my presence. It was impossible to tell even if he was awake or asleep.

"Well," I said finally, getting up.

That roused him. He started, and opened his eyes. "Sorry?"

"I guess I'd better be going," I said.

"Oh, are you sure?"

I nodded.

"All right, then." He didn't know what else to say: *Thanks for coming? Nice to meet you?* In the end he just stammered: "Ha– have we discussed everything?"

"Yeah, I think so." On my way to the door I had a brief tussle with my better nature. My better nature won. I turned, and asked: "O.K. if I take the notebooks?"

"Yes, yes, of course."

I was almost at the gate when I remembered there was something else I ought to tell him. It was painful, but it had to be done.

I walked back to the caravan and went in. He was sitting exactly where I'd left him.

"None of us can know for certain, of course," I said. "But I think you were right about one thing: my mother didn't mean to kill herself."

The front door was open when I got back to The Stumps. I walked in, calling: "Hi, I'm back!" There was no reply. I went into the kitchen, but she wasn't there. I couldn't find Sally in the living-room or the dining-room, either, so I stood at the bottom of the stairs and called again. Still nothing.

I went outside, thinking she must be doing something in the garden, but she wasn't. I was starting to feel seriously worried. Maybe she'd had a heart-attack in the bathroom, or was lying murdered on her bed.

And then, as I was passing the out-buildings on my way back to the house, I remembered the little cinema.

She was sitting in the front row, watching something on the screen: a circle of black-uniformed men, shot from above, closing in on a woman who was sprawled on the floor, trying to cover herself with a sheet. The effect was both menacing and oddly, geometrically beautiful – like watching a contracting iris slowly turning the world from light to dark. I knew I hadn't seen it before, but the style was unmistakable. It must be from the section of reel four that I had missed that morning.

"Oh, hullo!" said Sally. "I didn't hear you!" She seemed excited and slightly embarrassed, as if I'd caught her watching a blue movie. She got up, and hurried into the box to stop the film.

When she re-emerged, she said: "It's naughty of me, I know, but when I came back to tidy up, I suddenly thought I'd like to take another look at that crowd scene, before it all gets sealed away again for another thirty years. So I did, and then I found myself hooked, trying to figure out what was going on, and I ended up re-running the whole thing from the beginning."

She paused. It was too dark for me to see her clearly, but her head was angled so that the slab of light from the door just caught the top of her face. It had that proud-but-puzzled look you see on people who've just cracked a crossword clue they'd thought was too hard for them.

"I may be wrong," she said, "but I actually don't think it's such a muddle as everyone says it is. There is a kind of shape, if you look closely enough. I couldn't fit all the pieces together, of course, but I'm pretty sure I've got the basic idea. It's a bit strange, but –" She stopped suddenly. "Sorry, I expect you don't really want to hear this."

"No," I said. "I do."

"Well, that poor woman – the one we see at the beginning . . ." She dropped her voice almost to a stage-whisper. "Your *mother*, I suppose it's meant to be, isn't it? Or someone like her?"

I nodded.

"Well, it's all about her, of course. But the problem is, she doesn't really know who she is any more. Or was. Her life has been so . . . so

394

invaded, so taken over by nightmare, she can't tell the difference between things she's dreamed and things that have actually happened to her. She's like a fractured lens, that picks up fragments of different objects, rather than a single coherent image. She has memories, but they're totally inconsistent. The real her might have been any one of those three girls, or bits of all of them. But just because of that – just because you can never finally pin an identity on her and say she was this particular person – she sort of comes to represent *all* the people who lived through that . . . that unimaginably awful experience. Or *didn't* live through it, I suppose, a lot of them. She's no-one, and she's everyone. I *think* that's what we're meant to get from it. And that's why he was going to call it *Ordinary*." She paused again. "Sorry – I knew I shouldn't have started on this."

I was crying. I hadn't realized it myself till then. The tears were just trickling down my face like condensation on a window – so gently and unobtrusively, they hadn't penetrated my consciousness.

"No, it's O.K.," I said. "That's fantastic. Makes me want to take it home and try to finish it for him."

"Hm." She gave me a good-humored, tolerant smile – the kind you give a child who's taken the fairy-tale game too seriously and thinks her magic wand will *really* turn the family pooch into a lion. "Anyway," she said, nudging me towards the door, "let's go in. I don't know about you, but I'm about ready for a cup of tea."

Afterwards I asked her if I could check my e-mails. She took me upstairs to the little room she used as an office, and switched on the computer for me.

There were three messages from Hody, all in the same vein: *Where are you? What's going on? Did you meet your childhood sweetheart and decide to become Mrs. Hugo Maltravers?*

And one from Michael: *Dad didn't want to scare you, but he's been having some tests at the hospital. He just got the results and it turns out he's fine – but now he's crazy with worry about you. Please get in touch with him. And copy it to me.*

I clicked reply on Hody's latest, dated yesterday, and wrote:

My darling,

I am so so sorry. Thank God, though, that you're O.K. I'm O.K., too. Too much to tell you about here, but in a couple of days I can do it in person, because I'M COMING HOME just as soon as I can get a flight. I'll let you have the details the minute I have them. Oh, I can't wait!

Love you

M

I copied it to Michael, and clicked *send*.

XXV

London – September 1939

The King's delivered a wireless message to the Empire. Half an hour ago there was an air-raid warning. When I crack open the shutter and look out, London seems to have disappeared under a layer of soot.

So, finally, it's really started. It's almost a relief, after so much waiting. Odd, though, to realize that your whole conscious life has been no more than a parenthesis between two wars. Or perhaps simply a lull in the same one.

But this time, obviously, it's going to be even worse. We've got bigger bombers, now, and faster tanks, and more lethal gases. In two years, or three, or however long it takes, millions of people who are alive tonight will have been snuffed out. Millions more will be diseased or homeless or hungry. A few will be unimaginably rich. The rest will be wondering: *How did we survive, when X and Y and Z didn't?* And there'll be no logic to it. A country vicar's wife will burn to death with her children in an Anderson shelter. An illiterate Balkan goat-herd will become a black-market millionaire. A cannon-fodder conscript will be reported killed with the rest of his platoon and six months later walk into his parents' house. A girl will be raped and murdered. Her twin sister will escape to America and marry a Chicago beef baron. It's all so arbitrary, the only rational response – at least as far as our own lives are concerned – is a fatalistic shrug.

But oddly, I don't *feel* fatalistic. Appalled, horrified, frightened – but not fatalistic. In an uncomfortable, butterflies-in-the-stomach way, I'm even conscious of being (sounds shocking, I know) strangely exhilarated. This, I'm certain, is going to be the supreme test. For years I've been tyrannized by indecision and cowardice, tugging at the corner of the plaster, then stroking it back again at the first whimper of pain. Now I've got to be prepared just to rip it right off. If I don't accept my destiny when it's presented to me *this* time, I'll never have another chance.

I know it seems ludicrous – in the circumstances, even obscene – to talk about *destiny* in a universe which seems so totally indifferent to the fate of the human individual. But there is love, too, in the universe, and compassion, and the power to imagine ourselves inside other people's skins. And what I believe I'm called upon to do is use those things, as far as I am able, to make it – if only by a fraction – *less* indifferent.

And – let me state it categorically here, after all my obfuscation and backsliding, all my compromise, all my writing rather than doing – that's what I *do* believe. I have had signs. Something has chosen to alert me to itself. I don't yet know why, or what it wants of me. But when the moment comes, I must be prepared to dedicate my life to it.

And I will. On this most awful and momentous day, I swear it: when I see you again, whatever the cost, I will follow where you take me.

Now no more words.

Acknowledgements

I must begin by gratefully acknowledging the support of Arts Council England, for their generous assistance during the writing of *The Woman in the Picture*.

Thanks to the many friends who have contributed encouragement, inspiration or practical help, among them: Nicholas Alfrey; Sally Darius and Derek Robinson; Louise Greenberg; Tony Hipgrave and Sue Barlow; Cathy and Julian Milby; Muriel Mitcheson Brown; Colin Samson; Gabriele Schlick; Richard Skinner; and Steve Xerri. I'm especially grateful to Dominic Power, for generously giving me the benefit of his immense knowledge of film history, and for his intelligent and perceptive reading of the text.

I'm indebted for their professional advice to Kevin Brownlow; Ann Runeckles of Shepperton Studios; the late Ernest Dudley; Mark Etherington; Lindsey Moore and Richard Jenkins of the National Film and Television School; the staff of the Burnley Local Studies Library; the staff of the Museum of London; and – particularly – to Matthew Sweet, both for helping me find my way through the jungle of 1920s and 1930s cinema, and for letting me see an early copy of his hugely entertaining book, *Shepperton Babylon*.

Special thanks, as always, to my agent, the peerless Derek Johns, and to all his colleagues at AP Watt; and to everyone at Faber – Stephen Page, Rachel Alexander, Anna Pallai, Will Atkinson, Walter Donohue, Noel Murphy, Neal Price, Kate Beal, Kate Ward, and the rest of the team – for their unstinting kindness and support. I'm particularly grateful to Jon Riley, who saw the book through its early stages, for his tremendous vision and encouragement, and to Angus Cargill, who edited the finished manuscript with exceptional intelligence, perspicacity, tact and patience.

And thanks as ever, finally, to my wonderful family: to my niece and nephew, Catherine and Richard; to my sister-in-law, Margot; to my parents-in-law, Margot and Ralph Emerick; to my mother, for all her support, and her invaluable assistance as a researcher; to Tom and Kit, for their tolerance and encouragement, and for their generous and helpful comments on the text; and to Paula, for more than I can say.